A PRAYER FOR DELIVERANCE

Also by Christopher Chambers

SYMPATHY FOR THE DEVIL

A PRAYER FOR DELIVERANCE

AN ANGELA BIVENS THRILLER

CHRISTOPHER CHAMBERS

CROWN PUBLISHERS • NEW YORK

This is a work of fiction. All incidents and dialogue, and all characters, with the exception of some well-known historical and public figures, are products of the author's imagination and are not to be construed as real. Where real-life historical or public figures appear, the situations, incidents, and dialogues concerning those persons are entirely fictional and are not intended to depict actual events or to change the entirely fictional nature of the work. In all other respects, any resemblance to persons living or dead is entirely coincidental.

Published by Crown Publishers, New York, New York.
Member of the Crown Publishing Group, a division of Random House, Inc.
www.randomhouse.com

CROWN is a trademark and the Crown colophon is a registered trademark of Random House, Inc.

Printed in the United States of America

Grateful acknowledgment is made to the following for permission to reprint
previously published material.

The Custodian, Northern California Bible College: Excerpt from *The Congo Journal of H. L. Marks (The Custodian* 2002). Reprinted by permission of *The Custodian,* Northern California Bible College.

The Kellie Campbell Africana Library: Excerpts from *The Diary of Henry Francis Fy[i]nn, Sr., Expedition to Natal Shore and Zulu Kingdom 1821–1831.* Reprinted by permission of The Kellie Campbell Africana Library, Durban, RSA, 2002.

Design by Leonard W. Henderson

Library of Congress Cataloging-in-Publication Data
Chambers, Christopher, 1963–
A prayer for deliverance : an Angela Bivens thriller / Christopher Chambers.—1st ed.
1. Women detectives—Maryland—Fiction. 2. Government investigators—Fiction. 3. African American women—Fiction. 4. Death row inmates—Fiction. 5. Maryland—Fiction. I. Title.
PS3603.H35 P73 2003
813'.6—dc21
2002013982

ISBN 0-609-60850-9

10 9 8 7 6 5 4 3 2 1

First Edition

To my grandmother Louise

ACKNOWLEDGMENTS

Thanks again to my editor, Kristin Kiser, plus Rhoda Dunn, Claudia Gabel, and the rest of the Crown and Random House family. Love to my publicist, Antoinette Roach, and to my agent, Joanna Pulcini, for making this and *Sympathy for the Devil* happen. I am indebted to the patient staff of the Charlotte-Mecklenburg County Public Library for hunting down some very obscure items for me. Props to the many, many book clubs who've embraced me. You know who you are!

And last, a special thanks to an old South African gentleman whose name escapes me now. I met him on a New Jersey Transit commuter train from Princeton to Manhattan. I was weary, cranky, pensive—on a book tour in the thick of an anthrax scare, in the aftermath of 9/11. He smiled and told me I'd do fine, that I should be proud. But when I asked him about things I'd researched for this novel, the smile melted from his face, his frail hands started to shake, and our row of seats became deathly quiet. Then he recounted ghost stories from his childhood. And here we are . . .

A prayer for deliverance
From sorcery and shaman chants.
Rescuing me from the dancing feet
And jubilant drums, both pounding
With evil glee.
A prayer for deliverance
From the sin vexing me.
For I can fight no longer,
Lest I answer my own prayer.

—POEM FROM THE DIARY OF FATHER B.L. MARKS,
AFRICAN AMERICAN MISSIONARY IN THE CONGO, 1903

Shaka called his corps of elite palace guards amaSimba, *or
"Lion's Regiment." They hovered about their King with
Winter's cold in their eyes and bane in their hearts. The King's
half-brother, Prince Dingane, swore to me that each* umSimba
*was possessed by a lion-demon, conjured by Warlocks to purvey
Shaka's spleen. Though I am Baptised in the service of our Lord
and Saviour Jesus Christ, from what I have witnessed of these
warriors' bloodlust, I cannot contradict Dingane's words.*

—THE UNEDITED JOURNAL OF HENRY FRANCIS FINN, 1820,
NATAL PROVINCE PIONEER AND BIOGRAPHER OF SHAKA ZULU

A PRAYER FOR DELIVERANCE

1

A SCULPTOR ONCE CALLED HIM MICHAEL, named for an archangel in service to the sculptor of mankind. Michael stood fifteen feet tall. Burnished bronze, yet the texture of finely carved and sanded walnut. Tapered wings; a slender form, but also rippling with muscle and sinew. Serenely, resolutely, this seraphim bore another bronze figure—a mortally wounded hero—off to heaven.

Both warrior and angel lorded over the din of the cathedral-like station gallery, oblivious to the incomprehensible loudspeaker announcements, herds of cursing passengers and wailing children, and screech of dragged luggage swirling about their pediment. And, outside the stained glass flanking the statue's warm, fluid figures, a winter storm raged, wrecking Amtrak's timetables from Richmond to Boston. The only traveler unruffled by the chaos was an old black man ascending the escalator from the frosty platform. He was wearing a gray, moth-chewed tweed overcoat with the collar drawn up. A weather-beaten porkpie hat—the kind the old jazz musicians sported—topped his small head. The skin on his face and hands stretched like purple-black parchment. He limped off the moving stairs to the statue's base and peered up. A scowl twisted through the old man's face.

"*Inkanyezi,*" he hissed. But the angel above him wasn't real. Nor was it a woman.

A young redcap rushed over, pushing an empty wheelchair and calling, "Yo, chief—"

"I am *not* a chief."

"Look 'ere, man—you just got off the four-ten P.M. Metroliner from D.C., right?"

The old man shoved his hands into his coat pockets and nodded.

"Well, you see a coupla *sisters* waitin' down on the platform?" The redcap noted the old coot's accent. Caribbean? African? "Um . . . I mean black women," he clarified. "Got paged for this wheelchair. You think they still down there?"

The old man shuffled away, saying nothing. The redcap cursed to himself when he saw the man's feet. *Four inches of wet snow outside and more coming, and this motherfucker's wearing jacked-up sandals?* He then thought aloud, "And look at them crusty yellow toenails . . . like some damn lion's claws!"

Suddenly, the young man was doubling over in a pain that he could later describe as a white-hot fireplace poker rending his stomach. Gasping, he looked into the crowd. And there was the old man, snickering back at him.

A woman's stern voice broke the pain. "Where you *been?*"

The grimacing redcap felt instant relief and caught his breath. He jerked his head toward the woman's voice, then back in the old man's direction. Blinking didn't bring the elfin codger back. He'd vanished.

"Yeah, I'm talking to *you*," the voice snapped again. "We been waiting on that chair, down on that cold-ass platform, for fifteen minutes!" The red-cap, still stunned, wheeled the chair to a cocoa-skinned woman wearing a tan shearling-leather coat. Bobbed black locks peeked from under a white ski cap. "Brother, *work* with me," she sighed. "It's not for me. It's for *her*."

Attorney Carmen Wilcox's thumb pointed to a small woman, no more than five-two, who was coming up the escalator. She was wearing a black wool 1950s-style toggle coat that looked two sizes too large. A pair of Wayfarers hid eyes, almond in shape and color, that were once huge and dewy. Plump cheeks and dimples had given way to a swollen, taut heaviness. Her skin's usual honey-brown glow had blanched.

She was steadied by another woman: petite as well, with butternut skin, curly amber hair, green eyes. *"Angel,"* said Sharon Boissiere, "take off the shades so you can see."

Angela Renée Bivens shook her head. No one was supposed to see the tears, spawned by the cramps ripping through her uterus. No one was supposed to know she was there to kill her baby.

Carmen tugged a Berber fleece beret down over Angela's cold ears and fastened the toggle coat's peg buttons. "Ease into this wheelchair slowly, chile."

"I can walk," Angela replied, hoarse. She turned to Sharon. "And I can see fine."

Sharon parsed the truth from Angela's sallow face and whispered in her friend's ear, "You're running a fever. You have blood spotting on your panties—I saw it when I was helping you in the rest room on the train. Now sit." Sharon pulled off the sunglasses and folded them into her purse.

Angela squinted, even in the meager orange light. And, it being fruitless to fight, she lowered herself into the chair. With Carmen and Sharon running interference, the redcap plowed her wheelchair through to the 29th Street and Arch Street exit. As the redcap propped open one of the glass doors, Angela felt something pierce her. Not the pain in her abdomen, or the bite of raw wind tinged with snowflakes and taxicab fumes. *Eyes* stabbed her. Angela turned her head back toward the lobby to find them.

There. Yellow. Unblinking. Belonging to an old man who couldn't have been any taller than she. He was seated on one of the lacquered station benches, below the dark statue of an angel propping up a slumping nude man. The old man was wearing sandals. *Poor thing,* Angela mused, *he must be homeless.* Freezing. Alone. She smiled at him. He nodded, as if he knew her. His face was the last thing Angela saw before she fainted.

Angela awoke on an examining table. She was clad in a paper gown sopping with sweat. Cold metal stirrups clasped her bare little feet. She was alone.

Milky images of two lost hours invaded her skull. *Carmen helps my brother-in-law, Byron, lift me into his Range Rover. My sister, Pam, turns around, tries to smile, but I see her crying. Pammy . . . why are you here? You haven't recovered from what Trey did to you. Or to the boys . . . Byron Jr. . . . little Kobi. You all need to move outta Philly like you planned. And if you're here, then do Mom and Daddy know where I am, now, too?* And now she watched snowflakes swirl around her, tinted red by brake lights on the Schuykill Expressway. She could hear the beat of the wiper blades, car horns. Carmen's voice: *"We're almost there, Angel. Hang on. None of this is your fault."*

Angela banished the past scenes and sensations from her head and, instead, tried to focus on the tangible walls around her. Through vision blurred by both pain and no contact lenses, she fixed on a framed photo hanging a few feet away. Three African American men: her father, Sharon Boissiere's dad, and another doctor, displaying a trophy marlin on the deck of a boat down in Nassau, Bahamas. Must've been 1985, '86? This third doctor was younger. Handsome. Bracketing the photo were twin diplomas: Leslie Tyrone Collins, Howard University, B.S., 1977; Leslie Tyrone Collins, Meharry Medical School, M.D., 1981.

Now Angela was hearing voices beyond the green privacy screen. Pamela's. Carmen's. Sharon's. And, on a speakerphone raked by storm static, was her OB-GYN in Washington. Finally, there was the tenor monotone of Dr. Leslie T. Collins, as he asked: Could the FBI discover where she is? Could the press find out? Is she absolutely *certain* who the father is?

The unspeakable had been spoken. The disremembered, vividly recounted. *Yes, I am fucking certain who the father is.* Phosphor Thomas Williams III. *Trey.* Prince and young Doge of the Nation's Capital. Bewitching her with those dusky onyx eyes. Wrapping her in that hard body. Soothing her with that tender molasses voice. *Ah . . . melting the unmeltable* with the very lips that had tasted the blood of so many victims. Seven innocent teenage girls. A dozen PCP- and heroin-dealing thugs. Angela's friend Monique. And Angela's partner, Special Agent Kristina Trimble.

To Trey, these diverse souls were nothing but food for arcane gods and demons hatched in his mind as a tortured child. His—and that of his twin brother, Ganneymede. "Pluto." Cold Pluto. Sad, sick Pluto. The Bureau and the D.C. Metropolitan Police Department dubbed the twins the Venus Stalkers. *And I killed both of them.* Pluto, in a D.C. Metro station, driven to suicide—leaping from her reach into a train's crushing path. Trey, on that cold beach, waves pounding a frigid Delaware shore. Five 9mm rounds from her SIG-Sauer, point-blank. *Lord, have mercy on my poor soul . . . for being blind? For not stopping them sooner. For being an avenger, 'cause only you can avenge. And do you hate me now for wanting one more death?*

Angela began to bawl when this question, and a dreaded answer, began to cleave her skull with pain equal to the contractions racking her abdomen. And she realized, as she lay on that examining table, shivering, that life's clichés no longer applied to her. Yes, often the center holds, or "good" triumphs over "evil." Equally true, however, is that thoughtful, *brittle* people like her can't help but scour the patina from these cruel little conventions. And underneath, they discover that the center held because it bowed. That "good" cheated. So maybe if pain was perdition, why couldn't this baby be *her* redemption? A new life to mold: a happy soul that would never endure the childhood horrors that had bred its sociopath father and psychopathic uncle.

Thus Angela's eyelids clenched tightly as her voice took over what her mind whimpered: "Maybe this child . . . is innocent. . . ."

Words ceased when a massive cramp sliced through her viscera. Angela screamed. Her fingers gouged the paper cover off the table; her feet jerked out of the stirrups. Her eyes opened only as she inhaled to scream again. They caught flashes of Collins's salt-and-pepper goatee, his white lab coat, the physician assistant's hands adjusting an IV bag. In seconds, Angela was limp and sucking shallow breaths. She heard Collins once more.

"Angela, listen. You're at thirteen weeks, but you're hemorrhaging and presenting contractions. We think it's best for you to sign the consent form and—"

Angela squirmed to the edge of the table. "N-no . . ."

Collins, agitated, leaned closer. "You came up here for my discreet help. Not even your father knows I'm seeing you. Why did you wait so long?" When his patient twisted away, he shouted, *"Damn it, you are pregnant by a serial killer!"* He then got hold of his emotions. *"Sweetheart . . .* I'm sorry . . . listen, the procedure'd be over in twenty minutes. Not a soul would ever know. But if you *now* want to carry this fetus to term, we have to get you admitted to an ER immediately to arrest the contractions and save it." Collins turned aside to his PA and droned without any emotion, "Just prep her for suction curettage. She's hysterical and presenting an imminent mis-carriage anyway."

Angela gulped air. *Mommy . . . Grammie . . . help me.* But she had never been more alone.

Seven o'clock P.M., and near the corner of Ardmore Avenue and Lancaster Pike, the old man from the train station was trembling on the slushy curb. Falling snow weighted down his hat brim and encrusted his coat. Yet his eyes never left the warm glow and moving shadows in a window across an unplowed parking lot. The marquee below the window read: COLLINS, HALL & BLAUSTEIN, P.A. OBSTETRICS & GYNECOLOGY.

From his coat pocket, he pulled out what looked like a small squash or gourd. Dry, curled leaves were still attached to the tiny, withered stem. But this vessel was also bound and stitched with a tight weave of grass and black and silver beads. Caked on the rounded bottom was a material that looked and smelled like dead flesh tinted with red pigment. The old man balled a fist around the object and shook it, rhythmically, up at the snow-laden sky. Something hard and dry rattled around inside the vessel as he sang in a whispery voice and danced on frozen feet he could no longer feel. In the dirty-gray clouds, he devined the image of a brown face with a salt-and-pepper goatee. A white coat. But in no more than a second or two, that image dissolved into another vision: a sealed plastic bag in a steel box, marked by the white man's symbol "Biohazard" and printed with their language "For Pathology Lab Pickup. Collins, Hall & Blaustein."

The old man realized that the bag contained an unexpected gift. A *weapon*. And as he danced, he smiled at his wonderful fortune, showing a mouthful of teeth.

Spiked and yellow, like a crocodile's.

2

THE BLUE HERON WAS AN OLD Chesapeake Bay tobacco plantation converted into a four-star bed-and-breakfast. Dr. Leslie T. Collins
traced his lineage to slaves who had toiled on the estate. That was one reason—aside from its being far away from familiar, prying eyes in
Philadelphia—he'd chosen the inn as his occasional love nest. Sex with a
white woman named Beth Hooperman in one of the manor's nineteenth-
century rosewood sleigh beds was indeed luscious revenge. The sight of that
bleached-blond hair grazing his chest as she rode him, her pink skin against
his slick ocher, *Lord have mercy,* must've driven the ghosts of the plantation's
previous owners berserk!

 That night, the lovers climaxed with the usual grunts and pleas to the
Almighty. Both were doused in sweat; the air was thick with their bodies'
timbre. Les Collins detested air-conditioning, so the sultry breeze coming
off the brackish cove beyond the jalousies only steamed the suite even more,
enhancing Les's odor. That smell was a pheromone for Beth Hooperman,
she of Mainline Philly galas and crystal goblets of Fish House Punch in a
Schuykill rowing-club boathouse. And when Beth jumped off of Collins,
Collins jumped into the shower. In the faux-marble stall, he crooned
"Didn't I (Blow Your Mind This Time)" by the Delfonics. The song floated
him back, not to Beth's past of ivy columns and rugby chants, but to the
"The Yard" at Howard University: September 1976. He smiled, recalling the

7

cornrowed scalps and polyester. Gaggles of coeds wearing platform shoes, halters, and tight, flared jeans all sending him coy winks while he, Bryce, Carl, and Butch barked a dreadful cadence to the frat pledges marching in gold berets and black trench coats.

Beth, resigned to inhaling Collins's scent from the damp sheets, yawned and groped for her emery board on the nightstand. It lay next to her White House ID: HOOPERMAN, ELIZABETH B., ASST. DOMESTIC POLICY ADVISER. The photo on the badge didn't do her justice; her soon-to-be unemployed boss, Bill Clinton, had nicknamed her Amanda, for Heather Locklear's old TV character on *Melrose Place*.

"Les, baby," she called. "What'd you tell your wife?"

"American College of Obstetrics and Gynecology district meeting in D.C.," Collins yelled back through the soap lather. "What'd you tell your husband?"

Before Beth could answer, there was a knock on the door. Beth threw on Collins's wrinkled blue oxford shirt, floated to the door, and blithely opened it without either buttoning the shirt or checking the peephole. The hallway was deserted, but at Beth's painted toes lay a sterling silver tray holding a plate of homemade lemon-mint cookies and an icy pitcher of Blue Heron Inn raspberry iced tea, laced with Chambord. This was the inn's trademark turndown service snack. Nick of time, too. No room service at the Blue Heron after nine. Just booze on the boathouse deck. Beth retrieved the tray and set it on an oak linen chest at the foot of the bed.

"Leslie," Beth said, alighting on the bed and crossing her bare legs under her, "we need to seriously talk about your friend."

Collins sauntered out of the bathroom with a plush white towel wrapped beneath his middle-age paunch. He snatched a cookie off the tray, gobbled it down, and said, "Friend, as in Butch?" He turned to the mirror over the vanity table.

"Uh-huh. The convention's barely two months away, and your 'ace boon coon' is in jeopardy of losing a firm offer to join the ticket as Gore's vice president. This guy's blowing his chance to make *history*. Are you listening to me?"

Her lover was busy frowning at his reflection. Aging was a bitch.

Beth counted on her slender fingers. "Okay, three things. First . . . he's *never* disavowed his ugly statements about the President during the impeachment trial. Does he even accept that the *only* reason he and Carol Moseley-Braun became the *first* blacks in the Senate since Reconstruction was that they rode on Bill Clinton's coattails? Second, he says Al Gore needs to 'rethink' his explanation for taking campaign contributions at that Buddhist temple in California. Worse, he makes that comment on freaking *Larry King Live* right after he and John McCain and Russell Feingold introduce this laughable campaign-finance reform bill on the Senate floor. I swear this stuff's going to appear as sound bites in Shrub's attack ads."

"Shrub?" Collins replied as he splashed on some bay rum, killing his scent.

"Yeah, that's what we call that little retard George W. Bush. *Third* . . . you following this? Your boy's allowed Hatch, Ashcroft, and Helms to hijack our last-minute federal judge appointments, hang us with this stupid Elian Gonzalez thing and God only knows what other eleventh-hour witch-hunts Ken Starr left behind."

"So?"

"It distracts Reno and the FBI from going after the right-wing sickos who're blowing up cars and shooting people. Among them, doctors, Leslie. *Abortion* doctors."

Collins shrugged and slid onto the bed. Beth continued, "Our people in the FBI and AFT tell us these fanatics are connected to Timothy McVeigh, Eric Rudolph. Homegrown terrorists. And Shrub and the GOP get to act all sanctimonious and disavow—"

Rolling closer, Collins nuzzled Beth's long neck. "Baby, maybe Butch is more worried about what y'all're doing to stop this dude who had those fools try to blow up the World Trade Center with a bomb in a van. Same dude who goes and blows up our embassies in Kenya, Tanzania. Your boss didn't do much in reply except kill some camels with cruise missiles! What's the bastard's name—Bin Labben, Ali Baba?"

Beth shoved him away. "Don't be ignorant, Les! We got bigger fish to fry!"

Collins chuckled slyly. Met with a pout, he started nuzzling again, stopping only to wet his finger and trace it along Beth's thigh to her pubis. She didn't bristle and push him away. But even through the soft coos, Beth kept up a semblance of a lecture.

"Honey, all I'm saying is . . . *ooohhh, that's good, right there* . . . Butch is pissing off both us in the West Wing, and . . . *ah yeah, daddy* . . . and Gore's people in Nashville, and Gore's already down twelve points in the polls. God only knows . . . *ah yeah* . . . if Shrub wins, loonies like Rupert Murdoch, Dick and Lynne Cheney, and their oil-company CEO pals are going to run the White House . . . *faster, baby* . . . and Les—"

Collins whispered, "I'll talk to the brother, okay?"

The door to the hallway went ajar. Just slightly.

"Damn, Beth," Collins grumbled. "Ya left it open!" He climbed out of bed and pushed the door shut. As it swung, he felt a hot, bone-dry flurry on his skin. Strange—because the night air seeping through the jalousies had been muggy and mordant not five seconds earlier. Collins shrugged it off, grabbed another cookie, and slid back to his lover. She'd already poured a little tea. As Collins sucked a gulp from her proffered glass, he heard the innkeeper's wife's dog, Pepper, barking viciously outside the open window.

"You were saying?" Beth purred, parting the shirt to expose her breasts.

Collins lost his train of thought. He drizzled some cold tea on Beth's nipples and licked them clean. She snaked her hand into his coarse chest hair.

"Trickle that tea down a little lower, like a *goooood* boy."

"Yessum, Miz Liz-bett," Collins mocked, before burrowing into the linens to root at her genitals like a truffle hog.

After a moan, Beth giggled, "Cut your fingernails." Abruptly, the giggle twisted into a frown. Under the sheets, something was scratching her right calf, then her toe. "*Stop* it, Leslie!"

Collins pulled his face away from her groin. "What? My hands're up here!"

Both lovers held still. But the sheets at the foot of the bed continued to move.

Beth felt something like a razor's nick on her big toe. She was about to reach down and scratch it when the pain ignited. Searing her foot. Hacking its way up her leg to her heart, her lungs. Her thighs thrashed with such force that they knocked the 250-pound Collins onto the hardwood floor. There, Collins remained prone and paralyzed—eyes splayed in terror because he couldn't hear Beth shriek or cry for help. He heard only the ugly heaves of a constricted throat begging for air.

Collins wobbled to his feet. Barely ten seconds had ticked off the grandfather clock in the corner. Beth's body was already stiff, contorted. But the bed linens continued to wriggle. Slowly, gingerly, Collins gathered the covers, then swallowed hard and yanked them off.

A green snake—as thick and long as a baseball bat—uncoiled from Beth's right leg. It flicked its forked tongue at Collins and slithered back into the sheet folds.

Collins screamed himself hoarse as he careened, naked, into the hall, down the stairs, and into the inn's brightly lit foyer. The carpet runner slipped from under him. His body smacked the marble floor. Gasping, Collins jerked his head around. *Where are the fucking guests, the innkeeper? The damn dog? Didn't they hear? Didn't they see?*

The inn's front door started to open. Slowly. Creaking.

"Hey . . . shit . . . hey, there—*Help!* Anybody? *Hullo?*"

The reply was a rush of hot, baking wind, pushing the door wide. And the air *stank*. Like the zoo or the circus. Like *lions*. It desiccated Collins's throat and nostrils. Dizziness seized him. The lights, the foyer's walls, and the furniture swirled as if inside a kaleidoscope. As Collins groped for a hold, he swore he could hear the innkeeper's wife's dog again. The barking was at first garbled, then hollow. But a final yelp skewered his eardrum. And then, quiet. The wind ceased; the door stopped moving, and so did the torque in Collins's brain. Yet the heat and the odor intensified. Collins's head cleared; he started edging, crablike, to the stairs.

A gray object hurtled through the open doorway and splattered onto the floor. Pepper's body. Her bloody head hung from her neck by only a few strands of cartilage.

Collins spurted urine. But when the first chants from unseen mouths hit his ears, the dribble became a stream.

"*Umgomo . . . ukwenza . . . uku-zi Umthakathi . . . umgomo . . .*"

The chorus surrounded Collins. *But no one was there.*

The *thoomp* of wood beating rawhide kept time with each refrain. Louder. Like a regiment of voices. Soldiers' voices. Collins slid to the banister, tears streaming.

Again, like thunder: "*UMM-GO-MO!*" Boom! "*UUU-KWENZAAAA!*" Boom! "*UKU-ZI UMTHAKATHI!*" Boom! "*UUUMMM-GOOOO-MMMMOOO!*"

Collins heard the dull thud of bare, callused feet on the foyer tile. He looked above his head to the skylight, perhaps in a prayer for deliverance.

There, he saw black faces floating beyond the glass panes. Faces caked with gray soot. Faces with no pupils in their yellow eyes.

Outside, the crickets and frogs had been singing to the moon. Then they stopped, as if muted by a sudden, dread anticipation.

A man's high-pitched scream shredded the silence.

3

ASSATEAGUE ISLAND NATIONAL PARK, MARYLAND

PROFESSOR ALVIN MARKHAM LAY NAKED and restless atop his sleeping bag. His chestnut dreadlocks were spread, spiderlike, on his white pillow.

"We're missing the Aeneid Majorus meteor shower," he said with a heavy sigh. He fumbled for a bottle of Skin-So-Soft insect repellent. "Want some?"

Angela Bivens rolled over to face him in the pallor of an electric Coleman tent lamp. She was clothed: a mini–tank top and a pair of draw-string shorts. She'd let her hair grow from the short, boyish cut she'd worn for over a year. Shorn, in mourning. About the only thing relaxing on this trip was the sea breeze blowing through the dunes, and the lullaby of the breakers pounding the beach. Angela wished her tentmate would just shut up and try to enjoy those sensations.

Camping on the beach was a tonic, yes. And a gamble. But she figured twenty milligrams of Paxil taken with her dinner at Phillip's Crabhouse in Ocean City that night made it a safer bet. The tablet quelled the shudders and sweats that darkness, the feel of sand, and the sound of waves would have produced only a few months ago. She'd shot Trey on an old coastwatch tower, above the breakers. In a chopper's searchlight.

"There'll be other meteors," she whispered. "Try to sleep." Indeed, Angela had been roused from a dream. Or was it a memory? Far from the surf, she'd seen dew glistening like diamonds on pale green leaves of sorghum grass. Sunbeams tickling yellow pineapple lilies and magenta acacia blooms. Alien flora sprouting from a broad, grassy plain. And then, suddenly, a gray pall of dust and acrid smoke shrouding plain, hugging the ground. Gunpowder smoke, not from modern weapons. Yet there was no fear. No death. No signs of battle. Not yet.

Alvin smiled shyly as Angela mused over her dream, then he summoned a little courage: "We don't *have* to sleep."

Angela sat up, crossed her legs, and began rocking back and forth, eyes cold and steely. Alvin had first seen that pose and stare in Mexico, right after Angela's promotion to inspector, when she'd received the Medal of Valor from Janet Reno. Alvin had helped her attain that citation; he was the expert on Mayan astronomy who had profiled twin killers. Yes, safe, dependable Alvin. But each time she'd kissed Alvin, from the minute she'd discovered she was pregnant, her lips never felt the melting warmth she desperately wanted to draw from his mouth. His voice, though reassuring, didn't prick up her hairs with electricity. Whenever Alvin caressed her body, he was met with that pose. He'd been seeing it for five months. Gimme space. Lemme heal. Take it slow. For five months, he obeyed. Dutifully. Sweetly. A shoulder to lean upon when nightmares prowled. And a smiling face, to lie to, when he asked, "What happened in Philly?" Or, "Do you love me?" Now, Alvin was the one who was distant.

"Sorry," he mumbled, dousing the light. "G'night."

His tone prodded her out of the shell. "Aw . . . don't . . . *shit* . . . don't apologize."

In the darkness, Alvin asked, "If I'm not your man, than what am I to you, huh?"

"We're *comfortable* together. So I can't think of any place I'd rather be tonight than here." Angela wondered if she meant it. Or just wanted peace.

Alvin rolled to her and kissed her cheek. Angela, seeing his penis flaccid and thus feeling secure that Alvin knew his place once more, pulled his arm across her body. They lay like spoons until jolted by a commotion from an adjacent campsite: the seething metal-rap of Limp Bizkit's "Nookie" on a boom box, and the clink of beer bottles.

"Fucking surfers again!" Alvin hollered with pent-up frustration. He slipped on a pair of cargo shorts. "I swear I'm calling the park rangers on their asses!"

"No, I'll take care of it."

Just as Angela pulled her FBI medallion badge from her canvas daypack, someone shut off Fred Durst's screaming; male laughter and girlish whoops became shouts and curses. A pair of high-beam headlights bathed the tent wall. Before checking out for the weekend, Angela had reviewed a couple of Maryland State Police hot sheets concerning drug-related beefs between surfers and local rednecks. So much for leaving the job behind while planning a vacation. Two people had been murdered in Ocean City a month prior; this was a resort where handgun homicides were as rare as African Americans strolling the boardwalk. The racket across the dunes was probably just another high school graduation beach party gone sour, but Angela had prepared for the worst. She groped in her daypack for her SIG-Sauer 229 9mm as a gang of shadows rushed toward the tent, backlit by red and blue flashes.

"Stay down, okay?" Angela whispered, loading in a clip.

Alvin's jaw dropped when he saw the weapon. "Angie . . . *Angel* . . ."

"Quiet," Angela hissed. Someone was tugging at the outside flap zipper.

The flap parted. A woman's head poked in. Angela aimed the SIG, but quickly realized the woman was wearing a U.S. Park Service "Smokey the Bear" hat. The female park ranger yelped as she fell backward out of the tent, with Angela following, still two-handing the pistol.

The headlights belonged to the ranger's pickup truck; the red and blue lights flashed from U.S. Park Police Jeep Cherokees. Indeed, Park Police officers had circled the tent, and every single cop out there now had his or her hands on their weapon. Alvin crawled out, showing all his teeth and raising his arms like a POW. He approached Angela. Her chin dropped to her chest. The puffs from her lungs slowed to deep breaths. *Oh, God,* Angela cried inwardly. *What have I done?*

Alvin eased Angela's hands down to a nonthreatening position, then embraced her. Angela buried her face into his fleshy shoulder and gave a muffled, "I'm sorry, Alvin." She raised her head, seemingly composed, as Alvin called to the officers. "She's . . . um . . . okay." Most of the cops sighed. None snickered.

"Special Agent Angela R. Bivens, FBI?" asked a bemused Park Police officer.

Angela nodded. *"Inspector* . . . I'm Inspector now."

"Sorry. Look . . . uh . . . I guess we got the campsites mixed up and scared the bejesus out of you folks. You didn't leave the Bureau a CBR."

Alvin scoffed, "What the hell's a CBR and why'd you need it?"

"Can-Be-Reached number," Angela explained softly. "I just didn't want anyone to bother us, Alvin. *Now* do you believe me when I say how much I care?"

Sensing the uneasy repose, a Maryland state trooper edged forward and tipped his hat. "Ma'am, I'm Corporal Mike Reese, Salisbury Barracks. Would you come with me, please? We have orders to extract you, direct from your Deputy Director."

Angela freed herself from Alvin's hold and shut her eyes. *"Victor Styles."*

"Affirmative, ma'am." Reese aimed a flashlight beam at an olive-and-brown Maryland State Police cruiser parked on an oyster-shell path. "ASAP."

Alvin yelled, "Give 'er some space, man. And what about our stuff?"

Angela spoke in a pained, low voice—pained and low because she dreaded what Styles might have in store for her. "Corporal Reese, this is Professor Alvin Markham. Can your people escort him to a hotel?"

Alvin winced. "Angie . . . what's—"

She kissed him on the lips. Again, no warmth. "Al, I'm okay. Go with them."

"No, you're not okay," Alvin groaned as Angela grabbed her Orioles baseball cap and hooded windbreaker, then fastened on a pair of Teva sport sandals. *"Angie?"*

She ignored him, quickly wrapping herself in the windbreaker; some of the male officers and rangers were staring at what was beneath her tank top and shorts. Angela gave Alvin a final wave and a weak smile and climbed into the cruiser.

"So where're we going?" she asked Trooper Reese. "Washington, by chopper?"

"No, ma'am. St. Michaels. A bed-and-breakfast called the Blue Heron Inn."

4

BALTIMORE FIELD OFFICE SUPERVISORY SPECIAL Agent William "Bud" White was a fifteen-year Bureau vet who emulated his cop-flick hero and namesake, Detective Bud White—the brute with the heart of gold in the film *L.A. Confidential*. He was six-three, barrel-chested, and topped with close-cropped, dull brown hair. He checked his cheap, beeping watch with equally dull brown eyes. Angela had been in the rest room for almost ten minutes.

"One look at that black vic's body and she barfs?" White croaked.

Special Agent George Constantine Vallas smoothed back his layered black mane and answered in his adopted Ebonics, "Back up off a sister, huh?"

Vallas pretty much anticipated White's response: a mock yawn and then "Wake me up when you decide to become a *white man* again, okay, Agent Vallas?"

Vallas pressed chest to chest with the older White. "No shame in my game, Agent White."

Both men backed away from each other when they heard the toilet flush. Angela emerged from the rest room. Her eyes were pink and hooded.

"Ready to bounce?" Vallas asked her.

Angela nodded, with a sniffle, then faced White. "I want to see the room now."

They'd been inside the Blue Heron's boathouse. Outside, a phalanx of floodlights blazed along the plantation's riparian grounds. Insects swarming in each hot beam reminded Angela of the snowflakes in Philadelphia on the night when she'd last seen Dr. Leslie T. Collins alive.

The thoughts and images churned in Angela's brain as she limped by Talbot County cops who were stringing a path of yellow crime-scene tape from the boathouse to the inn. The officers gawked. In her sandals, bare legs, cap, and windbreaker, Angela resembled a summer-camp counselor, or maybe even a teen camper, given her height. No matter, because Angela Bivens was a virtuoso at the art of concealing a lava nucleus with a cool shell. But Vallas had grown hip to this act, and Angela could feel his eyes prying back her coating as she recapped the facts.

"So around ten-thirty P.M., two guests were on the boathouse deck having a nightcap . . . they heard a man screaming . . . then silence . . . then a splash out in the cove? They find Collins under the dock—"

"Split open like rotten fruit," White finished in a dead, mean monotone.

Beneath the mansion's front portico columns, White's people were interviewing dazed guests; an Evidence Response Team agent in a blue ERT cleansuit and surgical mask brushed past them, carrying a bloody white garbage bag with the word *Dog* scrawled in felt-tip on the evidence label. Inside, ERT's plastic drop cloths covered the foyer's marble floor tiles, and about a dozen agents and Maryland State Police CSI techies were quietly vacuuming bits of lint, grass, and dirt from every square millimeter of wall or floor. Great arches of blood painted the walls and speckled the ceiling; the volume and velocity meant arterial gushes. Angela smelled human urine and feces.

"Now, the dog was killed outside, yet found *indoors*," she recounted. "But Dr. Collins was stabbed indoors . . . I'd say his bowels and bladder evacuated, in fear, shock, right before the stabbing begins. Yet he ends up *outside* under the boathouse."

White and Vallas nodded their heads in unison.

"Unoxidized blood inside . . . none outdoors. Catch any trace with the luminol?"

Vallas shoved his hands in his chino pockets and replied, "ERT found blood droplets leading out of the foyer and down to the boathouse. That's it."

"Maybe I'm missing something," Angela said, brow furrowing. "There were what, half a dozen other guests, plus staff? This wasn't the wee hours of the morning, so I'm going to ask something elementary—*nobody heard or saw a damn thing?*"

"Upstairs, some guests say they heard a dog barking, footsteps, and shouting," Vallas said. "The innkeeper found the beheaded dog and all the mess in the foyer."

Angela posited, "So, after they killed the dog, the subjects must have dragged the body out on a nonporous tarp or litter of some kind, right?"

"Subjects?" White asked.

"No one person could've done this. Did the laser or infrared find nonconforming footprints or drag marks on the lawn or the path to the cove?"

White answered this one with an insouciant shrug and a mumbled "No."

Angela's eyes narrowed. "And that didn't strike you as peculiar?"

"Awright," White said with a sigh, "everything here is off the *Twilight Zone* scale—which I guess is why FBIHQ called in you and Agent 'Saturday Night Fever.'"

While Vallas rolled his eyes, Angela was rapt and sharp. "Agent White, I presume we're here because of the White House connection—and our expertise."

"Whatever," White droned. "All we've ascertained is that each of the guests in the house—with the exception of the gin-'n'-tonic drinkers on the boathouse deck—was either very sleepy or complaining of severe headaches between twenty-one hundred and twenty-two hundred hours, or in other words, after the concierge did the nine o'clock bed turndown service rounds. They serve iced tea and cookies."

Frustrated, Angela joined Vallas on the stairs. Both snapped on surgical gloves, sheathed their feet in blue paper shoe covers, and moved to Collins's room. ERT's Special Agent Leanne Manning was shooting digital photos of Beth Hooperman's body. White and his men followed upstairs, but remained in the hall. Immediately, Angela noticed that Beth's right leg was a deeper, darker blue than the rest of her lapis-tinted body.

"She's cyanotic," Angela commented, circling the bed. Angela spotted the tray of lemon-mint cookies and a broken pitcher of spilled iced tea. "Take samples."

"You thinking poison?" Manning asked. She motioned for a Maryland State Police criminalist to bag the cookies and take a few drops of tea. "Must have acted instantaneously if it was." Manning sighed. "By the way, got some weird smudges on a shard of this pitcher. The laser should be able to clarify the image, but the Print Lab'll have to fume it. I'd get the grimy residue analyzed as well."

"What's the grime from?"

"Looks like ash mixed with organic matter."

Vallas caught the twinkle of pavé diamonds on Beth's anklet. It drew his eyes to her mottled, blackened toes, and he poked the flesh with a gloved finger. "Ladies, check *this shit* out."

Angela crouched down to see two puncture wounds on Beth's big toe. "Snakebite? *Big* one. Some venoms cause severe cyanosis in the victim's skin. Gold star for Georgey. Someone better call Talbot County Animal Control."

Everybody but Angela jerked back and nervously scanned the floor. Angela calmly folded her arms across her chest. In her sixth-grade science class in Baltimore, she'd learned that copperheads and water moccasins were the only venomous snakes native to Maryland's disappearing wetlands. Neither packed this animal's wallop. And no snake will crawl inside a house and slither up two flights of stairs to attack a human deliberately. Not unless it had human help to enter and escape.

"George," she said, "contact Frank Lupo. We have to interface with the Secret Service ASAP. This wasn't a robbery gone bad or some random psycho."

Vallas locked eyes with her, then called out to White in the hall, "Agent White, you better advise the innkeeper, his wife, and their staff of their rights."

White loomed in the doorway. "You're not suggesting that they're suspects?"

Angela jumped in, "He *didn't* say arrest them. They need to be inked for elimination prints. We need hair samples, and then we should conduct closed, videotaped interrogations. Somebody on the inside clearly aided our intruders."

White's chest and neck swelled. *"Whoa* . . . you're telling *me* how to do *my* job?"

Bud White had just clowned a woman who was sleep-deprived and hanging on by the thinnest of threads. Before Vallas could stop her, Angela sneered, "Not familiar with my new title, Agent White? Inspector, Investigative Services Division. Know what it means?"

White chortled derisively, "Nah, enlighten me."

"It means I'm here to help you and the local police."

White poked his tongue into his cheek.

"And, if my help is spit back in my face, then I have the authority to stick my size-five-and-a-half foot in your *ass.* Don't you *dare* question my directions again!"

Unconcerned with contaminating the crime scene, White stormed into the room; Angela stood her ground. Vallas jumped between them, hollering, "Yo, you need to back yourself up outta her grill, else your big ass gets called on the carpet at HQ . . . not to mention, gets tore up, right here, *by me*, right now!"

White bit his lip, reversed course, and trundled away with his agents in tow.

With Beth still lying there, cold and rock hard, Vallas asked a shocked Agent Manning for privacy. Angela had already pulled herself into a corner, clutching at her own shoulders as Manning left, closing the door.

"Not cool, Angie. That *ofay's* in the top ten of everyone's bad-mother-fucker list."

"Not . . . not in mine," Angela muttered.

Vallas replied sternly, "On the real—it's time you tell me what's wrong." He pulled Angela's hands away from her shoulders. They were shaking. "Bad flashbacks again, about the Trey Williams case? Thought you were seeing Dr. Myers about that."

He'd put his butt on the line for her before; she owed him her trust. "I knew the victim." Angela peered down at Beth's eyes. They glistened with a death film. "Not Hooperman. *Collins.* Friend of my parents'. He took care of me after . . . Trey." Now she raised her eyes to Vallas's. "He is . . . he *was* . . . an OB-GYN, George."

Vallas was always a quick study. Yet Angela avoided his waiting embrace by willing some composure. She yanked off her gloves. "Look, um, call Lupo like I said. I'm gonna grab a soda outside. Collect my thoughts . . ."

Talbot County officers had set out a vinyl cooler of soft drinks for the CSI and ERT teams working the crime scene. Unfortunately, it lay in the wet grass next to the Medical Examiner's Dodge minivan, and the County Coroner—who had the very un–Maryland Eastern Shore name of Babu Kumar, M.D.—was about to zip Les Collins into a black body bag. Angela took a swig of ginger ale to settle her stomach. She ordered herself to detach. *Don't be weak. Don't get sick.*

Kumar asked, "Feeling better, I see? Many times, I pray for cases like this. All I get here is duck hunters shooting one another, or trailer-park women poisoning their boyfriends with antifreeze in their Budweiser. I must be more careful what I pray for!"

Amen, Angela commiserated. Kumar then pointed to Collins's corpse. "This gentleman was *filleted,* sternum to groin. Six feet of ileum yanked out. Penis and scrotum partially severed, then torn off . . . replaced in the body cavity. Very nasty, eh?"

Angela shot back, "How could this be done in a few minutes, no witnesses, no blood spilled after the initial attack indoors, no tissue remnants out here?"

"That is for *you* to answer, dear girl. Someone had a surgical background, or perhaps worked in a slaughterhouse." Kumar aimed his flashlight at Collins's torso. "The flat blade used to stab the victim the *forty-six times* I counted was also used in the mutilation and disembowelment. So we have thrusting motions here in the throat, chest . . . yet slashing motions there. Your Tool and Bladed Weapon Section should have a jolly time deciding what this was." Angela leaned closer as Kumar continued, "Notice the angles of the defensive cuts on his hands and forearms? I believe he was fending off at least two attackers while perhaps a third or fourth assailant was stabbing him. Now look here: contusions on his wrists. I'd say the fatal wounds were simultaneous thrusts under each armpit, into the chest cavity."

"Meaning two unidentified subjects must've grabbed each wrist and held up his arms for the others to stab him?"

"Clever girl. Perhaps with a sword or a spearlike weapon? You concur?"

Vallas hiked over to them. "Lupo wants you at HQ. Chopper's on its way."

Angela turned to Kumar. "I want your autopsy protocol, plus twenty-point toxicology and serology, in no more than thirty-six hours, all right?"

"Dear girl, this is still a local homicide. I may only copy you on reports, and tissue samples must go to the State Police Lab in Pikesville, not to Washington."

"This a federal investigation now, sir." That statement alone was usually enough to cow a local official. She still had no clue of the basis for FBI jurisdiction.

"I see." Kumar shrugged. "Then that explains why that disagreeable fellow, Mr. White, was so agitated when I found this?"

Angela and Vallas gaped as Kumar opened Collins's mouth and lifted Collins's swollen, black tongue with his ballpoint pen. There, embedded in the flesh, was what looked like a smooth gold coin. More, an irregular disk. Kumar plucked it out with forceps. Etched into one side was a figure, like the number 7. This clue juiced Angela like a terrier acquiring a scent, overpowering her grief for Dr. Collins, fury at White, and dismay at the ease with which she'd abandoned Alvin.

"We've seen this before, George. God help us, we've seen this before!" *So that's why Styles tracked me down.* Angela ordered, "Bag it, tag it, and messenger it to the Numismatic Section!" But Vallas had already pulled away into the darkness. Angela scurried after him and caught his arm, saying, *"The Archangels*. Their calling card!"

"I dunno, Angie . . . doesn't make sense. The coins we found in other victims were Denver-minted U.S. eagle dollars. That thing in his mouth . . . it's . . . Jesus, Angie . . ."

"Hey . . . *hey*. Look at me. What about it scares you so much?"

"We Greeks have a legend that the Orthodox Church disavows. See, in order for a soul to cross the river Styx to the Underworld, it has to pay a toll to Charon the Boatman. To this day, if a friend or relative dies, some folks still put a gold coin in the dead person's mouth before burial. Not a modern drachma coin. Ancient gold slug, like *that*."

His words gouged the fight right out of her. Cold and fear seeped back into the empty spaces. *Don't forsake me. Don't send another.* Not one more devil chronicling his torment in the language of corpses. Familiar corpses.

5

ANGELA HAD TROUBLE KEEPING PACE with Assistant Director Francis X. Lupo's long legs as she followed them down a blue-carpeted corridor on the seventh floor, toward the FBI Director's Suite.

"I don't understand why the Director needs a personal briefing," she complained. "Victor Styles was the one who shanghaied me for this case, yet now, you say he's 'unavailable'?" Indeed, the Deputy Director's office had been empty when they'd whisked past it a minute ago.

Lupo replied grimly, "Alfred Whiting's still missing."

"Look, I've had no time to prepare a proper status memo. Bud White's people haven't finished drafting the 302s. What am I supposed to say?"

Halting at the door to the suite's anteroom, Lupo merely shrugged and straightened his apricot-colored silk tie. At Angela's insistence, he had punted the old 1980s Gordon Gecko look he'd sported when he was Special Agent in Charge in the Washington Metropolitan Field Division—the D.C. Field Office or "Nest," for short—in favor of twenty-first century monochromatic ties and earth-toned, four-button suits. Yet with those charcoal eyes, the pug nose, cleft chin, and Ditmars Boulevard, Queens, accent, Lupo's image remained more a Cosa Nostra *capo regime* than the head of the FBI's new Investigative Services Division, or ISD.

The Director's receptionist buzzed the pair through to the anteroom; a dour-faced male aide closed the door behind them and asked them to wait.

Angela, voice low so as not to arouse the aide's attention, pressed, "You were the only person who knew I was at the shore for the weekend. And *how* would the Deputy Director of the FBI zero in on a local Talbot County double homicide within *an hour* of the bodies' being discovered?"

Lupo settled into the supple leather couch next to Angela and answered, "Somebody in the White House who keeps tabs on Elizabeth Hooperman tagged ol' Vick after the Talbot County police got to the crime scene and ID'd the victims. Finding that coin in Collins, well, that just cemented our jurisdiction. He wanted a press blackout on the male victim's ID. Why? I ask. You don't need to know, he says. Then he orders me to find you. *You*— to honcho the locals and the Baltimore Field Office."

"Why *me?* AFT and our Civil Rights Section's on the Archangel case, too."

The Assistant Director raised his palms. "Asking the wrong guy, Tigress. But he got pissed off when I told you you were taking a weekend vacation, somewhere on Assateague—beach blanket bingo with your physics prof friend."

"Frank, change the subject."

"Understood. See, at seven this morning, one of Clinton's little Stephanopolites from the West Wing called Attorney General Reno to get an update on Hooperman. Probably the same asshole who's Styles's contact. When the AG responded, she didn't have all the facts, blah blah—and that this was likely gonna be a parochial matter for the local cops and the Baltimore Field Office—well, the next call comes from the White House Chief of Staff. The AG rousts the Director outta bed. It's ISD's case now." Lupo then explained that Beth Hooperman was a political shark, well-published feminist, and doyenne of both the East Coast and Hollywood liberal elite. Her husband, a dotcom mogul in suburban Philadelphia, was a major fund-raiser for the Democratic Party.

Lupo said, "Look, ISD's job is to come in and do a 'Columbo' or 'Hercule Poirot' anytime the field offices are stumped, or when FBIHQ says so. Regardless of what you think about Bud White, this is the latter case, *capiche?* Besides, there's bizarre physical evidence to deal with. Right up your alley, Tigress. If it's not the Archangels, then, short of aliens or witchcraft, ya gotta tell me your theories."

After a yawn prompted by twenty-four hours of work, Angela's tone was low, timid. "Possibly the Archangels' MO." She wasn't going to offer Vallas's Greek legend.

"Listen, Hooperman was a juicy target for Amesha Spentas. Yeah, since you cracked their code, I'm using that name instead of Archangels. Collins musta been gravy for them—black, wealthy, having an affair with a white female who worked for Bill Clinton? His dossier says he did two hundred abortions last year. Your dad's a gynecologist, too, right?"

The aide reappeared. The Director was ready to see them. *Thank God,* Angela thought as she shot to her feet, smoothing out her suit skirt.

The aide escorted Angela and Lupo into the inner office. FBI Director Remo Donatello had showered after jogging in the midday heat. He was wearing a white terry robe and had a towel draped over his head like a boxer; he'd plopped down on a little divan opposite a fifty-six-inch, flat, digital TV.

"Inspector Bivens," he called, facing the screen, "and Francis Xavier— help yourselves to some cold Pellegrino, lemonade, or Cokes over on the bar. Ninety-something today, seventy percent humidity. God, another summer in Washington!"

"Mr. Director," Angela said, "are we expecting Deputy Director Styles, too?"

Donatello chuckled as he turned to face Lupo, "That's our little soldier, eh, Francis? All business. That's why she was promoted!" Angela noted the passive voice there—hadn't *he* promoted her? "Kick off those high heels of yours and watch the tube."

MSNBC's Lester Holt appeared on the monitor. *"Sources close to the Bush campaign tell NBC News that the FBI has now doubled the size of the Crisis Management Unit team sent to the Whiting family's Arlington, Virginia, home, thus confirming fears that Mr. Whiting has indeed been kidnapped. Alfred B. Whiting, former U.S. Attorney for the District of Columbia under the elder George Bush, and current campaign cochair for Texas Governor George W. Bush, failed to return home over ten days ago from a Memorial Day weekend retreat for GOP leaders in Bal Harbour, Florida. MSNBC will carry FBI Deputy Director Victor Styles's press conference live from Washington."*

Angela was at once relieved and disappointed that Styles was preoccupied. Donatello seemed to pick up on it. "Vick was anxious to speak to you," the Director told her. "But somebody had to douse this other wildfire, quick."

Now, Holt's partner, Ashleigh Banfield: *"Back to our breaking news—local police and FBI officials remain silent about the mysterious death of Clinton White House Adviser Elizabeth Hooperman in the Chesapeake Bay village of St. Michaels, Maryland. Mrs. Hooperman's body was found along with that of a male companion whom officials have yet to identify."*

With the remote, Donatello switched to the Fox News cable channel. Shepard Smith reported, *"Fox News has learned that Clinton staffer Elizabeth*

Hooperman's dead lover was a married, prominent African American physician named Leslie Tyrone Collins, who also has close ties to Senator Brian 'Butch' Buford, Democrat from California. Hannity and Colmes will have more on this newest disturbing Clinton scandal tonight at eight, Eastern time, and Bill O'Reilly will add his insights at nine, Eastern, on the O'Reilly Factor."

Lupo seethed, *"Son of a bitch!* Remo, I'll take full responsibility for any leaks."

Donatello waxed nonchalant. "If there's a leak, I'll presume it started in Bud White's shop up in Baltimore. He and his pals 'n' patrons are like hyenas waiting for a wounded giraffe to drop—and I guess I have a very long neck." The Director then yanked the towel off his head and began fluffing his hair. *Odd,* Angela thought. He usually wasn't *this* phlegmatic, especially over naked politics. Something was up. Still, she resolved not to tell them she knew Collins. How could she?

"Now listen, both of you," the Director resumed. "Only Attorney General Reno knows what I'm about to tell you. Regardless of who's living at 1600 Pennsylvania Avenue this time next year, I'm retiring as Director effective August thirty-first, 2000."

Angela leaned forward; Lupo's cleft chin sank.

"Mr. Director," Angela said, "why . . . why are you telling *me* this?"

Donatello chuckled. "I owe you, kiddo. After all the mess I put you through surrounding this Trey Williams thing? I trust what you got . . . right here." He thumped his sternum for emphasis. "Don't ask me to elaborate on your role anymore, all right?"

She nodded, but said, "Deputy Director Styles doesn't know?"

The Director winked and continued, "I have a legacy to protect. Problem is, the dike is springing leaks. Not enough fingers. All this and a presidential election to look forward to!" He stood, staring at Angela with those hooped, squinty eyes. "If these Archangels, Amesha Spentas, or whatever they're calling themselves, are responsible, we want you to dispose of it, fast and clean, understood?"

"Understood, sir," Angela answered crisply. Her eyes pledged her allegiance to the Director. She was part of his legacy, too.

Lupo shook his head. "Retiring? I shoulda seen this coming . . ."

"Nah, Francis, you wouldn't've. But it'll all be clear soon, because *you, paesan,* will be interim Director. Until the election settles things."

Angela stood from her chair; Lupo's head snapped back. She heard him mumble, "Get the fuck outta 'ere." Not an epithet when between Italian-American buddies, so the Director took no offense.

A second of painful silence passed before Angela intoned, "Bypassing Victor Styles wasn't an oversight, sir."

"Yeah," Lupo agreed, voice whispery. "And you're jumping me over Woody Sessions and Bob Scofield, too. They aren't gonna be happy, Remo."

The Director shrugged. "So? Half the time, Bob has no clue what's going on in the field offices. And Woody, he let me down big-time with this Chinese-spy mess at the Los Alamos nuclear lab. Yeah, he and his right-wing friends on the Hill break my balls, but he isn't the Prince of damn Darkness, right?"

Right, Angela thought. Woodruff Sessions was a Plano, Texas, native who headed the Bureau's National Security Division, or NSD: the spy catchers and terrorist hunters. Most of the agents in NSD were white males; Sessions was a personal friend of the Bush family and Republican House members Tom DeLay and Dick Armey. Robert Scofield had made his FBI bones as a protégé of former Director William Webster. He supervised the Criminal Investigative Division, or CID: joint FBI-DEA task forces, bank robbery, organized crime, and civil rights. Both men opposed the settlement of Angela's class action suit the previous year, which gave her what she'd always wanted—to be in the trenches as a field agent. And both men had opposed Angela's promotion to Inspector. Keeping Sessions and Scofield at bay, at least until the election, suited Angela just fine.

Donatello continued, "As for the *real* Prince of Darkness, our friend Vick, he's a lightning rod. Too tied to the liberal hobgoblins my enemies despise. Now, Angela, would you please sit back down . . . you're making me nervous standing there, kiddo."

"I'd . . . I'd rather stand for this, sir."

"For chrissakes sit, Angie," Lupo jumped in. He grabbed a bottle of Pellegrino and poured a glass for himself, likely wishing he had some Johnnie Walker Black plus a Zantac as a chaser.

Angela sat and convinced herself that duty, not fear, took over as she cleared her throat and said, "Mr. Director, I'll hold what you've just said in strictest confidence . . . and I'm ready to do what's necessary on the Hooperman matter."

Donatello smiled. "That's our girl. The game's turning on loyalty, now. Not skill or bravery. Candor will be a liability. You follow?"

She nodded. He clapped his hands.

"Good. Now that *that's* settled, you will now be the primary on Hooperman, with the Civil Rights Section and Bud White's people providing support." Donatello then patted his *goombah* on the shoulder, as if to remind him of something. "I'd talked this over with Francis last week, so the timing couldn't have been better. Vick was against it, but, hey, he can't *always* have his way. You need some help."

Once the reminder registered in his head, Lupo said, "Yeah, you're on rotation to receive a trainee from the Academy—did you get my e-mail?"

No such e-mail. And then Angela girded herself. Though she led a loose-knit team of ten agents that included Special Agents Vallas, Micklin, and Marcus Johnson, she, herself, worked alone. She refused to share her soul again. She'd done so with Kristi Trimble, and she'd let Kristi die.

"I'm sure you remember your salad days as a trainee-intern?" Donatello mused.

She did. Mindless, rote memorization of the *Manual of Investigative Operations & Procedures,* or *MIOP.* Being shunted from one bitter white male agent to another. Making photocopies for them. Making coffee for them. Enduring a total abdication of mentorship, yet targeted for cruel jokes. "Sir, given the complexity of every contingent piece of my caseload, I really don't think a trainee would be approp—"

"I think you'll be an excellent teacher." Donatello handed her a file folder that had been lying, innocuously, on an end table. "This trainee's in the top quintile of her class."

Lupo remarked, "Her section completed the Tactical Course down at Fort Bragg; her flight comes into Reagan National . . . when?" He glanced at his *padrone* for guidance.

"One-forty P.M. tomorrow, USAir, from Fayetteville."

Angela wondered why the Director of the FBI would have such detailed travel information on a trainee.

"I realize you're working on no sleep," Donatello said. "Just get her settled in. The Training Section reserved a room for her at the Marriott Courtyard in Foggy Bottom."

Addled, Angela had to read the name aloud: " 'Nadia Rose Riccio, born February fourteenth, 1977.' "

"We thought it best for her to use her mother's maiden name at Quantico," the Director said almost sheepishly.

"*We?*"

"Her last name is really Donatello. She's my daughter."

Congress had voted to close D.C.'s Lorton Prison in suburban Virginia. Most of the inmates had already been shipped to "privatized" human warehouses, far from their families, despite the lobbying effort from ex-cons like former mayor Marion Barry. But one block of cells remained stocked with black- and brown-skinned bodies: death row.

A balding guard, himself an African American, stood before a metal door covering the bars of a cell, twirling his brass turnkey in one hand while supporting a food tray with the other. "C'mon, niggah . . . ain't you hungry?" he grumbled. He couldn't see the occupant through the small slit. There was usually an answer: a grunt, a curse, a whimper. This time there was silence, so he taunted, "Sorry 'bout yo' appeal, Mistah Afrocentric *Joe College.* Yo' high-price white lawyer di'n't *really* think a Tom like Clarence Thomas was gonna save *yo'* murderous black ass, did he?"

Again, no reply. The guard set down the tray, unlocked and swung open the outer cover door.

Antoine Jones was hanging by the neck from an electrical cord that had been yanked from the broken ceiling light fixture. At six-four, Antoine's toes just about scraped the floor as he swayed, slowly.

"Ten fo'teen!" the guard choked into his shoulder mike as he tore open the cell door. "Unit twelve, block B!"

Jumping to the bunk-bed frame, the guard could hear the final burps of life from Antoine's twisted trachea. He pulled out his penknife. Not too smart, that guard. As he cut into the hard rubber cord, his knife blade hit the live copper leads inside. The guard fell hard to the painted concrete floor, dead.

That slice sufficed to snap the cord—leaving Antoine crumpled on top of the fat hack's body. Before Antoine's eyes caught the blur of the prison SORT squad crashing into the cell, they focused on the far wall, on words scrawled there, faintly, in pencil:

AMA SIMBA UKU ZI UMTHAKATHI

And on the dank cell floor, below the writing, lay a torn, empty envelope. The return-address read:

Maynard V. Mullinix, Esquire
Grunton & Williams, LLP
1800 K Street, N.W.
Washington, D.C. 20005
ATTORNEY-CLIENT PRIVILEGED/CENSOR EXEMPT

With the cell secure, the SORT goons departed, leaving a trauma nurse to attempt CPR—on the fat guard, not Antoine. Regular hacks were already shoving Antoine's limp body onto a rusty gurney. Yet no one in the cell appeared to notice an old-fashioned Polaroid on the floor next to that envelope. The hacks stepped on it, over it, around it; kicked it as if it were a discarded gum wrapper. Or maybe they *couldn't* see it. It was a picture of a white man's hand. Just a hand. Freshly severed at the wrist.

6

JUNE 13, 11:15 A.M.

OFFICE ASSISTANT JERRY LOPES PEEKED his head in the door. He was barely five-seven, muscular and tanned, with spiky black hair. His left ear was pierced by a tiny diamond stud: a gift from his boss.

"Inspector Bivens? Sorry to disturb you . . . your father called again, and we got some new file materials for the Hooperman matter, plus a Latent Print Lab Chain of Custody pouch for a glass shard from a broken pitcher at the Blue Heron Inn?"

Angela didn't answer; instead, she rotated, slowly, in her office chair.

"Um . . . your dad's pretty upset I'm screening your calls."

Jill Scott's "Love Rain" was spinning on the CD player perched atop a wood-veneer bookcase by the door. Jerry knew something of his boss's past with Trey Williams, thus he figured the song was providing Angela's distraction: *The rain was fallin' and I could not see that he became my voodoo priest / And I was his faithful concubine.*

Angela wasn't in a gray fugue; rather, her brain was choked with the data spilling off a ream-high pile of printed reports and typed memos on her desk. Images from surveillance photos were plastered onto the movable dry-erase board that obscured her view of the Hoover Building's atrium. On her credenza, two laptops augmented her desktop computer, all pulsing with streaming video. Jerry thumbed down the volume knob on the CD player and called again, *"Inspector?"*

31

Perhaps that title, *Inspector,* hadn't sunk in, even after five months. It was payoff at worst, a canard at best, all so Donatello and Styles could shellac over the Bureau's utter abdication in investigating the murders Trey Williams had committed. Perfect buff-and-polish job, especially when the media and Congress discovered that the very agent so cynically assigned to tow the line and round up the "usual suspects" had been sleeping with the perpetrator while she slowly unraveled the truth.

Finally, Angela looked up at Jerry. "What is it now?"

"Inspector, also . . . we got a FedEx from Dr. Kumar in Easton, Maryland—the Collins autopsy protocol. Plus, our own lab sent up some prelims on Elizabeth Hooperman's tox and serology. Does this stuff go in the new tub with the items from the Baltimore Field Office?"

Angela shook her head. "No. My in-box."

Jerry pursed his lips when he saw the stainless steel mesh tray weighted by a layer cake of folders and Redweld tubs, plus pink and canary flimsy form copies. The FBI still wasn't quite a paperless crime-fighting machine.

As Jerry turned to leave, he added, "Oh, and Dr. Myers called right after your dad. You canceled your appointment last Thursday because of your beach camping trip, so she wants to see you in her office before you pick up Agent-Trainee Riccio."

"Yeah . . . she already e-mailed me. Twice."

"Inspector Bivens, um, your dad's calls . . . he said he wanted to talk about Dr. Collins. Did you know this victim, personally?"

"No. I think he was a chief resident at the hospital where my father was on staff. Years ago, in Baltimore. I'm not sure."

Jerry cocked his head. "Hmmm, I guess it'd compromise the investigation if you knew him well, huh? More so if you knew him and didn't disclose it."

Angela managed to smile. "Are you going down to the canteen?"

Jerry smiled back, nodding. "You want me to order some lunch?"

She scanned the burnt, crusted bottom of her coffeemaker's carafe. "Actually, run to Lawson's on Eleventh and K and get a pound of vanilla French roast, finely ground."

"Decaf this time—*please?*"

Shaking her head, she handed him a crisp twenty from her purse. "And I want all my change back." She laughed.

Jerry ducked out, but in less than thirty seconds, Angela heard his voice again, this time on the intercom. "Security says Ms. Boissiere and Ms.

Wilcox are down at the Ninth and E Street checkpoint. They aren't on your calendar. Shall they send them up?"

Angela cleared the visit, then said in a strained, detached voice, "If Professor Markham calls, put him in my voice mail. Say I'm in a briefing."

Maybe Jerry felt the vibe over the intercom, for he answered, "If he loves you, he'll wait. If *really* loves you, he'll move on. You got some dragons to slay, gurl."

Angela chuckled to herself, then gibed, "Boy, go get my vanilla French roast!" In the ten minutes it took for Carmen and Sharon to clear security and knock on the office door, Angela slid the dry-erase board into a corner, facing the wall, then scooped up the loose materials on her desk and shoved them into her cabinet and credenza: form 302 evidence-witness reports, interview transcripts, bomb forensics memos from the Bureau of Alcohol, Tobacco and Firearms (AFT or BATF) National Laboratory Center in Rockville, Maryland. And it all pertained to one phrase Angela had scribbled in green marker, on the last bare patch of the board. *Amesha Spentas.* The mother of all dragons on her caseload.

The words *Amesha Spentas* had first been written in chalk on a Dumpster outside an abortion clinic in Mobile, Alabama, on Christmas Day, 1999. A brick of C-4 had reduced the clinic and adjoining offices to singed splinters. Same for another clinic on January 17, 2000, in Lima, Ohio. Five people died. Two weeks later, as Angela lay on Les Collins's exam table, the FBI's elite Hostage Rescue Team had stormed an abandoned hunting shack in the North Carolina high country. The shack was a hiding place for fugitive Eric Rudolph, the suspected Atlanta Olympic Park bomber and murderer of a nurse and a police officer in a Birmingham abortion bombing; the land records listed the cabin as the property of a dead cracker named "Gabriel." Pinned to the battered, bloody body of the imam of the Third Avenue Mosque & Community Center in Flint, Michigan, was the word *Raphael.*

At a Jacksonville, Florida, gay bar in March 2000, amid the gore produced by flying shrapnel from three pipe bombs, the word *Uriel* was drawn on a cocktail napkin. "Michael" was the sender of a postcard to a Jewish appellate court justice in Florida who'd reversed a local judge's decision allowing the Ten Commandments to be posted in classrooms. The postcard threatened the judge's children. He was childless, but a day later, his two prize dalmatians were beheaded and gutted, just like the dog, Pepper, at the Blue Heron. *Azreal* was spelled on a sidewalk in the blood of a black student leader on the Indiana University campus in Bloomington in April 2000. He'd been shot in the throat. He survived, but was mute for life. Police found a laundry ticket with the word *Jophiel* written on it, in a planter outside the home of a reporter in Boise, Idaho. She had been researching a story on the Posse Comitatus, skinheads, and neo-Nazi survivalists in the Rockies, and the nameless allies helping them infect the Internet with hate. She'd been gunned down on Memorial Day weekend, right before Alfred Whiting disappeared, and as Les Collins and Beth Hooperman doubtless made their plans for a rendezvous. And the reporter, like the student in Bloomington and the imam in Flint, had a gold dollar coin shoved under her tongue.

Only three more, Angela thought as Carmen and Sharon sauntered into her office. *Abdiel, Chamuel, and Zadkiel.* She'd broken the code, all right. *Amesha Spentas* was ancient Persian for "the archangels." Such seraphim didn't bear heroes to heaven or watch over train passengers. They could be your neighbor grumbling about school prayer as he mounted his riding mower. Or the pimply kid at the video store counter with empty, raisinlike eyes. Or a quiet Gulf War vet, like Tim McVeigh. Impossible for Angela to track, because no one wanted to racially profile clean-cut white boys.

Angela forced a wide Miss America smile and exchanged cheek pecks with her friends; they were distracting her from sending these archangels to hell. Carmen and Sharon sat on the couch and quickly mopped their glistening foreheads with tissues yanked from their purses. Both women wore floral-print dresses with flounce hems, and strappy heels sans hose. Only nudity would have provided relief in that heat.

Carmen said, "Awright, Missy Thang, grab your stuff. We *be* out for some lunch. Time to decompress you."

Angela shrugged. "Um . . . ladies . . . I-I can't."

The more reticent Sharon added, in her soft monotone, "We've got reservations at Timothy Dean's at the St. Regis. Some lunch, then high tea. No excuses."

Carmen leaned forward, levity pushed aside. "We saw the news, and the front pages of the *Post,* the *Washington Times,* the *Baltimore Sun.* Everybody's cranked on this Hooperman woman and the White House connection, but *we* know better. And we know you, honey. You didn't tell your superiors you knew this man. As if you aren't already under crushing stress. We don't want you to drift away from us ever again."

Angela sighed. "I said I can't." She rotated away from them in her office chair. Still afraid to show weakness to the two people who had bucked her up at her lowest.

Sharon countered, "It's no crime to ask for help. Now, c'mon, it's my treat. My big law firm salary's got to go to something besides paying my condo fees."

"If not lunch," Carmen added, smile returning, "then take a break tonight. We'll check out that new place off New York Avenue, Dreams. Paint some M•A•C on our already pretty faces, throw on our summer hooker dresses—yeah, I know you got the stuff in your walk-in closet 'cause I was with you buyin' it in Nordstrom at Pentagon City two weeks ago, and don't front!" Carmen coaxed a brief giggle from Angela. Decompression was tempting.

"First off," Angela said, "I'm not going to Dreams to stand in line with youngsters and gold-*teefed* folks, okay? How 'bout a girls' night out next week. Alvin can tag along."

Sharon wasn't smiling. "Why buy clothes if you never go out? Why buy sexy dresses if you won't wear them for your boyfriend? Sorry, your *friend*. I bet you haven't even told poor Alvin you're okay since you had him carted away on that beach."

"Hold up . . . why are you tripping? And 'poor' Alvin?"

"Angel, he called me like four times over the last two days. Worried sick."

"And so why would he call *you?*"

Sharon rolled her green eyes. "Because *you* won't take his calls."

"Because work's kicking my ass! It's TV and headlines for you. It's real for me. Real blood. Real bodies. Alvin understood that I had to get back into the war long ago. Yes, we have our quality 'alone' time, and what we do then isn't anyone's biz."

"You're the one tripping now," Sharon huffed, twisting away from Angela's squinted eye. "So his consolation prize is being token man on girls' night out?"

"Like Monique used to say, 'Hang with the cats, gotta learn to meow.'" Angela ground her teeth, realizing that quoting their murdered friend was harsh. Lack of sleep, pressure, secrets—all frayed that last thread on which Angela danced.

Carmen interceded. "Angie-Boo . . . listen, the fact that Al was frantic is all you need to know. He told Sharon they pulled you right out of the tent to take you to that bed-and-breakfast. And seriously—and look at me when I'm speaking to you, chile—have you even spoken to your mother and father at all? Les Collins, Lord . . . it was *Les Collins*. Angel, we don't care about real bodies, real blood. We love and care about you."

Sharon stood up. "Alvin doesn't want to meow. He wants to bark." Sharon then shrugged her sun-blushed beige shoulders. "On second thought, Alvin's no dog. Nor is he a crutch. He's a man who cares about you, like we care."

Carmen stood, too. "Love means *trusting* that someone won't pick at your scabs, honey. We won't, and we know all your scabs."

Angela lowered her glance. "Alvin doesn't know one of them."

Angela raised her eyes when she didn't get a response from either of her friends. But she did notice Sharon now distracted by one laptop screen. On it was a logo of a bald eagle perched atop a swastika. In Gothic font:

`"cyber Reich."`

Below scrolled a banner:

`"The Lord God won't bring a runaway government under his heel by himself. It's up to his chosen white children, to use the government as his footstool."`

The inset box showed another site:

`"www.america4ever.com."`

"We think they've been doing recruiting for the Archangels," Angela explained. "These sites give the addresses of ACLU lawyers, and abortion doctors and clinic workers. The Supreme Court's overturned the injunctions that shut down the sites."

Though Carmen and Sharon nodded along, their faces were drawn and tight, as if indulging their friend was painful. When Angela finished her lecture, Carmen gave her a thick hug good-bye; Sharon gave her a weak buss on the cheek. Quietly, they left. Angela could see them striding down Pennsylvania Avenue, arguing, gesticulating, as they disappeared into the heat shimmer. *They'll never understand what I've been through. But I do love them.* Yet Angela knew what lay beneath the patina of that cliché, too. It didn't matter how much you loved someone—a friend, a family member, a spouse, or a lover. What mattered was how you acted when you were with them. *And I acted like a fool.*

She checked her watch. The passive-aggressive approach to avoiding an appointment with the Bureau psychiatrist, Sylvia Myers, entailed digging into Beth Hooperman's toxicology report. Kumar opined that a nerve toxin caused death by both asphyxia and coronary infarction; the FBI Lab confirmed it. The toxin was snake venom. The culprit was a member of the elapid family, whose members include cobras and coral snakes, rather than the viper family. Angela sent an e-mail to ITC; she had to query through the arcane and bug-infested Automated Case Support System, which meant her research request might or might not reach a technician.

```
Request forensic referral at National zoo and/or smithsonian:
Herpetologist/venomous reptiles. urgent. special compartmen-
talized info/confidential messenger to deliver victim serol-
ogy, tox, and crime scene photo, case NO. ISD2001-0049,
Hooperman/Collins upon contact.
```

From research months ago, Angela knew that Zadkiel, one of God's seraphim, laid the Lord's punishment on adulterers who also committed murder to further their trysts. Entwined around the archangel's staff were two snakes, as on the caduceus. The old Persian, Greek, and Roman myths named the snakes as green cobras.

Angela yanked off her glasses and tossed them on her desk blotter. Oh, no, no rest for her. No mending ties with her girls, no rescue of Alvin's heart. Just dragon-slaying. And not with a sword. Here, the slayer had to plod through paper, laptop screens, photos. She e-mailed Numismatics, though Vallas had likely double-checked on the progress of the analysis on the gold coin found under Collins's bloated tongue. She had no compunction about triple-checking. Took up an extra two minutes. Two minutes of dodging from self-examination, till there was another knock on the door, followed by a low, husky voice, like an older Lauren Bacall or Kathleen Turner.

"Figured I'd have to come down to lasso you, dear."

7

FBI Psychiatric & Medical Division

DR. SYLVIA MYERS, M.D., PH.D., TOOK a deep drag from the Virginia Slims Menthol 100 clamped between her stubby fingers while Angela scanned the slip from the prescription pad. Dr. Myers may have spoken with the Bacall- or Turner-esque sexy-and-sandpapery tone, but she sure didn't look like either of the actresses. She was even shorter than Angela: a squat, apple-shaped white woman who sported an extra chin. Always adorned in a short-jacketed Chanel suit, fabric matched to the season. Silver bangles and charms had jingled on her little wrist when she'd reached across her narrow desk to hand Angela the prescription.

"I know what this is, Sylvia," Angela said after reading the word Risperdal. "It's for schizophrenia and disassociative episodes. I'm just down, a little panicky." She tossed the slip back onto the desk, next to the large, humming ion-air filter that allowed Dr. Myers to circumvent the regulations against indoor smoking.

Dr. Myers said, "Paxil's not going to help with these waking dreams of yours."

Angela gestured to the long, plush, forest-green couch along the wall, still decorated with spent tissues. "I only mentioned my grammie Lucy once in this session. And, hey, I didn't even talk about Trey and Pluto. That should be enough for OPR. No need for psychotropic meds. Lord, just give me some Zoloft. Not *this.*"

Dr. Myers studied Angela's earnest facade. "The Office of Professional Responsibility doesn't monitor our sessions; your visits are purely voluntary." Dr. Myers leaned forward, and Angela could see the fine lines around her eyes and mouth fracture the plastered layer of Estée Lauder foundation. "Angela, every minority female like you, indeed every woman, period, has learned that working here is a marathon, not a sprint. Sounds cliché-ish, I suppose. But it seems to be a lesson you must relearn."

Sounded like what Sharon had said, and it made Angela chafe. "No offense, but what do you know about being a 'minority' female?"

Myers rocked in her chair. "Ahhh. Never too late to assign your therapy to Dr. Hill, a black woman. Perhaps she'll get a breakthrough."

" 'Breakthrough'? This is the first I've heard that word." The smoke was getting to her. "Look, are we done here? I mean, I get irritable and weak if I don't get food, and I have to get some before I go to the airport."

Myers crushed out her cigarette. "Cards on the table? You are suffering from *severe* post-traumatic stress disorder, punctuated by anxiety attacks and depression. Have you been functional? Yes. In the half a year I've been treating you, you've driven yourself to excel in no less than three major investigations, from stock fraud and money laundering to domestic terrorism. But overcompensating for *loss*—that's not the prognosis that gives me pause, Angela. What scares me is what happens when you eventually begin to *de*compensate. Spiral downward. You're *brittle*. Risperdal's our insurance policy."

Angela's back stiffened. "The Bureau depends on me. *Everyone* depends on me."

Dr. Myers asked, "How long will you indulge these twin demons?"

"I thought we were done with Trey and Pluto."

"Not them. *Your* twin demons. Attributes. One is guilt. The other's not so easy to quantify. I studied philosophy, too, dear. Self-forgiveness is our first step."

"When I was eleven and my friend Michelle took her cop father's service .38, shot herself . . . my parents told me to 'forgive myself.' Easier said than done."

"We both know your guilt has its genesis with this childhood trauma, dear. Losing your friend. Not *protecting* her at that moment when you found her, in the playground, and those boys had coaxed her to take off her clothes. Or even avenging her for all the cruel teasing heaped on her. But that's just prologue. Guilt now flows from victims of all the crimes you investigate, and not simply the ones who've died, but ones who've been de-frauded, harassed, abused. It flows from Special Agent Trimble, whom you still refuse to talk about. And it ricochets daily off this wall through which you won't break: *forgiving yourself for loving Trey Williams.*"

Angela's eyes moistened, and she cursed herself for it.

"Dear, I'm sure a little human piece of him existed, somewhere."

A quivering smile grew on Angela's face, even as glistening tears tracked down her cheeks. Yes, there was some little human piece of Trey. *Ha! Like twenty-three chromosomes worth?* A bloody mass of tissue, long ago chucked in Les Collins's garbage.

Dr. Myers snapped off a tissue from a box on her desk and handed it to Angela. While her patient blew her nose and collected herself, Dr. Myers said softly, "You were a sociology major in college. So you would recall what *DSM-IV* says is the most dangerous weapon a hyper-antisocial personality like Trey Williams wields, because he wielded it at you. They have the abil-ity to winnow into your soft, secret places. And who's the most vulnerable? Ironically, someone who feels she has to be so hard, so in control, as to mask the lack of control in her own life . . . well, Trey, like any addictive behav-ior—and I include workaholicism—gives false warmth, like a dram of brandy during halftime of a freezing football game. Vulnerability's no char-acter flaw, dear."

"Let's deal with the real world, okay? I show weakness to these men, I'm out."

"Keeping you 'in' the FBI's game is what I'm here for."

Thinking herself composed, Angela grinned and quipped, "Right. You said two demons. So what's my other one?"

"Deafness." Dr. Myers swiveled to her credenza to grab another ciga-rette. "You see, dear, something's been calling you. Tugging. You've been re-sisting it for the last six months and that's causing turmoil inside you. But, dear, you try to quiet the call with your robotic adherence to duty. Duty and *listening* aren't the same thing."

"You sound a lot like my grammie. When I was in college, she said, 'A spirit talks and you got wax in y'ears."

"Interesting. Let's take that further."

"Sure." Angela laughed. "Okay, Grammie said that I got an old soul. I al-ready told you . . . months ago . . . how she said a woman's soul's got two parts, boy and girl. Still, both sides are old, from another time. Not rein-carnated. Just old. One's fierce, brave, restless. The other one's practical, nurturing, protecting." Then Angela's brow tightened. "Dual. Like my so-called demons. Like Trey and Pluto. Look, may I go?"

Dr. Myers shook her head quickly as she lit up another bone. "One last thing." She exhaled and the ion filter consumed the smoke. "The recurring daydream you mentioned at our last session. Has it changed?"

"I told you I'm hungry and I'll be late."

Dr. Myers rocked in her chair. "Look at me . . . and relax. *Breathe.*"

Angela mumbled, "No," but Dr. Myers kept coaxing her in that voice. Ever softer. Making Angela sigh. Loosening her tight back muscles. Causing her eyes to blink out the gray bookshelves, then close. Flooded with color. With movement. "It's sort of like before, Sylvia," she said, narrating. "You know—dry, hot places with exotic names that I seem to know and yet can't pronounce. But . . . well, now, no dew or flowers, or that acrid smoke. Now, I hear cattle. Moos and bells clanking. Dogs barking. I see mountains. Tall grass. *And someone else.*" Dr. Myers kept rocking, and Angela kept talking, time lost. "It's a little boy. I'm handing him leaves, blossoms, oils. He's grinding them up in some stone cup."

"Like a mortar and pestle?"

"Uh-huh. He seems to know more of what he's doing than I do. He knows it will make people well. He looks like *me*. Smaller. Masculine. I mean, I only see my hands, his face. Not our bodies, when we talk . . . *without speaking*. And I'm sad because he's going to lose me. He'll have to survive. And he knows it, too."

"You mean you'll lose him?"

"No. *No.* He'll lose me."

"Dear, wake up."

"*No.* There's a waterfall. I hear a waterfall. And I see gold shimmers on the eddies. No foam or whitecaps. Just gold shimmers. People dance. Two men. I can't see their faces . . . but I know they're men. They're ugly. They stink. I smell them. Stink like corpses, Sylvia. On the opposite riverbank, below the waterfall . . . shit . . . a woman. I can see her because the boy sees her. Then, in the eddies, the gold eddies, something big, black, thick writhes up, splashes up. An animal. Like a snake. Like a big number 7 in the water. Head bent, like big number 7."

Angela's eyes opened. Dr. Myers said, "Dear, when did these dreams begin? Late November, after the Williams brothers were dead, and you were in the hospital, or late January, when you applied for emergency leave and never told us why?"

"I don't recall." Angela was going to stonewall if the questions probed deeper.

"You want to have children someday, right?"

Angela nodded. "I think more about a son than a daughter, like in the dream. I like the name Michael. Michael's the name of an archangel. A protector and minister to the afflicted. But not an avenger. Or who fights evil with evil's tools, ya know?"

"Interesting." Dr. Myers stopped to scribble on a legal pad. "One of your cases . . . bombers, killers, using the name Archangel."

"That's classified," Angela chuckled. "And the reason why I will always be employed."

Dr. Myers took a puff from her menthol. "And why I will, too, dear. Same time, next week?"

8

CLOSE TO TWO O'CLOCK, NINETY-SIX DEGREES, and air like soup. The wrong day for Sweet Pea's air-conditioning to tank. The white '97 VW Cabrio suffered Angela's curses all the way up the ramp to the vaulted main terminal of Reagan National Airport. With no cold blast to unglue her thighs from the griddle-hot upholstery, Angela had little choice but to drop the convertible's top; wind wash quickly euthanized the humidity-ravaged remnants of her salon coif. Angela pulled a rescue bottle of Infusium out of her glove box, ran some through her wild sorrel hair, and flipped up her FBI parking decal. *No, Sylvia, I don't have demons to indulge. Just memories to overcome. Never recount.*

"Hey . . . yeah, you!" came a raspy female voice, emanating from the blessed shade behind a concrete pylon. "Weren't you supposed to meet me at the gate?"

"Huh?"

"Lemme see some ID and we'll be on our way, 'kay?"

The words grated like sandpaper as a young woman sauntered into the glare, dragging her roll-away bag. Her hair was a burst of red waves, literally the color of flames, and the locks flared around her circular, freckled face like a corona. Angela raised her sunglasses to get a better look. The girl was hardly a sylph: a black, knit-cotton halter dress clung to a thick and chesty body. Her skin was pale pink except on her arms, fore-

43

head, and shoulders, where sunburn had darkened the pink to coral. She was maybe five-four, but platform slides—black to match her dress—gave her at least another two inches of height. Ceramic, black bangles clunked on each wrist; a silvery chain hung around her neck, ending in what looked like a tiny silver cylinder dangling within her sun-tinted cleavage.

"Uh-huh, I'm Nadia Riccio." Angela could see her rolling her eyes behind Prada shades. "So, ya gonna help me with my luggage or what?"

Because Angela's reaction was too slow to suit her, Nadia swung the heavy bag into the VW's rear and climbed into the front seat. She slipped her bare feet out of her slides and propped them up on the dash. Nadia's toenails were painted glossy black; a rose-thorn tattoo ringed her right ankle. Angela stared, openmouthed.

"Christ, it's like the Amazon meets the Sahara out here, like frigging Fort Bragg. So how 'bout pulling up the top and pumping some AC, huh?"

Angela sucked in a deep sigh before extending her hand. *Be cool. Be polite. If you read this little trollop, you'll get busted.* "Welcome to Washington. I'm ISD Inspector Angela Bivens. And I'm sorry—the AC's broken. Old car."

Nadia gave a lame handshake. "So, aren't you like a GS-14? Pop and Janet Reno must be paying you enough so you can go to CarMax for a new ride."

Sweet Pea peeled off onto the George Washington Parkway, skirting the Potomac, with Angela grinding her molars. It got worse. On the way to the airport, Angela had been grooving to a new, buttery R&B singer named India Arie on WPFW.

"Aw, this is mad cool, but ya mind if I switch to WHFS?" Nadia changed the station, without permission, finding Len's "Steal My Sunshine." "Yeah . . . this was my spring-break jam, senior year in college." Nadia bopped her head. "I think I showed Panama City that we Sarah Lawrence women freak as hard as those silicone sorority bubbleheads. Got any spring-break horror shows to share?"

Not the memory Angela wanted rattling in a sore head: Virginia Beach, 1988. She and her AKA sisters with very big eighties hair and very small bikinis. Them, flirting while Guy and the *School Daze* sound track slid out of a boom box. Her, trying to relax and read Maya Angelou while being accosted by flexing brutes tattooed with keloidal Greek letters. That pried up Angela's sluice gates. *"Excuse me,* Agent-Trainee Donatello—"

"Riccio. I go by Riccio, honey."

"Well, I go by Inspector Bivens, *honey*. Your daddy isn't here for you to hide behind—let's get that straight, right now, okay?"

Nadia didn't answer. She just yanked a pack of Newports out of her leather tote bag. By then Sweet Pea was crossing the 14th Street Bridge out of Virginia; Nadia cocked her head to the jets roaring above, over radio noise.

"God, I was like five years old when that Air Florida plane crashed into this bridge. Remember that, in all the ice and snow? Pop was down here working for some House committee; Mom was a good Italian housewife, wasting a master's in art history. The day of the crash, Pop told my mom that he wanted to run for New York Attorney General. I remember 'cause my baby-sitter, one of Pop's interns, was listening to Howard Stern that morning." Nadia lit the cigarette and took a puff. "Howard got kicked outta D.C. for making asshole comments about the crash. He moved back to Manhattan when we did. And a year later, my mom walked out on Pop. She's now assistant curator of the Guggenheim, ya know."

"This train of thought got a caboose, Agent-Trainee Riccio?"

"Yeah, it does. I'd have thought you'd be the *last* woman in the Bureau to judge a book by its cover. *Choo-choo.*"

So the child had some depth, Angela figured. But too much attitude. "This song playing on the radio," Angela baited, "the one that's giving me a migraine? It samples an old disco tune, 'More, More, More,' by the Andrea True Connection, 1975. Anybody your generation listens to have one original musical idea?"

Nadia took a long drag before tossing the cigarette into the wind and scoffing, "Christ, get real! Ever heard of Moby or my girl Eve? Nelly Furtado, Nikka Costa?" Then she grinned. "By the way, Andrea True was a porn star in the seventies—like in *Boogie Nights*. The 'More, More, More' refers to more *dick*, I suppose."

Angela smiled and let the song play; Nadia'd redeemed herself with cleverness. But once Angela was distracted with a freeway snarl, Nadia locked her clasped hands between her knees like a little girl on the first day of school. Scared, yet eager.

Angela's pager tweeted just as a caravan of Gray Line double-decker tour buses wedged the VW into the No Parking lane around the Lincoln Memorial. Nadia made faces at the sweltering tourists while Angela checked the readout.

CODE 371 ALERT. RETURN FBIHQ W/ TRAINEE RICCIO PER DEP DIR V. STYLES BRIEFING/PRESS CONF RE WHITING. MAIN DOJ BUILDG 1630 HRS.

Whiting was not her case. What was Styles up to?

"Hey, are those places Sequoia or Tony and Joe's still on the river in Georgetown?" Nadia asked breezily. "I'm hungry, and we can beat the yuppie and Eurotrash happy-hour crowd if we hurry."

"Change of plans."

Nadia was expecting Cosmopolitans, fried calamari, and grilled-shrimp Caesar salad. Instead, Jerry escorted her to Angela's office and sat her down in front of a green cafeteria tray of wilted chicken quesadillas and a diet Snapple iced tea from the Hoover Building canteen. Yet Angela wasn't met with a crescendo of bitching as she typed out a memo on her desktop. Rather, Nadia yanked some tiny earphones and an MP3 player out of her tote bag. She'd downloaded about a dozen Korn, Rage Against the Machine, and Nikka Costa cuts. Angela could hear them blasting as Nadia retraced her lips in Hard Candy's Burnt Cherry lipstick.

"Ms. Riccio, you're hot, tired, hungry. So am I—more than you can imagine. But in ten minutes we're going to the Attorney General's Press Room at the Main Justice Department Building. The Whiting kidnapping. In the meantime, I prepared a briefing memo for you on my Hooperman case." The document popped off the laser printer.

Nadia scanned the memo and said with a yawn, "So why do we have to go to this Whiting thing if we're on Hooperman—Amesha something, right?"

"Spentas." It was a wonder the child could think with those rave lyrics blasting in her head. "You are a trainee. You go where I say you go."

Nadia slurped down her Snapple and shot back, "Don't take things out on me."

Angela would have loved to rip Nadia's earpiece out of her ears. Instead, Angela spoke gently, as if to herself. "As an ISD Inspector and a divisional liaison, everything connected with major felony investigations is what I do. It's *all* I do. Now please come with me. I'll have my assistant send your luggage to the Marriott." Slipping her linen jacket back over her sheath dress, Angela noted, "And I think you should grab a blazer from your bag. Something to cover yourself?"

But Nadia ignored Angela and instead spun her chair, slowly, to peruse the spartan, functional office. No little toys or geeky coffee mugs. No Dilbert dolls or photos—not even of family, friends. And the last woman to win the Bureau's Medal of Valor didn't even have it on display. Nothing personal, other than the CD player on the cabinet. Nothing to convey any warmth.

Nadia's eyes narrowed, and in a gravelly voice she whispered, "P. Thomas Williams really, *really* messed you up inside, didn't he?"

Angela could only summon a weak, fake smile. In one sentence, Nadia had chiseled through the shell. The trainee stood and proffered her earphones. Mute, and without question or protest, Angela inserted them and listened. Korn. "Freak on a Leash."

Something's taken a part of me / Something lost and never seen.

Angela handed the earpieces back to Nadia. "We're wasting time. Follow me."

Frank Lupo met Angela and Nadia in the mosaic-tiled corridor leading to the AG's Press Room. George Vallas stood beside him. They looked like father and son. Of course Vallas was cheesing, heavily, and flashing that sexy grin. Nadia rolled her eyes, but Angela noted a tiny follow-up smile.

Lupo didn't spot the MP3 player hanging at Nadia's waist; it was hidden by the navy hopsack blazer that provided some professional cover to her clingy dress. "On behalf of your ol' man," he greeted, "we're glad to have you on board."

Nadia mumbled something in Italian under her breath: *"Sei antipatico."* From Angela's old Quantico Berlitz course, she knew it meant "You're tiresome."

Were Nadia anyone else, Lupo would have pulled up on her right there and burned his black Sicilian eyes right through her skull. But this was the boss's little girl. The same boss who had just anointed him successor.

Lupo pulled Angela aside and in a harsh whisper said, "Screw this little brat for the moment . . . *riccio* means 'porcupine' in Italian. Now listen, the Crisis Management Team's picked up a lead on Alfred Whiting."

"Ransom?" Angela asked. "Still doesn't explain why we're—"

"Unh-unh," Lupo interrupted. "A direct tie to the Archangels, or at least that's what Styles thinks." As Angela swallowed hard, Lupo swung back to grab Vallas. "Into the Press Room, kids—you, too, *Miss* Riccio. You got a box seat for this." He then commanded everyone to the Press Room.

"Why keep the media up in here, Skipper?" Vallas quizzed as they walked.

"If you can manipulate the press to serve your needs," Angela jumped in, "you can seduce anyone."

As Vallas reached for the Press Room doors, he said, "Deep. Your quote?"

"No, Styles's. He taught me that when I was in law school at NYU. He was my adjunct trial advocacy professor."

Lupo grunted. "Yeah, and the danger with these goddamn dog and pony shows isn't the release of sensitive info or intell, it's what happens if there's a monster fuckup—pardon my French. Right in front of the cameras. Back in '82, I was assigned to the Gambino Family Task Force out of the New York Metro Field Division. My boss was in the middle of assuring the press, our team, and the NYPD that all was quiet within La Cosa Nostra when, suddenly, everybody's pager started going crazy. John Gotti had just clipped 'Big Paulie' Castellano."

The group entered a room sardined with FBI agents and chattering reporters; dozens of TV equipment cables snaked in like jungle vines. Some of the reporters had been across the street at the Hoover Building for Styles's earlier press conference. Lupo flanked the empty podium with his successor at the Washington Field Division, Special Agent in Charge Claude Baker. The mulberry-skinned Baker was wearing his signature paisley bow tie, starched white shirt, and gray, double-breasted suit; he'd headed the Violent Offender Apprehension Team based at the Miami–Metro Dade Field Office. He'd tracked Gianni Versace's killer, Andrew Cunanan, and helped save Angela's sister and nephews from Trey in Delaware. Baker nodded at Angela as she took her seat.

CID Assistant Director Bob Scofield then came to the podium to welcome the press. Lupo was eyeing him nervously as he spoke. No wonder, given that soon Scofield would be reporting to him. Scofield was tall, gaunt, squinty; Angela always thought he looked like the second Darrin on *Bewitched*.

Angela watched Styles appear from a rear door with two of Janet Reno's Department of Justice lieutenants. Six people were now crowding the podium. No women, of course. Spotlights from the cameras rinsed Styles's caramel skin to a pale orange; he was squinting through the glare. He was looking for someone. And he found Angela quickly enough. She averted her eyes and put on a stone visage. But Styles stared right at her and smiled, slightly, as he spoke. His voice was deep and mellifluous.

"Now that we're *all* here . . . at approximately two P.M., Eastern time, we received an anonymous cell-phone call informing us that Alfred B. Whiting was alive and well. We managed to trace the cellular 'footprint' to a corporate account: the Richmond, Virginia, law firm of Grunton and Williams. Our suspect is Maynard Vincent Mullinix, age thirty-four, born in Charles County, Maryland. A litigation associate in Grunton's Washington, D.C., office. Details and photos will be released as necessary."

Angela heard gasps, mostly from the reporters. Once the elder Bush had exited the White House, Alfred Whiting had left the public sector for a stint as managing partner of Grunton's D.C. office before working on the younger Bush's presidential campaign.

"We have issued an all-points on suspect Mullinix. Based on other intelligence, we believe he's holding Mr. Whiting within the metropolitan D.C. area." Styles paused, piqued at Angela's lack of eye contact. "The implications of the Grunton connection are manifest: even in the absence of a ransom demand we have a botched kidnapping . . . politically motivated. Our CID and Crisis Management Unit intelligence has confirmed this. We believe suspect Mullinix is a fellow traveler with violent right-wing domestic terrorist groups."

Louder murmurs. *Nexus, Victor,* Angela thought. *You're too slick to go public without one.*

"Anticipating the press's likely attempt to analogize this to the Richard Jewel situation after the 1996 Atlanta Olympics terrorist attack, wherein an innocent man was profiled and arrested, I am revealing that exigent circumstance and consensual searches of the suspect's office and home are occurring as I speak. Less than two minutes ago, I informed Justice Department officials that so far, in plain view, right-wing paraphernalia, documents, have been found, along with a credit card receipt for a gas station in Bal Harbour, Florida. And . . . two gold coins. U.S. Mint, gold dollars—the 1995 Denver series used in recent politically motivated homicides. Found under the victims' tongues." Now he was skewering Angela with his stare. "Yes, two coins. Our confidential investigation, coordinated by Assistant Directors Lupo and Scofield, indicates that there may be two to three additional victims, based on the pattern discovered by our Medal of Valor winner, *Inspector* Angela Bivens."

At last, Angela locked eyes with Styles as fifty pairs of eyes turned toward Angela. *I don't need the limelight, Victor. And now the fucking Archangels know who I am.* She nodded to him, anyway, as he continued,

"The Inspector's investigating a probable terrorist homicide within this pattern, associated with the murder of White House aide Elizabeth Hooperman. Based on confidential intelligence, we do not anticipate that Mr. Whiting will be harmed. We do, however, anticipate a breakthrough within the next hour, and that is why we wish to share this information with the media, as an aid to our efforts to bring Alfred Whiting home safely, as well as to flush out suspect Mullinix and those who would aid and abet these acts. Sorry, *alleged* acts."

While Styles pontificated at the rostrum, an agent worked his way down the aisle, crouching. He tapped George Vallas's shoulder and handed him a document.

"Like magic, from Numismatics," Vallas whispered in Angela's ear, "about that coin on Dr. Collins's tongue. Might not really be a coin at all; definitely not Amesha Spentas." He looked over to Nadia. "You catching this, rookie?" He winked.

Nadia, seated on Angela's left, didn't even acknowledge him. She'd snaked one MP3 earpiece out of her blazer pocket and had been grooving to Korn again, with the volume turned way down. Vallas sighed and whispered, "The National Institute of Standards and Technology in Gaithersburg says it's gold all right, but a primitive smelt and hand-hammered. So much for my Greek connection, huh? Check it out."

Angela scanned the report, tuning Styles out as surely as Nadia had. The gold ore in the disk had been mined in South Africa, " 'possibly the Witwatersrand–Howick Falls veins in KwaZulu-Natal,' " Angela read audibly, forgetting her surroundings.

Styles called out, "Is there something you'd like to share, Inspector?" Angela jerked up and froze like a deer caught in headlights. "Ladies and gentlemen of the press," Styles crowed, "the Inspector's expertise is a function of tenacity and talent, not age. Our new blood." Camera lights swallowed her.

Styles waited with a delicious smirk—until his pager vibrated on his waistband. Then another pager tweeted in the corner of the room. And another. Three more. And cell phones rang: a choir of furious beeps and chirps. Angela watched Frank Lupo punching his own thigh. Déjà vu, from 1982. Just as he'd warned.

Nadia jumped up. "Hey . . . what the hell's going on?"

Disgusted, Angela yanked the MP3 earpiece off Nadia's head and cranked up the volume to hear what was so distracting. Korn again. "Freak on a Leash," a redux.

Angela hit the power button and grimly told the trainee, "Do you know what these lyrics mean? I do. In the field. On the streets. Learned it in a very short time. Now it's your turn. And I *pray* it doesn't 'mess you up inside' as much as it's done to me. Welcome to my world, little girl. Let's go."

9

IN THE BURNING TWILIGHT

CHUNK-CHUNK-CHUNK! CHUNK! . . . CHUNK-CHUNK-CHUNK!

No other rifle in the world sounds like that: a semiauto AK-47 illegally modified to automatic fire. Pluto Williams had fabricated one for his twin brother, and Angela's thigh had taken a 7.62mm round from it that night on the beach in Delaware. The noise nested in Angela's ears like an old song, though muffled by the roar of helicopters and the bulletproof glass of the midnight-blue FBI Ford Expedition in which she hunkered with Nadia, George Vallas, and Special Agent Robert Micklin.

Dusk's long shadows and ten-foot stands of fern trees offered a modicum of cover; Micklin had pulled the Ford into a rutted gravel lot abutting Jefferson Davis Highway in Alexandria, Virginia. Sweat beaded on foreheads and soaked clothing underneath Kevlar and blue FBI field windbreakers. The windows had to stay up and the engine on a low idle. The AC was barely puffing. Nadia nestled as close to Angela as possible without touching. Her hands shook as she tried to light up a cigarette. Angela tugged it out of her hand and shoved a blue FBI field windbreaker and a Kevlar vest onto her lap.

About thirty yards ahead, the main squadron of vehicles—other blue Expeditions, armored Chevy Suburbans, beige Crown Victorias, and a dozen Alexandria PD black-and-whites—had churned to a halt. They clustered before two narrow, decaying structures that lay along the oily, coffee-ground-like sand of a Potomac River tidal pool.

Angela squinted through a blazing sunset toward the twin shells. Judging from the ruins of their carved cornices, chiseled molding, arches, and bloodred masonry, she guessed they were pre–Civil War vintage. Alexandria PD said they had been used as warehouses since anyone could remember. And always dead, dilapidated, as if they'd been cursed. Inside one of them, Alfred Whiting's kidnapper clambered among platforms of broken mortar, twisted wrought iron, and smashed bricks. Unseen. Firing on the Alexandria SWAT officers and FBI Hostage Rescue Team agents struggling into assault position. A pale, chubby young lawyer with thinning blond hair. Four young children and a stay-at-home wife. Angela squinted, harder. It didn't fit.

CHUNK-CHUNK-CHUNK-CHUNK! Nadia whipped her head from side to side. Angela reached out for her. *She was you, not too long ago.* Nothing wrong with being scared. Equivocation, not fear, got you killed— and only experience taught you that.

"Drew, do they have a ten-twenty yet?" Angela asked. Drew was the nickname Micklin had gotten when he, like Angela and Vallas, had been promoted to FBIHQ from the Washington Field Office. HQ staff said he resembled a taller Drew Carey on steroids.

Micklin shook his head. "Gosh-darned rubble's really good cover from both ground or air." Micklin, a member of the FBI's "Mormon Mafia," never cursed.

Vallas turned around from the front passenger seat. "Ain't our party, Angie. We lay here in the cut and observe the sit-ref as backup."

"So we stay here and roast?" Nadia asked, dismayed. "I thought ISD was part of the Archangels thing? This guy Mullinix's one of them, right? DD Styles as much as said it. Come on, is somebody going to clue 'the rookie' in here?"

Vallas replied, "I don't like sittin' here an' getting capped without being able to answer back, know whut I'm sayin'? But that's standard ops."

"We'll have our crack at Mullinix," Angela assured her. "Sit tight and learn."

Vallas smiled. "Yeah, plus, I gotcha back, rookie. No worries."

"Oh, I feel so much safer now."

Snickering, Vallas passed Angela and Nadia two throat mikes and ear-pieces. "I figure HRT's gonna get a couple of those softball-sized camera-audio links inside the warehouses. State-of-the-art spy shit. You can toss 'em in like a grenade."

Nadia affixed her mike and did a sound check for Vallas. "I practiced at a live-round sim at Hogan's Alley, down in Quantico, ya know . . . maybe three weeks ago."

Angela affirmed Nadia's anxiety by handing her a spare SIG-Sauer, a nylon holster, and a clip of 9mm ammo. "Good. Then you're rated on a SIG 229?"

Nadia jerked a nod, then loaded and nervously holstered the weapon. "I mean . . . a simulated town, hostages, wow . . . it's not like . . . like *this*, ya know?"

Angela said, "I hated Hogan's Alley. Sucked at those sims. Want some gum?"

The small talk calmed the rookie. A bit. Angela hunched forward between Micklin and Vallas. "Lemme see the Crisis Management Unit dossier on Mullinix." Now Angela was thinking aloud. "This man made the cell-phone calls that bring half the FBI down on his own ass. Is anyone else besides me asking *why?*"

Micklin brought up the field dossier on the Ford's built-in laptop. "No criminal record," he reported. "Married his high school sweetheart from La Plata, Maryland."

"One generation from white trash, then," Vallas grumbled. "No wonder."

"Jesus, guy," Nadia scolded, "I thought we were supposed to detach."

"Good girl," Angela said, play-smacking Vallas's head. "See that—he writes freelance articles for *The Weekly Standard* sometimes . . . Young Republican VP when he was a student, on scholarship, at Washington and Lee. Voted for Ollie North. Wife says he listens to Rush Limbaugh and reads Ann Coulter. Damn, Drew—*you* listen to Rush. Okay, here's something—ATF flag on a registration form for a gun show in Fredericksburg. Assault rifle, semiauto Kalashnikov. Incomplete history re mental illness, drug abuse. No peculiar debts or discernible shylock problems. So what drives this guy to—"

CHUNK-CHUNK-CHUNK . . . PA-DING! A stray round ricocheted off the pavement and gored the Expedition's cargo hatch. Nadia stayed crouched until Angela eased her up. She was fingering the little silver cylinder that hung around her neck; Angela could see it sparkled with minute filigree and likely held something Nadia wasn't ready to share with anybody.

Suddenly, the laptop beeped; new data filled the screen. Nadia, maybe anxious to show she was as unflappable as Angela, noted it first. "See that—he did death-row appeals pro bono. If he was such a white-collar Hitler Youth, then why waste time on saving black convicts, huh? Or maybe just lost one and snapped?"

"Print that, Drew," Angela said. A color printer in the Ford's cargo area spit out a hard copy, which Nadia grabbed. Angela plucked away the sheet.

"Hel-*lo*," Nadia protested. "I get props for helping, right?"

Mullinix had indeed lost a case. *Very* recently: JONES, ANTOINE F., DOB 10/07/73, CAPITAL MURDER FIRST DEG RAPE/ASSAULT CONVICTION DC SUPERIOR CT: 12/27/92. AFFIRMED DC CT OF APPEALS, 04/28/93; NEW TRIALS DENIED, 06/30/93, 10/27/95; DEATH APPEAL REJECTED 06/05/00 JUSTICE CLARENCE THOMAS SITTING IN CIRCUIT, AFFIRMED EN BANC 06/06/00

Antoine Jones? The name tickled Angela's memory, but in the adrenaline-soused moment, she drew a blank.

Micklin tapped his earpiece and jostled Vallas. Apparently one of the tiny robot drones had got an audio fix on the shooter. Vallas switched to a feed from the Command Channel. After a few seconds of static on everyone's earpieces came the *POP-POP-POP* of HRT's suppressing fire, and then . . .

"Make me stop . . . make me stop. Jesus make me stop." The voice was wheezy, broken, and dripping in despair. Micklin, frowning, said, "Huh? Is he talking to the negotiators?" Angela shushed him as Maynard Mullinix's horrific rant charged on: *"I gave him the gift. He told me the Lion came . . . to murder the lies. B-but he's a lie. A fucking lie!"*

Crisis Management Unit Chief Ed Groom's voice came over the channel next: *"Gift? Does he mean Whiting? Get a video fix on this lunatic, damn it! Video!"*

Mullinix's screams to Groom's hostage negotiators trailed after the frenetic police chatter on the frequency. *"I'll be marked . . . under my tongue . . . my balls ripped out!"*

Angela and Vallas crossed wide-eyed, knowing stares. "George," Angela gasped, "get any-damn-body on the Command Channel . . . *now!*"

"Make me stop! Kill *me . . . before . . . the Inkanyamba's gold's . . . under my tongue!"*

"The *what?*" Angela said. The *Inkanyamba*. Mullinix pronounced this alien word correctly. Yet, more disturbing, *how did I know he did? From a dream? A memory?* "Fuck the Archangels, George—do you have a damn link?"

He did, but neither Crisis Management Unit Chief Groom, nor the HRT Commander, Paul Trask, would take the incoming call. Eight months ago, when Trey'd taken Angela's sister and nephews hostage, Trask's impetuosity had almost gotten them killed. Angela heard Claude Baker's calming voice next. As Special Agent in Charge of the Washington Field Office, he was in tactical command.

"There is a kill order on this subject. Word came down less than a minute ago."

"What . . . from who? Not from Styles or the Director! Not the Justice Department!"

"From AD Scofield. Clear the channel, Angela, you copy?"

"Copy, Command, but, I'm . . . I'm coming down to the CP." She rousted Nadia and told the startled rookie, "Ring the bell—school's in session."

"Hey, I'm not going out there!"

"Angie, don't do anything crazy," Vallas counseled. "Rounds are hittin' close."

"They've got to see the intell on Jones and hear me out about Les Collins, the coin." She switched back to Baker. "Sir, please, *please* do *not* allow Trask's people or Alexandria SWAT to take down Mullinix." She opened the SUV's door, to Nadia's horror. "Please patch in Frank Lupo."

CHUNK-CHUNK . . . CHUNK-CHUNK. Micklin and Vallas pleaded for her to return. But Angela was their team leader. Dauntless, she yanked the daughter of the Director of the FBI out into the heat and noise. Yes, school was in session.

Exasperated, Baker replied in her ear, "Negative on the patch to FBIHQ. Lupo's been apprised. A kill order is not clearance to assassinate a suspect! If he can be taken alive, Trask will do it. But we aren't risking agents or the hostage to do so."

With one arm, Angela tugged Nadia toward the blue van that was the CP; with the other, she kept her finger to her earpiece. "More politics? Whiting to be kept alive, but a suspect we need to interrogate is expendable? We can save both, sir. No one has to die tonight!" She glanced over at her terrified trainee, who looked utterly out of place with a cotton dress under her Kevlar and wedge slides on her feet. "Keep down and stay close to me. Easy strides. We're almost there."

They reached the police pickets and the van. Crisis Management Unit Chief Groom threw open the doors. He was wearing a pink polo shirt under his own vest. "Damn it," he fumed, "your own people and Civil Rights said these Archangels operate in tight, self-sufficient cells. The best we could hope for are leads on accomplices in the Bal Harbour snatch."

"If Mullinix were some right-wing terrorist, and he isn't, then why the hell would he snatch *George Bush's* cocampaign chair? Elementary. Did anyone *ever* stop to think about that? Now listen to Mullinix's ravings." The lawyer's fractured screams grated their earpieces. "He tipped us off. He wants to die. We gotta find out why." Now she raked everyone in the van with her eyes. "He described perfectly the MO in my Hooperman case. The mutilation of Dr. Les Collins. And I need—"

Baker cut her off when he realized who was huddling behind Angela's small body. "Good Lord, Angela—that's Nadia Riccio! She was to remain with your team!"

"No, sir, my strict orders were that she was to remain with *me,* at all times."

Groom growled, "Yes, he wants to die, so he'll kill his hostage, all right. Your investigation, any Archangel linkage, is secondary to preventing that."

Baker took her arm. "Angie, *please.* Now take your trainee back to your vehicle."

Angela led Nadia to a river shore strewn with cans, bottles, and slimy green algae blooms. A safer route back to the Ford than directly across Jefferson Davis Highway. Then Angela halted and unholstered her SIG.

"There's the Ford. I'll keep in contact, okay?"

But Nadia stood her ground, head shaking.

"I had to pry you out of the Ford, but now you're going to jump bad? *Go!*"

"All those men . . . they still don't give shit about you, your instincts. Like you're a trainee . . . and I guess I'm just some brat on a field trip!" A helicopter swept across the setting sun and lingered above like a giant hornet. "See that? I bet it's there to keep me safe, not to cover Mullinix, or even you! So no, I'm staying. I need to learn. I need—"

Abruptly, Nadia's resoluteness morphed into a frozen cower. Angela watched Nadia's eyes tilt to the ground.

Rats.

Brown and gray, slick with river oil. Not a few, scurrying and squeaking willy-nilly. But scores. In a few seconds, hundreds. Silent, but for the gnawing and scratching on the grit and rocks as they marched in seeming lockstep, noses all facing an open, rusted iron hatch in the warehouse wall. The mass looked like a living carpet of wet fur, rolling up from the shore.

Angela could see Nadia's face scrunch in terror every time a hairless tail passed over the bare toes peeking from her slides. If they stood out there like scarecrows too long, they could be inviting targets for either Mullinix or uninformed sharpshooters. Mullinix found them first. A burst of the AK's rounds exploded into the gravel, forcing a rat stampede. The fetid, four-legged army coursed into the warehouse—pouring over the mortar and bricks, driving Angela and Nadia before them. The two women tumbled through the iron hatch, missing its teethlike rust stalactites by inches. Both hopped to a rubble heap once inside: an island in a sea of rats and heat-stewed garbage. They aimed their weapons at the squealing horde, knowing that a mere ten bullets in each clip would not save them.

From high on a rusted catwalk, above the shrill calls and the women's own panting, came a laugh, and the rats quieted, as if an attentive audience. Angela peered up and heard the *cla-clink* of an assault rifle bolt sliding back.

A man moved into a finger of the twilight burning through the rotted ceiling rafters. Ribbons of dried brown blood painted the sweat-soaked jacket and trousers of his gray business suit. What little blond hair he had stood on end as if he'd been charged with static electricity. And he was aiming the AK.

"Oh . . . *shit*," Nadia muttered.

"His soldiers, you see," the man wheezed. "They came for me . . . and the gift."

"Easy . . . easy, Maynard," Angela said. "W-we're not SWAT. Not here to hurt you."

"Not here . . . to *hurt* me," the man parroted with a bizarre sneer.

Angela was now hearing shouts in her earpiece, then, *"We got a ten-twenty! Inspector Bivens is in there . . . in contact . . ."* Then Paul Trask's bellowing: *"Crazy little bitch needs to be back at HQ with her shrink! I want an OPR disciplinary hearing when this is over!"*

Mouth bone-dry, hands shaking, Angela called to Mullinix, "Be calm. Yeah . . . that's it. We need . . . to talk. But first, where is Alfred Whiting? Is he alive?"

Mullinix whispered as he nuzzled his AK's magazine, "He was supposed to be meat for the Lion's Regiment. Called by the Lion himself. Not now . . . not anymore."

Though unnerved by the rifle and the rats, Angela said, "Suicide-by-cop isn't the way to settle this, Maynard. Let me help you. I can protect you from the SWAT people outside . . . *and any who wants to put a gold under your tongue.*"

But Mullinix howled, "Tell that little bitch to watch where she puts her hands!"

Nadia, body quivering, lips moving silently, had reached up to grasp that tiny silver tube once more.

"It's okay, Maynard . . . look at me. Look at me. She's young and very scared. A student. You remember when you were a law student? I was a law student."

Mullinix grunted, "Fuck the cheap psyche job. Better she gets shot . . . than die like this!" He kicked a stray rat off the catwalk into an ocean of its brethren.

Angela tried to salvage as many bloodless seconds as possible. "Please, listen. Tell me about why someone would try to . . . to castrate or mutilate you. Put gold in your mouth. You said 'Inkanyamba's gold.' What is *Inkanyamba?*"

"Creator," he chuckled, as if she should have known. "Lives in the waterfall."

Even in that terrible moment, she remembered her dream. And Mullinix ranted on, oblivious to the HRT agents and SWAT officers now using the distraction Angela—and the army of rats below—provided to scramble into final position.

"He said the Lion would come—to murder the lies. But it was a lie." Mullinix's face contorted. "A fucking lie!"

"The Lion? The waterfall? Was all this about you trying to save Antoine Jones?"

Mullinix laughed maniacally. "*Save* Antoine?" The rats' mass squealing began anew, almost in reply. He lowered the AK's barrel, very slightly. Angela kept her SIG cocked, at her thigh. Ready. Nadia released her pendant and inched up her own weapon. Angela held out her palm, meaning "be cool." But she could hear Nadia's voice—more a chant than mumbling. It sounded like "Goddess protect us in your bubble of light." Repeated and disjointed as the murk, stench, and the heat collapsed the warehouse into a claustrophobic nightmare.

Mullinix muttered, "This wreck of a building . . . *this* was the place his children came and died." He studied Angela's face, smiling intently. "*Your* children."

As a swooping chopper drowned out the squeals, Mullinix motioned with the AK to a seething clump of rats in a black corner. The clump was about two feet high, maybe six feet long. Something under the clump appeared to be moving. Suddenly, an arm punctured the writhing net of fur and teeth. An arm with no hand. Several rats clamped on to the macerated flesh at the wrists, holding on for dear life as the stumpy limb whipped back and forth.

Mullinix cackled above the din of the rotor blades. "You know, next month, that son of a bitch was going to recommend me for partnership!"

Nadia cried out and drew her weapon down on the gorging rodents.

"Nadia, no!" Angela shouted.

POP-POP-POP! Nadia sent three rounds wildly at the floor. Angela whipped her SIG from her hip in an arc. Mullinix had already leveled the AK and was one muscle twitch away from firing. But Angela beat him on the trigger. Shell cases jumped madly as she fired two wounding rounds: one struck Mullinix's shoulder, another hit him in the thigh. Both spun him back to edge of the swaying catwalk before he could get off a burst. Though he still gripped that rifle, his body was canting at the catwalk rail. Below, the rats seemed to gather, waiting impatiently for his fall.

Angela heard in her earpiece, *"Damn it, Inspector—get clear!"*

"No!" Angela screamed. "He's down! Do not take the sh—"

A ruby dot lit Mullinix's chest as he recovered to crouch and return fire. *POMP!* The dot exploded into red mist. Mullinix bellowed in pain, dropped the AK, and fell flat to the catwalk's wobbly grating.

"Look!" Nadia gasped.

Angela's jaw locked as she and her trainee watched the tide of rats ebb from the building, seemingly disappointed that Mullinix didn't drop to them. Or perhaps an invisible pied piper called them to retreat. Their squeaks were replaced by the barks of HRT agents and Alexandria SWAT officers crawling through gaps in the brick walls.

Angela jumped over to Nadia, who was now vomiting at the sight of Alfred Whiting's convulsing body. Most of the flesh on his cheeks had been chewed away; his nose was a lump of bloody cartilage.

"Look at me—you all right?" Angela shook Nadia's shoulder but got only a blank stare in reply. Angela left her to an HRT agent and climbed to the catwalk.

Mullinix's eyelids fluttered as Angela bent close to him. He choked up blood and clutched Angela's hand as if the bullets he'd taken were succor.

"I need an EMT up here!" Angela yelled as red bubbles and bloody froth popped on Mullinix's lips and nostrils. And then Mullinix muttered something.

"He c-came . . . to m-murder the lies . . . but the *other* is here." He spit up blood. "The Lion . . . and the Crocodile. Even the arc-archangel's afraid . . . oh my God . . ."

Angela had heard the delirium of imminent death before; yet these words weren't utterly alien. Archangels, like Amesha Spentas? But the rest made no sense. Not here, not now. She shouted, "Where's the EMT? Jesus, hurry!"

But the pained breaths ceased, displaced by a wash of terror. Then the light went out of Maynard Mullinix's eyes.

Below, EMTs worked on Alfred Whiting. Disheartened, Angela called down to them.

"Is there anything on his tongue, like a piece of metal?"

"No, ma'am," answered an EMT fighting back his own nausea. "Because he hasn't got a tongue."

10

SWEET PEA ROLLED UP CONNECTICUT AVENUE, top down to the hazy night sky. An MPD motorcycle rode escort.

"So what did they talk about in the debriefing?" Nadia asked in an uncharacteristically deferential tone. "I mean, I saw SAC Baker, that guy Groom—they took you to the Alexandria PD headquarters and the reporters followed you all there."

Angela didn't answer, but her hands left glistening sweat stains on the steering-wheel grip. A year ago, at the Henry Daley Building in D.C., she'd been at ground zero of another shoot-out where hostages had died and the perpetrators had thrown their own lives away. The scene at the warehouses had become a harsh, glaring media circus, just like at the Daley Building slaughter. But unlike at the Daley Building, no one was proclaiming Angela a hero tonight.

"Nadia, Alfred Whiting died an hour ago at Walter Reed Army Hospital."

"Did you tell them about the rats?" Nadia rejoined.

Angela cut her eyes at the trainee. "I couldn't stop them from killing Mullinix . . . and the hostage is *dead*. Doesn't that mean anything to you?"

"Then . . . then I fucked it up for you."

"No. I did. Myself. Two deaths, so, no, *pardon fucking me,* I didn't tell them about the rats. There was nothing to tell. Nothing. And you will not bring it up."

"Jesus Christ. I'm just trying to . . . *look,* you put me in danger out there."

"You disobeyed my order to go to the van."

"So it was my fuckup, like I said. They can't blame you, right?"

The light at Van Ness and Connecticut turned red; the motorcycle cop up ahead signaled that they were getting close to the safe house, a high-rise at Connecticut and Davenport. Remo Donatello didn't want his little girl, who was supposedly not to receive special treatment, staying at the Marriott now. Rather than detail a gang of agents, Donatello demanded that Angela watch Nadia personally. And Styles seemed perfectly content with the decision. Just as long as Angela was in his office by nine-thirty the following morning. *Seeing Victor would almost be a denouement after all this shit.*

After a signifying sigh, Nadia asked, *"He* lived up near here, didn't he? I mean Phosphor Thomas Williams the third."

Yes. Up Connecticut, past Brandywine, then take a right on Davenport—the route she'd take to Trey's when there was too much weekend traffic on Broad Branch and Rock Creek Parkway. Never once did she go back to that house. The Metropolitan Police Department's Detective Sergeant Brett Mallory had told her that the brick mansions on Davenport were still festooned with Realtor signs. The house at 3002 Davenport remained as dead and sealed as a mausoleum. Angela would have fought Donatello tooth and nail had she known the safe house was this far up Connecticut. Yet Nadia—this blind, snapping, hungry fledgling—had been dumped in her care, and she could do nothing about it.

The light turned green. Nadia posed, "Agent Bivens . . . sorry for being such a bitch just now, 'kay? I'm still a little jumpy. I'm entitled, I guess, right? I just . . . just want to ask you a personal question?"

"Does anyone ever say no to that?"

"You might."

That brought a smile to Angela's tight, tired face. "You want to know how I could have an affair with a serial killer."

Nadia shook her head. "Nah, I want to know what it was like to empty a clip into someone you'd been *in love* with, monster or not."

Angela's foot slid off the clutch pedal; the VW shuddered and almost stalled. "You need to think about what you're going to say when you're debriefed tomorrow morning, all right? No rats. My mistake. Now let's try to get some rest."

"Ya know, people at the Academy . . . and some of the female agents you were in that lawsuit with? They said you were serious, but not like this."

"Like how?"

"They said, after you won your medal for stopping the Williams brothers, all that other stuff with the drug crews, you started acting spooky and in need of therapy."

"Tomorrow, you can just run back to Quantico on Daddy's chopper and provide some more gossip, okay?"

"Chill, lady. People call *me* spooky and in need of therapy, too. Happy now?"

The response was an arched eyebrow as the VW pulled up to an apartment building, behind the MPD motorcycle cop, who'd already dismounted and scanned the sidewalk.

Angela parked Sweet Pea in front of the lobby entrance. "Special Agent Alex Guzman will be parked in the Taurus across the street. No outgoing phone calls tonight, okay? Incoming will be monitored. We're in apartment 1206, with a change of clothes, fresh linens, and a stocked fridge." Angela reached across and unlocked the passenger side door.

"Hey, aren't you coming?" Nadia asked.

"Have to make a call first. Guzman will take your stuff in."

Nadia met Agent Guzman at the glass revolving door; she kept looking over her shoulder, frowning, as she spun through it into the large, sparse lobby. Angela kept watching her, too, as she tapped out her home answering machine access number on her cell phone. *The snapping fledgling's hungry. But I ain't her mommy.*

Two rings, two messages. The first message was dead air until Angela heard, *"Okay . . . well, I guess we—the people who love you—don't rate a CBR number, either, huh?"* It was Alvin. Breathless, agitated. Patient, understanding, kind, wonderful Alvin. *"Your parents called me. And Sharon called me . . . and Carmen Wilcox drove by your place and saw one of those blue FBI vans parked at the corner of Fifth and Constitution with some motherfucker taking one of your garment bags out of your apartment! Your gay-fabulous assistant wouldn't tell me where you were! Yet we all see you on TV, covered in someone else's blood! Outstanding job, Inspector Bivens! Sooo damn proud of you!"* There was a pause. *"I-I can't roll like this anymore. God, if that sounds fucking selfish, then so fucking be it!"* Click.

Angela bit her lip. The second message: *"Angel . . . I-I'm sorry. I care about you so damn much. But what voice is calling you away from me? You always have my CBR."*

It took five of Guzman's radio pages to coax a tearful Angela out of her car.

*   *   *

The bedroom door swung wide open and the hallway light sliced Angela out of the red-duvet-covered quilt's cocoon. She snatched the TV remote off her pillow and waved it. "Was, uh, the TV too loud?"

Nadia stood in the doorway, backlit by the hall light. "Um . . . I just wanted to see if you had any nail polish remover." She was wearing a blue, veil-hemmed tank top. Her rear end was biting a pair of blue, bikini-cut panties, into a thong. She carried a ceramic ashtray in one hand, filled with acrid butts, and a steaming mug of something that smelled like wet grass in the other. Nadia set the ashtray down, then rose and checked her painted nails. "Can't have this color on these at headquarters tomorrow. Tight asses would complain."

"Look under the sink in the bathroom."

Angela started rubbing her eye sockets with the balls of both hands. She hoped the gesture and the answer would give Nadia an easy cue to depart. Nadia didn't. She moved closer, stepping gingerly as if sneaking up on someone already asleep. She could see Angela's face, bright with the twenty-six-inch TV's glow.

"Yeah, I looked under there. Nothing. Hey . . . uh . . . you okay?" After Angela nodded, Nadia said with a snort, "All's that was under the sink was like ten boxes of tampons and an humongous jar of Noxzema. Some clueless men stocked this place." She paused. "You mind if I sit?"

"I do. I'm tired."

"Why'd you have the TV on, then?"

I'm not a deranged harpy. I will not act like one now. Angela leaned over and turned on the lamp on the nightstand. She looked away when Nadia saw her swollen, pink eyes. Her Howard University Bison T-shirt was soaked with sweat.

Nadia plopped down near the foot of the bed anyway. This was a full-size, not a queen, so the women were almost face-to-face. Nadia crossed her pale legs under her.

"God, this time last year, I was draining apple martinis at Man Ray, down on West Fifteenth in Manhattan. My going-away party before orientation at Quantico. Jeez, Sean Penn was there that night, 'Mr. Big' from *Sex and the City*, and that model Tyson Beckford. But he doesn't do anything for me. Not that black guys aren't hot, but, well—"

Angela cut her off. "You should request reassignment. I'm sure your father's considered this a mistake already."

Nadia stretched her stout legs back out across the bed and proffered the mug. Angela took it. The brew was greenish brown. "G'head," Nadia insisted. "Sage, a little chrysanthemum. Mugwort for clear thinking." She smiled when Angela frowned after sniffing the powder sprinkled on the mug's rim. "That's frankincense."

"As in 'We Three Kings' frankincense and myrrh?"

Nadia nodded; Angela sipped some. It may have smelled like stewed lawn clippings, but it tasted like hot root beer. Not bad.

"The stuff makes you calmer. Think better. Put past trauma in perspective."

Angela instantly swung the mug onto the nightstand and rolled onto her side, away from Nadia. "Good night."

"Okay . . . okay," she heard Nadia whisper. "I made the tea because I was afraid to close my eyes." Angela closed her own. This sounded horribly familiar. "I saw rats when I closed my eyes. I heard screaming. Rounds popping off . . . that guy Whiting's face. The tea refreshed my mind, not my body. Christ, I was in the tub for an hour scrubbing off the smell of blood and cordite." Tugging on the loose corner of the duvet, she entreated, "Pop didn't assign me to you; I *requested* you."

Angela peeked up from her pillow.

"Yeah. I sent Pop e-mails and had genuine tantrums until he said he'd hook us up on the next rotation." Nadia's attitude melted into a wide, freckled smile. "I've wanted to work with you ever since I saw you on TV at the federal courthouse on Third and Constitution, where you beat Pop and Janet Reno in your suit. You tried to look all meek and humble . . . the same way you're looking all rough at me now. But you had this bearing, this *beauty* . . . as natural and spiritual as those *rats* today were *unnatural.*"

Angela rose up on her elbows to click off the television. "Go away."

"I'm not some Italian-American princess, 'kay? Well . . . maybe a little. I went to high school at Chapin in Manhattan—ever heard of it? I worked *hard* to get over on those preppies and cocaine-hoovering Upper East Side tarts. And I graduated from Sarah Lawrence with a three point six GPA in women's studies and lit, enduring a bunch of whining bitches with fucking eating disorders and Bronx thug boyfriends."

Angela pinned up her dry hair. "So there's more to you. Whatever. But why join the FBI? Your version of pissing off Daddy with a 'Bronx thug boyfriend'?"

"I went to Quantico to find out something about myself. That I wasn't my mom, nor was I what Pop was trying to make me."

"My old partner, Kristi, said the same thing."

"Too many guys out there think we join up either because we gotta prove something to them, or we're dykes." Nadia got a bit reticent after that last comment.

Angela cocked her head toward the ceiling fan. "Think about what happened today. You don't know me. Damn, *I* don't even know me anymore."

Weird agitation seized up Nadia, balling her fists, tensing her back. She sounded as if she was going to cry. "Jeez . . . I'm like twenty-three freaking years old. How will I ever figure out this mess, if you haven't by age thirty-three?"

Angela drained the mug. And, yes, she did feel warmer. Not like the grimy heat baking the night air. Rather, hot Ovaltine warmth, from when she was a girl and had come in from playing with Pam on infrequent Baltimore City Public Schools snow days. Her head didn't hurt anymore. Her heart was more willing to share what was in what her grandmother called an old, split soul. "I'll answer that question you asked in the car," she said. "About P. Thomas Williams. See, the opposite of love isn't hate. It's indifference. Sure, indifference can be mean, but love and hate are the *same*. If I told you that I was indifferent to Trey when I discovered the truth about him and his brother, and that I pursued Trey and then killed him, all because that was my *job* as an FBI agent, I'd be lying. And I'd be dead. So would my sister and my nephews. Loving Trey came so easy. Thus, so did hating him. Therefore, shooting him—"

"—was easy?" There was a bit of awe in Nadia's tone, until she whispered, "But watching his eyes as your rounds dropped him . . . that's what tore you up?"

Angela nodded.

Nadia perched up on her bare knees. "Why haven't you *really* been attached to a guy? Just curious."

"I've had lots of relationships." Angela sighed. "One, now, I suppose. Almost had a fiancé after college. He was eye candy, and I was silly-acting back then, because I thought that's what men wanted. He really didn't 'get' me. None of them did."

"And yet the one who really 'got' you eventually wanted to *get* you."

Angela yawned in the darkness. "That's some irony for your ass, huh? Now let me flip—that thing on around your neck. You were chanting, holding it. Something about a 'goddess'?"

Nadia fingered the tiny cylinder, smiled, and then fell on her back, her red hair cascading off the edge of the bed. Angela pulled away, just a bit.

The physical contact made her uncomfortable. "C'mon . . . up. Go to bed. And thanks for this tea."

Nadia swung her legs around. "What do you believe in? God, Jesus, the Virgin Mary? I do, but there are other things that, like, swirl around the 'normal.' The conventional. Based on faith, yeah, and just as powerful. Sometimes, older. There're animals with the behavior to swarm. Roaches, flies . . . and rodents. But what those rats did, this was unnatural. Twisted. What I keep near my body"—she patted her chest—"is a charm. Keeps my faith in the *spirit* of what's natural."

Nadia rolled off the bed, scooped up the ashtray, and made for the door. She turned before departing. "Glad we talked. Our tea will give you sweet dreams."

The bedroom door closed behind her; the hall light blinked out.

"Our tea?" Angela said to herself as she switched off the nightstand lamp and sank her head back into the pillow. *No sweet dreams for me, rookie. Waterfall. Mullinix said waterfall. Inkanyamba. My mind will race all night.*

The warmth of that tea pervaded every muscle now. And suddenly, Angela didn't fear the dark or see death and shame in the shadows. Quickly she could smell Grammie's spoon bread and sugar-crusted yams . . . and greens smothering a big ham hock, and a pot of kraut: a whole Baltimore Thanksgiving meal. Yet no turkey—Mommy had dried it, badly, and she was cursing at the old GE oven, not herself, so Angela watched her father herd Pam and some rusty-butt little male cousins into Mommy's old silver Ford LTD wagon. *We going, Pammy, to get some crabs and ribs at Sea King way out Liberty Road 'cause Mommy messed up the turkey. Daddy, it's okay to be mad 'cause we hungry, too! Can we stop at Baskin-Robbins afterwards? Here's a hug if you say yes! Oh, this dollar's so I can buy my friend Michelle some sherbet on accounta her mommy won' let her have any 'cause she's too heavy. I think she's pretty and I'm the only one who says so. Michelle's house is on the way. Please, Daddy?* Sweet dreams, indeed. And silent ones, for, strangely, her family moved in pantomime; the only sound she heard other than her own voice speaking to them was rattling. And clacking. And scraping. Like dice hitting a floor, scooped up, shaken, and dropped again. Yet somehow, something soft and dear whispered to Angela that they weren't dice at all.

11

SHAW-TRINIDAD NEIGHBORHOOD

EIGHTH AND Q STREETS, N.W.

THE KNUCKLEBONES HIT THE VINYL FLOOR. Dry, baked, and gray—yet they stank as if still moist and spackled with rotting flesh. A dim yellow glow from the greasy bulb over the stove-top gas burners illuminated wrinkled, purple-black hands with long, cracked, yellow nails and gnarled joints. These hands passed over the bones, then parted. Scooped them up. Dropped them again. Weathered lips sang a canticle.

"*Uuuum-nyaaaaa-ma.*" And then the lips translated to English, with a heavy accent, "Darkness. It sing to de a Ama Simba. They wake and dance to his riddems . . . wit flesh *afire. Umnyama sizi suwbona Inkanyamba, iki su Inkanyezi.*" Darkness, one gift from the Inkanyamba and bane to the star angel. Archangel. Filmy eyes studied the scattered pieces within a circle of gray soot and blood painted on the floor.

The hands pulled back to naked black thighs as eyes scanned the cramped kitchen and fixed on a steak knife beyond the blood circle. This old man, this bone seer, touched the blade. It was warm, still dripping. Next to it, on a sheet of aluminum foil, was the severed head of a neighborhood stray cat. The animal had been hiding beyond the cracked windowpane and stained vertical blinds, in the stands of ferns laden with strange fruit: empty forties, spent hypodermic needles, and used, brittle condoms. Hiding, indeed, from rats emerging from holes dug into row houses waiting to be gutted for white urban homesteaders, with their Starbucks and Kinko's.

The bone seer rose slowly, achingly, to shuffle into a small bathroom. He checked the opaque plastic container into which he'd dropped two Polident tablets. Five minutes and the teeth he detested would be clean. He tried to urinate but could only strain out a painful dribble. His jaw slackened when he saw a single dark brown droplet mingle with the piss. His own, not cat blood. He cursed, in English, as he eased into the boxers and tank undershirt that hung over the stained tub. "Where de fuck . . . is de *thikoloshe* . . . him wit my medicine?"

In the bedroom, an ancient black-and-white TV set danced with silent images. The volume was broken, but he didn't need sound to understand. The bones told him everything they were going to say, and his mind heard their voices while he searched for his work slacks, white socks, and black, rubber-soled oxfords: *It's five-thirty A.M. and time for our first Sky One Metro Traffic Report. Beltway traffic's delayed at the American Legion Bridge. Accidents on I-95 northbound at the Occoquan and on the John Hanson Highway.* Banalities. But then the lips of the black woman on the screen moved, speaking a silent, vital truth as the old man carefully drew one of his socks over clawlike toenails.

The suspect has been identified as attorney Maynard Vincent Mullinix, of Falls Church, Virginia. We will update you after the FBI's press conference later this morning . . .

The old man smirked as he slipped on a cotton work shirt that matched the trousers. The name patch above a pocket read SAMUEL. He started to button it as his mind heard: *According to FBI Inspector Angela Renée Bivens . . .*

The bone seer stopped buttoning his shirt.

. . . who was on the scene with suspect Mullinix before he was shot by Alexandria police and elite FBI Hostage Rescue Team agents, Mullinix was the attorney for condemned killer Antoine Jones. The former Howard University student, awaiting execution for the 1992 slaying of a female student, made an unsuccessful suicide attempt in his cell Monday afternoon. Inspector Bivens made the revelation yesterday but the comment was withdrawn through an FBI spokesperson. Now sports. The Orioles dropped another to the Chicago White Sox last night . . .

The old man tucked in the shirt and moved back into the bathroom. At the mirror once more, he swallowed hard. As hard as his wrinkled, mole-dotted eyelids clenched. The bones had told him to rein in his sorrow, rage. Taught him to be patient. So he'd waited, for almost ten years, until the clatter of bones, the smell of fetal blood, the chants of voices long dead, called him.

The bone seer positioned the Polident-soaked appliance in his mouth, summoning happy memories so he could smile. These teeth always hurt when he smiled. They were all white and square, just like Chiclets gum on the candy shelf.

"Good morning, sah," he said, beaming into the dirty bathroom mirror, practicing his best English. "De red Lexus SC 430 convertible? . . . Oh, no, sah, it doesn't get dis humid in South Africa. Durban is on de Natal coast— *wondahful* sea breezes. I watch AIDS concert you sponsor in Sun City. Eric Clapton and Paul Simon, Hugh Masakela, Miriam Makeba, Johnny Clegg. You are my American hero, sah. Owning TV, owning rap music songs, and buying our victorious NBA team . . . deir name again? Oh, yes. *Wizards.*" The phony smile straightened; yellow eyes narrowed. The voice lowered to a whisper. "An' will you be having lunch wit my heroes Mr. President Clinton and Senator Buford tomorrow? No—a *funeral?* Oh, my Gott, I am so sorry for your loss. So he was a doctor, eh? From Philadelphia?"

Footsteps, creaking through the dark hallway, broke his colloquy. "*Thikoloshe?* You late," he hissed.

The man hung in the bathroom doorway like an immense black spider. His head, half-braided, half-puffed with a waning Afro, barely cleared the portal. Sticklike limbs poked through a dingy Baltimore Ravens jersey and low-riding, hole-stippled gym shorts. He was wearing bedroom slippers. Indeed, his own yellow eyes were still crusted with sleep as he grunted, "I tole you don't call me that. Yo, take your shit."

Lemurlike fingers offered two Ziploc bags, one containing a moist, black leafy matter that looked like old redneck snuff, the other held small mushroom caps. Bloodred. The old bone seer smiled. "*You are thikoloshe.* Came to me, willingly—I no have to find you. I see you de *amathambo.* De bones. An' you appear. But *nevah* be late."

"Ain't your muv-fucking slave. Yeah, I do your shit, but I ain't no—"

The pain, though brief, brought blood to the lanky man's lips, along with silence. No, he wasn't a slave. He was more. He'd seen the cat's head on the kitchen floor. The bone seer had schooled him, teasingly, that the white sows, the wicca, cavorted with cats. They called them Familiars. Master and servant took the communion of the bloodred mushroom, on a vinyl floor, as the sun rose over a dying husk of a neighborhood called Shaw-Trinidad.

12

NADIA WAS WHISPERING AS SHE and Angela took seats opposite the Deputy Director's secretary, a silver-haired, thick-armed black woman named Bettina Perri.

" 'Weezy Jefferson' over there's too busy checking out a shirtless Shemar Moore in her *Essence* magazine to pay attention to us." Nadia then cut her eyes at Victor Styles's office door. "Word around the campfire at Quantico is that he's your mentor . . . or something more."

Angela crossed her legs. "Campfires are for ghost stories or lies."

"Which is it with you?"

Angela sighed. "Your dad's aide'll be coming for your debriefing soon. Remember to speak with authority, answer forthrightly, don't embellish."

Angela then looked Nadia up and down. Her fiery, curly red hair was drawn into a straight bun as tight and severe as Angela's, though she let two ringlets dangle at her temples. She wore a white cotton tank—no bra—under a calf-length, metal-gray, embroidered silk dress topped with an almost shear peach blouse. "I thought I told you to wear a suit," Angela scolded. "This isn't MTV's *Real World.*"

"I don't do *uniforms.*" Nadia gestured at Angela's outfit: a beige, silk-cotton, four-button, tailored pants suit; coral blouse collar overlaying the jacket lapel. Beige flats. A summer uniform.

Angela dodged her trainee's look by focusing on the oil portrait of

Thurgood Marshall hanging over Bettina's desk. Not the grizzled old Supreme Court justice with bulldog jowls about to surrender his seat to Clarence Thomas, but young, handsome. A wave in his slick sepia hair; a finely trimmed mustache. Resplendent in his uniform: a cutaway and ascot, circa 1967, as Lyndon B. Johnson's Solicitor General. Still, Angela noted a taste of disdain in his eyes, as salty as the mixture of dolefulness and antipathy pouring from J. Edgar Hoover's brooding portrait in Donatello's anteroom. Maybe these two colossi understood on whose walls they hung and weren't happy.

Donatello's aide arrived, peeking from beyond the glass-curtain wall abutting the hallway. The trainee stood up with aching reluctance.

"I won't request a reassignment," Nadia declared, "I swear I won't."

"You might not have a choice. *Learn to take orders.*"

"You haven't—especially when the orders are bullshit."

"Nadia, *go.*" Angela smiled. "Thanks for the tea."

As Nadia and her escort departed, a buzzer rousted Bettina from her magazine. She lifted her bulk from behind her desk and silently, almost disdainfully, ushered Angela forward, through the door into Victor Styles's inner office.

"Mr. Deputy Director," Angela called after willing up a shell of bravado. "What wonderful surprises do you have for me on this hot, nasty morning?"

13

KING COMMUNICATIONS CORPORATION

13TH AND F STREETS, N.W.

"GOOD MORNING, SAH!"

Bryce King jumped—a little startled. "Oh, yes . . . good morning, uh?" He scanned the name patch on the shirt facing him. "Samuel." Then he smiled, embarrassed that a creaky-boned old man, barely an inch or two over five feet tall, could sneak up on him like that. Maybe he was light-headed from his dash into the Ready Park garage. He'd attended a break-fast seminar across the street at the National Press Club Building; the garage bottomed-out King Communications Corporation's seven-story of-fice tower. In 1987, he leased two floors, turning a storage closet into a tiny cable-TV production studio. Now he owned the whole thing, as well as a recording soundstage in suburban Maryland, and a state-of-the-art, four-thousand-square-foot studio complex in Los Angeles.

"Yes, sah, Samuel Ibhebesi. So will you be going to lunch wit my hero de senator . . . perhaps Mr. Clinton? I love your stories, sah, about so many famous—"

"Samuel . . . Sam," King interrupted, wincing and reaching for his cell phone, "I have a limo on its way, so I just want to know, will my car be squared away?"

"Lexus coupe, clean and waxed and ready, by two P.M., sah." But soon Samuel's gleaming white smile curled into a pout. "Oh—you aren't happy wit de old shine?"

"It's not that. I'm leaving for Philadelphia. A friend's going *home* . . . let's just say."

Samuel Ibhebesi nodded solemnly.

A massive, champagne-colored SUV turned the corner from 13th Street. King put away his phone and stepped to the curb, shielding his eyes from the morning glare. A younger parking attendant with the name patch MUSTAPHA ran out with a valet ticket and opened the driver's side door. Out stepped a portly, bald man wearing a white clerical collar and black smock under a tan, double-breasted gabardine suit. His face and bare head rippled with folds of flesh, like a human shar-pei; the flab hung from a man once an athlete as a teen, now a gourmand in middle age. A contrast to the lean, tall King, draped like a twenty-five-year-old *GQ* model in a close-tailored, taupe Armani suit. Bronze skin smooth but for a few worry lines on the forehead.

The fleshy cleric planted himself on the sidewalk with brown-and-white, jute-mesh spectator shoes. He shook King's hand, then yelled to Mustapha as the SUV pulled into the dark garage and started down the ramp, "Hey, man! That's a Cadillac Escalade V-8 with a custom transmission, so be careful!" The man cursed when he heard gears grind, then peered up toward heaven for dispensation for the utterance. He turned to King. "Lord, these immigrant Africans come here, take decent service jobs from native folk trying to survive, don't bathe, never seen a bottle of Listerine, don't speak a passel of English, then turn around and call us who've built this country 'cottonpickers.' "

"Carl," King said with a sigh, "this is Samuel . . . Samuel I-heb-beb— never mind. Just Samuel. He's from *South Africa.*"

"Uh-huh. You look like you're at the short end of the Good Book's three score and ten, Samuel. Shouldn't you be retired . . . not working no minimum-wage job?"

King tried to be polite. "Samuel, this is Carl O. Davidson Jr., bishop of the African Methodist Episcopal Diocese of Delaware-Maryland-D.C. and Northern Virginia. His home parish is the Druid Hill AME Tabernacle in Baltimore."

"Ah, yes, sah—on cable TV! Your KCC-TV dos de gospel show from dere every Sunday morning. Praise Gott! Bless you, Bishop!"

Bishop Davidson rolled his eyes, thinking the old man ignorant. He snorted, "I gotta find another sponsor, now that KCC's moving the main production studios to New York, eh?"

That part Samuel understood. "You . . . you are leaving, sah? KCC was born here in Washington, our capital."

A black Lincoln Town Car limousine pulled in front of the building. Davidson edged to the curb; King took his arm. "Hang back a little, Carl. We got time." King then indulged Samuel. "Sam, yes, we're selling the Maryland studio, but the corporate offices will remain right here in KCC's 'cradle.' We'll shoot our shows and record our music elsewhere. It's called growth. That's what makes America great, right?"

Davidson added, "Yeah—I remember granddaddy here, now! You're that detailer Bryce was crowing about! Makes cars shine like a brand-new nickel, and sweet inside, no matter the accumulation of Cuban cigars, chili-'n'-kraut half-smokes, broken wind, and exposed un-Massengill'd feminine genitalia!"

King cracked up and patted Samuel on his crooked back. "Fifty bucks excluding tip, Carl. Carnuba wax and chamois on the outside. Inside, not a crumb on the carpet. I've even seen him collect *every* speck of dandruff, hair, whatever, from the headrest with tweezers when Les was down last year. Now that's pride in your work."

The bishop sank his blubbery chin. "Yeah. We better get moving."

The gloom infected King. He patted Samuel again, then climbed into the waiting limo with Davidson. As the limo sped to 14th Street, King turned to see Samuel waving good-bye.

"Nice old dawg," King opined. He looked toward the sweating bishop. "You given any more thought to the homily for Les? I haven't spoken to Veronica as yet about the eulogy. Then the fraternity's wanting some input, too . . . then we got the media to deal with. Worse, the Talbot County coroner and the FBI won't release the body until tomorrow. I'll try to pull some strings."

Davidson gestured toward the limo driver with his head; King took the hint and pressed the button, raising the privacy pane.

"So what's this about the FBI putting Angela Bivens on this thing with Les and that White House harlot Hooperman?" asked the bishop as he reached for a blue bottle of Ty Nant water in the minifridge.

"I'm researching the matter." King exhaled loudly, as if in pain. "I was friends with Trey Williams's late uncle Hector Baptiste. Trey did a lot of work for us, too. Called in some chits with Tariq Witherspoon and what's left of the African American National Congress. Neither he or anyone else at the AANC was aware of Bivens's involvement."

"Bitch's a walking little scourge. Clinton withdrew Witherspoon's cabinet nomination at HUD because of her. And the AANC's nothing anymore."

"Carl, Clinton withdrew Witherspoon's nomination because of the fool's association with a serial killer. Be right. Be fair."

"Well, I *thought* Bivens was supposed to be ostracized. Persona non grata."

"Grow up, huh? She's been *in-cog-negro* since January, *voluntarily,* only surfacing for work." King poured some bourbon in a tumbler with a lot of ice, took a slow sip, and continued, "Question is, why's she on this? Les knew her parents, Randy and Barbara Bivens. And before he died, he was itching to tell me about something related to her."

Davidson waved his hand. "Irrelevancies, m'man. What *I* wanna know is—are you prepared to press Victor Styles about this murder investigation? Maybe even get Bivens off the case? Hell, you got enough money floating around this town to buy anything, and after your merger with AOL Time Warner happens—"

"I told you to shut up about that! Letting you in on that violates about seven securities regs and two statutes. Besides, no info's flowing from the White House; Gore and Hillary've put Bill on lockdown until November 7th."

Dribbles of mineral water collected in the folds of the bishop's chin as he drank, then hissed, "Victor Styles. Lawwwd, I *hate* that smug, slick, broke-wristed—"

"We *all* do. He's a necessary evil: the ogre guarding the wall."

"The faggot ogre's asleep at his post, 'cause I know it was some right-wing McVeigh-type Klan-Nazis that slaughtered Les. Word is that the FBI's been on that trail for months . . . years. You above all should've known that!"

"I'd been on Les's ass to stay away from that bitch. And the abortions, Lord, after he did my daughter's two years ago, I pleaded with him to stop!"

"*Word,*" the bishop grunted. "White folks be out there picketing his office in Ardmore like flies to dog poop. And, Bryce, *any* black man with power and money's gonna be on the radar screen of all them folks who hate Butch Buford."

King smiled. "We do love our conspiracy theories."

"Ain't no theory, man. You own a cable network, play golf with the President of the United States, tennis with the CEO of Time Warner, cut hip-hop hoodlums' records, and got a million-hits-a-year Web site, but you don't watch the news?"

"I do—I'm about to turn on CNBC's Squawk Box to check our stock price."

"Didn't you see what happened in Alexandria last night? Damn, Bryce! Alfred Whiting's *dead*. Yeah, *he was found*. Ready for this? Kidnapped by one of his own associates. Some kinda internecine right-wing beef, not personal." Davidson paused. "Bryce, you in a haze? This white boy handled *Antoine Jones's* death row appeal."

King muttered, "I heard he tried to hang himself at Lorton. *Damned* if that would've put everything to bed. . . ."

He switched on the TV. Like a punch line, CNN Headline News previewed an FBI press conference, to be held by Deputy Director Victor Styles.

Davidson grabbed for a Cutty Sark minibottle to mix with his water. " 'Woe to thee that spoilest, and thou *wast* not spoiled,' " he recited, nerves showing, " 'and dealest treacherously, and they dealt not treacherously with thee.' God have mercy on us."

King cut off the TV. "Calm down. Let's focus our thoughts and prayers for Les, and his family." King suddenly smiled to diffuse the tension. "And besides, you're going to come home to a *very* clean Escalade."

14

IN THE LEOPARD'S TREE . . .

"NO SURPRISES THIS MORNING," STYLES PROMISED. The Deputy Director was in shirtsleeves, with his $100 silk tie yanked away from his collar. He'd retreated behind a two-hundred-year-old walnut desk, built and carved by a freed slave named Thomas Day in North Carolina. A seven-foot wardrobe with clawed feet dominated one wall beside a lighted display case holding a priceless plum-blossom-patterned seventeenth-century Kabuki robe. The Japanese artifact was from Styles's personal collection. He'd somehow relieved the Smithsonian of Thomas Day's creations.

Styles threw his feet up on the desk. So much for a treasure. But this wasn't insouciance; he groaned, slightly, as he massaged his graying temples. Everything, a little stilted. Off. Not the usual demeanor of the man who *always* strode and spoke, with ally and enemy alike, as if he were a leopard. Prowling silently on padded paws, primed claws.

"William White attended our seven A.M. breakfast briefing. I apologize for letting the Director saddle you with him."

"He's everything I hate about these mediocre white boys who think that *I'm* the one who's incompetent, or that I'm a bitch whenever I try to assert myself."

"What White and his ilk lack in tact, they more than make up for in stupidity, right?" Styles seemed impressed with his joke. "Want some juice, fruit, bagels?"

"No, thank you. I do, however, want to know what's going on. You're the one who called this meeting."

He rocked in his chair. "Ah, yes . . . the kill order on that man Mullinix."

"Victor, standard procedure is to save the hostage and take the subject alive. Wounded, but alive. That's an HRT directive. Were we pandering to the Republicans: save Whiting and make sure no one finds out why Mullinix *really* snatched him?"

"Glad to see you're outgrowing your Joan of Arc righteousness. If Governor Bush were to win this November, he'd certainly have named Whiting to the Supreme Court. The rumor floated was that he'd be Attorney General. No. So losing him in a shoot-out would hurt the Bureau. But Whiting had skeletons clattering in his . . . *closet*. Among them, Mullinix. Uh-huh, right-wing *and* bisexual. Imagine my *shock*. Essentially, Whiting subjected Mullinix to quid pro quo sexual harassment. Plum assignments, partnership track, in return for . . . favors."

Angela's mouth hung open.

"And Whiting's tastes were piquant, to say the least. You've seen *Pulp Fiction*?"

"That's why AD Scofield convinced the Director to authorize a kill order? Shooting a man because he could embarrass Whiting *or* Governor Bush?"

Styles finally grinned that feline grin. "Amazing, eh—when the outlandish holds true? Unfortunately, we couldn't have foreseen that our suspect was going to turn Whiting into a rodent Happy Meal. But Scofield also had legitimate reasons to propose the kill order, based on the intell."

"And when do I get to see this intell?"

Styles quickly rose from his chair and leaned, hard, over the antique desk. "First, I want to hear theories on how Amesha Spentas is tied to Hooperman/Collins."

Angela swallowed hard and answered, "It's not Amesha Spentas."

Styles came around the desk and stood above her. Angela stiffened her back in her chair. "Then it will be." He pulled away from her, toward the huge picture windows, looking out to the Archives Building. "It *must* be, do you understand?" When he didn't hear a response, he repeated, louder, "I said, *do you understand?*"

Angela twisted around in her chair, more mesmerized than shocked at what he'd just said. She'd never seen the leopard scared. Leopards feared only lions. "Are you asking me to manipulate facts that don't exist, Mr. Deputy Director?"

Styles faced her, angered. "Pin the Hooperman and Collins murders on these right-wing terrorists. Make sure that we tie the Whiting kidnapping into this. The evidence tends toward a massive hate-crime conspiracy orbiting around the Archangel murders and bombings, anyway, *my dear*, so I'm *not* asking you to fabricate or manipulate a good-goddamn thing!" He quickly composed himself. "Angie, I'm hardly the monster you think me to be. Remember, the FBI has been politically compromised from the day J. Edgar Hoover took over as Director. Hell, the Mafia and every president from Calvin Coolidge to Nixon knew about his garters and stockings. Hoover did a lot of evil dirt, but, in the big picture, it served the Bureau. Made it the traffic cop of political power. Be *grateful* I'm the bastard I am, because 2000's going to be dirtier than 1960, when the Chicago and New York Mob families were behind JFK, thanks to his daddy, and the Miami Mob, Jimmy Hoffa, and a bunch of right-wing billionaires like Howard Hughes backed Nixon. Nothing's changed in forty years."

He dropped a blue file folder on Angela's lap. She recognized the document as a DCS-1000 report: the FBI's "Carnivore" wiretap for e-mails. It was hard to hold back a gasp when she read some of the names and activities outlined in the document. High-ranking Republicans and party donors. Evidence that *might* indicate obstruction of justice, and money laundering for known antiabortion and hate groups.

"Victor, this information's way beyond the search warrant's scope. It's illegal."

"Ah, yes, Carnivore has peculiar design flaws, doesn't it? Taps and collects more information than authorized. But, Angela, why let all that good intell go to *waste?* With some digging, we can show that this money highway reaches to the Archangels. Check the other documents. Two of Mr. Mullinix's clients, while he worked under Mr. Whiting, appear on my little list. You see the cash outlays coinciding with the Archangel 'Azreal' shooting in Indiana, and the 'Jophiel' murder in Idaho? I think they were funding the perps' escape. Perhaps plastic surgery, expunging records . . ."

"Then this file must go to Director Donatello."

Styles glared at her as he traced his mustache with a slender finger. She knew damn well he wouldn't do that. Angela was needling him—tugging him back to when he'd assigned her to the murders Trey and Pluto were committing. When the victims were poor blacks and Latinos who didn't fit his plans, or drug dealers who needed to be gotten rid of. When he'd subordinated his own suspicions about Pluto and elevated his bizarre affection for Trey. Why? Politics. Stinking politics.

Attempting a poker face, Angela said, "You promised no surprises."

"I lied." He loped back to his desk. "In your debriefing transcript, you mention an Antoine Jones as being pertinent to Maynard Mullinix. Can you elaborate?"

Angela sighed. Relieved, indeed, because Styles was frightening her. "Last night, at the safe house, I logged on to ITC and did some Nexis searches. Antoine Jones was a student at Howard University when he was convicted of murdering his estranged girlfriend, an African student named Jewel Ngozi. She was homecoming queen, Miss Howard. Police found her in the Omni Shoreham Hotel after an alumni party. Fractured skull, mutilated. They arrested Antoine in his dorm room as he was packing his bloody clothes and some personal items of hers in a plastic garbage bag. There was an issue as to whether statements he made constituted a confession, and if so, voluntary."

"Indeed," Styles intoned, stroking his chin. "Wasn't that Bryce King's party?"

"Bryce King—the CEO of KCC? Strictly speaking, no. It was good scandal for the media, but wasn't an issue in the case. It's called the Friends of DaFellaz Party. King's frat brothers, alums, are on the planning committee each year. Even I attended often. The court admitted Jones's statements against interest. That, plus the physical evidence doomed him. And, he had a federal public defender who just passed the bar."

Styles was now sitting on the edge of his desk, pointing a remote at the giant antique wardrobe. The office lights dimmed, the automatic blinds were drawn. He slid off the desk to open the wardrobe's cabinet doors. "This was a federal capital case, correct?" he said to a bemused Angela. Inside the wardrobe was a thirty-six-inch TV monitor.

"Uh, yes, federal . . . are we watching something? You see, it would have been a D.C. Superior Court murder case, but the victim was a foreign national. Plus, they found a stolen .22 in his dorm at Drew Hall, registered in North Carolina." She paused when she saw Styles power up the DVD player and slide a disc into the open tray. "Jones was a dream come true, turned nightmare. Born in a Virginia prison infirmary to a junkie mother. A rich, white Virginia family adopted him. He was dean's list at Episcopal High School, and the number one college basketball recruit in the nation. Gave up both the Ivies and big basketball schools to attend Howard.

Changed his name to Shaka Seven. I was a senior when he announced his intent to come to the university. By the time I finished law school, he was on death row."

"Watch the screen," Styles said, unconcerned with the end of the story or Angela's emoting. "The Protection Unit of the Capitol Police has monitored four dozen death threats against this man. His name's volleyed about by the men and women in the Carnivore file I just gave you. As an enemy."

Styles played a segment of PBS's *The Charlie Rose Show*. The host, ever polite and mercurial: *"My guest is Senator Brian Buford of California. Senator Buford is an architect of the McCain-Feingold-Buford Campaign Finance Reform Bill. He was author of the Civil Rights Restoration Act of 1993, and the Buford-Wellstone-Hollings Prescription Drug Act of 1999. He serves as Senate Minority Whip, though oft-times publicly at odds with Minority Leader Tom Daschle and Congressional Black Caucus Chair Representative Maxine Waters of California. His work of nonfiction, recently published by Random House, is titled* The Ghost of Hiram Revels Speaks: A Ouija Board on the 'Third' Post-Reconstruction Era. *Hiram Revels was the first African American elected to the U.S. Senate during Reconstruction and was the last for a hundred years until Carol Moseley-Braun of Illinois and yourself. Welcome."*

Buford smiled and corrected Rose. *"Actually, Charlie, Ed Brooke of Massachusetts, a liberal Republican, came in 1967 and served two terms."* Buford's voice flowed in sharp tonics and dominants, like a well-tuned trumpet. Thin eyebrows rode high across a sweeping forehead. His tea-colored skin carried a tinge of California suntan. His hair was cut in a conservative, rounded "fade" as was Styles's, and, like Styles, gray tickled his temples. Angela recalled a *Newsweek* piece recounting Buford's enlistment in the Navy when his father couldn't afford Howard University's tuition. At age nineteen, he won a Purple Heart and the Navy Cross for the 1974 rescue of the crew of the cargo ship SS *Mayaguez* from the Khmer Rouge on Koh Tang Island, Cambodia. Déjà vu: JFK's *P.T. 109*.

When Rose asked Buford about the *Mayaguez*, Styles paused the DVD. "Buford hates Kissinger, Brent Scowcroft, and Donald Rumsfeld. He claims the rescue was a PR farce cooked up by those three when they worked for Gerald Ford, after the fall of Saigon. A lot of Buford's close friends were killed or abandoned on Koh Tang." Styles fast-forwarded. "Pay attention to this part."

Charlie Rose: *"I'm struck, indeed fascinated, that you use the Phosphor and*

Ganneymede Williams 'Venus Stalkers' case as one example of 'denial' in the African American community."

Angela straightened up in her chair.

"Charlie, I see no difference between serial killers and young black men like that seventeen-year-old gang leader who made national headlines a week ago by walking into the backyard cookout of the mother of a rival drug dealer and machine-gunning the guests. Eight people died; four were toddlers playing in a blow-up pool. Yet some folks call these thugs mere capitalists, as if, but for race, resources, and parental nurturing, they'd be Bill Gates. No, there's something decayed in them. Last month, a teacher at a Baptist school sexually assaulted seven children. No one did the background check that would have uncovered his past criminal convictions. Why? Because the pastor lamented that since there were so few black male teachers available, they felt compelled to hire him. Worse, Charlie, was their justification: 'This is something only sick white men do.'"

Styles paused the image. "He's a gem, to be polished, preserved, protected."

"You said that once about Trey . . . and look what he turned out to be."

Again, something a little off, a little incongruous. Styles didn't bite back. "There is only *one* person in this government whom I admire and respect more than Brian Buford." His eyes washed over Angela. Perhaps in moral envy. "When young Buford returned to college from Cambodia, he and *Leslie Tyrone Collins* became frat brothers."

Another poker face, though her heart thumped faster. "Really?"

"The Senator's already asked me when Collins's body may be released for a funeral. I told him that, as primary, that's Angela Bivens's call."

"Twenty-four hours, maybe?" She was speaking as softly as Styles. Stunned.

"Whiting's funeral's at Arlington, tomorrow. We'll get you his tox and autopsy results on time, don't worry."

The Deputy Director returned to his DVD player. Angela mulled what he was up to next. Another Charlie Rose clip?

"I want you at Collins's funeral in Philadelphia. Buford's attending, and based on the intell, we don't want the Archangels visiting. Thomas Hooperman's holding his wife's memorial service the same day. The President's attending that one, so the Secret Service will likely annoy the Philly Field Office for strategic assistance." Styles paused to stroke his chin again. He didn't even blink at her. "Thus, watching Buford falls on you.

Talk to his friends. Bryce King, especially. They might have some insight on Collins."

"Insight?" Angela replied, enduring his stare. "There's more to this, Victor."

"So true. I presume your parents will be going to Collins's ceremony. They can ride and lodge with you, on our dime. Better for you to return with loved ones."

Return? That sucked the moisture out of Angela's mouth. Styles slid in another disc. The TV screen glowed with a greenish night-vision image of a snow-covered parking lot. A Range Rover pulls up to a handicap ramp. A white woman in scrubs and snow boots rolls down a wheelchair, as two black women and a black man get out and ease another woman wearing a toggle coat out of the vehicle. Pamela Bivens-Willis follows everyone up the ramp, arms folded against the cold. Watching her life's horror on TV felt like a billhook ripping Angela's stomach down to her knees.

Styles's voice lost its satin pitch. Now it was frosty, brutal. "I knew your father and Collins were friends. Did you really think you could soft-pedal it? As for these images, they are from routine protective surveillance tapes under the Access to Clinics Act of 1997. But I get the DVD dubs, because there were people in the West Wing who were nervous about Collins's affair with Elizabeth Hooperman. Asked me to do enhanced checking up on the good doctor. Imagine my surprise. You got dumbfuck careless, perhaps in grief. Unfortunately, the Philly Field Office has the original videotape."

Angela gripped the sofa armrests, mouthing random words as Styles spoke.

"I'd recognized Ms. Wilcox," he said, "but I thought Pam and your brother-in-law moved to Boston? Fortuitously, they hadn't." Styles leaned close to Angela's contorted face. His eyes were opalescent. The leopard spirit had returned; Angela was a gazelle dragged onto a baobab tree's thorny limb. "Collins did you a favor."

Eyes welling with tears she vowed she'd never let Styles see, Angela whispered back, "Go . . . to hell."

"Satan said it in *Paradise Lost*—heaven and hell are just states of mind."

Styles wasn't going to devour her. Just keep her impaled on thorns, high up in his tree. He buzzed Bettina to ready one of the press rooms on the Hoover Building's second floor. "Imagine what would happen to your career, to the Director's *legacy*, if this got out. Oh, I'd be able to patch my ship, sail on. You'd drown, *Angel.*"

Angela looked up at him, eyes red. Defiant. "You should be talking to Dr. Sylvia Myers, too. No, motherfucker . . . you should be in a rubber room, with Antoine Jones!"

"Sticks and stones. And stop wasting time with that female gnome Myers. You already understand your flaw. Digging out the devil in the details, like a terrier. But sometimes, he's right there in front of your face. Sound familiar?"

"Yeah . . . yeah. I see *him* now."

His catlike eyes narrowed. "I don't want to hurt you. You aren't bound to Donatello or Lupo. No, *our* fates are strung together, inextricably." The liquidy voice returned. "Remember what I said about the Bureau being the traffic cop for power in this town? Do you want sinister motherfuckers like Woody Sessions—cronies of Dick Cheney or John Ashcroft—working the intersection? Gore loses, we lose."

Angela turned away from him as the bile started welling in her throat. "You're going to lose, regardless of who's elected." She caught herself before revealing why.

Styles sighed. "Ah, drama. Well, Bush's winning might be our own fault, really. Arrogance, hubris. Though, it'd be interesting to see these puffed-up, slick, corrupt fools like Jesse Jackson or Bryce King without Clinton's tit to suckle on. Or mine." He pointed to the blue file. "Whether we ever find the Archangels or not, at the very least I want indictments for conspiracy on their sponsors in that file, by Election Day. This, along with keeping Butch Buford alive long enough to get on the Democratic ticket, should suffice to salvage this train wreck of a campaign Mr. Gore is running."

"And you'll extort me into helping you?"

He smiled. "You know what I'm doing is best for the Bureau. For us. Much is at stake." He squared up his tie, pulled on his suit jacket, then asked, "By the way, when you returned from the Blue Heron Inn for a meeting with Lupo and Donatello, what did you all discuss? I was hip-deep in Whiting, dealing with Scofield and Sessions."

Angela shook her head. "We talked about . . . Nadia. Agent-Trainee Riccio."

"I see. I'm sure you scared her to death. She'll be reassigned, no doubt."

Donatello had already told Angela: survival, above all else. Slicing against everything she'd been taught, from childhood to that day. Everything she'd fought for.

The Deputy Director headed for the door, then paused and said, "By the way, this conversation remains between friends. Secret."

As he held a finger to his lips in a mock "shush," Angela whispered, "The murders—the MOs, physical evidence— Jesus, Victor, something else is going on here that won't connect to Amesha Spentas . . . or your fucking 'hit list.' "

"Convince yourself otherwise," Styles admonished. "The connections are palpable. It's not like we're dealing with voodoo or anything."

15

EVIDENCE CONTROL ROOM A-7

"BY THE WAY, I PICKED UP the ticket vouchers for Philadelphia," Special Agent Marcus A. Johnson told Angela. Johnson was a baby-faced young black man who had come over to FBIHQ from the Washington Field Office, where he'd been Lupo's aide. He slid toxicology screens on Alfred Whiting and Leslie Collins across a broad faux-walnut conference-room table. "These are for you, too. Glad you're flying, 'cause Drew here doesn't like the train, or driving."

Micklin complained, "Hey, Marc, I drove out and back from my uncle's farm to the Tabernacle in Salt Lake a hundred miles every week when I was prepping for my missionary summer before I started at BYU."

Johnson chuckled, "I meant you hate driving in and out of East Coast cities with all our traffic and 'ethnic' types!"

"Both of you, quiet," Angela commanded. Her eyes remained on a lap-top screen. "I swear you're both worse than my nephews . . ." Her voice trailed off as her search results scrolled down the screen.

"Automatic case support system entries?" Johnson asked. *"Hello?* Inspector?"

Angela raised her head. "Just doing my own research. Something Mullinix said, before he died. *Inkanyamba.*" She sighed, hard. "It's a giant snake with the head and mane of a horse that lives in a river called the Mfolozi, in South Africa. British explorers and Boer homesteaders first documented it in 1856."

"Boers?" Micklin asked. "Dutch, right? Locked up Mandela?"

Johnson explained, "No, Drew, they been called Afrikaaners for the past fifty years and been oppressing black folks for damn near two hundred. So what's this African Loch Ness monster got to do with our case?"

With her eyes still on the screen, Angela answered softly, "It swims with its head upright in the water . . . looks like a giant number 7. The Bushmen first saw it, and later, the Zulu. The Bushmen said it was born . . . in a waterfall. Just like Mullinix said. Howick Falls, in KwaZulu-Natal. The Zulu say the falls are where all life . . . and magic, witchcraft . . . began. The Creator? Just like Mullinix said . . ."

Micklin said, "Howick Falls? KwaZulu? Isn't that where we think that gold they found in Dr. Collins's mouth came from?"

Angela nodded blankly.

Squinting, Johnson pulled his chair closer. "An African sea serpent . . . Zulu gold—not something skinhead terrorists, or a crazy lawyer, would mess with, right?"

Finally, Angela turned away from the laptop to face her agents. "Exactly."

Johnson stood up and checked his watch; his way of dealing with Angela's bizarre trance at the conference room table. "Inspector, um . . . you wanna go over this tox analysis. Pretty strange stuff. We may have to get the actual samples down to the Advanced Mass Spectrometry Lab, gas chromo, maybe even an enhanced electron-microscope scan. You have to get the samples sealed in chain-of-custody pouches and personally—"

Angela held up her hand while gulping half a can of Mountain Dew. The drink was chock-full of caffeine. She swiveled in her chair to Johnson. "You aren't leaving here until you explain these prelim reports to me." Angela didn't conduct meetings the way she'd seen some white females in charge do. The male underlings loved the smiles and the chirpy, insipid cheerleading. Maybe Johnson had thought his ordeal in the evidence room was wrapping up.

"Both Leslie Collins and Alfred Whiting's liver tissue showed trace amounts of two unknown agents," Johnson said, rolling his eyes. "One was a compound resembling a variety of the psilocybin mushroom."

"These men were drugged with identical compounds? Magic mushrooms?"

"Uh-huh. Here's the weirder stuff. The other substance was an alkaloid-like molecule nobody's ever seen before, which is why we need mass spectrometry. The mushroom compound was in the Blue Heron iced tea: it showed up in Beth Hooperman as well. Kumar and the Maryland State

Police Lab were right—the source of the alien molecules appears to be microscopic grains dusted on the cookies Collins and Hooperman ate. Definitely organic. Scary."

"Yes . . . scary. I want strict chain of custody on these samples. Do not breathe a word of this to anyone outside of this Division, got it?"

Johnson rolled down his shirtsleeves. "Now, can a brother get some props for this lead? You've had us cooped up in here, integrating these files, for the past two hours."

"No praise for doing your job correctly, Marcus Aurelius," she said. "But nice work. I'm assuming you have plans for the evening?"

Johnson mugged at Vallas, who had been lounging quietly at the windowsill all this time. The sun, low and fiery red through the blinds, set his body with a corona.

"Marc and me were gonna hit Grits and Gravy at State of the Union," Vallas said. "Ya know, Soul Kitchen, floating party. Seventies funk, eighties party rap—Al Green and Sly to your personal faves Eric B and Rakim?" He grinned that sexy grin when he saw he'd coaxed a smile from his team leader. "You never come out with us anymore. Every night it's either work or a Blockbuster video and couch-snuggle with your boy the professor."

Angela purged the final reference from her head and shot back, "Gimme ten more minutes of brainpower before I unleash you two on the females of the Nation's Capital. Both Collins and Whiting were high when they were killed?"

"Hell no!" Vallas exclaimed, popping off his window perch. "Far beyond high. Try raving buck-wild hallucinating! You got an unknown mushroom extract that mimics lysergic acid. *LSD.* Mix that with a superalkaloid nobody's seen before . . . *damn.* Talk about trippin'!"

Angela pondered aloud, "And a snake. Totally alien MO to what we've seen. Oh, yes . . . a hate crime, *Victor.* But what kind of hate?"

"Pardon?" Johnson said, confused.

"Nothing. Micklin, anything more on this snake . . . and the neurotoxin that killed Beth Hooperman?" Angela's brain had upshifted. Dozens of thoughts all at once. Whiting was a false gift. The Lion? A lion's regiment? And she now needed to talk to Antoine Jones. When was he scheduled for execution? One of the hundreds of pieces of paper scattered about Evidence Control Room A-7 listed July 22, 2000, right? She stood up, expelled a deep, cleansing breath, and did a yoga stretch.

Micklin opened his Palm computer and recited his notes from the small screen. "The lady at the National Zoo whom I spoke to was like the Captain Ahab of herpetologists. She wants this snake badly. Apparently, it's an unknown subspecies of the elapid family's *Dendraspis augusticeps*. The green mamba. Native to southern Africa."

Southern Africa. Like the gold. Convergence. Just not what Styles had envisioned.

"She says from the Blue Heron evidence, this animal had to be *at least* three feet long, maybe twenty-five pounds? Certainly not your waterfall snake with a horse's head, but still huge. I'll cross-ref with labs, wildlife parks, Bureau of Fish and Wildlife."

"Maybe Customs and INS," Angela added, mind calmed but still clicking, "in case somebody from the Motherland came in with a pet in his or her suitcase."

Micklin nodded. "The herpetologist said they'll name it after you."

Johnson quipped to himself, *"Dendrapsis sistahwidnolifeandanattitudinus."* He pursed his lips when he realized Angela's hearing was better than average.

"Been chugging *Haterade* in this heat, I see? Highly counterproductive, Marcus. Now, you have anything for me from Tool and Bladed Weapon?"

"Sorry. Um . . . Tool and Bladed Weapon's still stumped on those wounds on Dr. Collins. Nothing like past Amesha Spentas victims, including that judge's dogs down in Florida, but they did find metal shavings in the rib bone—like you said they would, given the depth of the stab wounds. Plus some tiny wood splinters. Analysis on the shavings and splinters is tomorrow morning, right after we get some feedback on those latent prints from the Blue Heron . . . the ones on the pitcher. By the way, everybody disagrees with this guy Kumar's hypothesis that spears made these wounds. Yes, they found wood suggesting the blade might have had a handle, but no known spear makes a thrusting pattern like that. They say, more a broadsword thrust."

Vallas added, "When you wanna kill somebody, you run up on 'em and cap their ass. Or blow them up with chemical fertilizer or C-4 or a pipe bomb. But *this?*"

The evidence control room door burst open. It was Lupo. And he was fuming. With his thumb, he gestured to Micklin, Vallas, and Johnson.

"Moe, Larry, Curly . . . beat it!"

Lupo slammed the door behind them. "What the fuck is all this, huh? *What the fuck is all this?*"

"Frank . . . I know I've been out of contact with—"

"I'm doing the talking, here!" He paced during the diatribe, his thumbs and index fingers extended in *L*'s as his arms jabbed the air. "It's bad friggin' enough that that *testa dura* Styles blindsides me and pulls my division onto Whiting directly, through you . . . without as much as consulting me, and announces it on national TV at a damn press conference. At least you had the good taste not to be on camera. But what pisses me off, Tigress, is then you go hiding from me and start working on these files, pulling in other agents I haven't authorized to help you. You don't even disclose that your parents are friends of a homicide victim!"

"Frank . . . listen, you knew Whiting was being folded into Amesha Spentas—"

"You don't get it, do you? The Deputy Director does not have the right to unilaterally detail my agents, without even a consult. Look, I got yanked into a useless goddamn executive committee meeting today, and ya know what? Remo turns around and backs Styles's play. I'm in the godforsaken position, then, of siding with Woody Sessions and Bob Scofield. I don't even look like I have a handle on my own division's activities or agents! Was Remo kidding when he said I would be taking over? Was he goddamn kidding?"

All she could muster was "I'm sorry."

That stalled his pacing, but not his spleen. "That's all you got to say? *Madon!* I depend on you. We all do. 'I'm sorry.' Not 'I'm gonna do right by you, Frank'?" He knelt down in front of her. The gesture scared her. "What'd Styles say to you, huh? What is going on with you two? Come clean. *Did you tell him what Remo told us?*"

"No, Frank. I'd never do that to you."

He stood erect. "Uh-huh. Here's the drill. Till I start to feel warm and fuzzy again, I'm allowing the other divisions full access and input into your investigation, rather than in a support role, and that doesn't mean what we've already been doing with Civil Rights on the hate-crimes angle. Styles can bitch and moan all he wants. You'll share case materials on Hooperman and Whiting with Claude Baker."

"I have no problem with that, as the Washington Field Office has been—"

"And, Bud White's being detailed from Baltimore to HQ to take charge of all physical evidence in these matters."

"No . . . no . . ."

"It was Sessions who suggested it. Bud's got a background in national security matters, antiterrorism methodologies. Coexist. That's an order."

Angela shot to her feet. "You'd be jeopardizing this investigation!"

"Don't flip my script, Angie! Nah, 'cause I'm goddamn Vesuvius tonight, and I will blow. Have Vallas secure this room, understand me? That includes lab results, samples. White gets custody and control of the whole nine yards. *You stay away.*" Yet he softened just a little, like an angry father. "You put me in a bind. Make me trust you again. I'm beggin' you. I don't like relying on mooks like White any more than you."

Angela turned away. Lupo, too, was in survival mode.

"White's coming in from Baltimore tomorrow morning at ten," Lupo said, tone now even softer. "Get the chain-of-custody envelopes containing every bit of testable evidence ready for him. Use the downtime to cool your jets, recharge."

"Frank—"

He cut her off. "Go home."

Lupo stormed out, likely before he'd start commiserating. With the door open, Angela could see other staff, frozen in the hallway, mouths agape. She fell back into her chair and spun aimlessly. No hollowness. Just numb. Helpless. And helplessness was worse than anything she could endure, short of a bullet. Maybe this was what Sylvia Myers meant by decompensating? Very close to it. She was about to reach for the table console speakerphone and press Dr. Myers's number when Vallas slinked back in.

"Room's not soundproof," he tried to joke.

"Gimme a moment, George."

"The Skipper's just trying to start some shit. Flex his muscles. I'll go talk to him."

"White's goons will mishandle the evidence, manipulate the case files . . ."

"Politics, right. Means somebody's gonna monkey with this stuff no matter what. Gus and Tasia Vallas didn't raise no fool on the West Side of Chicago, now."

Angela smiled. "So what are you saying?"

"We keep doin' what we doin'. Fuck White. It's what the Skipper would want, with a wink. Starting with this." He handed her a pink flimsy: a copy of the autopsy analysis of Maynard Mullinix's stomach contents. "Ghosty shit, in light of your little story about this African Puff the Magic Dragon."

"And magic mushrooms," she said to herself as she scanned the sheet.

Mullinix had ingested ginger, ground black-tea-leaf residue. Traces of subtropical mandrake-root extract. Mandrake? Angela's bouts of insomnia led to a lot of late-night Discovery Channel and TLC viewing. Mandrake was a favored ingredient in love philters, witch's brews. *Tea.* Angela chuckled until she read aloud from the flimsy. "Mugwort extract, sage, undigested chrysanthemum petals . . . frankincense. *Oh my God.*"

"What?"

"Find Nadia—Agent-Trainee Riccio. *Now!* I don't care if you have to call the Director's house. Then page me at home."

16

CHI CHA LOUNGE

18TH AND U STREETS, N.W.

FLUNG OPEN TO THE SULTRY NIGHT air, Chi Cha's bay windows gave full access to the still broiling sidewalk. Checking IDs was next to impossible, thus the lounge heaved with under-twenty-one summer students as well as legal, sweaty bohemians, yuppies, and buppies, fueled by sangria, imported beers, spicy tapas, cigars, clove cigarettes, and hookahs fired by apple tobacco.

Angela watched the mass of conviviality as she idled Sweet Pea at the curb, top down. She'd sloughed her suit slacks and flats for a white cotton sleeveless shell, black capris, sandals. The breezy summer attire belied bottomless thoughts. As this was the confluence of the Adams-Morgan, Dupont Circle, and U Street Corridor neighborhoods, a parking space on a summer night would be as elusive as the Loch Ness monster. Or the Inkanyamba? She flipped up her FBI parking decal and went in.

Angela navigated through hot, tightly pressed bodies dressed in everything from silk to T-shirts, Manolo Blahnik mules to Birkenstocks. She found her targets, in the corner, beneath faux-crumbled brick and mortar. Five attractive young white women, lolling on two velvet sofas around a metal table. Three wore short, cotton print sheath dresses. Very J.Crew. Very Chi Cha. A fourth, wearing abbreviated denim shorts, had her long, bare legs stretched across Nadia Riccio's lap. Her blond hair was styled in a wispy pageboy. Not unlike Angela's, months ago. The rose-thorn tattoo ringing the blonde's ankle was identical to Nadia's. Both young women wore those neo-hippie scarf-tops, barely covering their breasts. Angela watched the trainee stroke the blonde's calf, then, slipping off the girl's thong sandal, the arch of her foot, delicately. Lovingly.

Angela approached; Nadia quickly withdrew her hands and lit up a cigarette. Angela smiled and said hello. Nadia expelled a puff of smoke tinged with animosity.

"And who's *this?*" asked the girl with her legs still on Nadia's lap.

"No one who matters anymore," Nadia said, looking Angela up and down. "Heard you got spanked today. And you're on hiatus? Join the club."

Angela said, "No hiatus. Not for me . . . or you."

"Really?" Nadia took another drag. "Pop says you told Styles you didn't want me around anymore."

"That's not true."

"You calling my father a liar?"

"No, I'm calling Styles a liar. Your father's merely misinformed. May I sit?" The patrons were crowding Angela as they laughed, smoked, swayed to the samba on the speakers.

"Pop lies, too. He's reassigning me once he comes back from Budapest from some Interpol thing. Yeah, takes off tomorrow. He's pretty pissed about some blowup among the Assistant Directors . . . caused by *you*, no doubt. But when the going gets tough, Pop gets going."

Nadia motioned with her head to the other girls; they slid to open a space on one of the couches. They met Angela with giggles of discomfort, then meek yet polite introductions. They were friends of Nadia's from either Chapin or Sarah Lawrence. All working for lobbyists, associations, or law firms. They seemed like followers. Sheep.

Finally, the one resting on Nadia swung her legs off and extended her hand, sharply. No follower here. "I'm Arianne Shipley. Of the Charlottesville Shipleys." She'd added a playful Southern accent as a joke. But what sucked in Angela was not her teasing. It was her eyes. Sharon Boissiere had green eyes, but this girl's were a pure, creamy jade. Magnetic. "I bet *you're* familiar with our most famous long-dead relative."

Angela played along. "And who would that be, Ms. Shipley?"

"Sally Hemmings!" she guffawed. "Actually, no. But hey, you're the celeb here."

Angela smiled, embarrassed this time. "You follow the FBI in the news?"

"More so, I follow strong women." Arianne tousled Nadia's red hair. "Actually, some students did a report about you in my class."

"You taking law or criminology courses?"

Arianne's snicker sounded more like a cat's purr. "I teach second grade at the Lowell School in Northwest, and am pursuing my master's in education at Georgetown. The little girls in my class think you are quite the hero. So do *other* little girls."

"Stop it, Ari," Nadia grumbled.

"Well, then, welcome to our *circle.*"

The others gasped at the word *circle;* Nadia crushed out her cigarette.

"Oh, Naddy, chill." Arianne faced Angela. "We relax here whenever my *Miss Porcupine* comes to town. Her name means 'porcupine,' you know."

A waitress brushed by. Angela asked for an extra ceramic pitcher of sangria for the table, then asked, "Nadia, can we go somewhere and talk. Briefly?"

Nadia shook her head.

"Ahhh, no secrets here, Sister Bivens," Arianne said beguilingly, stretching her legs like a waking cat. Angela sensed that the "sister" sobriquet wasn't an attempt to be racially mawkish. "Share some tapas with our circle. You look *hungry.*"

Angela searched the tabletop, but not for the Spanish finger food. A cocktail napkin was in front of Nadia. Someone had etched a pentagram on it, in felt-tip. Nadia quickly crumpled the napkin. To the left of the table candle was a plastic cup of water. No lipstick marks on it, and a small pile of salt was beside it, no more than three or four pinches. Bracketing the salt were two plastic cocktail swords that had once skewered olives or maraschino cherries. Now they were daggers, on a play altar.

Angela revealed, "I did some on-line homework before coming here. Santeria. Animism. Homeopathy. And book excerpts: *The Golden Bough,* Phyllis Curott's *Book of Shadows,* Marta Vega's *The Altar of My Soul . . .*"

"Certainly all my coffee-table books," Arianne chuckled. "So?"

"So maybe now I can trust all of you—especially you, Agent-Trainee Riccio—to tell me what I'm dealing with here."

Angela pulled a folded photocopy out of her purse and slid it to Nadia. The rookie read, gasped, then pushed it to the other girls around the table. When Arianne took it, she smiled knowingly, then stuck out her tongue in a mock retch.

"Ewww, gross. Stomach contents? Shall we help her out, ladies?"

After the waitress had brought more sangria, one of the girls explained, "The mandrake in the tea is a catalyst for a *spell*. Protection . . . from evil."

"Like that thing you all are wearing around your necks?" Angela saw the same filigreed cylinder pendant on each girl. "European and American wicca have a goddess at the center of their crafting. Inside your charm is a message from that goddess."

Arianne broke the tension with a cackle—a fake witch's laugh from many a cartoon or Halloween fable. "So here we are, poor little rich, bored white chicks thinking they're witches, huh? Tabitha, Sabrina, Samantha— those are our real names!"

"Shuddup, Ari," Nadia hissed.

"And by the way, a charm can also be a spell, rather than a necklace. They teach us that in witch school—don't you watch *Charmed* on the WB?"

Nadia cut her eyes at Arianne, then at Angela. "So *now* you wanna talk about rats, huh? Hey, maybe I emulated you and expunged that 'irrational' shit from my brain. Maybe I *am* a little rich girl playing at some fad. Spooky. In need of therapy?"

Arianne's mood turned frosty. "And what *else* would you consider a 'fad,' Naddy? Me?" She gestured to the other girls, who quickly scooped away the water cup and the salt, then blew out the candle. Her green eyes flashed. "I'd really appreciate it if you'd leave." Arianne's slender arm hooked around Nadia's freckled shoulder.

Angela watched Nadia peel off Arianne's embrace. The other three silent, preppie girls seemed relieved by this coup. One motioned for the waitress to bring Jägermeister shots. And then, barely audibly under the music and crowd banter, all, save Arianne, recited, " 'An' harm ye none, do what ye will.' "

"That's from our Wiccan Rede," one girl explained. "Unbreakable rule."

"But there are some people out there who don't believe in keeping nature's rules," said another. "They pervert the magick."

Arianne finally resumed command. "Not magic, okay, like David Copperfield in Vegas. M-A-G-I-C-K. Perverting rules against, say . . . hmmm . . . seducing rats to swarm? You, who deals with serial killers and gangsters and terrorists and drug dealers—can you handle that?" She draped herself on Nadia once more; Nadia kissed her hand.

"Ms. Shipley, anything that leads me to the truth, I take very seriously." Angela leaned closer to Nadia. "Tomorrow, I'm in Philadelphia, so I need you to go to the Hoover Building, sixth floor, ISD Evidence Room A-7 at oh nine-thirty. Pick up evidence samples and walk them through a lab test battery, keeping chain of custody and control. Vallas will call you at oh eight hundred, all right?"

"Fuck procedure, huh?"

Angela dropped back from the table.

"Yeah, you heard me. I'm not stupid. I know what's going on in HQ. So now you want me to just trash the stuff you claim you stand for: Fidelity, Bravery, Integrity. F-B-I. The slogan on that badge I get when I graduate. *If* I graduate?"

Arianne chimed in as the other girls eyed Nadia. "You need Naddy because if she helps you and gets caught, she's the Director's daughter. She won't get punished. But trust me"—she kissed Nadia's cheek—"her daddy doesn't need a new scandal."

Angela sighed. "It's not like that."

"Liar!" Nadia screeched.

Angela reached across the table, across what was their little wiccan altar, pried away Arianne's slender fingers, and clasped Nadia's palm. Her almond eyes never once peeled away from Nadia's amber-brown ones. Slowly, the trainee began to smile.

"Oh, great," Arianne huffed. "So now what—you've bonded? You're like a short Batman with tits and Naddy's Robin? Wonder Woman and Wonder Girl?"

"Just trying to do the right thing, Ari. You know that. And besides, she's not Batman. She's that Claymation chicken in *Chicken Run*. 'Ginger.' Brave. Never gives up."

"How sweet," Arianne teased. But when the waitress arrived with the shot glasses of dark liqueur, she snatched one right off the tray, raised it, and told Angela, "Then you protect my Naddy, 'Ginger.' And you'll seal it with a libation, for the goddess, since you interrupted our first attempt."

Everyone drank. The stuff tasted like licorice and burned.

Nadia scribbled a phone number on another napkin. "I won't be back at the Marriott tonight," she simpered.

Arianne added, "I'll make sure she's awake."

Perhaps to recover from the conversation, as much as pee, Angela stood. "Will you all excuse me? I'll be back— I want to hear more about magick."

"More than happy to educate you," Arianne said as Angela slid around the table to find the rest room.

She pushed through the bodies toward the alcove across from the bar.

But immediately, she stopped dead. There was Dr. Alvin Markham, blocking her path. Little amber-haired Sharon Boissiere was right behind him. Sharon carried this look of hyperventilated surprise, the opposite of Alvin's glare. It looked as if Sharon had been holding his forearm, and not as a means of navigating the crowd.

"Hey, Angel . . . we tried to call," Sharon proffered.

Angela shucked her teeth and huffed, "Yeah. Really. Coincidence. Bye."

The professor ground his molars, then let loose, "Oh, that's good, Angie!"

"Al," Sharon whispered. "Let's not show out in here."

"*Al*'?" Angela intoned, hand now on one hip.

"Why didn't you pick up your phone? Did you listen to your voice mail?"

"The ringer was turned off. I was on-line, I was reading. Busy." All this time Angela was looking right into Alvin's brown eyes. Easier, because he was wearing new contact lenses, rather than his "granny" specs. His chestnut dreads were tied back. He was dressed in the summer casual khakis and linen and tee and slide sandals of the lone brother always seen among the white models in the J.Crew catalogs Arianne's "circle" seemed to shop from. Not like he dressed whenever he was with her. A bit sartorially challenged, like many academics are. No, Sharon had been teaching him style points. Behind everyone's back? And Angela's subconscious fear became a conscious voice.

"Green eyes more to your liking? Or you just couldn't be *patient* for me?"

Sharon's reticence disappeared. "Angel you are *so* wrong on *so* many levels!"

Alvin patted Sharon's shoulder. Angela couldn't understand why that gesture made her fume. "It's okay," Alvin assured, almost sweetly. But then he faced Angela as he continued addressing Sharon. "You don't have to explain *jack* to her. She's the *Angel*. Sherlock fucking Holmes. Let her figure shit out!"

Common sense rushed back in, but it was too late. "Alvin . . . I'm sorry and—"

"No, Angie, listen! I am here by coincidence with Sharon: a friend, just a friend. A friend I made through you. A friend I talk to, share with, because so often you don't share a goddamn thing with me . . . and you could be lying next me. At the bar sits a colleague, in town from Stanford, and his wife. And, yeah, you were the topic of conversation because, like fools, we're worried about you."

Angela backed to the wall, arms raised as if under attack from an invisible boxer. "Where's Carmen? Y'all, look, I'm sorry I clowned just now. Please."

"I'm not hearing it, all right? Had you bothered to check, you'd have gotten a voice mail from her telling you to either meet her and her friends at the Uptown Theatre to see *The Perfect Storm* or go straight to Chi Cha and hook up with us."

Sharon fought to keep her eyes dry. "I carried you, Angel. Literally, remember?"

Angela's lips stiffened. She prayed Sharon wouldn't be so venal as to reveal what had happened in Philadelphia, in the snow. She prayed Sharon wouldn't be so venal as Angela was now. But little Sharon pulled away to the bar, and Angela's own tears started to seep.

Alvin watched Sharon leave; he sighed. "Decide. Am I your boyfriend, or a crutch? A medical appliance."

"You are my *friend*, Alvin. Like Sharon, but . . . but more. Boyfriend? Not . . . not such that you can make demands of me. *No one* makes demands of me, all right?"

"Look at me—*have you been taking your meds?* Look at me, Angel!"

She sputtered, "What is up with you . . . saying stupid shit like this in public?" Angela raised her hand to his face. "I'm out."

He reached for her hand. "So, it's like that? I'm a companion, nothing more, and you're done with me? Refreshed, renewed . . . healed, huh? Ready to shoot some bad motherfuckers for Uncle Sam? Or maybe ready to find some new big, black, bald man to fuck, 'cause you *can't* fuck me, right? At least not fuck with passion. Nah, out of thanks. *Friendship.*"

She pushed him off. "Stop it . . ."

He backed away. "Ya know, somewhere in that ten-volume set of tomes entitled *The Long-Suffering Black Woman,* I hope there's a three-sentence blurb for the long-suffering black man . . . on how we gotta endure your baggage and scars. You have a nice life, Inspector Bivens. *This* corny, naive brother is through with it."

Alvin folded into the crowd, leaving Sharon and his friends at the bar stunned. Angela crumpled against Chi Cha's cold brick wall. *No! Make things right!* she cried inwardly. She broke away from the wall and followed Alvin onto the street. She caught Alvin just down the block, in front of the Results Gym. She took his hands, squeezed them almost purple tight, so breathless it was hard to speak. He released himself from her grip. She saw pained bewilderment like that on her own face and embraced him, and pressed a wet kiss on his dry lips.

A mistake. The spirit exhorting her didn't have a kiss in mind when it said make things right. For the first time since January, Angela was learning how to hear. Learning how to *listen* would be much harder.

17

MORNING, EIGHTY-EIGHT DEGREES FAHRENHEIT

ANGELA OPENED HER TERRY ROBE and let it fall to the tiled floor. Slowly, her palm wiped a clear, squeaky swath through the condensation on the bathroom mirror. With a shaky finger, she traced a scar on her thigh. A track from one of Trey's bullets. Puffy, ugly. She finished with a pat on her belly, where a fetus once rested. Also compliments of P. Thomas Williams III. The last man she'd made love with. Until now.

Did I allow Alvin to make love to me? No—allowed him to fuck me? Unh-unh . . . I fucked him. The bathroom door opened. Alvin, also nude, came in behind her, encircling her small, stiff body with his arms. A flurry of Joshua Redman's tenor-sax solos from the CD player in Angela's living room floated in with cooler air. Alvin was the only person who listened to her Joshua Redman CDs, bridesmaid's gifts from Monique Mallory when she'd married Brett, the cop. Angela was indifferent to Joshua Redman.

Alvin nuzzled her neck and whispered, "You are so beautiful. But, hey, I know you've gotta pack for Philly. Do your FBI thing, huh? Thank you for letting me into your life . . . all the way." His kissed her and they stood, looking in the mirror. Him smiling serenely. Her about to shed a tear. Before the tear could fall, he released her and grabbed for a spare toothbrush near the soap dish. "You got no food anywhere up in here, but we got time. Breakfast at Morning Edition on East Capitol? Hell, I'll even run you up to the Steak and Egg on Georgia Avenue."

She said nothing. Instead, she reached for her hot curling irons by the sink.

"Angel," Alvin asked with a mouth foamed from Colgate, "who were those white girls you were with at Chi Cha . . . the one's hanging all off of one another?"

"Friends. New friends."

"Uh-huh."

She faced him. He was now slipping on a Stanford University T-shirt: one of a few articles of clothing he kept at Angela's apartment in case he was staying over after a night of Thai carryout and Blockbuster video rentals. "I don't love you. I don't think I could grow to love you. Not in the way you need me. Not in the way I need to. I-I am *so* sorry, Alvin. I see all this bad around me and I am not a bad person, but it saturates me so often. I . . . dunno . . . I loathe my job sometimes but I stick it out because some-one has to do it. Someone has to protect . . . fight. Stop the pain and pun-ish those people who start the pain. But what about my pain? Or my friends' pain? My family's? *Yours?* I'm not . . . not so good at stopping that, huh? And the only person I punish there . . . is me."

Alvin stood, motionless for few seconds. She touched his arm; it just dangled. Maybe he'd agree; he'd curse her. Maybe he'd stand mute and she'd have to push him to answer. He did worse.

"Tell me something," he said in a raspy monotone. "When my dick or my tongue was in every crevice of your body, did you close your eyes?"

Angela's mouth hung open.

"Sure . . . I recall you did. Who were you dreaming of? The niggah I helped you and the Bureau hunt down? The niggah who's always inside your head? Yeah . . . the niggah who did *this!*" He poked at the bullet wound on her thigh. She slapped him. Jaw clenched, he fled the bathroom, and Angela hunched over the sink, hands perilously close to the burning curling irons. Weeping. Joshua Redman drowned out her cries. And Alvin Markham's.

The professor was gone by the time Vallas called to confirm that Nadia had arrived at HQ. Alvin had toted out a Hecht's shopping bag full of his belongings to a waiting cab. Angela finally removed the Redman CD when the cab sped away, replacing it with D'Angelo's *Voodoo* album. The syrupy voice, the vision of his chiseled body, cornrowed scalp, white teeth—all wallpapered over her pain. She started to dress, put on her makeup. Be an FBI agent, not a feeble victim.

And exactly one hour later, Drew Micklin pulled a blue FBI Taurus into the same spot where Alvin's taxi had idled. Angela's parents were safely stowed in the backseat, dressed for mourning. Air-conditioning blasted them like a polar wind. Outside, little white girls wearing Limited Too flip-flops and little black girls wearing Payless jellie sandals skipped rope together on a furnacelike sidewalk.

The first thing Barbara Bivens said to her daughter was "Remember when you and that fat little child Michelle—the one who committed suicide—jumped rope *all day* out in the heat down at the corner of Sequoia and Hilton Parkway? I swear I thought that child was going to have a coronary, but there you were, helping her along, despite all those other little hellions laughing at her." The second thing: "I hope you'll be bringing Professor Markham up to Pam and Byron's in the Vineyard for the Fourth of July. You two need to make your ferry reservations soon."

18

"DADDY, *PLEASE.*" ANGELA COULD HARDLY hear Nadia's voice in the hands-free earpiece of her cell phone. Randolph Bivens, M.D., was droning just as loudly as the idling turboprops of the De Havilland Dash 8 in which Angela sat. "Okay . . . Nadia, you there? I'm nervous about using cells, but if you have to move with the evidence, fine."

"No choice. Your assistant, Jerry, told me that the asshole Bud White and his goons were hunting for stuff in the evidence room. Now they're looking for me, and Lupo's like super-hydrogen-bomb pissed. Better for me to talk as I walk this stuff through, rather than just leave it down here in the lab."

Angela's father's mouth revved with the plane engines. "We've been sitting here waiting to take off for half an hour. I told you we needed to get to the gate at least an hour before this flight just in case we needed to reschedule."

"Nadia, hold on." Angela leered at her father. "I told you, none of this 'show up at the airport the night before' mess, okay? We're late anyway, so just relax."

"Relax, huh—like *you?* You should be investigating the airline industry. And why did we have to come down to D.C. just to fly to Philadelphia? We'd be there now if you'd let me drive. My taxes are paying for limo service and plane tickets?"

Barbara, seated behind Angela and next to Micklin, scoffed, "No, we'd be lost if we'd taken your dirty ol' car. Remember, I drove the last time we went to Les and Ronnie's house."

"You mean Les and Ronnie's *castle?* You got more complaints about our house?"

"Oh, Lord, Randy stop."

"Folks—" Micklin said, attempting a mediation.

Barbara kept snapping, working her head. "I say *wonderful* we're skipping I-95 traffic! Agent Micklin, my husband would vacuum coins out of a fountain if he could get away with it. It took a *death* to get him to take time off from his practice!"

Angela turned around. "Hey, I'm working here."

As her father mumbled something under his breath, Angela opened her palmtop and jotted down the information with the stylus as Nadia relayed it.

"Okay, AMS and gas chromatography confirmed the two hallucinogens in Dr. Collins's liver, matching his and Whiting's toxicology and serology results. One source is a plant, another is an animal."

"Animal?"

"Yeah . . . hold on. Okay. They did confirm lysergic acid from the mushroom, but it wasn't psilocybin. It was *Probocybin fungi.* Get this . . . it's native to, and I'm reading, 'the temperate highlands and subtropical coastal forests of South Africa and southwestern Mozambique, and thought to be extinct.' "

"Africa again. Good girl. Now get to this animal stuff, quickly!"

The flight attendant suddenly announced they'd been cleared for takeoff. "Please make sure your seat belts are securely fastened"—she paused when she saw Angela on the phone—"and please turn off any personal electronic devices."

Dr. Bivens nudged Angela when she didn't comply. As the plane lurched onto a taxiway, the flight attendant moved down the aisle toward their seats. Angela pressed Nadia. "Are you there?"

"Inspector, my name's Aaron Silverman, a tech three. Agent Riccio's viewing an electron microscope sample of a neotenic parasite, a larval flatworm. We found a few hundred of them, dried and sprinkled on the cookie plate. This animal's alkaline secretions are used as a very powerful narcotic in some parts of the world."

Nadia got back on the phone. "Hard to pronounce. *Polystoma umthakathi?*"

"*Umthakathi?* Scan and e-mail the report. Now, get over to latent prints and—"

The flight attendant reappeared, smiling. "Miss, please turn off the cell phone and stow the palm device, thank you."

With an eye roll, Angela said, "I have to go." Then, in a hurried, furtive whisper: "Get your palmtop ready . . . I'll e-mail you from the plane."

The Dash 8 lifted off at a steep angle; National Airport's runways looked canted like aircraft-carrier decks. Even through the haze, the view of the Mall, the monuments, and the milky Potomac snaking through the green hills and vales of Maryland and Virginia was beautiful. And lost on Angela.

She said the word again. *"Umthakathi?"* Alien, yet, somehow, it rolled off her tongue. Familiar. And in seconds, she was shifting uncomfortably in her seat. Pain had reflected outward from her core to her abdomen when she repeated the word, as if it were a ghost of the cramps she'd suffered the last time she'd traveled to Philadelphia.

"Reenie," Barbara Bivens inquired as the plane banked over the Chesapeake Bay. "You all right?"

"She should have eaten something besides that banana," Dr. Bivens grunted.

"I'm . . . I'm fine, Mommy."

The props' drone dropped to a fine hum, the seat-belt sign switched off. They'd be descending into Philadelphia in twenty-eight minutes, the female pilot announced. Grabbing her tote bag, Angela motioned toward the rest room. "Won't be a moment."

Angela shut and locked the door, sat on the toilet cover, and pulled out her palmtop. She extended the antenna and logged on through the wireless modem, hitting instant messaging once she connected. After a half a minute that seemed like half an hour, Nadia replied:

```
e-mailed abstract of the worm analysis to you. i'm now down
in latent prints and bud white's looking hard for me.
;-(we've got the blue laser going on this piece of the ice
tea pitcher from collins's suite at the blue heron. we have
to hurry.
```

Angela wrote with the stylus; the software converted the handwriting to text:

```
stay focused. work the evidence. don't worry about bud white.
vallas has your back.
```

The plane hit a little turbulence; the humidity had been breeding five-mile-high thunderstorms north of Wilmington, Delaware. The "Please return to your seat" sign flashed yellow. Angela braced herself against the sink. A knock on the door jarred her. Her father. "I'm okay, Daddy," she responded. "Just a little airsickness."

She hurriedly sent another message:

```
After you get a clarification on those prints, make sure to
check on the analysis of the metal fragment and the wood
splinter, then call me tonight.
```

Nadia:

```
He just refumed the glass. one came off right on the tape.
send to IAFIS for an ID? But there's something strange. The
techie says the ridges are degraded.
```

Angela tapped the sink with her stylus, her heart racing as she waited for another line. The next instant message came up on the tiny backlit screen:

```
closest thing they've seen to that are ID prints for corpses.
```

"What?" Angela said aloud. Before she could write out a reply, the next line came up:

```
Burn victims. They're saying—are you ready for this?—prints
are consistent with those lifted from dead burn victims.
```

Angela:

```
victims, plural? As in multiple latents from different
subjects?
```

There was no reply. Exasperated, Angela dug out her cell phone and punched in Nadia's number.

"Christ, is this from a Skyfone?" the surprised trainee answered.

"Listen." Angela inserted her hands-free piece as she scribbled notes with the stylus. "Have them take a sample of the so-called burned-fingerprint material back over to the AMS and see if it's indeed dead or charred flesh. Someone's screwing with us." She checked her watch. "We're running out of time . . . get over to the Metallurgy Section ASAP and guard that metal sample."

"They've already sent it off to the NIST in Gaithersburg, like with the gold."

"Good. Where's the wood piece?"

"Carbon dating. I showed some initiative. I figured you wanted the sample dated, the wood identified? Thought you'd be impressed. The guy's got the prelims."

A rap on the door fractured Angela's concentration. "Nadia, hold on. Um, hullo . . . I'm not feeling well. Be done soon."

"Ms. Bivens, open the door." It was the prison-matron tone of the flight attendant. "The first officer's been picking up radio-frequency waves from the cabin. Please turn off the device and come out, *at once.*"

19

WALNUT STREET UNITED CHURCH OF CHRIST

RITTENHOUSE SQUARE, PHILADELPHIA

THE FLORISTS WERE STILL OFF-LOADING bunches of lilies and yellow roses from two vans parked at the curb. Less demure arrangements headed up the grayish limestone steps to the church narthex: hot-pink-dyed carnation wreaths, powder-blue papier-mâché crosses. Mementos from older patients and an earlier phase in Leslie Collins's life, when he lived on Belmont Avenue in West Philly and could only dream about Chestnut Hill, or cocktails at the Union League. Now, past and present, Chestnut Hill and West Philly, his daughter's Bryn Mawr crew team and the daughters of his street-gang cohorts, filed, silently, into the church. Angela viewed the crowd from the window of a tan Crown Victoria, compliments of the Philadelphia Field Office.

"Sound check, Angie," Bob Micklin said, tapping her shoulder.

She adjusted her earpiece and heard Micklin count to five.

"It's all work for you, huh?" Dr. Bivens scolded. Her father was trembling a little when he said that. Aside from the horror with Trey, she'd only seen him tremble at funerals. *But who was he to talk about "it's all work"?* Still, she wasn't as angry as her thoughts conveyed. He had to deliver the tribute on behalf of the American College of Obstetrics and Gynecology, the Meharry Medical School Alumni, and the Lambda Nu medical fraternity. Angela's mother stroked his shoulders to calm him. She'd donned a black, broad-brimmed hat with a black lace veil; Angela could barely see over it to talk to Micklin in the sedan's front seat.

"I want a clear channel when Agent-Trainee Riccio calls me," she said.

"Sorry," Micklin answered. "We need all channels when Senator Buford's en route, unless you'd like to tell me why Ms. Riccio's call is so darn overriding?"

"Later, okay?" Angela then glanced at her mother. "I'll watch Daddy, don't worry." Angela smiled, touched her father's hand, and opened the car door.

When she'd left the airport, Angela had witnessed black, anvil-shaped thunderheads marshaling across the Delaware, ready to strike Center City. But a stubborn dome of bright, baked air kept them at bay for now. Angela put on her sunglasses against the glare and pointed her parents toward solemn ushers wearing gold gloves: undergraduate members of Collins's fraternity from Temple, Penn, and Drexel.

Micklin joined her, announcing, "Air Force One landed at McGuire Air Force Base. Secret Service is choppering 'Bubba' in for Beth Hooperman's funeral." Micklin tapped his earpiece. "Hey . . . Philadelphia PD says Senator Buford's just left the Ritz-Carlton. They're handling security for the wake at the Union League."

Angela turned and spied a group of middle-aged black men only twenty feet down the block, huddled near a line of limousines. A tall man at the fringe was a celeb, Dr. J, legend of the 76ers and now a prominent businessman and speaker. One was a portly cleric, draped in a white and purple cassock and surplice. He was wiping his bald pate with a handkerchief. At the group's center stood a slender man with salt-and-pepper hair. Angular face, darting eyes. The rest of them she'd seen on the covers of magazines like *Black Enterprise* or *Fortune* or *Forbes;* others were physicians her father had mentioned.

"Excuse me for a minute, Drew."

Angela stepped slowly toward the group. They divided like supplicating servants as she approached, black patent leather heels clipping the concrete. The mogul named Bryce King, and the bishop named Carl Davidson, stood their ground.

Angela extended her hand. "Gentlemen, my condolences." King took her hand and shook it firmly, saying nothing. Davidson took a heavy breath and shook her hand, too, weakly. "If you need anything, just say the word."

The Bishop scoffed, "No handcuffing to interrogate us about Les? Get some dirt, leak it to the white media?"

"I'm sorry, Bishop Davidson."

"Carl, stop. Remember who and what you are, and why you're here today."

"Ain't no thing, Bryce. I have a low pain threshold, so she's only got to whoop my ass once and I'll tell her where all the runaway slaves is hidin'."

The power elite, still circling the wagons around Trey's sullied memory? Angela backed away. Micklin's voice in her earpiece halted her tactical retreat. "Buford's here."

A black Chevy Suburban rumbled to the curb right in front of Davidson and King. Senator Brian Buford stepped onto the sidewalk; cops and aides kept the reporters off the church steps and cleared them from the sidewalk. He was beaming an amiable, serene look. He hugged King and then Bishop Davidson, slipping them a frat handshake in the process. Then, unexpectedly, he turned to greet Angela.

"I heard much about you, but never met you," he said, smiling despite the somber moment. "Glad you're here. My best to Victor."

Once Buford withdrew his hand, King turned him around. "We need to talk."

Angela excused herself. Yet as she moved away, she felt a gentle tug on the sleeve of her suit jacket. Buford. He started to whisper while crouching to meet her ear.

"Don't let them intimidate you. You were, *and are*, doing your job. You were, *and are*, a hero to many people. Don't forget that."

He's good, she thought cynically. Just like on *Charlie Rose*.

"You and I know what it's like to take a human life in the line of duty. I was just a boy on Koh Tang. Killed five people: two real close. One, with my knife, as close as we're standing now. Like we were making love . . . apt, because she was girl, younger than me. Her RPG killed my Master Chief, ripped up our patrol boat. She was aiming another at a Marine chopper. You've seen it . . . when your eyes meet, and one of you has to die? There is no worse feeling of terror . . . even if you're the one doing the killing."

Angela nodded, her cynicism neutralized by his voice, his eyes. He was like Hector of Troy, the shining-helmed hero from *The Iliad*. But the Trojans lost that war.

Angela moved up the steps, turned, and peered over her sunglasses at the three old frat brothers. She watched them point fingers and scowl at one another, halting or smiling only when a friend greeted them, or they knew a pod of paparazzi was aiming telephoto lenses. She would have heard this exchange, had she been closer:

Davidson grumbled to Buford, "Cavorting with the enemy? And you, a war hero?"

"Carl, other than an expanded ass, you haven't changed since college. Back then it was clotheslining running backs on the ball field, or beating our frat pledges till blood oozed through holes in your damn precious, sacred paddle. Tell me, how *did* a cruel, vicious sonovabitch like yourself become clergy?"

"Bryce, you need to check Mr. Clean here. He got room to talk. A *politician!* Ha!"

Buford dropped his arm on Davidson's doughy shoulder, smiling, so cameras would see, but his tone was like that of a dog guarding its food. "You and I're supposedly in the same business: serving people. But you forgot that once the five-figure tithe checks and talk-show honoraria rolled in. And let's not forget the lonely widows, the buxom choir members, the nubile teenage girls in Vacation Bible School: pussy, pussy everywhere, and no time to do the Lord's work, eh?"

The bishop hissed, "Don't forget—we *own* you, motherfucker." Davidson spun around, surplice whirling, and entered a side metal door, screaming for an acolyte to fetch him a cold drink.

Bryce King glowered at the senator; sweat was now running off both men's faces, staining collars on $200 custom-tailored shirts. But neither budged, and Angela witnessed the standoff.

"Butch, you are not the pristine, Jimmy Stewart–type you think you are."

"And, Bryce, you are not the big man on campus you were thirty years ago. Today, however, you don't push me around. So get out of my fucking way."

"So you're the big man, now? Well, fuck you if you leave the fold, like that Bivens girl. And your latest games? Tearing down Jesse Jackson over his personal problems, trashing the AANC over Trey Williams? Half the Black Caucus is voting with the Republicans against your campaign finance bill because it will short-circuit their own fund-raising; the other half's ostracized you over your Byzantine little turns to the right. Some folks don't even want to sit in the front pews with you today."

"I'd laugh at you if I wasn't about to break down and cry over Les. And the front row—that's for people who loved Leslie Collins. Not for self-aggrandizing fools."

Angela watched King laugh. But she didn't hear his tone of disgust. "You sound like Victor Styles now."

The Senator moved to embrace the media mogul. From a distance, all looked fraternal, loving. "Let me tell you something that Victor Styles knows damn well," Buford whispered in his friend's ear. "I'll deliver California to Al Gore. I will deliver the minivan crowd in the suburbs to the Democratic Party, even in the South. Ironic, eh? Me, a black man? No, me—war hero. Small businessman. Honest lawyer. Family man. The type of voter you and your ace Bill Clinton forgot. So you go in that church, chill those spooks out, and tell them to ride on my back on Election Day."

Buford kissed Bryce King's cheek and broke away, bounding up the steps past Angela without even a glance, as his aides chased him inside. Bryce King followed, until he reached Angela.

"Can I help you with something, Mr. King?"

King smiled. "We've all been friends since the Senator went away to the Navy, freshman year at Howard. You remember your friends on the Hilltop?" She nodded. "A bond nothing will sever. *Nothing.* But the Senator's got to realize, on this day of loss, that there are people who wish him harm. We're his refuge. Yours, *too,* if you're smart."

He walked inside, leaving Angela alone. That's when the first rumblings of thunder started in the east, and the hazy, sunny sky began to boil gray. That ghost pain in her abdomen commenced as well, as the first raindrops spattered on hot stone steps.

The choir ended with a rousing version of "Goin' Up Yonder," though it was almost drowned out by rain on the church roof. And the speakers—all fifteen of them, including Angela's father—were upstaged by the lightning exploding beyond the towering stained-glass windows. Angela sat between her parents, arms linked with both, while she chewed on an Anaprox from her father. The cramps in her uterus had gotten worse, but tears of pain can be confused for grief. Yet this pain intensified with each boom of thunder, each flash that lit Les Collins's open coffin. The mortician had to be a true artist. As much of an artist as the person who carved up Collins.

Bishop Carl O. Davidson perched himself at the pulpit's rostrum. The homily started softly, with praise, with anecdotes. Then the preacher's inflection and cadence changed and the theatrics began. And down to a whisper again. Forgetting her horrible discomfort, Angela swiveled around to see everybody, including white people, seemingly mesmerized by Davidson's oratory. Maybe spirits indeed answered his call to lift Collins to heaven.

Suddenly, Davidson broke into a coughing fit. People in the pews gasped. Davidson apologized, sipped water, and tried to remember his place. He was swaying, stammering. Eyebrows rose, murmurs started. A thunderclap boomed overhead; church lights flickered, the choir band's amps buzzed with feedback. More gasps. Rectors whispered orders; ushers and acolytes scrambled. Bishop Carl Davidson was coughing again. Sweat glistened such that people in the distant rear pews of this massive holy house could see it twinkling off his cheeks. He made a final cant at the rostrum and the huge, open, leather-bound Bible. His eyes appeared focused on something invisible, as if it were floating down the aisle. He cried out in an almost canine yelp, clutching his chest with his right hand, as his body smashed into the rostrum.

"Oh my God, Reenie!" Angela heard her mother cry.

Angela stood and tapped her earpiece. "Micklin . . . talk to me!" He acknowledged as she saw two cops, a rector, and Bryce King struggle to the pulpit.

Now there were shouts, bawls, but no one in the pews really moved: none to aid, none to flee. Fifteen hundred people sat for those few horrible seconds, aghast, until somebody yelled, "He's had a heart attack!"

Angela pushed through stunned choir members toward the altar, halted, and turned. Over two hundred doctors were in there, yet Angela saw only three run up to join her father. Bryce King had already yanked off Davidson's surplice; Dr. Bivens pushed him aside and checked the Bishop's pupils and pulse while another doctor checked his throat and began chest massage.

Angela screamed to Micklin in the mike, "Ambulance's ten-twenty?"

"Called . . . ETA three to five minutes."

She checked and waved. "Okay, keep Senator Buford with you!"

"Ten-four." There was static, then, "Hey . . . there's a two-way call in ISD channel, from your trainee!"

Davidson was foaming at the mouth. Angela couldn't break away. *"Shit.* Close the channel and have her call me when we've stabilized here, you copy?"

Dr. Bivens shouted, "Can they take him at U. Penn Trauma Center?"

One of the doctors who'd clambered up to the Bishop's body replied, "Too far . . . but Thomas Jefferson's ER is right around the corner—two minutes, maybe?"

As if to extinguish their hopes, thunder crashed above their heads. The lights flickered in the church after another crash of thunder, then winked out. The real screaming began. It was early afternoon, yet black as tar outside. Angela spotted the magenta flash of the EMT and fire rescue lights through the stained glass. In another minute, the EMTs—soaked by the rain—made their way up to the pulpit, led by a firefighter with a huge flashlight. Two other firefighters followed behind the crew with a gurney. Angela pulled her father away from the flailing hands, IV bags, and portable defibrillator contacts. She hugged him and pushed him back toward her mother, who was embracing an inconsolable Mrs. Veronica Collins.

Angela spun around to see Senator Buford, eyes wide as plates, panting. He'd broken away from his frightened, confused aides; Micklin ran up behind him.

"Bishop Davidson is getting the best care possible," Angela assured Buford. "They're taking him into the rectory . . . apparently there's a tunnel there to the Barclay Hotel next door . . . they can take him right to an ambulance in the garage."

"I want to go."

"No," she answered, pushing her five-foot-two frame to block him. "Sir, please go with Special Agent Micklin, here."

Flashlight beams lit Bryce King's form, trailing the gurney and the EMTs. Angela followed them into the rectory, through a library, and down a ramp into the bowels of the church. Emergency exit signs lit the mouth of the long, cavernous tunnel. Yellowish lights were strung above, down the tunnel's length.

Angela caught up with the breathless King. He backed up to the wall and slid down to the floor till his knees touched his chest. No more the arrogant, aloof media titan—equally at home with Master P and Missy Elliott as with Barry Diller and Sumner Redstone. He was crying.

"Mr. King," Angela said, bending over him, "take my hand. It's okay."

Though the EMTs had long since disappeared into the dim tunnel, both Angela and King lifted their heads and turned, for they could no longer hear the echo of footsteps, radio calls, and feedback, or the squealing of the gurney wheels. Just the patter of rain from the other end of the tunnel. And then the rush of wind. Not a wet wind driven by the summer downpour.

No. Hot, broiling, devoid of any moisture.

King stumbled to his feet, wincing. "*Urghhh* . . . you smell that? What the hell . . ."

She did. The breeze stank like soiled animal cages in a fly-by-night circus. Angela called to Micklin. "Bob, I'm in the tunnel in the rectory base-ment and . . . I . . ." She paused. The stench worsened, burning her throat and nostrils.

"Agent . . . B-Bivens," King stuttered, "I'm feeling . . . dizzy. Maybe I should sit."

"Angie . . . Angie?" Micklin called in her earpiece. But she didn't answer. Her eyes were clouding. She felt a little light-headed. The tunnel lights looked as if they were twirling, slowly at first, than a little faster until she slapped her palm against the cinder-block wall as well to steady herself.

She heard a thud down the tunnel, then another. And sounds like foot-steps. Like *bare feet* on painted concrete. Dozens of them.

"EMTs c-coming?" King muttered, loosening his tie.

The thuds grew louder, nearer, as did the patter of feet. And . . . *whispers.* Low, coarse, like many men. Punctuated by . . . *laughter?*

The wind swooshed by, brushing by her lips, her breasts. Tingling the fine hair on the back of her neck. And carrying that stink.

Shuddering, whipping from side to side, Angela called, "Mr. King?" She couldn't focus and it wasn't simply from fear. She swayed and slurred like a drunk.

One whisper flew into her ear. Her mind heard, *Si-ya-nik-hum-bula.* She spun to catch the source. Instead, she saw that King was gone. Footsteps behind her on the stairs meant he'd abandoned her.

The whispers stopped. As did the wind. Dead silence.

Her equilibrium draining, Angela frantically called for Micklin. "Bob, you copy? Is there . . . there another EMT unit down here? Tell them . . . the fire department . . . to check for a gas leak . . . maybe when the power went out . . . something happened."

She tapped her earpiece. Static answered her.

Then, from deep inside the tunnel, in perfect succession, each bulb exploded.

Angela dropped to her knees. Hand trembling, she reached around for her SIG as the last bulb popped six feet ahead. One second. Two. Three—she waited, swallowing hard when she heard breathing from the darkness. *Wheezing.* Like that of an elderly person. Smoke and ozone from the fried bulbs mixed with the lingering stench, making her breaths labored. Angela heard shuffling steps coming out of the black corridor.

There! Someone. Small, almost elfin. Closer now. Wearing some sort of hat. Maybe only ten feet away now. Yes, an old black man, clothed in a grimy seersucker suit jacket. Wrinkled blue trousers. His arms were raised; his sleeves billowed as he shook a vessel in each hand. Shaped like large squash? Inside the right vessel, something dry rattled. Inside the left, something viscous and wet swished, slopped.

"F-FBI . . . identify yourself," Angela sputtered, squinting. She raised the 9mm as the figure closed in, shaking those vessels faster. "I said . . . i-identify your—"

Her voice trailed off. The figure came into the light from the emergency exit sign. Angela beheld yellow eyes. And a smile. Full of pointed fangs, as yellow as the eyes.

"Oh, God . . . God . . . Freeze!"

Too late. The figure waved the vessel containing something wet. Angela's lungs loosed a howl they'd let escape only once before: on Les Collins's examining table. The pain was no longer a ghost. It shredded her abdomen and dropped her to the floor, heaving, screaming, writhing. Her eyes felt seared by white heat, white light. Her ears heard someone shuffling closer, wheezing, crouching. Arthritic joints cracking.

Then, a rebuke. *"Inkanyezi! Uku-zi inyama, Inakenyezi! Ama zi fufuyama, Inkanyezi! Umdomo, Inkanyezi! Ama zi Ama Simba . . . Ama Simba, Ama Simbaaaaaa!"* The next sound was a mouth, gathering saliva. A spitting noise. Foul moisture spattered on her cheek, and footsteps moved away.

The white light in Angela's head blacked out, melding with the darkness of the tunnel, there, deep below Rittenhouse Square.

20

IT BEGAN AS IT HAD BEFORE:

Dew glistening on the pale green leaves of sorghum grass like diamonds, sunbeams tickling yellow pineapple lilies and magenta acacia blooms.

And now Angela knew it meant dawn, in this field.

Dawn, where a little boy frolicked, nude, brown-skinned. Giggling. His soft voice calls the meadow "Ulundi."

The word and laughter vanish like vapor. Now smoke. Gunpowder smoke. Almond eyes in a small head see the field, changed. The field where mother battled to save her children, not just her son. All of her children. From king to soldiers to crookback old hags and plump babies. She is lost . . . to those eyes. Lost to yellow eyes, yellow teeth. Pointed like a crocodile's. The soft voice whispers its name. Umthakathi: *who waves the* ishungu, *or gourd, holding burnt bones and condemned souls. The soft voice whispers a mother's name. Her role: diviner. Shaman. Like all the women of her kind, she's called* sangoma, *who wave the* ishungu *holding the spice and root spirits. Ground mandrake and nightshade. Cinnamon, ginger. Leaves of grass and skin, woven for the kings of her people from the beginning. Gifts of the Inkanyamba, who dwells in the falls. Who plays no favorites, for the serpent is also the source of the* umthakathi's *power.*

She is the star angel of the sangoma. *And she is lost . . . she is lost . . . forever. To me. I speak now. Do you hear me?*

Now I am alone, mud stipples my cheeks except where tears have tracked them clean. I want my mother . . . I miss her. I am only three seasons weaned from her nipples. My feet are cut by briers and brambles. But no one will hear my cries because they're swallowed by the moans and screams of dying men, on Ulundi. Can you hear them? Listen to the rustle of black, sinewy arms sprouting through the smoke mist like charred saplings. Two thousand warriors—the amabutho, *of whom I wanted to be when I grow up, Mother. When I am circumcised you'll bless the scar and you'll teach me everything you know. I am running now, Mother. I'm screaming, too. So frightened. I stumble into the thick brush and shelter of a donga. And in the ravine, I'm not alone. Listen again. That man with the potbelly and ivory head ring you called Great Fire is weeping. He was not like his grandfather's brother, the one for whom the* umthakathi *spoke the charm of* mfecane. Mfecane: *"the crushing." A spell that brought that king you called Shaka his empire. Our empire, now crumbling like dry dung on our pastures. I hear another man crying, too, over his brave dead soldiers. A lean general, with plumes of ostrich and gold adornments and cowtail. And I hear more cries. The* izigodlo, *the young women with pert breasts and round rumps who always peered at you with curiosity, sometimes contempt. Sometimes envy. Those royal wives and handmaidens, huddling at the fat man's feet. Their whining sounds like the drone of bees.*

Now I hear strange noises across the field, from over the donga's *western lip. No more guns, or man-made thunder. These are the white men's shouts and bugle calls and drums, and my mind can spy the red coats and white pith helmets of their army. Not the ones who wear the slouch hats and beards and who speak the other white man's tongue, called Dutch. Those who have hated us since you were born, Mother. Those who tricked the men in the red coats and white helmets to help them steal our pastures, our cattle. Who ring their wagons against us and sing their hymns that sound like phlegm clearing a throat. They are burning our homes. Though I am hid in the* donga, *safe with the fat one who whispers your name as much as I do, I flinch from morning sunlight that glints off what the fat man calls "bayonets," "cavalry sabers," and "'lance tips"; it blazes up the burnished brass of the monsters on wagon wheels that spew fire. Pop-pop-pop-pop-pop. I once heard a white missionary call the monsters "Gatling guns," and they mowed down entire regiments of the* amabutho *like a sickle on a dry millet field. Months ago, we danced when the Great Fire's regiments wiped out the red coats at the place called Isandlhawana and routed the cavalry of their white queen . . . whom you called Victoria, at Hlobane, taking many horses as prizes. This morning, in the meadow called Ulundi, after you were lost to me forever, our soldiers hollered their battle cry "uSuthu!" and pounded the handles of their* iklwa *stabbing spears against their rawhide shields as they charged. In futility.*

And now the general pleads, hoarsely, to the fat man, the Great Fire. But the fat man wants to stay. He says there is a child. Not me. A girl. He wants to kill her. He wants me to watch. Because he says you have failed, Mother. He says you are dead. He calls to the soldiers and they bring her. She is naked and smiling and tiny. Small hands and dusty little toes. And, Mother, he has a knife. Can you hear him say the words? "This child is innocent." But it must die, anyway. Remember the words?

He doesn't strike. He calls for the general to bring the old creature, to watch his seed die. The creature's weak, Mother; you nearly killed him. He sneers and calls me inyanga. *And laughs: "Your herbs will not heal a burned soul, boy." I almost pee on myself as I cower behind the general's leg. The creature then slicks his long, scarlet tongue—the only moist thing on his body—across his fangs and smirks at the Great Fire and his men: "Can you hear the lions' roar? It's the roar of the Ama Simba . . . celebrating your defeat. My coven's spells helped close the white queen's ears to your calls for peace—and summoned the Lion's Regiment from the un-speakable place to hobble your troops before her army's guns. Now I suck my vengeance from your soul as a hyena sucks marrow from a doe's crushed bones!"*

I peek from behind the general when I hear the creature's laughing at us no more. He'd seen his little girl. And he's squealing like a piglet. The girl rushes to me—because I am a child like her? I hug her, Mother. But the soldiers tear her away and she screams. Listen to it! The general holds up the old creature's head, while the fat one, Great Fire, raises a knife . . .

Mother . . . Mother? Do you hear me? I am shaking and so scared because the girl's crying and the old creature shouts, "Fool! My body is but a vessel. We are forever!"

The fat man mumbles, "Forever . . . ends here." And then: "Because your seed dies here. As sangoma *to* inyanga, *mother to son. So your kind lives, father to daughter. Soon, you die, too!"*

The knife sweeps down toward the little girl's neck and—

Mother! A gunshot!

On the donga's *edge, a white man atop a brown horse reloads his short rifle and aims it at our fat king. Five blue-coated lancers ride up beside him, followed by their leader brandishing a pistol. The fat king, one whom you served, has lost all nerve and spirit, Mother. He drops his knife, as red coats pour into the* donga *like termites. They yank me away from the others. They cut the bonds of the old creature and shove the little girl into his sticklike arms. They call us "Kaffirs."*

The leader groans in disgust at this old creature and pushes father and child off to a red coat with golden stripes on his arm, and big, bushy lip hair, but none on his chin. And this bushy-haired one snaps a salute, barks at the younger red coats with no stripes. One grabs my hand. Throws me into a wagon with other chil-dren, sick old people, women, and wounded amabutho. *You can't hear us weep-ing anymore, Mother. But can you hear the fat king's wail?*

Listen. He's on his knees. He hears the whistle of a dry, hot wind. It scours Ulundi. And in that foul blast, he hears the Ama Simba roar.

And he whimpers your name . . .

21

"*. . . INKANYEZI!*" ANGELA SHOUTED.

A hand took her own and squeezed. She felt a lumpy pillow cradling her head; a stiff mattress under her back. Her nose sniffed institutional disinfectant. Her eyes darted around, saw the EKG monitor, the IV bag. Blurry faces gathered above her.

"Easy, Angel. Daddy's here." And there was his face. Haggard, but smiling. "You're at U. Penn Hospital, baby. Mom's down in the cafeteria, on the phone with Byron and Pam. She'll be up to sit with you after these gentlemen leave."

Angela lifted her head when she heard a coarse, familiar voice ask, "What did she just say? In-ka-na-ye-whatever?"

Bud White. He was shaking his head. Angela shut her eyes and opened them, hoping White was as spectral as the dream she'd had. He was still there.

Micklin chuckled, "Bet you feel like Dorothy, waking up back in Kansas."

"God . . . my head . . . I recognize you, Scarecrow." She paused and then looked at her father, still wearing his suit from the funeral. "And you, Mr. Wizard." She peered at White. "And the flying monkey king."

"I'm not laughing, Inspector," White growled. "We have a certified Code Blue."

Angela grimaced, less from the full-body ache than what White had re-vealed. "Code Blue?" Then Angela's eyelids popped wide. "Oh, *no* . . . Buford . . . is he okay?"

"Senator Buford's fine," Micklin said. "But we can't—"

White broke in, "Code Blue. *Classified.*" That meant there were people in the room who weren't authorized to hear the details. A nurse dressed in yellow scrubs circled from behind a short, balding man a gray suit. Next to him stood another short man, swarthy, wearing a blue uniform and a white cap; a Philadelphia PD officer guarded the doorway, whispering to a young black man in a navy blazer. The nurse said sharply, "None of you, except Dr. Bivens, should be here."

Angela looked over at her father, squeezing his fingers tighter. She blocked out the others. "Daddy . . . I heard words . . . in a dream, that be-came a nightmare. But it was really a memory."

"Just relax, honey."

"No . . . I heard the same words in the tunnel. But the dream, or at least part if it, has been going on for months." Now, she focused on Bud White. "Why are you here?"

"Because of the Code Blue, and to take your place as primary agent in this task force until you mend."

Micklin piped in meekly, "He came up last night. That's Eugene Fowler, SAC of the Philadelphia Field Office. That's Deputy Fire Chief Arturo Rojas over there."

"I'm Detective Eric Goins, Philadelphia PD," said the black man in the blazer.

"W-wait," Angela grunted, trying to lift her head. "Daddy . . . what day is this?"

"Reenie, you've been here since yesterday afternoon. Detective Goins's people found you passed out in the tunnel. You've been in and out of con-sciousness, mumbling these, well, strange words, for four hours."

I've got to focus. Wake up . . . stay in control. But her body was limp. "Victim?"

Goins nudged White aside. "Bishop Carl O. Davidson Jr., age fifty-four. Inspector, can you tell me—"

"Wait. No prints or physical evidence . . . except a gold disk on his tongue?"

This time White answered, "Yeah. And the disk had a 7 etched on one side."

"Not a 7. The river snake, swimming to the falls. Howick Falls." She opened her eyes. "South Africa. A mother . . . a child, fighting a man with teeth, like a crocodile. Full of hate. The smell was like lions. Hot, dry. I heard them coming. Not lions. *Men."*

White whispered to Fowler, "Aw, she's lost it. I've got to report this to HQ."

Fowler spoke up, "You were found with your weapon drawn. Why?"

"An unidentified subject. But his eyes . . . his . . . teeth, like my dream . . ."

White snickered; Fowler masked his incredulity with a jerky nod.

Chief Rojas cleared his throat and said, "Philadelphia Electric confirmed that the storm shorted out a pump on the Barclay Hotel's gas main. That was what knocked you out. But it doesn't explain what happened to my guys."

Dr. Bivens pleaded, "No, not this again—*please* let her rest."

Angela watched her father turn away, florid and flustered, as Fowler explained, "Rescue Unit 347 of Pumper Company 52 responded to the cardiac call at the church. *This* happened five minutes after you saw them in the tunnel. The corner of Nineteenth and Spruce Streets, no more than a block from the Square." He handed her an eight-by-ten photo of an EMT unit, crumpled into a concrete wall like a red and white accordion. Blood was spattered on the shattered windshield and mangled dashboard.

"Oh my God."

Goins jumped in. "At least fifty miles an hour when they hit the wall. Like they . . . like they crashed *on purpose*. Both EMTs died on impact."

Fowler rejoined, "And this is what happened to Bishop Carl Davidson." He handed Angela two more photos. Her stomach sank. On the pavement ten feet from the unit's open rear doors, a gurney was tipped over on its side, with Carl Davidson still strapped into it. His body had been ripped open. Groin to chest. His penis was missing. His entrails and what looked like quarts of brown blood ran in the gutter, mingling with rainwater and the leaked oil and gasoline from the wrecked ambulance.

Angela pushed the photos back into Fowler's hands, whispering hoarsely, "Check my bloodwork, do a tox screen on my hair. I wasn't . . . wasn't gassed. And there was someone in the tunnel. Black male, five-three to five-five, maybe sixty-five to seventy-five years old—"

"Hold it," Goins said. "You want our facial-composite technician up here?"

"Yes."

"*No,*" Dr. Bivens said. He looked to the nurse. "Page the chief resident on this floor, stat. I want these men out! Her blood pressure's low and she's barely sentient."

"I'm afraid we can't, Dr. Bivens," Micklin stated, stepping forward to try to calm him. "Sir, we need ten minutes alone with her." Micklin repeated that to the nurse.

Randolph Bivens tried so hard to sound harsh. "I despise this life of yours, Angel." But he kissed his daughter's forehead anyway, and Micklin took him out.

Angela cleared moist eyes with her thumbs. "Where's Bryce King?"

Goins recounted, "Mr. King left for D.C. before we could get a statement. His lawyers called not too long ago, affirming that there was no one down in the tunnel but the rescue unit, him, and you. The excitement of the moment made him dizzy."

"He's wrong. Or lying. And there were other footsteps. Detective, have your crime scene unit do a thorough—"

Fowler raised his hand as he moved closer to the bed rail. That's when Angela's head cleared enough for her to remember Styles's awful extortion threat. Gene Fowler: this was the man who had the master surveillance tapes of Les Collins's office. Her heart skipped and the EKG picked it up.

Fowler didn't outwardly appear to recognize her. Why would he? She calmed, but her respite lasted barely a second before Fowler asked Chief Rojas and Detective Goins to leave. Rojas was all to happy to oblige. Goins slapped his notepad on his knee and filed out, huffing, "This is still a local homicide, and we will press it."

"Yeah, you do that, *Den*-zel," White mocked as the door closed. "Think he's sweet on you, Inspector?"

Fowler explained, "I've been on the phone all night with Washington." He then cut his eyes at White, with disdain. "They sent Supervisory Special Agent White to liaise with my people. Clear things up . . . though, this South Africa issue wasn't part of your briefing, Agent White."

While squinting at Angela, White replied, "No, sir. Perhaps we have some weird convergences. Flukes, even. The fact remains"—now he was addressing Angela—"Philly PD and our ERT found symbols, written in blood on the EMS unit. No prints from it. We ran it against your files. Pretty close to the Hebrew letters sounding out the word *Cha* or *C-H-A.*"

Fowler added, "The beginning of the word *Chamuel.* That's one of your Archangel names, correct?"

"Hebrew? These animals wouldn't use Hebrew letters."

White countered, "Aren't these names pretty much Hebrew-derived?"

"For God's sake, I saw an old black man in that tunnel!"

Fowler gripped the bed rail and said, "Agent White briefed us that in your field notes, shared with the Civil Rights Section, angel Zadkiel had poisonous snakes as his retainers? Mrs. Hooperman died from an aggressive neurotoxin in a snake bite."

"Why don't you let me speak to the Inspector alone, sir," White offered.

Fowler sighed heavily and nodded. He called to Angela as he departed, "I didn't mean to upset you, Inspector. We're all on the same team here."

Angela grinned. There went either a diligent, honorable man or a fool.

"Alone at last," White needled as he pulled up a chair.

"I got nothing to say to you."

"Oh, yeah, you do. You made me look like an idiot at HQ. Lupo consented to putting me in charge of the physical evidence, the forensics, for both Hooperman and Whiting, but your slick move—"

"So you'll hit me with possible violations of the MIOP? Impeding an investigation? Insubordination? Feed me to OPR, like that HRT asshole Paul Trask's been dying to do since he almost killed my sister and nephews?"

White guffawed. "You should get an Oscar. You know damn well that sealing the chain-of-custody carriers under your signature is proper protocol, even if Lupo told you that's *my* job. But then you get your trainee to ferry the lab tests through—Director Donatello's daughter? She takes those results, plus whatever evidence your ISD team was processing, seals the test results, again under your signature. I wonder how she got it, *seeing that you were in Philly*. But, hey, section twenty-five of the MIOP: she can refuse to relinquish chain of custody to me unless you, as her supervisor, clear it. We can't even find her now. Styles hasn't ordered her to cough the materials up . . . and I look like a pussy because I have to beg."

Angela smiled. The little witch learned fast. "You don't like me, eh, Bud?"

"I don't dislike you, Inspector. I hate what you represent. What people like *you* and those who shove you into the limelight are trying to do to guys like *me*. 'Diversity.' 'It takes a village to raise a child.' Bullshit slogans." His hard frown softened. "But you know what, if you have an alternate theory of these homicides, we should compare notes. Yeah, would right-wing scumbags suddenly be using African crap in their MO? Let's discuss those test results, so I don't look like a retard again next time I brief AD Scofield and AD Sessions."

"Thought we were 'all on the same team.' You didn't mention Frank . . . or Styles."

He was now so close, she could smell a Philly cheesesteak on his breath. "What's Victor Styles up to? We've been getting nibs of intell on possible expansion of this Archangel task force to include RICO counts, laundering, conspiracy? Ugly, preposterous rumors about certain individuals."

"So you're my buddy now, Bud?"

He smiled and nodded.

"Then pass me that bedpan over there and lift me up."

He growled, "Not funny. So what's the play—you going to try to shoe-horn your way back into the primary agent spot, like you got shoved onto the Whiting kidnapping? Kick me back into a 'support' role? Use the test results as leverage?"

A wonderful strategy, but Angela was trapped in a hospital. Helpless. Out of the loop, yet roped into dreams, now nightmares, that were themselves prophetic and even connected to tangible evidence. Angela struggled to hide from White the anguish boiling inside her as she lay on that bed. *Crossing Over with John Edward*, Dionne Warwick's "Psychic Friends": What would White's joke be as he harpooned her credibility? And there was Styles, holding a terrible secret over her head. Angela remembered that word Arianne Shipley had used. *Magick*. Witchcraft. *I wish I could blink my eyes and everything would make sense. I'd know why two men were butchered. If the Senator's next. And what my place is in all of this. Who's calling me? Do you know, Grammie?*

White's dull brown eyes rolled over Angela's face. Angela's eyes were shut, yet her lips still moved. Somewhere between his words, and her thoughts, she'd fallen asleep. He ground his teeth and stormed out. At least she was out of the way. Time was his ally, and he was going to slay the dragon, be it Amesha Spentas or Victor Styles.

22

EVERY TEN-TO-THE-HOUR, a nurse invaded the room to check Angela's vitals. Not that Angela could sleep anyway. Nor did she want to. Visions of Davidson's body haunted her almost as chillingly as the yellow eyes and teeth in the tunnel. The same eyes and teeth in a little boy's admonitions. Even without that child in her dreams, the yellow eyes, at least, stung Angela's memory. Yellow eyes meant pain.

"Zulu," she whispered in the dark. Now another word seeped back into her brain. *Umthakathi:* a tiny worm that carried hallucinogenic poison? *No, an enemy from my memory . . . or a dream? I'm listening, now, to a boy. And I'll call him Michael.*

The door latch to her room clicked. Quarter past midnight, so it wasn't a nurse. Angela clutched her top sheet. *Daddy?* A figure crept into the room and up to the bed rail. Angela slowly moved her hand down to the nurses' station call button. But then she saw a freckled smile in the glow of the EKG and sniffed an amalgam of pungent Jean Paul Gaultier eau de toilette, cigarette smoke, and cinnamon gum. Eyes still closed, she whispered, "Is that you, Sabrina the Teenaged Witch?"

Nadia whispered back, "Is there any doubt, Ginger the Brave Chicken?" She clutched Angela's hand. "Figured Bud White would come here to rattle your cage about the evidence brouhaha . . . the rookie did good, huh? Followed the letter of the rules without breaking them."

"You preserved a piece of me in this case, but I've got to get back to Washington. How'd you get away?"

"Pop had me on lockdown, but, hey, this girl's got da skillz. Vallas told me what happened. You, the tunnel. Bishop Davidson. I think the goddess's abandoned us."

Angela propped herself up on her pillow. "I'm going to ask you another favor."

Nadia sat on the bed. "Way ahead of you. We can be packed and outta here in ten minutes."

Angela smiled. "First, tonight, do you have your laptop or palmtop?"

"Nah . . . when I took Pop's car, I—"

"You what?"

"Yeah, his BMW 740. Hey, he insists on leaving me spare keys, and the security detail doesn't give a fudge 'cause they got the thing LoJacked anyway. They have no clue why I'm here, I'm sure."

"Who else knows you're here?"

"Your girl Carmen Wilcox. Weirded-out that I found her number. She seems pretty cagey."

"She is. But worried sick, too, no doubt. Listen, how can you log on to the Info Tech Center's remote server in Savannah?"

"Get real. Tons of cybercafés open late down on South Street."

"I forgot I'm a dinosaur at age thirty-three. Help me up so I can call my parents at the Sheraton Center City. I want my dad to make sure someone does a full screen on my blood, urine, and hair samples. There's a Detective Goins who seems pretty conscientious."

Nadia plucked a hair from Angela's scalp. "Now we got one." She wrapped it in a tissue and put it in her shoulder bag. "So, what do you want me to look up?"

"Three terms. Don't ask how I know how to spell them, or pronounce them. *Si-ya-nik-hum-bula*. Another is *Inkanyezi*. The other is part of that term for the worms—"

Angela noted Nadia's head dip slightly in the dull green glow of the EKG and bed control panel. "*Umthakathi*. I already know what it means."

Angela switched on the lamp over the bed. "After the dreams I've been having, I'll believe anything you tell me."

"Remember our circle, at Chi Cha? Unnatural people, perverting nature? Causing rats to swarm, attack? Poisoning, drugging, driving people crazy before they kill them? That's a black magick spell. *Umthakathi* is Zulu . . . for 'warlock.' "

A chill shot across Angela's back, bared by the loose hospital gown, as she whispered, "I know."

"How? I mean . . . have you been talking to Arianne? She's the one who clued me in. I swear she doesn't want to get involved, but . . ." Nadia was almost panting in excitement. Or fear. "The *amathakathi*—that's plural—are males. Warlocks. Necromancers. Sorcerers, and I don't mean fucking Harry Potter or Gandalf the Grey. I mean real heinous assholes. Like the *boucur* in Haiti: voodoo shamans who drug people into zombies, kill with poisonous snakes. Conjurers in Jamaica, who call out evil *jumbies* and *duppies*—poltergeists. Hexers, who work the roots in places like South Carolina, to cause illness or kill. *Your people* got *years* on us wicca with our Stevie Nicks–looking peasant blouses and Birkenstocks and our herb teas, swear to God. Think I'm nuts?"

"No," Angela whispered, leaning off the bed for Nadia's hand. *But they are my people, aren't they? Calling me in my mind?*

"You need two experts, I figure. One normal one—to give you the hard facts, what all this Zulu stuff means. The other, well, Arianne had spoken to this woman in Georgetown because, like, that philter you said was in Mullinix's stomach really freaked us out. Her name is Youssa. Owns an herbal apothecary and gift shop up on Wisconsin and P. She's from Burkina Faso. Used to be called Upper Volta. She's, um, *a witch*. She clued us into what this stuff means. *Umthakathi*. She said she'd help. I mean, seemed *real* hell-bent on helping, ya know?"

Suddenly, a cramp struck Angela like a Lennox Lewis jab to the stomach. She groaned as she felt sticky, hot moisture between her legs. She stumbled out of the bed, barefoot and in a flimsy hospital gown, dragging the IV stand toward the bathroom.

"Oh, shit, you okay?"

"My period . . . just ran up on me. Never happened like this. Way out of sync."

Nadia gasped. "Never ever? Oh, *no* . . ."

"What?"

"I have some stuff with me, more tea. But it's in the car."

That's when Angela understood. Contact with that old face in the tunnel, and in the dreams—it brought the breakthrough, pain, the flow, all at once. And finally she remembered eyes—yellow eyes in 30th Street Station, when she went to Collins's office, in the snow. Crumpled to the cold floor, cupping her hands to her face; Nadia rushed to her side.

"Him. I know him. I saw him. Six months ago. Help me . . . to the bathroom."

No time for false modesty. Angela sloughed off the gown, searched for the toilet paper and a box of generic hospital feminine napkins. Nadia tended to her nervously. "We aren't trained for this," the trainee mulled. "Facts and forensics. Computer models, wiretaps. This isn't about that."

Angela eased herself onto the toilet seat. "I told you I'd believe anything."

Nadia sighed. "Okay then. Save some of your menstrual blood. *Save it for Youssa to use.* I'll get a cup with cover off of your service tray."

What Nadia said didn't corrode what she'd been taught any more than the duplicity and cynicism tumbling from Styles's full lips or White's dry, thin ones.

Nadia returned with a blue cup. "There's a Baccarat crystal vase of white roses on the windowsill. From the Lenny Kravitz–looking guy I saw you with at Chi Cha?"

Dourly, Angela shook her head. How would he even know she was there, so soon? Nadia left to give Angela the privacy to collect a few drops of blood, then urinate. Angela called out, "So, who're they from?"

Nadia had walked over to the window; the bouquet softened the antiseptic smell of the room; the white petals reflected the moon glow through the blinds. "This card has a United States Senate logo on it. From Senator Brian Buford."

Angela flushed. Now two of his friends were dead. Time to speak to him, and that bastard Bryce King. No games. As she waddled back to her bed, Nadia pulled out a single rose and brought it over.

"Sorry if I started out as a pain in the ass. I guess I should tell you, I did a little research on what happened to your partner, Agent Trimble. I still wanna be with you."

Angela sniffed the rose; a thorn pricked but didn't draw blood. "Metaphor for you, eh? Close to your ankle tattoo."

Nadia bobbed her head, perhaps unsure of her next thought. It seemed coquettish. Angela reassured her, "Never mind getting out of the car. *We'll* be fine."

"Yeah. Um . . . hey, why're you letting me in? I mean, to your life, like you did with Trimble?"

Angela remembered spring break, 1988, reading a poem in the Virginia sand while her sorors flirted. Maya Angelou. *Nobody, but nobody / Can make it out here alone.* "I'll wait for the next nurse check, then get dressed. Meet me back here in two hours."

Nadia swung an embroidered sisal bag over her shoulder. "Umm . . . by the way, Ari showed me an article in the *Post* yesterday about Mullinix's client Jones . . . Shaka Seven? They moved up his execution date three weeks. The shrinks claim it was a bogus suicide attempt. Ari was really freaked out by that, too—don't know why."

"We're going to interrogate Mr. Jones. Now, make sure the cop down the hall sees you leave. Flash that FBI ID and show some cleavage. I want them to think this is all legitimate; that you're here to brief me, whatever. Then we go home."

Nadia mused, "It was hot today. Like inside those things in the chemistry lab?"

"A crucible," Angela replied, recalling Styles's metaphor.

"Yeah. Everything burns in there, together. Burns dirty, too."

23

BY ANGELA'S CALCULATIONS, A FOUR-INCH-high swirl of Dickey's soft vanilla frozen custard on a cake cone would last three minutes before melting into yellow goo. "No better authentic custard in this world, George," she told Vallas after lopping off the creamy peak with her tongue. "From Coney Island to the Santa Monica Pier."

Vallas's shades hid the worry in his black eyes. "I'm not so sure about this stunt, Angie." He shed his suit jacket and swung it over his shoulder as they walked. "Your briefing starts"—he stretched his shirtsleeve to check his watch—"now."

They turned the corner at 17th Street and Farragut Square. About a dozen bike messengers had taken refuge from the hammerlike sun in the few trees shading the square. Through her Wayfarers, Angela peered up, admiringly, at the statue.

"David Farragut," she said. " 'Damn the torpedoes—full speed ahead!' "

Vallas shot back, "Mind you don't get sunk. Styles, the Skipper, all of them read your report, which basically says, 'Whoops, ain't the Archangels. Maybe some other group, maybe some pattern killer who thinks he's from the Motherland. I'll get back to y'all when I figure it out.' "

His cell phone beeped. He passed it to Angela. "*Miz* Riccio, for you."

"Inspector . . . I mean, Angela? Bad news. ITC confirmed: *inkanyezi* isn't on the system. None of the linguists could make a match. But they say it's Zulu, like *Inkanyamba,* and *umthakathi.* Like *si-ya-nik-hum-bula.*"

Si-ya-nik-hum-bula—we remember you.

Angela fought off the inner chill those words conjured. An awful chill, despite the blazing downtown heat and humidity.

But then she saw two familiar faces moving through the heat shimmer on K Street, toward the Farragut North Metro entrance. Squinting beneath her sunglasses, she fixed on Sharon Boissiere and Alvin. She in a white camp blouse and tapered suit skirt; he in cargo shorts and a Hawaiian shirt, his dreads bouncing as they walked, quickly. They were anxious to get on that subway. Anxious, because they'd both spotted Angela. Angela tried to speak, as if they could hear her all the way across K Street, above the cacophony of traffic and pedestrian shoe leather. Alvin took Sharon's little arm and they disappeared into the dark of the station. Sharon was still looking over her shoulder. Deadpan. And Angela just stood there, numb, as melted Dickey's custard dripped onto her hand.

"Angela?" Nadia prompted. "I said, good luck today."

"Uh-huh . . ."

"When Pop comes back from Budapest, I'm gone. I'll call you tonight. Bye."

Angela was still holding the cell and cone aloft when Vallas said, "You okay? Makin' a mess, baby." He took her hand and playfully licked off the melted custard. And yet, still she said nothing. Not even an acknowledgment, or recoil, from Vallas's intimacy. *I've lost them,* she thought. *No, they lost me. And that's why I shouldn't lose my mind. Dragons to slay. Work to do.*

After smacking his lips, Vallas said, "You're gonna get me fired. Yo, Angie. Attempt to pay attention, as this is *yo'* party, not mine."

Angela whipped around. "Yeah . . . um . . . you'll be fine. Trust me."

She bit into the cone. A dab of custard got on her nose. Grinning, Vallas wiped it off with his thumb. "You get me involved in this shit," he said after licking his thumb clean, "and I always trust you, right?"

He tapped her nose with the sucked thumb. That contact brought a smile. A smile that was better than a Paxil, diffusing the anxiety, the distraction of *loss.*

Within thirty seconds, Vallas's cell sounded again. This time, Angela could hear Lupo rant.

"Yeah, Skipper, I found her. We're on our way. Yeah, I understand this means my ass, Skipper. My ass always belonged to you, so kick it hard." He clicked off. "Motherfucker's pissed. Ya happy now?"

"I won't be happy for a long time." A forlorn comment, made in a wistful tone. It was as much for Alvin and Sharon as it was for Vallas. And for the Bureau. And for a child whom she only saw and heard in her dreams. He would have loved to taste the cold creaminess of Dickey's custard, in that hot, magical place where he lived.

Lupo paced with his hand dug deep in his pockets. Styles's eyes tracked him as if he were a human metronome.

"*Crap,*" Lupo growled. "Tigress, you're pulling crap here."

Angela sat calmly on Styles's leather couch, legs crossed. She looked over at Styles, still seated at his desk, fingering one of his *hanto* knives. They were used for ritual hara-kiri when a samurai or lord failed or was shamed. Indeed.

"You have my memo," Angela said to Lupo, though she was peering at Styles. "You have assessments of the physical evidence. No crap. We do not have a Zadkiel and Chamuel incident. We do not have a related political or grudge kidnapping with Mullinix and Whiting. But the cases are related." She paused, chilled by Styles's glower. "I think we have hate crimes, all right, but in the purest sense of the word *hate*. I want a free hand to pursue research on this South African tie."

Bud White had been languishing in the corner. "So you're saying it's a so-called black thing, or whatever these hip-hop kids have on their T-shirts these days?"

Bob Scofield, officious, icy, glossed, "What Bud here is saying is—"

"I know what he's saying, sir, and, crudely—he might be right."

Woodruff Sessions smoothed back his white mane and smiled. He was deeply tanned, perhaps dangerously so; his cheek was marred with the scar from a precancerous keratosis. His drawl was reminiscent of an old Mercury or Gemini astronaut from *The Right Stuff*. "Frank, Mr. Deputy Director— note the item in paragraph six, about the wound patterns on Dr. Collins and the Reverend—"

"Bishop, sir."

"*Bishop* Davidson. My apology. Heck, African American preachers back home're usually called reverend. Anyhow, looks like the ITC folks had to dig deep in the encyclopedia. An *iklwa* stabbing spear: 'Developed by the Zulu and the primary infantry weapon of the Zulu army or *Impi*, under the reign of Shaka, 1818 to 1828.'" Sessions shrugged, still grinning. "And this part's very interesting, Inspector: 'Radio carbon-dating of the metal fragment found embedded in victim Collins's fourth left-lateral rib put the fragment's age at almost two hundred years old. Impure, high-sulfurized steel, primitive smelt, like the gold slug or disks in victims' mouths.' And this—'Twilight Zone,' in Supervisory Special Agent White's lexicon: 'Wood sample found in wound is indeed ash, genus and species unknown, but from a family associated with the deciduous forests of temperate African highlands. Tree from which this handle was hewn was at least *four hundred years old when cut.*" The emphasis was Sessions's. He settled back in his chair and faced Styles. "Your prodigy's onto something worth exploring."

Slowly, Styles slid the *hanto* back into its woven-silk scabbard. So slow, yet with a practiced technique, that everyone watched. Like his own tea ceremony, or Kabuki. "Naturally, Woody," he said softly, "if there's a perceived foreign nexus—South Africa, maybe—your division will still demand a role in the task force?"

Sessions sighed. "We are still dealing with terrorists of sorts. And two victims are friends of Senator Brian Buford, who sits on the Senate Foreign Relations Committee, and who's minority chair of the Select Sub-committee on Intelligence and Terrorism, so, yes, I'd like to keep my people in the loop. Buford may be a potential victim. Maybe not for the reason we *all* seemed to envision, catch m'drift?"

"Oh, I catch it, Woody."

Scofield, voice shrill, emotionless, counseled, "We still have a credible threat from the Amesha Spentas group. Are we suggesting spinning off Inspector Bivens, perhaps most of ISD, on this 'African' track, while we continue the task force's work with the Archangels? And I would be happy to remove the Alfred Whiting component of this matter from the Inspector's plate. Allow her to explore these alternate theories."

"Bob, I don't see a theory, yet," Lupo said. "I don't see a why. Just specu-lation on how. And no who. Yeah, apparently you were mumbling some strange African words in the hospital, brought on, maybe, by the hallu-cinogens found in Dr. Collins, Mr. Whiting. But how did the EMS unit in Philly crash? Nothing from the paramedic and EMTs' autopsies indicates hallucinogens, yet they plow their unit into a cement wall. The firefighters were clean, too. Now, we've already established a connection in the Hooperman-Collins murders between the Archangel Zadkiel and a snake. This could include this *thing* you reported Mullinix talking about—Inkanyamba, right? Written in blood on the EMT unit . . . 'cha'—*Chamuel.*

You're asking us to ignore this? Come on, Tigress, it's not your job to de-bunk investigative tracks set from the top."

Angela hid her pain that one of her mentors was attacking her. "Nor is it my job to ignore anomalies, or alternative, probative theories. And I'm not convinced that's *cha*, in Hebrew letters. The rest is . . . coincidence."

Lupo's eyes narrowed, and Angela knew she'd stapled a fat hint to his forehead that she was hiding something. She'd always told him, there was no such thing as coincidence in the Federal Bureau of Investigation.

Lupo looked to Styles. "Maybe we should call the Director in Budapest? We got an impasse he needs to break. I'm inclined to keep the task force as presently *tasked.*"

"No such impasse," Styles replied in a contemplative croon. "The Inspector's work is thorough. Thoughtful. I'd like to speak privately with you, Frank and Angela, then memo you, Bob, and you, Woody, along with Dick Wasserman in the Civil Rights Section and Assistant Attorney General Miller once I make a decision."

Scofield frowned. "We have seven more agenda items to cover, and Director Donatello returns the day after tomorrow. I hardly think it's pru-dent to adjourn."

But Woody Sessions, chuckling, beady chestnut eyes darting, patted his colleague's arm. "C'mon, Bobby, I think we've made our point, and the Deputy Director will adjust the investigation accordingly. Victor, I'll wait for your call." Sessions gestured to Bud White. "Buddy, why don't you skip on down the hall with us."

Once alone with Lupo and Styles, Angela declared, "I'm doing my job. Period."

"Is that what you call hijacking evidence . . . hell, hijacking an investiga-tion? Lemme tell you something, those two guys—they aren't your friends. They're thinking about making us look bad. Blood's in the water—the election—and they are sharks."

Angela glanced at Styles and warned, "Do we really want to have this conversation *here*, Frank?"

"Oh, don't mind *me*," Styles intoned.

"Our roaring lil' tigress. Full of surprises today. So what other spells have you cast, huh? You come see me when you're in a more loquacious mood, okay?"

Lupo stormed out of Styles's office, leaving Angela to confront the leop-ard. And the leopard's eyes were burning with a soft, silent rage.

"So who will get an anonymous tape in the mail—Greta Van Susteren? Geraldo? Me going to abort the child of a serial killer, tended by a man who becomes a victim in one of my cases. A case you shoveled me into and then turned up the fire?"

Styles fumed, "Wouldn't be so brave if you didn't have an ace. So throw it."

"I wouldn't have to pack an 'ace' if all of you would just focus on the truth. Too many bodies out there, unavenged, because of politics."

"*Truth?* Lupo stated correctly: these machinations about Africa—yes, you have some direct evidence, but you personally have to have some root in them for you to posit them as theories. So I'm asking you—*why?*" Styles pressed his forefinger to her temple; she didn't flinch. "Zulu spears? *Come on!* What's really in that head of yours? I've decided that, if you force, I'll send a dub of that surveillance tape to CNN."

Angela remained erect in her chair. "I will call Carmen Wilcox and have her send the *Washington Post* a microcassette tape she's been holding for almost a year. You, in your condo, telling me how you suspected that Pluto Williams was involved in the Venus Stalkers murders, yet did nothing about it, and why. So we all suffer. *Fuck you.*"

Styles's face went blank. "Touché," he muttered. "You'd be dangerous at poker."

"First, I want you, Scofield, Sessions, even Frank, off my back. Free hand to pursue my leads wherever they reach."

"Vague, but I understand."

"Whatever, Victor. Then, I want you to have the U.S. Attorney for the District of Columbia obtain a material-witness order for Bryce King."

Styles glared back her. "You want me to convince the U.S. Attorney to move a court to issue what is, in essence, a body attachment?"

"Only for an interview, to corroborate what happened in that tunnel. And release any background he has on who would want Collins and Davidson dead."

"You realize the man's not only rich, but has a fan club in the White House?"

Angela rose from the couch. "I realize from our previous talk that you seem to dislike him. What's he scared of—what's more frightening than being the next friend of Buford's to be butchered like steer?"

"Not a clue. Anything else?"

"Research assistance. A contact with knowledge of South Africa."

"It's a 'black thing,' eh?"

"Precisely."

He reached for his phone, yet, as he punched in a number, he spoke lyrically, "There's no deliverance from the crucible once the lid closes. Not from melting heat or the flame. Sooner or later, even angels get burned."

24

BEHOLD, AN AFRICAN DUSK

SAMUEL IBHEBESI GAWKED AT THE evening sky. Almost nine o'clock and still light up there—a pale yellow pallor, as jaundiced as Samuel's eyes. And the sun endured, vexing the city with some final, noxious waves of heat, mixing with car exhaust and bus fumes. Then, a wind swept through the monuments. Dry, broiling—not the usual humid stillness. It made Samuel smile. Behold, an African dusk.

The streetlamps finally buzzed to life; Samuel sighed and wiped the grime and carnauba wax from his withered fingers. At least the police had towed that fat minister's Escalade out of the garage. Samuel had stayed late to pick up some overtime, parking cars at some after-party launching a new pay-per-view channel on King's cable network. The actual reception was held down at the Southwest Waterfront, where King moored his sixty-five-foot sailing yacht, the *Def Zephyr*. The theme was tropical *Survivor,* and Samuel snickered at the guests arriving in loud Hawaiian shirts, lascivious bikini-topped and spandex-bottomed outfits, ludicrous safari gear. The white people among them were silly looking enough, but the *akotha*—black American "cottonpickers"—much sillier!

A blue Ford Explorer pulled onto F Street. Two men in suits got out. They were so tall and clean. Those bastard Afrikaners in the Bureau of State Security, or BOSS, before apartheid fell, dressed like that. As Samuel backed away from their looks, a limousine pulled into the garage. Bryce

King climbed out with his wife. He wore a blue blazer, pink silk shirt, white duck slacks. No silly costume, Samuel mused, though his wife's fat rolls munched hungrily on her floral sarong and bandeau.

King's grim, lifeless eyes spotted Samuel. He told his wife and their entourage to meet him in the lobby. The two men in suits descended the ramp.

"*Sawunbona, nkosi abaBryce King,*" Samuel greeted. "*Ninjani?*" When King frowned, Samuel explained, "It mean 'Hello, boss. Howa you?' The party is not good?"

"Cost me two hundred and seventy-five thousand dollars to block off half of Maine Avenue, rent the River Club, and feed these millionaire-thug ballplayers and rappers, thieving politicians, my own deadbeat family. Not a soul consoled me about Les or Carl."

Samuel put his hand on King's shoulder. "I, too, have lost people I loved. You mustn't take it out on dose round you. Perhaps, sah, I can help?"

King nodded, muttering, "I'm open to anything, Samuel."

"Please . . . follow me to my locker, den."

One of the men in suits called, "Mr. King, sir? I'm U.S. Marshal Scott Reed. I'm here to serve a material-witness order on you to make yourself available for an interview, with counsel present, at the FBI's Washington Metropolitan Field Division at—"

King hollered, "You with Bivens? Meddling bitch can't let me grieve in peace?"

Reed handed King a blue-backed court order. "Nine A.M., Monday, Mr. King."

The marshals trundled up the ramp to F Street.

"Muthafuckers," King mumbled as Samuel led him to his rusted locker. Samuel unlocked the padlock, opened the door, and handed King some moist, leafy matter that looked like old redneck snuff.

"*Umodi,*" Samuel explained. "Chew it. Taste like licorice. You feel good."

King chuckled, then put a pinch in his mouth. Instantly, he sighed, as if succored, content. "Um, hey . . . this stuff isn't like coca leaves or opium, is it?"

"No, sah. Your head will not ache, and you will deal wit de ache in your heart."

Samuel then removed his sopping, stained workshirt and reached for a fresh, pressed one hanging from a hook in the rusted locker. King gasped. Painted across Samuel's thin, wrinkled, dry, purple-brown skin and the protrusions of his spine and scapulae were nubby strips of pinkish flesh. Samuel felt the mogul's eyes rove. Calmly, he faced King, buttoning his new shirt as he spoke.

"Dese marks are why I leave South Africa."

"My God, you were whipped like a dog! Torture, by the police?"

Samuel shrugged. *"Naaaah, sah.* By my own people. I am Zulu."

"Old beefs between Mandela's ANC and King Buthelezi's Inkatha Party?"

"You are very well informed about my country, sah. But dese t'ings, you could not possibly understand." He paused, yellow eyes shut. "I was born near Howick Falls. Huge-tower-of-water place. Enchanted place. But I see much misery. My first wife died . . . childbirt'. My second, she shot by police and BOSS agents . . . dey t'ink she was a Communist. She was schoolteacher. So my children, my gems, I scatter dem, like seeds in wind and I am chaff. I remain alone." His eyes opened to find King leaning against a concrete piling, head thrust forward. Not the phony nodding and insouciance he usually showed persons he didn't deem "important." "My t'ird wife . . . so pretty, young, soft. She had a job as a clerk with a hotel in Durban; I work farm labor, and part-time as a cook in Howick. Lawd, sah, she would come back by bus, seven-hour ride, ev'ry Sunday, just to lay wit dis old bag of bones. Like I have been old forever. It was a Sunday, sunrise, we hear de goats' bells clang. Smell de cooking fires stomped out . . . smoldering coals. Den a lorry horn."

"Lorry?"

"You call it a truck. Full of King Buthelezi's boys. Dey drag us naked from bed. Urinate on us. Push me down into goat dung . . . t'rash me with bicycle chain till I am a bloody mess . . . a bloody mess. One man, he take a can of petrol and pour it on my wife. I am broken and eyes swollen and lips blistered, but I scream for her. Burn me, instead, I say. But dey men look to a woman in de lorry. Evil eyes, she. They call her *sangoma.* Dem *sangoma,* de devil cunts dey are. Shaman."

"Shaman, as in witch doctor? Voodoo priestess?"

The old man nodded. "She wave her hand. Speak curse. Dey burn my wife . . . so young, so soft. Burn her till her body black. Limbs break off. Stir her ashes in my face. Leave me. Nineteen ninety-three, I escape to Durban. But all de time I t'ink of my children. How some came here, to America. I come here. My new home. Now, sah, I must get back to work. Mustapha, he need help parking dese cars."

King released a slow breath. "But why did they do it?"

Samuel closed the locker and clicked the padlock, then smiled. "Oldest reason: because I was different. Dat is all I will say."

"Okay. And what about your kids—you ever hook up? They visit?"

The old man sank his head, mumbling. King patted Samuel's slouched shoulder, then walked to the metal door to the lobby level. He halted there and called, "Sam . . . Samuel? I understand. Thanks."

King jumped, for the old man's reply sounded like a whisper a millimeter from his ear. *"Dere are t'ings you cannot understand."*

And, as King's entourage greeted him in the lobby, Samuel Ibhebesi grinned and added, "But you will. Soon."

25

BEHOLD, AN AFRICAN NIGHT

NUMBER 3056 MASSACHUSETTS AVENUE, N.W., was a two-wing, Georgian-style mansion in the middle of Embassy Row. Angela watched the valet drive Sweet Pea away as the floodlit green, black, red, white, and blue flag of the new Republic of South Africa fluttered above in the furnacelike breeze. The sky was raven black but for the Milky Way's starry ribbon. She'd never seen a sky like that within the haze and bright lights of the capital. Jasmine and coriander perfumed the wind, rather than the usual garbage and exhaust-fume stink of summer.

Under that night sky, Angela had donned her best and seldom-worn summer party gear: a floral bustier in ruddy orange, green-gold, and blue, a knee-length slit orange skirt trimmed in gold, taupe mules that made her five-foot-four, rather than her tiny five-two.

And as that flag flapped above, Angela knew Woodruff Sessions's NSD people had been following her. Champagne-colored Chryslers. Blond white guys named Mike or Todd wearing gray suits with American-flag lapel pins. So easy to spot. Angela accepted her clandestine "escort" as the price for clueing Styles into her own vulnerability. *I'm not the little gazelle dragged up on a tree limb.* Perhaps Styles was even proud of her machinations. After all, he called her his prodigy. His soldier.

Angela roamed under a stone arch connecting the mansion's wings, into a courtyard and garden. Strung across the courtyard entrance was a huge red banner with white lettering—SOUTH AFRICAN MILLENNIUM RELIEF FUND FOR AIDS ORPHANS—and inside the garden were three tents. One was huge, covering a stage bathed by colored lights. The other tents were packed with people: white and black, white Armani dinner jackets and Vera Wang gowns mingling with gold and green headwraps, crimson bu-bus, and fine linens and prints in intricate patterns. Bold-colored, geometric Ndebele weaves hung from the tent walls.

A black South African Marine sergeant, resplendent in his white, silver-spiked pith helmet and green sash, inspected Angela's FBI badge, snapped a British-style salute, then escorted her into the swirl of bright lights, the aroma of roasted yams, beef, and herb-rubbed goat, and the cacophony of music, clinking champagne flutes, and banter. She heard that harsh Boer Afrikaans, spoken with that weird South African English, which, to Angela, sounded like an Australian accent. But the Xhosa and Swazi dialects sounded familiar. And she knew Zulu immediately. Somehow.

Ladysmith Black Mambazo was on the stage, ebullient, high-stepping, and singing a cappella to a Zulu township cadence. Angela'd seen them with yet another ex-boyfriend ages ago, when she was in college, at the Merriweather Post Pavilion outside Baltimore, when the group was touring with Paul Simon for his *Graceland* album. Before she had faced something old and terrible in that tunnel, Zulu had been just another exotic language to Angela. Not anymore. The Marine reappeared and said, "Her Excellency Dr. Helen Tambo, and the Consul General, Dr. Jan Durnkloopf, can speak with you for fifteen minutes." With that, Ladysmith Black Mambazo ceased singing, and the orchestra struck up the South African national anthem, "Nkosi Sikelel'i Afrika"—Lord Bless Africa. The Marine saluted and Angela sang along, having learned the lyrics not in a dream, but at Western High School in Baltimore, where conscientious American children protested over Soweto, Sun City, and clamored for Nelson Mandela's release.

Angela eyed the Ambassador's party as she sang. Helen Tambo was a tall, slender black woman wearing a gold-lapis headwrap and matching bu-bu gown with balloon sleeves. Her spouse was a squat white man in a tuxedo. Durnkloopf was a leathery-skinned Afrikaner with gray-streaked blond hair. His spouse was a young black woman in a sequined, strapless column dress. *Behold the new South Africa*, Angela thought. The Marine soon escorted her indoors.

Angela leaned against a red-felt billiards table, nursing a fruity South

African Chablis and scanning the fauna artwork on the walls. Wildebeest, hartebeest, nyala, springboks, Thomson's gazelles, eagles, cheetahs, massive white rhinos, majestic elephants. And lions. Even less glamorous hyenas, wild dogs, meerkats, and boars. *"Hakuna matata,"* she murmured with a grin, thinking of those last two species in Disney's *Lion King*—her nephew Kobi's favorite film when he was a toddler.

She whipped around when the Ambassador and Durnkloopf entered the room.

"We are happy to help the FBI," Dr. Tambo said. "We've heard of you, Ms. Bivens, but most impressive was this referral from Victor Styles. Is he coming tonight?"

Shaking the Ambassador's hand, Angela said, "He sends his regrets, Madame Ambassador."

"Mr. Styles was posted in South Africa, you know, after leaving your Navy JAG, as part of the delegation helping us draft our new criminal code, and then as an observer in our first true 'one-man, one-vote' election."

"Er . . . yes, he told me about that. Now, tonight I need some background on the words, the terms, history that I—"

The Consul General cut her off. "Why don't we sit?"

They retired to three soft leather chairs behind the billiards table. Durnkloopf spoke again: "I am an expert on the Zulu, having served as an aide to former President de Klerk on Zulu affairs, and as liaison to King Buthelezi. The details of your queries were, to say the least, interesting." He pulled a pipe from his white dinner jacket pocket. "May I?"

Both women nodded. So long as it wasn't a cigar. He lit the pipe and said, "We'll start with something easy. That word *inkanyezi* stumped even our Zulu consular staffers. No such word."

Angela noticed the Ambassador stiffen a little at Durnkloopf's declaration.

"Now, the other item . . . that rather savage and arcane custom of slipping a gold coin under the dead men's tongues might well be some American terrorist cell's contrivance, but the practice is identical to that originated under the rule of Shaka kaSenzangakhona. Thanks to popular myth and films, you know him as Shaka Zulu. Interestingly, the word *shaka* means 'intestinal beetle,' not great king or warrior. This man regimented every aspect of Zulu life, literally, all toward the goal of turning a trivial tribe into masters of a great empire. By the time he was assassinated in 1828, he'd done so, but also steeped much of southern Africa red."

The Ambassador leaned forward, earnest. "To this day, my Xhosa people and Afrikaners alike speak of this period as *Mfecane*. The 'crushing.' A historical metaphor, like you Americans speak of 'the Civil War,' or 'the Depression.' "

Angela shifted in her chair, masking her horror with a nod. *Mfecane* was a word from her dreams, but there, it meant an evil spell. "Madame Ambassador, Dr. Durnkloopf . . . the history's a fascinating and pertinent backdrop but—"

"I'm a diplomat by training," Durnkloopf interrupted, smiling, "not a cultural anthropologist. And Her Excellency is a barrister." Durnkloopf's smile soon disappeared. "So, please, bear with us. *Mfecane* indeed has a spiritual meaning as well. The lore is that sorcery aided Shaka's ascension as paramount king—analogous to English myths . . . Arthur becoming king of the Britons with the help of Merlin. Such is the 'magic' called *mfecane*. Attributes of this legend are the gold coins, those words you remembered, the use of the green mamba snake as an instrument of death—all tied to a battalion of Shaka's personal bodyguards called the *Ama Simba:* the 'Lion's Regiment.'

"Remember how I said the society was 'regimented'? The Zulu army was called the *Impi*. The Impi was made up of twenty regiments of nine hundred to twelve hundred men each, called *amabutho*. They were grouped by age and marital status. Young women even had their own regiments. The Ama Simba were the most loyal, fiercest troops: Shaka's Green Beret, *and* his Gestapo. They would slaughter their own families if the King so ordered. And when they assassinated another chief or some political rival of Shaka's—including women and infants—they would mutilate the corpse and place the gold disk under the tongue. Gold mined from Howick Falls, which is now a popular tourist stop. Gold appeased *Nkulunkulu:* God. After a warrior takes a life, he must cleanse himself ritually, with water and ashes, or the victim's spirit will haunt him. That's not always practical, because you'd be bathing for days. This was a pious Ama Simba shortcut that grew into a macabre joke, just as Shaka's paranoia grew. Indeed, the word *simba* isn't Zulu for 'lion.' Apparently, Shaka desired that an exotic mystique attach to his bodyguards."

"But, sir, if *Nkulunkulu* is God, then what is the *Inkanyamba?*"

Durnkloopf guffawed. "Been watching *National Geographic* specials, eh? Our local 'Nessie.' The serpent is called the Creator, not because it's the source of all *life.*"

Angela finished his thought: "Because it's the source of all *magic.*"

Durnkloopf took a quick draw on his pipe and nodded. "Quite."

"Thank you. And why was Shaka assassinated?"

Ambassador Tambo answered that one. "My girl, for the same reason Caesar was: fear. Or possibly on orders from the British at the Cape Colony. Absolute power makes one insane. The colorful yarn is that Shaka allowed the Ama Simba to become possessed by the *amafufuyama:* demon spirits, or *poltergeists,* in Afrikaans." She chuckled heartily. "Fairy tales I tell my daughter when she's off to summer camp!"

Durnkloopf added, "Uh, yes, well, Dingane, Shaka's half brother, was behind the plot. He spread the rumor that witches had corrupted Shaka and the Ama Simba. Ridiculous to us, but not to nineteenth-century Zulu. Dingane killed Shaka; the Impi hunted the renegade Ama Simba down. Burned them at the stake."

Angela leaned forward, deadly earnest. "Tell me more . . . about witches."

"It's lore, as Her Excellency joked, but . . . well . . . when Dingane's son, Mpande, became king, he continued the wars against my ancestors, the Boer Voortrekkers, journeying northeast from the Cape to the Transvaal to escape British rule. Our only defense against Mpande's Impi were our *laagers:* circles of wagons. The symbol of my people."

Angela saw the Ambassador frown slightly. Old wounds still had scabs. Durnkloopf, oblivious, continued, "Mpande wanted to finish us off because he had more pressing problems with the witches' coven allied with his dead uncle Shaka."

"Umthakathi."

"Why, yes. Warlocks, more accurately. Literally, 'night sorcerer.' Bone seer."

Angela winced.

"You seem . . . pained. Do you need a drink?" Ambassador Tambo asked.

"No, ma'am. Doctor, please go on."

"When Mpande died, he left the Zulu empire and its war with both the warlock coven and the Boer to his son, Cetshwayo."

Just as in the tunnel under Rittenhouse Square, the fine hairs on Angela's neck rose. "They called him . . . Great Fire?"

"Yes . . . yes. You *are* a learned young woman, Inspector. Cetshwayo was a fat, jolly sort. More fraternity boy than Zulu king! But he could speak and write some English and Afrikaans, and he was a converted Lutheran.

Legend holds that the coven—the *amathakathi*, cursed the Zulu nation upon Great Fire's taking the *Inkantha*—the weave of grass, beads, and flesh that, even to this day, is the symbol of royal office. Zulu oral history is specific and striking: backtracking, you find that the day of the curse's utterance was the day, in 1877, that Cecil Rhodes and the Natal Governor-General, Sir William-Bartle Frere, decided it was time to eliminate the last great black nation blocking Rhodes's Cape-to-Cairo railroad. No favor to we Boers, for the price of eliminating our blood nemesis was that we, too, would become subjects of Queen Victoria, and thus our gold, diamonds, and pastureland would be hers. On January eleventh, 1879, a British army invaded Zululand. But in one of the first battles of the war, the Impi, under the brilliant generals Isingwayo and Mavumengwana, destroyed over one thousand crack British regulars at Isandlhawana. The product of white arrogance, like your Custer at the Little Big Horn. The morning of the battle, there was a partial solar eclipse." Durnkloopf's eyes widened. "Portents, you see, conjured by *amathakathi* to convey a sense of a hollow victory. The eclipse aided the Zulu advance on the British position. Though there was another victory at Hlobane, there came defeats, and finally, the climactic set-piece battle the British hoped for, on a broad, grassy field."

"Ulundi."

"Again, you amaze me. Yes. July fourth, 1879. Massed breech-loading rifles, Gatling guns, rockets, artillery . . . versus raw courage. Though the outcome was never in doubt, when Cetshwayo was captured, he swore that the tide of battle turned on evil spells."

Angela stood, smoothed her skirt, and nodded respectfully to Ambassador Tambo. "Your Excellency . . . Dr. Durnkloopf. I don't mean to sound impertinent. But that is not what I wanted to hear about Ulundi. Something *else* happened there. Something having to do with this word no one seems to know. With the *Inkanyezi.*"

Teeth clenched on his pipe, Durnkloopf growled, *"There is nothing more."*

Dr. Tambo shuddered as Angela walked up to the seated Durnkloopf, recounting with a heaving chest, "A psycho-reactant mushroom, native to South Africa, supposedly extinct. A green mamba snake. Tiny parasites called *Polystoma umthakathi*, whose distilled essence creates violent hallucinations. A dead white lawyer who, for some reason, can tell me about the Inkanyamba! A Lion's Regiment. Wounds on my victims that match a Zulu spear. And, Mr. Consul General, my blood tests from a recent hospitalization . . . *Probocybin fungi* molecules . . . the same mushroom . . . but inhaled, as if it had been burned like incense." She was right on top of him. "Look at me, Mr. Consul General. I need to know . . . for my own sanity as much as to solve these murders—*what the hell are you people hiding?*"

"Jan," the Ambassador broke in. "Tell her."

Durnkloopf's blue eyes narrowed. "I told her I wasn't an anthropologist!" He knocked his pipe into an ashtray, mumbling, *"My God . . ."*

Her Excellency locked eyes with Angela and spoke, stern yet low. "Inspector, please sit." Angela obliged. "We are building a new nation. A modern nation. But still a nation of extremes, of conflict. Of opposites that go beyond race. We cannot afford to be known as a people that still believes in *witchcraft.* The whole 'witch doctor' stereotype . . . if you couple that with the horrid folkways regarding sex, marriage, women, property—and superstition—that pervades the countryside, that only magnifies our HIV and AIDS catastrophes, the shame of having the world's highest fetal alcohol syndrome rates, our shootings, lootings, rapes, political strife within what was my own ANC. Or, between the ANC and the old Zulu Inkantha Party." She cleared her throat. "Ms. Bivens, we have deceived you. *Inkanyezi* holds mythic meaning in KwaZulu-Natal."

Durnkloopf stood and moved to the mantel below the animal paintings. As he studied the lions, he said, " 'Star angel' is the literal translation. Figuratively, *archangel."*

Oh my God. Angela swallowed the rest of her Chablis.

"The *inkanyezi* was a very special *sangoma."*

"I'm familiar with that word. The *sangoma* . . . is a woman."

"Yes. They are the Zulu diviners, shaman."

"A witch herself?"

"Aw, maybe 'good' witch," Durnkloopf chuckled, "if you believe in that distinction. Their power descends mother to son; the son becomes *inyanga,* or herbal healer. Minister to the sick. A daughter of his, in turn, becomes *sangoma,* and so on. Before the British and Zulu clashed at Ulundi, the myth holds that an *inkanyezi* faced the coven, *amathakathi.* They, who summoned the *amafufuyama*—the dead Ama Simba—back to this world to weaken Cetshwayo's regiments. The *inkanyezi* was killed. And so the Zulu lost. The British took one surviving warlock prisoner, and after that—"

"After that . . . there is a psychopath out there who thinks he's a witch, and he—with help from others—is murdering people."

"Bloody ridiculous," Durnkloopf scoffed. "Is this why Mr. Styles sent you here?"

Angela rose again and reached for her beaded evening bag. "Your

Excellency, Mr. Consul General, I think I have enough, now. But I would make one more imposition." She faced the now trenchant Afrikaner. "Specifically from you, sir. Our INS is a joke . . . but your office can provide me with detailed requests for passports and residency changes from KwaZulu-Natal. I need them for the past five years."

"Lord," he cackled, "why not make it *ten?*"

"Ten it is."

Durnkloopf jerked his body from the mantel. *"Girl, you are daft!"*

"Jan!" The Ambassador exclaimed. "Do not forget that she is my guest and this is *not* your old South Africa! You will not call her 'girl.' " Tambo looked up at Angela. "Your request will take time. May I contact you through Mr. Styles?"

"No."

"Somehow, Inspector Bivens, I didn't think so." After a deep sigh, Tambo revealed, "Unfortunately, witch-hunts have been used as an excuse for political assassination and terrorism. If you have an enemy, accuse him or her of witchcraft. The local *sangoma* have lost their credibility as spiritual fonts. They are most analogous now to Madame Defarge in Charles Dickens's *A Tale of Two Cities.* They have directed persecutions and pogroms . . . and sat back, watching Zulu villagers set automobile tires aflame around innocent people's necks, the same way Madame Defarge knitted at the guillotine. So you must understand our official silence."

"No, ma'am, I do not. Masking dirty laundry, or an evil, only makes it fester and stink. I've learned that much." Angela then scanned her thin gold and silver evening watch. "But thank you, Your Excellency, for your insight and patience."

Another South African Marine escorted Angela out of the library and into the hot night air. He called on his radio for the valet to retrieve Sweet Pea, parked almost down to Sheridan Circle. Angela looked in the sky when the Marine departed. A yellow, waxing crescent moon had risen. The same crescent that, almost a year ago, Trey and Pluto Williams beheld as the squinted eye of the Feathered Serpent. Squinted, as if complicit in their killing spree. *Now, behold, an African sky,* she thought to herself. She removed her mules and carried them as she scampered, barefoot, down Massachusetts to hunt for her VW herself. She could not endure another moment under that sky, alone. Unprotected. No silver charm around her neck, like Nadia's. No layer of cronies and secrecy, like Styles or Bryce King. Her only armor was her soul. A brittle steel soul.

26

Madame Youssa's Holistic Remedy & Herbal Shop

P Street & Wisconsin Avenue, N.W.

"ABSOLUTELY NO COINCIDENCE?" ANGELA pressed Nadia. She peered back at the Dell monitor screen next to the cash register when Nadia shook her head. There it was, a $37.51 charge on an American Express Optima card, June 3, 2000. Maynard V. Mullinix. Four grams, ground African mandrake root and nightshade.

"Pas de coïncidence," came another voice, deeper than a female alto, almost masculine. There was no such thing as coincidence. *"Ça, c'est* magick."

Angela looked up at Youssa Ogamdoudou. Regal, oval face, narrow nose, drawn-on eyebrows. Skin a burnished, flawless bronze, like the statue of Archangel Michael, in 30th Street Station. Pearl-white teeth. Eyes like pearls, too: black pearls, set in gleaming white ones. Youssa stood six feet tall; Angela had embraced Janet Reno when the Attorney General awarded the Medal of Valor, so extrapolating the height from that wasn't hard. Her hair was close to shorn; she wore a long, hooded cotton cardigan over a turquoise tank top and West African Mende-print wrap skirt. The brown feet strapped into weathered sandals looked twice the length of Angela's.

"Ask the young wicca here. This man, he know the craft, the charms. Or he *bewitched* by them." She pointed a slender, waxy finger at Nadia.

Nadia had been leaning on the clear Lucite countertop. Perspiring profusely, lips quivering. "This . . . this is why I called you when you left the embassy. I'd already set up this meeting through Ari, right, but then Youssa tells Ari she recognizes Mullinix from the news. I checked Automated Case Support—CID'd run Mullinix's credit card purchases. They didn't bother to come here. Fucking . . . creepy."

Angela looked to Youssa. "What do you remember about this customer?"

"You believe in dreams?" Youssa replied. "Zulu call them *amaphupho.*"

"Please answer my question, Ms. Ogamdoudou."

"Embassy give tourist guides. Youssa give *truth*. That what you really here for."

Sighing, Angela settled back on the little stool at the register and scanned the display inside the transparent counter. She saw crystals of every hue, from creamy pastels to sharp emeralds and ruby, for every affliction and mood. Wall shelves sagged with bins of charms and rings and amulets, powdered holistic cure-alls and mineral salts. Wreaths of dried roots and herb leaves hung about the shop, mingling with the scent of jasmine sticks smoldering in censers and dozens of burning candles. Thank God for the aroma and the air-conditioning Youssa kept full tilt. A prophylactic for the pungent musk emanating from a storage room Nadia called "the fetish place."

No, not the fetish one might think of when watching HBO's *Real Sex,* as Nadia had clarified when Angela had arrived. She did so, not for levity, but to underscore the dead seriousness of Youssa's craft. Fetish, in the ancient definition of that word. An accoutrement of African animist magick, which was the mother of Santeria and voodoo.

Angela said, "Nadia, you understand that NSD agents have been ghosting me, right? They'd be pretty tickled to report back that I'm in a voodoo shop."

Nadia pursed her full lips. "Not a voodoo shop. Arianne said you'd be testy."

"Testy? Tomorrow, we prepare for interviews with . . ." Angela paused. Identities were classified to civilians. "Our subjects." Angela felt a sudden twinge in her stomach. She looked to Youssa, who was smiling wryly.

"He call himself Shaka Seven, for the Zulu king and *sept,* for *le numérologie.* Seven, it cannot be divided." Angela's mouth slackened as the witch seemingly mined her thoughts. "Bryce King . . . and, informally a senator."

Eyes searching the floor, Nadia muttered, "No secrets . . . among the craft, 'kay?"

"I need to speak with Ms. Ogamdoudou alone. Go hang in Thomas Sweets across the street. Have some ice cream. Call Vallas and give him our ten-twenty. *Do it!*"

"Go, wicca . . . your teacher will come directly," Youssa reassured. "She will be *changed* when she come by. Say not to Ari Shipley what we do here. That is for we."

Nadia pouted like a rebuked child as she departed.

"*Et maintenant,* the truth about man who kidnap very important fellow?"

"I want to hear observations, facts."

"Facts . . . they perceptions we agree on, *non?* How we see, touch, smell."

"Are you a philosopher as well as a witch?" Noting the sarcasm in her voice, Angela said, "I'm sorry. I've had a difficult evening. Week. Year. *Life.*"

"Of course you have, *petite chérie.* And Youssa, I was graduate student in engineering at l'Université de Abidjan, in Côte d'Ivoire. Ivory Coast. But INS, it want engineers from Eastern Europe, Australia, China. We come here, they give us green cards only to drive cabs, make Slurpees, park cars, eh? I open shop."

"I see. And why didn't you come forward when you saw Mullinix's face on TV?"

Youssa laughed heartily. "Knew you'd come. But this white man Mullinix, he troubled when I see him. He say he get dreams, like you. But *not* like you." She stopped laughing. "Youssa no pry unless they come to put *le charme noir,* or curse, on me. And they won't. Youssa is powerful witch. *Alors,* you troubled, not because of *umthakathi.* No, because something calling you." Her great, mannish hand clamped on to Angela's. She sniffed the air. "I boil you menstrual blood in pot with finch egg, feather *fetoushe.*"

Angela broke Youssa's grip. "I'm not being rude. I need context, not mumbo jumbo."

Youssa smiled slyly. "Context is, you give up monthly blood, willingly, *petite.* Sit. Drink some tea." Youssa lowered the blinds on the shop's plate glass and returned to the counter to pour some tea off a small hot-plate. "Lipton, nothing more," she joked.

Angela sipped the warm tea, closed her eyes, and surrendered. "Who am I?"

Youssa took her now trembling hand. "You lose a part of you—long ago, and recent. That when dreams begin, *non?* After the cold, blood. Snow and screams . . ."

"*Oh my God.*"

"*Bon,* keep praying to God. Keep faith in Jesus. *But trust in Youssa.*" Youssa crouched to Angela's eye level, deadpan. "Are you *la mère, ou sa fils?* Ah, you have old soul, she drink the power from the Inkanyamba's falls.

Same water night sorcerers drink. But it is not she who calls you. It is the son." When Angela twisted away from her on the stool, Youssa grabbed her bare shoulders. "*C'est l'esprit.* From *l'Afrique.* Voodoo and Santeria—they are fruit of African tree. *Tout l'esprit,* it begins *en Afrique.* You Americans are lectured from when you little girl that you must sit in a pew and listen to some preacher—him, a male—drone about God, about Jesus. We scream, we dance, we burn the herbs, to *become* God. To reveal *l'esprit.* You are mother *and* son. Son calls you. *Listen.* He say he grow to be great healer. But he also say, you die, long time ago . . . as great witch. You die—as *inkanyezi!*"

Angela covered her mouth, weeping, overwhelmed by the irrational, the fantastic. Everything she'd been trained to discount, ignore. "No . . . no . . . you're telling me a warlock is killing these people, not a lunatic who thinks he is? And me, I'm . . ."

"*Ma bébé . . . écoute-moi.* The warlock, night sorcerer, taste red mushrooms, make him strong. Black mushrooms, make victim crazy. Weak minds weaker. Guilty minds more fearful. Smell of the lions in the wind, when burnt. You smell in tunnel, eh? With elixir of worms, mushroom make mind soft for monsters, demons. *Amafufuyama.*"

"Wait. You admit your magick, is pharmacology, nothing more?"

"Ah, and pharmacology, it is magick. Cocaine, LSD, heroin, PCP, make you see monsters, kill family, sell own precious punanny, drown babies, *non?* You take little pink pills, tell you mind what to feel? *Umthakathi,* he practice what Zulu call *umbhuelo* . . . it mean 'harmful medicines,' see? So he very real, *petite.* He flesh. But do *not* make mistake of confusing the pharmacology and cruel motives for killing, with magick. *Both* real! As real as our flesh! Now, come with Youssa . . ."

She dimmed the outer shop lights, then opened the door behind the counter. The room was narrow, lit only by a long, sputtering fluorescent tube. Dust and lint rose like a cloud. No AC vent. The stink assaulted Angela's nostrils. All around her were stacks of skulls, skins, and feathers of just about every small mammal, bird, fish, amphibian, or reptile native to the African continent, the Caribbean, and Central America. Mummified monkey paws. Putrefied lion's penises. Above the organic remnants, on upper shelves, sat mahogany and teak statuettes, dozens of them. Other cultures might call them tiki gods or small, carved totems; they were inlaid with gold and copper and beadwork. The animal remains were the "day fetishes." The wood effigies belonged to the night.

Angela cupped her hand over her mouth to stifle a gasp when she saw the ugly little wooden warriors, feeling an electric chill crackle up her spine to the base of her skull. *I've seen things like this before. In dreams . . .*

As she shuddered, Youssa explained, *"Les fetoushes,* they tools, like flour or baking powder to make cake. Bones, day fetish to see the future, divine truth, fortify loved one. Night fetishes, to guard, to watch . . . to control. Or kill. Zulu also use *ishungu.* A gourd. Hollow. Either good or bad, depend on what you put inside."

"The man in the tunnel," Angela whispered hoarsely, "had something like that."

In the meager light of that hanging single tube, Youssa looked up at the night fetishes. "Zulu use same fetishes as these, here. Youssa import these, along with day fetish. Smuggle, actually. Youssa more scared of U.S. Customs than sorcerer."

"I won't bust you. But . . . what's that little fetish, there—a half-rat, half-man?"

"Make rats crawl, attack. Need animal blood as fuel. The roach and ant fetish, with the evil smile there—it make bugs swarm. Or, *assagai* or spear-carrying fetish, it make machines go out from a man's control. All machines. Gun, computer. Even car or truck. Youssa seen it. Truck crash in Niger River because sorcerer say."

Angela gulped air. "Any vehicle? Even"—she paused—"an ambulance?"

Youssa nodded grimly. "Truth, *petite chérie."* Then the witch laid an old leather-bound, eight-column bookkeeping ledger on a stack of eagle skulls and opened it. It wasn't an account book—it was filled with old photos and news clippings. "There," Youssa pointed. "Me as a girl apprentice to a wizard. He stands with me in his best suit and tie at Le Grand Marché Fetoush. The Fetish Market. All the magick sold there, *nowhere* else in all Africa. Now, South African government close down fetish markets, but not shops of *inyanga*—the herbalist healers. Poor people have no health care without they. But *sangoma,* they are around for the tourists. Some even bless killings. See? Strife start in 1982, after a great *inyanga* die at one hundred ten years of age."

Angela read the obituary clipping. Dr. Michael Dginshwayezi. Pastor of the First Lutheran Church of Ladysmith. Practitioner of ancient folk healing, which he learned as a child before the 1879 war between the British Empire and the Boers. The next lines stung her eyes, yet she read it aloud: " 'Orphaned, he was a witness to the surrender of King Cetshwayo. Raised and educated by missionaries, and called to God's service at age seventeen, Dr. Dginshwayezi's works for the poor and afflicted of the Natal Province and his Zulu kin brought him the name 'Michael, Archangel of KwaZulu.' He told many generations of parishioners that he owed all he was to Jesus Christ' "—she swallowed hard—" 'and his mother.' "

The eyes in the photograph looked clouded from cataracts. But Angela had seen them before. Nascent and bright. Loving. Eager to learn. She retreated into a clean corner while the sputtering tube painted macabre shadows through the night fetishes and animal carcasses. Youssa pulled her back out to see another page. The article was from a Washington, D.C., African American newspaper, *The Informer,* dated April 2000.

Youssa said, "My English better when I read. 'Buildings slated for rehab into luxury lofts and riverfront office space once housed the Neal & Co. Alexandria City slave pens . . . by 1849 processing five hundred human beings a day as fodder for wholesalers and traders . . . across the Potomac from the hallowed halls of democracy. Though in the Nation's capital, slave ownership was legal.' Now, read this part to Youssa."

Angela recited, " 'Jefferson Davis Highway.' Oh, *shit* . . . this was where Mullinix kept Whiting. The warehouses . . . *how did you know?*"

The witch smiled.

Angela's pulse raced as she read on. " 'Neal & Co. paid bribes to U.S. Navy and Customs officials, allowing them to circumvent the law prohibiting slave importation from Africa after 1808. Contraband shipments contained captured peoples from the central Congo River region, Southern and East Africa, rather than the traditional Middle Passage sources of the western coast. This was necessary to meet the demand for human chattel generated by new Red River sugar and rice plantations in Louisiana and Eastern Texas.' "

"Votre grandmère, where her family come?"

"Virginia . . . and Nacogdoches, Texas. It's near . . . Louisiana."

Youssa shut the book. *"Pas de coïncidence.* You ancestors, you children— they bought and sold there, they die there."

Mullinix had said it, too. *His children . . . your children, died here.* What did that mean?

"Wickedness not born in the night sorcerers, or ghosts. Demons. Lucifer." Youssa touched Angela's forehead. "Wickedness spawned only here." She then touched Angela's breastbone. "And here. Greed, lust, jealousy, rage. Demons, ghosts—they the maggots and flies on this garbage heap, and they are what live on long after we die. *Amafufuyama* live on after Shaka's Lion's Regiment die. Not so hard to believe now? But take heart, *chérie*—goodness, it live on, too. *Votre grandmère . . .* she live on, in you."

"If you could see, sense these events before they happened, you could have—"

Youssa's pearl-white eyes narrowed as she cut Angela off. "Could have what? Walked to FBI and say Youssa a witch. Youssa can help? Tell Janet Reno, and police, about *les fetoushes?* Ha! Even many young wicca learn craft because they outsiders, or they think it exotic, or they vegetarians and do yoga and this just part of a fad. Arianne, not so. But she exception. Like you."

Angela broke out of the room to suck in fresher air. She rested beneath a rack of multicolored, beaded pouches, like purses with attached belts. When she looked up at the little pouches, her heartbeat slowed, a bit. Her lungs calmed.

Youssa followed her out of the fetish room. "They called *ibheqe.* Zulu use for holding things for someone they love. This like a 'love letter.' Colors mean 'I ache for you,' or 'Please answer me.' Most made now for tourists; some Zulu girls still make them, send to boyfriends. But this here, a hundred years old. Belong to *sangoma;* she make for her fiancé, *oui?*" She took it off the rack and handed it to Angela. "*Sangoma* opposite of *umthakathi.*"

The comment brought Angela back to her quick gloss of *The Golden Bough.* Sympathetic versus contiguous magick. Contiguous magick means you have to be in contact with someone through touch. Sympathetic magick means you need something intimate of a person's.

"*Umthakathi* take hair, nail clipping, dandruff. Zulu say *insila.* But better than semen, menstrual blood, is *flesh.* Nadia bring you blood for me to read."

"So does that make *you* a night sorcerer?"

"Ha! *D'accord,* what embassy say make better sense to brain, what Youssa say make better sense to heart. Now, you better prepared in both. Now you almost whole."

"*Whole?* Um, Nadia's waiting." Angela hurriedly slipped back on her mules. She left her card on the counter and rushed out through the shop's jingling front door.

"*Ngiyabonga, Inkanyezi,*" Youssa bid, in learned Zulu. "*Yenza okuqondile.*"

Be well, Protector. Now go do what is right.

27

SECURE IN HER SOLITUDE, YOUSSA sat at the shop's counter, puffing on a homemade cigar as long and thick as the cardboard tube in a roll of paper towels. The sweet, lemony smoke mingled with the waxy odor of seven fat white candles, and seven black ones, lit all around the shop. Both scents battled the pungent stench of the monkey skulls and shrike feathers Youssa was reading. Youssa sang for Angela Bivens in the tongue of ancient Mali: the Tuareg, ancestors of her people the Fulani. Sang, alone, until the phone rang.

She laughed after she answered. "Go to Giant after you shift, pick up gallon of OJ, Rice Krispies, whole chicken. No, not a *live* chicken! *Merde*, you tease me too much!" A figure approached the door off the sidewalk. "Hold on, girl." She cradled the phone on her shoulder, snuffed out the cigar in an ashtray. "We closed!" She returned to her conversation. The shop door opened. "I must go. *A bientôt*. I tell you who's on Jay Leno."

The visitor was tall, black. Sunken cheeks, pointed chin. Mustache twisted almost in a macabre Fu Manchu. Hair braided, now all the way, and dropping what looked like shiny black tentacles on his narrow shoulders. His tank top was soaked through with sweat, and wet mesh showed the outline of his ribs. He was a wraith, in Nike Airs.

"G'wine home, boy. Police no want black men on street, disturbing white folk in Georgetown." With one hand, Youssa scooped the stink fetishes into a drawer between her computer monitor and the cash register. With the other, she groped under the counter for a .38 Smith & Wesson snub-nosed she'd purchased after two men had robbed and murdered the employees of the Starbucks one block up Wisconsin.

But the tall, spiderlike man didn't move. "Uh-huh," he muttered. "You doin' the 'read.' The bitch was here, wasn't she?" He stepped forward. In the candlelight, Youssa saw his rotted teeth grit beneath snarled lips. "You play me, you suffer."

Youssa stood up, keeping the gun to her side and her horror masked, for she finally smelled *it* in him. He wasn't a dope fiend or thief. *"Mon Dieu . . .* he send you?"

The spidery man smirked. "He? An' who's he?"

Youssa recoiled. "He?" wasn't a question. It was a statement, inside a riddle, and it ripped away her resolute mask. She raised the gun. "Magick . . . no hurt Youssa . . . in here." She cocked it. "And you . . . you goddamn not hurt Youssa either."

He took another step, scowling, sweating. "Got all these dumb white bitches and faithless muvfuckers fooled? You wid your tarot cards and roots and *doc-tor-of-ho-me-o-pathic* shit. You nothing but another African come here for the hustle!" All of the candles in the shop blew out simultaneously.

"Stay back! I powerful witch . . . from the day the village matrons come for me as little girl, to cut me, circumcision, and I have *le fetoushe* make knife go away!"

But her chants of protection were matched by his shrieks of laughter, in the dark.

"What did you tell Bivens?" he growled. *"We* need to know. *Don't fuck with me! Does she believe?"*

Now he was blocking the counter, and Youssa's back was pressed against the door to the fetish room. She squeezed the trigger. Two rounds exploded through the plate glass, producing neat, cracked holes, not the shower of shards that would bring the police immediately. The earsplitting pops were enough, however, to send pedestrians on the still bustling sidewalk to the pavement. But the spidery man had dropped from sight, and the shop door was wide open, bells jingling. Youssa yanked the door to the fetish room open, then slammed it shut behind her. Body braced against the door in the blackness, she could hear her pulse in her throat. But he was gone, and she could wait for the cops.

Soon, Youssa heard scraping noises, then clicking, beckoning from the rear of the nasty, narrow room full of dead things and wooden effigies. There—beyond a gray steel door connecting to the alley loading dock. Youssa cursed the intruder. She still had the .38.

Through shadows, Youssa moved to that rear door. Listened. Silence, then more scraping, clicking. Not metal on metal. Something organic. Erratic. She didn't dare turn on the light now. Fortified by another song, she tripped the dead bolt and swung open the heavy door. She aimed the gun. Nothing out there but Dumpsters and her red Civic. Indeed, only the noise of traffic on Wisconsin broke the still of another humid night.

Suddenly, the alley's safety spotlight unit, strung on a telephone pole, began to flicker. In the strobelike beams, Youssa saw a silvery moth swoop and flutter. Nothing odd in the summer. But more fluttered into the light. Hundreds. She froze. *Thousands.* In a blizzard. Wings *clicking.* She clutched for a tiny bag hanging from her neck, beneath her tank top. Chanting, she scanned the Dumpsters . . . for rats. Relieved that she saw none, Youssa edged back in, locking the metal door behind her. Chuckling nervously, she finally popped on the fluorescent light. A second passed, and it exploded.

Youssa ran to the inner door to the shop. It was immovable, as if welded. And she smelled a breath fouler than the dried day fetishes piled in the creeping, murky dark. Her gasps turning to screams, Youssa threw herself back at the rear door, but it, too, was fused shut.

The scraping noises started anew, outside. Followed by whispers, inside.

Eyes wide and adjusted to the dark, Youssa saw shadows move on the upper shelves. Little ones. With painted faces and sharp copper teeth set in thirsty mouths.

28

FRIDAY, JUNE 23, 2000

THE FLORIDA AVENUE GRILL, 8:45 A.M.

VICTOR STYLES LOUNGED IN A BACK booth. The legendary soul-food eatery brimmed with diners—blue-collar workers, students, and others who, like Styles, had donned professional suits. And it popped with their cackling banter, sharp clinks of coffee cups on saucers, forks on plates of country-fried steak and grits. Country sausage, scrapple, towering hotcakes. Or spicy hash drowning in ketchup, or cloudlike biscuits, smothered in butter or bursting through a blanket of gravy.

"Hold up," said the waitress with a sigh. "You want *what?*"

"Yogurt, a bran muffin . . . and café au lait, if possible."

"Honey, you can get that mess downtown. We can get you somethin' ta *eat.*"

"Yogurt, a bran muffin . . . and your *house* coffee. And privacy."

"Well, excuse me, then."

"Yes," Styles intoned, sliding a crisp $50 bill toward her, "excuse you."

The waitress snatched up the fifty. She was sweating. Everyone in there was. Harsh morning sunbeams filtered in through the blinds, allying with the heat from the kitchen grills and stoves to battle the phalanx of old Carrier window air conditioners. The AC was losing. Yet this brother, suit jacket still on, was cool as ice. As she moved away, she brushed against another man in a suit. She smiled, almost doing a curtsy. Others risked whiplash turning their necks so quickly. But Bryce King didn't smile back. Always smile back, he'd tell himself, not because you want to, but because you have to make Jamal and Jamika Q. Public think they are always in your heart. The faces of KCC's Asian, Dutch, and British investors took up more space in King's heart than those of the legions of teens watching hip-hop videos on his network or buying CDs off his Web site. But this morning, his face was sallow, gaunt. Once-darting eyes were drawn into their sockets. Almost breathless, he edged into the booth opposite cold, *cold* Victor Styles.

King growled, "Could you have picked a *more* public place?"

"Folks here keep their mouths shut. Besides, doesn't it bring back sublime memories of the ol' Hilltop?" Styles gestured toward the Howard University campus. "Legend is, you thought up KCC in this very booth, over two wings, fries, and gravy, for a media-marketing term paper. Fred Smith dreamed up Federal Express like that, at my alma mater, Yale."

"I play tennis with Fred Smith . . . and you are wasting my motherfucking time."

Styles yawned. "I have dossiers on most of the chumps in the autographed photos on these walls. I learned the hard way that those whose names we drop seldom drop what they're doing to help us. So—how may I help you?"

King's haggard face contorted. "You snide faggot mother—"

"Decorum, Bryce." Styles frowned when he studied the mogul's face. "You sick?"

"My two best friends are dead, Victor. One murdered while I was burying the other. And your people haven't a clue why or who. No, let me rephrase—the *white men* in the Bureau certainly know who. And why. And couldn't give a shit."

"No more coffee for you."

"Kiss m'ass," King hissed. "And Butch, a brother I have staked my wealth, my rep, my very life on, won't take my calls. His way of dealing with this, with the right-wing army besieging us, is to act like a Republican whenever the lights go out. Then two U.S. marshals serve me with a court order in front of my party guests—and I find out you sent them, as part of this 'investigation.' You, motherfucker. *You.* Is this a joke?"

"So much for grief over your friends," Styles said, dabbing his mouth with his napkin, "and righteous indignation over our apparent incompetence, inattention to your needs? You're going to be a for-real billionaire, not a paper one. And you owe much of that to me. Knocking down enemies, or thorny FCC, SEC, IRS problems."

King gnashed his teeth and shooed away the waitress when she came to pour more coffee; Styles continued, "Angela Bivens's theory that we are *not* dealing with the Archangels may start to gel some minds at the Hoover Building, Bryce. We can scheme and posture as to whodunit, but the fact remains, we have to stop who did. Elizabeth Hooperman was not the target. Les was. Then Carl Davidson. Perhaps, soon—Butch."

King slammed his palms on the table, exposing a shirt pocket. Styles saw what resembled a spreading, moist wine or red-ink stain. His mind couldn't accept that it was blood. King noticed; he snapped his suit jacket back over his breast.

"What's wrong with you?" Styles probed, head askew. "Are you injured?"

"Goddamn it, no . . . what are you doing to resolve our problem?"

"Your life's likely in danger, too. That's *your* problem, correct?"

"Angela Bivens. I meant Angela Bivens is our problem."

"She isn't my problem. People like Woodruff Sessions or Orrin Hatch, Tom DeLay, Dan Burton . . . George W. Bush. *They* are my problem."

King shot forward in his seat. *"And we have the means of derailing all of them!* Bivens was on this so-called Amesha Spentas case for months, and *my* friends in the Justice Department and the White House look at the same evidence you and she do. Victor, that little bitch has gone mustang on all of you. Rein her ass in."

"Little bitch, yes. As in a terrier. Once she's in the rat hole, she doesn't come up till she's got something in her jaws."

"That's what I am? A rat?"

"Okay, wrong metaphor, but the right context. We are on the verge of a civil war within the Hoover Building. Donatello has utterly abdicated. The only way for me to keep the peace, consolidate my position, was to give her as much leeway as possible. A long leash. But you don't care, do you? In the end, it's all about *you*. A cult of self-importance: you and all the niggers like you, Bryce—and I include our white pal in the Oval Office as a 'nigger.' Fuck the long term, fuck the plan. *Après moi, le déluge,* as King Louis XV once said. Or was it Elijah Muhammad? After me, the deluge."

"You're fucked."

"I may just *be*. Each of the other Assistant Directors wants a piece of anything Bivens digs up. Each but Frank Lupo. I have no idea what game he's playing."

King suddenly started pawing under his jacket, at the stained spot. At first Styles blanched, but the look quickly frosted into a scowl. "You asked for this meeting, remember? We obtained a court order to interview

Antoine Jones as well. Uh-huh. And Angela's started field research on South Africa. Now Bryce—clarify that for me."

King slumped backward, still pawing at his chest. "You let her waste time digging up old wounds? A boy goes berserk and mutilates his girlfriend. Has ties to drug dealers and—"

"*Shut up!*" Diners glanced at the booth, and even Styles paused and swallowed, shocked at his loss of cool. "I could care less about a convict! *I'm talking about a girl named Jewel Ngozi, from South Africa.* I am adding two plus two and the answer 'four' is frightening to me, Brother King. Almost as scary as the prospect of George W. Bush in the White House."

"A dead coed," King mumbled. "I had nothing to do with her."

"So you remember her? Well, you and your four-hundred-dollar-an-hour lawyer had better."

King lunged across the table to claw at Styles's lapels. Unfazed, not the less by King's weak grip, Styles whispered, "Relax. Breathe. People are *star-ing.*"

King released him, slumping back into his former pose. Desperation wasn't vintage Bryce King, and it was then that Styles fully noted the hollowness of King's eyes, his dry lips. Wrinkles on what had been smooth skin for a fifty-year-old man, as if something was gnawing at him. Draining him.

"Bryce, it was you who started me on this road, ten years ago. I was no saint, but I wanted to change the world and you corrupted that for me. I'd left Navy JAG—the employ of Trey Williams's demonic father, Admiral Williams, and lived in New York, but you met me at a rap music industry party in L.A., remember? I was visiting my mother, who still lives quietly in the shadow of Crenshaw Mall in Baldwin Hills. I'd then been sired by one Rudolph Giuliani, U.S. Attorney for the Southern District of New York. You and I talked about the power of information; you related how this civil rights bullshit was pointless. For real power, we had to play ball like the white boys: sometimes on the dirty end of the field. Already jaded, I guess I concurred. Then comes October seventeenth, 1992. You called me in New York. Needed 'background' on the U.S. Attorney for the District of Columbia. *Urgently.* You asked that, if it existed, I deliver it, in person, to Congressional Country Club in Maryland, before your golf outing with Ron Brown, Vernon Jordan, and then-Governor Bill Clinton. You said 'we' needed an ally inside the FBI. I had the credentials. I knew Giuliani and former Attorney General Dick Thornburg liked my work despite my politics and would provide recommendations. But you revealed how I could slip in before the election and no one in the Bush administration, or then-Director Webster, would oppose it. You said, 'It relates to the quality of mess you dig up, my brother.' And I was the one who found out that Alfred Whiting was a faggot. *And I helped you blackmail him,* God help me."

King chuckled through visible pain. "God help you? You loved it. Before Clinton was even elected, that errand made you an assistant FBI director at age thirty-seven."

Styles leaned in, voice barely a whisper. "My *dirt* on Whiting coincided with the murder of a young African student, found shot, skull bashed in, ripped to pieces, in the same *fucking* hotel where you and your frat brothers had your annual homecoming alumni jam. Two plus two equals what?"

"The request . . . coincided . . . with an *election*. Not a murder, you idiot!"

Styles pushed his plate away somberly. "And that brings us full circle. Angela Bivens is here to protect you—and Brian Buford—from peril. I can't manipulate the investigation beyond what I've already done. I'm trapped. You will be, too."

"I want you to retract this court order and protect *me,* yes. And I want Bivens to protect us *all* from neo-Nazi terrorists and the conservative scum who bankroll or apologize for them. So what the fuck is this bitch really looking for, Victor?"

Styles's smirk returned. "Ahhh, there're only three beings in the universe who can answer that. You, her . . . and God. As for God, well, I'm sure we'll hear from him, real soon."

King stood up with a grunt. "You left out one other person. Butch."

"Yes, we all want to leave out the Senator, don't we? Angela *won't*. But fear not—they are kindred spirits, you know. Unlike us, they don't revel in backstroking through the pool of bullshit that is this city in an election year."

"You must have *something* to hang over her?"

Victor Styles played with his fork and mumbled, "No."

King pushed through the diners waiting to be seated; Styles watched him limp out into the sun that boiled the fresh asphalt on 11th Street and tumble into his waiting limo. Still scratching at his chest with fingers now sticky with blood.

"Leprosy, I hope," Styles muttered to himself as he signaled for more coffee. But the waitress's attention was riveted to something lurid on the local morning news. Styles twisted to view the TV over the luncheonette-type counter.

"*. . . identified as Youssa Ogamdoudou, aged thirty-six, a native of Burkina Faso in West Africa, who lived at 780 Butternut in Takoma Park, D.C. Police say the victim owned and operated an herbal medicine and gift shop in Georgetown, yet her body was discovered by a security guard in the construction zone of the new D.C. Convention Center, off N and Tenth Streets, N.W. Metropolitan Police Homicide Detective Sergeant Brett Mallory stated that there were indications that the body had been moved to the site from a block of gutted row houses in the adjoining Shaw-Trinidad area, once known as The Jungle, but refused to comment as to the basis for that observation.*"

"Oh, Angela," Styles muttered to himself. " 'What hath God wrought?' "

29

SHOULDERS SQUARE TO THE OPPONENT. Uppercut, pivot. Jab. Jab. Hook. The son of a bitch staggered. Finish him. Roundhouse kick to the solar plexus. A chimeric enemy embodied in that hanging heavy bag groaned, died. All to the doggerel of Public Enemy's "Don't Believe the Hype" pulsing from Angela's boom box. Angela's cassette was over ten years old, purchased when she and her classmates had protested a corrupt and ineffectual college administration. The only bright spot on campus back then was the arrival of a freshman basketball phenom named Antoine Jones.

Angela tore open the Velcro binding of her Everlast boxing gloves with her teeth, then tossed the empty, moist gloves to the sandaled feet of her friend Carmen Wilcox. Carmen had been leaning against the padded wall, forlorn and silent while Chuck D's angry rhymes pumped. Her summery tie-dye headwrap and black knit tube dress spoke volumes against Angela's spandex workout pants and jog bra. Exhaust fans kicked up a cold gale, sending chills up Carmen's body. Angela's steamed with heat, dripped with sweat. Kicking away the small, stale-smelling boxing gloves, Carmen popped out the cassette and said, "I blame myself, Angie-boo. You've been under so much pressure. Collins, then hospital, sparring with Styles, and Lord . . . Sharon and Alvin didn't help matters, and I *swear*, baby, I didn't know what was up with them."

Angela grabbed for her towel. "No one's fault . . . though are you taking all this shit on yourself as some way of saying I'm responsible? Responsible for driving Sharon and Alvin together? For being crazy, tired, confused, maybe—for what I just told you? You're my friend and I love you. I even love Sharon and I damn sure love Alvin more than he'll ever understand. I love my parents, my sister, but why do I think I'd get the same bullshit thrown at me if I told them the facts, my reality, that I told you?"

After a weighty sigh, Carmen demanded, "What are we supposed to say—that we are all behind you when you come at us with some story that you are some sorta reincarnated witch-doctor-priestess Buffy the Vampire Slayer? And there's some *wizard* out there, murdering people? Aw, Angel, aw naw."

Angela mopped the sweat from her face and arms as her mind struggled to render an explanation that made sense of what couldn't possibly make sense. "You my girl, Carm?" she posed, doe eyes wide, needy.

"Oh no you didn't! You *know* this sister here's had *your* back . . . held your hand and been your advocate and A-number-one fan from the day I answered your ad for a roommate down in the East Village when you were at NYU Law and I was at Columbia, to suing the FBI . . . to Trey, all that death, all that misery . . . to an abortion—oh, sorry, *miscarriage*—to seeing you tear through this old-boy network like a comet, and finally . . . *awww.*" Flustered, flushed, Carmen raised her hand and turned away.

Angela placed her hand on Carmen's bare brown shoulder. "You're my anchor."

Carmen faced her, eyes wet. "Then call Dr. Myers, sweetie. Please. Your mother says you haven't even been up to see your dad since that horror at that funeral!"

Angela grasped her friend's wrists, pulling them to her sweaty chest. "Someone is sending a message in these murders. A story. Just like Trey and Pluto told a story. A new devil."

Carmen yanked her arms free. "No . . . *no!* Angie, I kept begging you to slow down. So did your parents, Alvin."

"Listen. All that's changed is the weapon. Spooky, yes. Crazy, yes. But it's just the weapon. What hasn't changed is what I do. Gather the facts. Marshal *my* weapons. Find out why the bad people are doing what they do. When you find out why, you find out who, and I stop them cold."

Carmen waved her off; Angela slinked to the padded wall and slid, sideways, down until she was a heap on the vinyl mat. For a second, one tick, her heart felt as if it shrank in her rib cage. Carmen wiped away a stray teardrop and squatted with her, resting her head on Angela's shoulder.

"This is no delusion," Angela said softly. "This man who practices witchcraft must have help. Followers, acolytes. They killed Hooperman to get at Collins. They killed those paramedics in Philly to get at Bishop Davidson. I can't help but think they will come after me. That's why I want you all to keep your contact with me to a min—"

Carmen moaned into Angela's flesh, "Let me take you home."

"I'm showering here and I have work to do. Frank's piling what the Civil Rights Section claims is Amesha Spentas info on me. They've gotten intell on an 'unspecified threat target within the nation's capital,' plus background on three firefighters in the company that answered the call at Collins's funeral. Seems they'd been using Philly FD servers to visit the Cyber Reich Web site's anti-affirmative-action link." Angela mocked, "Some Irish and Italian firemen are racists? *For real?* Frank's wasting my time."

Carmen eked out a slight smile. "I get so scared for you. Take time off, then go back to your roots, and I damn sure don't mean what this Madame Youssa means by *roots,* or what your weird-ass little white trainee might relate, cool? I mean forget the ghost stories and the insidious political conspiracies and take care of the plain ol' nastiness and death still out here on the street. Lemme tell you my own story, about a seventeen-year-old client of mine from over in the old Simple City Crew's territory in the Potomac Gardens projects. He's a good boy but he's going away for life because of a dealer . . . six-foot-seven bastard named Stringbean Coy. A college dropout. Your school, Howard. He slit the throat of the witness who could clear my client. Threw her eighteen-month-old baby girl off a fucking roof. Cops still got a citywide on him. Still haven't found him. He was high on red-devil love boat: liquid PCP. But the folks in the neighborhood swear, 'No—he bewitched.' Got the roots worked on him. Born under an evil star and all that madness. Wanna hear more? Cops found some poor woman in Shaw-Trinidad. Her face torn up. Eaten, they say. Found her over by the new Convention Center: the Jungle, where white folks wanna gentrify. There're tangible horribles out there, honey. They're there without you having to invent new ones."

Angela nodded along. "Carm, there's no hierarchy of horribles. But this case . . . this case has something *calling* me. Me. My spirit. You claim to be a spiritual person, but you won't trust me."

Carmen stood up and pleaded, "Call Sylvia Myers. *Please.*"

The words felt like knives, cutting Angela's heart out. Despondent, near tears, she fumbled in her gym bag for her cell phone, handed it to her friend. "Go ahead, you call her. The number's programmed. But if you do, I'm . . . I'm not your friend anymore."

As Carmen squeezed her fingers around the phone, it tweeted furiously. Surprised, she tossed it back to its owner.

It was Nadia. Her usual dry, gravelly voice now rang high-pitched, broken. Wet.

"You have to come to the morgue . . . you have to come *now!*"

30

ANGELA PUSHED THROUGH THE SWINGING double doors into Examination Bay Number Two, still dressed in her workout suit. Carmen followed. Meeting them was MPD Detective Sergeant Brett Mallory, huge, bull-necked, and bald. Pyoung Park Chun, M.D., D.C. Chief Medical Examiner, a pale little man dressed in pale green scrubs, sat at a metal desk, reviewing a clipboard.

Carmen said, "Maybe I should wait for you up in the observation room?"

"No, Carm, Dr. Chun won't mind, right, Dr. Chun?"

"You have lost none of your impetuosity, Special Agent Bivens," Chun said, shoving his hands in his lab coat pocket.

"*FBI ISD Inspector* Bivens, now," Angela told him. "Where's Nadia Riccio?"

Chun motioned with his head toward the glass door leading to the "freezer."

Angela pulled on a pair of surgical gloves and walked in with Brett. They found Nadia in a corner, sobbing in between gulps of water from a paper cup. A morgue techie lounged in a metal chair beside her, bopping his head to the loud percussion and raucous lyrics of D.C. "go-go" music, thumping out of a small radio.

"Kill that shit," Brett barked to the techie.

When Brett barked, even large men hopped to it. The music cut off, and

Nadia rushed to Angela. The trainee buried her face in Angela's shoulder, cries muffled.

"I-I heard on the MPD scanner . . . I can't find Arianne anywhere!"

"It's okay . . . you have to learn to stay in control." Angela straightened Nadia up, dabbed her face with a Kleenex.

Brett said, "This trainee called me directly. She says you'd interviewed this vic night before last?"

"She's not a 'vic,' asshole!" Nadia screamed. "She's our *sister!*"

Angela patted her protégé into silence; Brett rolled his eyes and relayed, "Third District patrolmen took the call late Thursday night. Found her in a brick pile on the Convention Center site. But we think she'd been killed down a few blocks. Wanna see why?"

The techie opened one of the steel doors in the wall and slid out a body drawer. Youssa lay naked, gray, cold. Eyelids sewn shut. Angela covered a gasp with a gloved hand, for Youssa's nose was gone. Chewed off. Just like Alfred Whiting's. Nadia spun back into the corner. Something else. Youssa's ears were missing, and when Angela opened her mouth, just on a hunch, she found no tongue at all. The shock and sorrow ebbed, replaced with a wave of rage.

"I want to see the case jacket, Brett. Now!"

But Brett explained, "Not your jurisdiction, 'less you tell if and why she's a witness in a federal investigation."

"Then tell me why you think she was killed blocks from the Convention Center. This woman had a shop in Georgetown. You seal it as a crime scene?"

"Yeah, apparent robbery. She scared someone off with her .38. Listen, brutal shit still happens down in the 'Jungle' in Shaw-Trinidad. M to Q Streets, crossed by Tenth over to Sixth. You still got many abandoned buildings and bare lots for crack ho's giving blow jobs to junior gangstas in return for rock or heroin. We found grit and debris on her clothing consistent with that location. One more thing: the rat population's *big.*"

"Rats?" Nadia suddenly muttered.

"Yeah. Scenario is, crackheads hopped a Metrobus over to G'town, for a night of thievin' in the heat. She scared 'em away, they returned and snuffed her, somehow took her back to the Jungle, left her for the rats, but then freaked and decided to dump the body elsewhere to throw off our case."

Wrong theory, Angela noted. She snatched the police report away from Brett. Youssa was found fully clothed, her ID and $6 in her sweater pocket.

The torso had no visible wounds except for contusions and soft-tissue injury from being dragged and thrown onto hard surfaces, like pavement.

"Get Chun in here," Angela commanded. "Any idea of cause of death?"

"You know what killed her!" Nadia shouted.

"Agent-Trainee Riccio! Go up to the observation bay and stay there!" Angela's voice softened. "Try to find Arianne Shipley . . . any of Youssa's relatives, all right?"

"Nose gone . . . so she can't smell *it* out," Nadia mumbled, arms clutching her own shoulders in the freezing, white-tiled room. "Ears gone . . . because she didn't listen to warnings. Tongue ripped out, because she spoke to us."

"What the fuck was that?" Brett pressed as Chun came in, brushing by Nadia.

"Nothing. So you think rats ate the cartilage?"

"The problem is," Chun said, interposing his small frame, "no traces of rodent dentition, fur. But we did find this." He focused his penlight and pointed with a rubber-gloved finger. Angela saw tiny slivers and splinters of wood, some ocher, some black. "We tested some samples . . . curious, we saw traces of brown dyes, lead-based black paint, shellac, and linseed oil on the extracted splinters."

Brett scoffed, "Hold up—you sayin' me a rabid Ethan Allen dining-room chair bit off this lady's face? This ain't you, Doc. Sounds more like my girl here."

"I'm getting *worse*, Mallory. Wait here."

Angela exhaled a slow, steady breath in that cold, dead room. *Wood? A wooden weapon—bladed paddle of some kind? No crackhead . . . maybe an immigrant asshole did it because his African machismo demanded it?* Nothing fit, until Chun returned with two sample vials containing dead moths.

"What the fuck is this?" Brett yelled, waking the dead.

"The trachea was totally occluded by them. We even found insects in the mouth, pharynx, esophagus, sinuses. Some were not stuffed in the victim— moths are very delicate. Many insects in the victim's mouth were still alive, as if they *flew* into her mouth after the wounds were inflicted."

Angela said, "Cause of death . . . along with shock from blood loss . . . was suffocation from the insect mass in her throat?"

Chun nodded nervously. "But . . . moths don't swarm, like rats or roaches."

"These did," Brett spoke up. "Angie, what's goin' on?"

The fetishes, Angela muttered inwardly.

*   *   *

Earpieces were plugged into Nadia's bopping head as she looked up to see Angela standing in the observation room, arms folded. Angela turned to Carmen.

"She spoken since she came up here?"

"Not to me. Made some calls. I think Youssa's sister's coming down. She lived with her." Carmen then sighed and said, "Angel, I am so, so sorry. I was wrong."

"It's okay." Angela knelt by Nadia's chair. "Did you find Arianne?" She had to yell, the music was so loud and Nadia's trance so deep. Nadia didn't answer. Somehow, the rebuke took Angela back to her old days at the "Nest," the Washington Field Office, in her Crim Squad Room. Distrust and distance were the only things she shared with her partner, Kristina Trimble. But soon, shared burdens and shared horrors meant a bond.

Finally Nadia pulled out on earpiece. The song sounded like rhythmic screaming. "This band's called Disturbed. Aren't fake-ass clowns like Limp Bizkit." Then Nadia turned off the MP3 player and rested her chin on steepled fingers, feigning interest in what Angela was about to say.

"You got to get it together. Cope. This isn't helping find Youssa's killer."

"Pop's back from Budapest last night. He's sending me back to Quantico, then some fucked-up place, within the week. All this, and Youssa's . . . gone. So fuck coping."

Angela bit her lip to control her anger. "Nadia, you shared some things in your closet with me. That means you trust me."

" 'Closet'? Freudian slip?" Nadia leered over at Carmen. "This what she says about me to all of you?" Nadia jumped up. "I need to find Ari. *She* believes."

"Agent-Trainee Riccio! We have interviews to prepare for!"

Nadia gave Angela the finger.

Lifting herself from the carpet, Angela sneered, "Arianne's gonna cry a river when I bite that finger clean off!"

Nadia double-blinked. "You got *no* right, you cruel *bitch.*"

Carmen cautioned, "Angie . . . let's go, okay?"

"No! Nadia, look at me. We owe it to . . . to *our sister*. And you are an FBI agent."

The trainee stopped in her tracks, breathing heavier, with eyes a little wetter. "I'm hungry. Can we get some food? Then go to the shop . . . check it out?"

Angela nodded, smiling.

Carmen sighed. "When you're done, where y'all want to eat?"

"Grab Mallory. But I don't think he'll have an appetite once he starts listening."

"Pardon the smell, miss . . . he's soiled himself coupla times last night. Had to hose him down an' Pine-Sol the whole damn cell. Ain't nah open windows, neither, in the interview room, on accounta him bangin' his big head on the glass. See—they all covered and sealed till he be gone."

"Um, thanks," Arianne Shipley said, slinging her macramé purse off her shoulder to hand it to the corrections officer.

"And sorry about the heat. AC system's old." He opened a folding chair. "And about how dark it is . . . he says the light hurts his eyes." The CO then pointed to the figure in the gray shadows. "Can't hurt nobody no more. Especially hisself."

The CO closed the door. Across from Arianne, Antoine Jones perched on the edge of his chair, his torso wrapped in a straitjacket. His legs remained in padded shackles affixed to the bottom of the bed rail, with only enough slack for him to stand and hop one pace. He wore orange Department of Corrections scrubs and was barefoot. Arianne noted that the left pajama leg was slit, and a slender tube led from his thigh to an IV bag tethered high above the bed.

Following her eyes, Antoine laughed, "Ironic, huh? They feed me with an IV tube . . . and they'll kill me with one, too." He refocused on her face. "So they say I'm faking being crazy, but the motherfuckers treat me like I am."

"I wish I could touch you," Arianne whispered. *"Hold you."* She leaned forward. "You're going to get out of here, I swear to you."

Antoine's brow and mouth contorted as if a dry retch or pained belch was coming. He then jerked his head away and cursed.

Arianne touched her balled fist to her mouth, fighting back tears. She mumbled, as if feeling his pain, "I know it's torture for you to be like this . . . for so long. But it will end. *She's coming.* Soon. Very soon."

Antoine stood up and tried to move forward; Arianne recoiled as both the shackle chain and the IV tube snapped taut, holding him at bay.

"Mullinix failed. That bitch's my only hope." Antoine's eyes drooped; his bound shoulders sank. "I don't wanna die like this," he whimpered. "I *can't* die like some mad fucking dog." He fell back into the chair. "You better go."

"Tony . . . I mean, Shaka," Arianne said, standing on her long, lithe legs. "We're forever . . . and I won't fail you, baby."

31

THE WINDOWS IN THE INTERVIEW ROOM were fused shut with dull matte white paint; an ancient Carrier AC wall unit puffed warm air that carried the must of stale farts. Still, Angela studied the photocopied pages of Antoine Jones's trial transcript pages intently, until rousted by her trainee's labored breaths and shifting chair. She looked over to see Nadia's eyes fixed on the hard-water stains on the ceiling tiles as she slurped from a bottle of cold Evian.

"Relax . . . professional," Angela counseled.

Nadia wiped a dribble of water from her chin. "I'm not nervous about this guy. I'm thinking about what we saw Saturday, after the morgue, at Youssa's shop. Bullet holes in the window. She obviously scared someone off, okay? Someone real, flesh and blood. But that big scary black cop with the wrinkled bald head shows us the fetish room—they found blood spatters in there. Hers. He jokes about maybe she did it as part of some kind of ritual? I told you he'd just think what you said about the *umthakathi* was bullshit. How long'd he laugh before he even started to listen?"

Angela sighed hard as Nadia spoke. Saturday, they'd tensely picked over lunch at Thaiphoon in Dupont Circle. Brett discounted everything they told him about the *umthakathi*'s spirit, yet accepted everything about the pharmacology. This was the mistake Youssa had warned Angela not to make. When they went to the shop and inspected the fetish room, Angela noticed that the top shelf seemed a little light. Brett chuckled when she climbed up on a footstool to find circles of clean space surrounded by dust, where several of the little statues had reposed. No blood up there, so she'd kept her thoughts to herself.

"Angela," Nadia said, nudging her mentor back. "I'm here on borrowed time. Pop wants to discuss my reassignment tonight."

"You're mine until then."

"Yeah. Hey, you trust that cop, Mallory?"

"Trey and Pluto Williams murdered his ex-wife, my friend Monique. And Pluto shot Brett same day he killed my partner, Kristi Trimble. That's why he walks with a limp. *I trust him.*"

The gray metal door swinging wide cut off Angela's dodge. A U.S. marshal wearing a black BDU, black combat boots, and web-belted sidearm holster entered, followed by a D.C. CO toting a shotgun. A third CO pushed in the wheelchair carrying a prisoner wearing bright orange scrubs; padded shackles clasped his ankles and wrists. Angela stood up when she saw that the man's head wobbled and swayed like rag doll's, supported only by the foam and nylon of the brace secured around his neck. Angela moved to the chair. Antoine Jones, aka Shaka Seven, former power forward for the Howard University Bison, was almost her height even when he was seated. She reached to lift the prisoner's chin.

"I wouldn't get too close," the marshal warned.

"What's wrong with him?" Angela demanded. Antoine's pupils were pinpricks. Angela then looked back toward Nadia. The trainee just stared, jaw slack, body rigid.

"The brace is from his old neck injury from him trying to hang hisself, ma'am," explained one CO, handing a clipboard to the marshal. The marshal, in turn, said, "Yep, naproxen for the neck injury doesn't mix well with the Depacote we give him to stop him from crying like a baby."

"He's useless to us in this state. Agent-Trainee Riccio, please—"

As if roused by either Angela's ire or Nadia's name, Antoine Jones raised his head slowly, muttering, "I'm here. Lemme speak."

The marshal shrugged and took a seat near the door; the COs departed. Nadia moved her trembling fingers to a laptop and activated the wireless modem. She also switched on Angela's microcassette recorder.

"Interview . . . with prisoner Jones . . . Antoine."

"Shaka Seven!" Antoine slurred. "Warrior. Indivisible."

Angela reached back and placed her hand on Nadia's. "You okay?"

Something about Antoine had indeed rattled the trainee. She wouldn't look at him, though he seemed to struggle to make groggy eye contact.

"I'm fine." Nadia rewound the cassette and recorded a calmer introduction.

Arms folded, Angela stooped to Antoine's eye level, speaking loudly to catch his somnambulant sways. "Mr. Jones, I am Angela Bivens, Inspector, FBI Investigative Services Division. This is Agent-Trainee Riccio. You are here pursuant to a material-witness order issued through the U.S. District Court for the District of Columbia."

Antoine nodded, looked down at his wrist shackles, and muttered, "Not talkin' about Maynard today . . . I tried to kill myself, to deprive my persecutors . . . of the satisfaction." His eyelids fluttered. "I was a kid when they arrested me. Gonna get juiced before I'm even thirty years old."

Angela turned to see Nadia cringe as he spoke, then faced Antoine again and asked, "Did you and Attorney Mullinix ever share what scared either of you the most? About life, the case . . . *anything?*"

"Maynard's dead—who cares what he's scared of. Me, I won't die on my back. Jewel wouldn't have me in heaven if I was so weak. I'm a warrior. Die on my feet. For Jewel."

"Yes, tell me more about Jewel Ngozi."

In his slowly watering eyes she could see crushing sadness, hidden behind fear. She'd seen something akin to that before—in Trey Williams's brother, Pluto.

Her tone was soft, almost motherly: "She was your heart, wasn't she?" But when Antoine smiled and nodded, her voice became blunt and steely, like a heavy wrench: "Then why'd you almost cut out *hers* . . . and bash her skull in?"

Antoine's eyes widened as big as eggs; calmly, Angela circled back to her seat, opened a blue file folder, and paraphrased, "She'd been strangled, blunt-force trauma to the head. Her sternum was cracked and her heart was almost torn from the pericardial sac. Puncture wounds through her uterus and cervix. Somewhere in that process, she died."

Antoine sank his head into his cupped hands, weeping.

"You crying for her, or for yourself?" Angela pressed sternly.

"You the FBI," he sniffled. "You tell me."

"The Medical Examiner found the equivalent of two tablespoons of baking soda in her vagina . . . along with your semen."

Nadia's hoarse voice broke through. "Baking soda? Why?"

Antoine stammered, "Oh, you . . . will find out soon enough."

Angela said, "There was also an eleven-week-old . . . fetus . . . in her ruptured uterus. No one bothered to do a DNA test on the baby . . . I mean, on that *tissue*. The science was still young in 1991–92. You admitted it was yours, like you admitted you were in the Stephen Decatur Suite of the Omni Shoreham Hotel having sexual intercourse with Jewel, then had a violent argument. You screamed to the arresting officers taking you into custody, 'It's my fault. I did it.' And you repeated it during questioning."

"*I never confessed*," he wheezed. "Cops, FBI, wouldn't let me eat, sleep. I know they planted that double-deuce. Belonged to one of m'boys, 'String.' I was crazy, been drinking, taking B-12 shots from ball practice . . . too broke up . . . scared."

"Scared of *what?* Your utterance gave D.C. Homicide and the Bureau the support to search your dorm room in Charles Drew Hall, where they found the .22, illegal . . . used in a robbery down in North Carolina, bloody Air Jordans, a note from her saying you're paranoid, violent, and that she was afraid of you."

Against Angela's orders, Nadia spoke up again, her voice still weak. "Why did your teammates nickname you A-Murda? It was in the file, but no one—"

"Agent-Trainee Riccio, please let me do this. Thank you."

Antoine answered anyway, "Fools who don't know the *true* me . . . give me that name on the court, with the refs. Just on the court. See, brought up by white family, I went to prep school. Dudes think you're soft. Had to make my rep. I stopped jumping bad when I met Jewel. Girl got my head right. I changed my name."

Suddenly, his pained scowl morphed into a blissful smile, as if an image of a nineteen-year-old with dark, flawless skin, like oiled mahogany, swam out of his memory and materialized in the hot, stale air. Oval face that ended in a sharp chin. Eyes and teeth that gleamed white from that warm black face. Heavy yet supple body curves. Tapered fingertips. Perfect chocolate toes.

Angela washed Antoine's sallow yet dark face with her eyes, and the sensation seemed to compel the prisoner's words.

"Jewel . . . she was an exchange student from Durban," he said, fighting for lucidity. "She was Zulu. Ah, that accent and smile. Nothin' like the princesses or gold diggers up in ballplayers' faces. Met her at a Pan-African Coalition thing sophomore year. Me and m'boys where there peepin' the word on the Diaspora."

It wasn't the time for a wry grin, but Angela gave one anyway, saying, "Or to pick up girls, maybe? Nothing's changed too much on campus."

"How you know?"

"I graduated from Howard, class of '89. I remember when they recruited you."

Angela's personal touch seemed to calm both Nadia and the prisoner. Antoine narrated, "She was speaking on that Zulu-versus-Mandela, black-on-black shit in Natal. The girl set it off, comparing it to the genocide on the streets of D.C., among the crews. First month here, the AKAs and Deltas make a mad play for her, but my Jewel pledges Zeta. Too warm a person for stuck-up AKA heifers."

Angela sighed. "I'm an AKA. Alpha Chapter at Howard."

Antoine pulled up a weary smile. "So, then, Miz FBI-AKA, you already know why she came to HU. 'Cause that dude at KCC-TV, he ran a scholarship fund and—"

"Hold up—*Bryce King?*"

"Back then, everybody knew King's boy Bill Clinton was gonna whip Bush Sr. and Perot. Get new black faces in the House of Representatives and Senate, too. More parties. More drugs. Power needs trophies, and King and his boys loved to hit it with students. When wifey was out of town, he'd walk the Yard, the Blackburn Center, maybe with some dean or a trustee, for cover. Then he'd have these coeds who interned for his TV station make the contact. On his dates, he'd have some faggot pretend to be the girl's boyfriend, then he'd roll as the older third wheel. Guess now that he's bigger than Ted Turner, he doesn't have to scheme for young pussy anymore."

Angela leaned forward, with Nadia waiting on her words. "He seduced Jewel?"

Antoine's head snapped back, despite the brace.

"Wake him up!" Angela shouted.

But the marshal just sat there, silently scoffing. Nadia shot up, ran around the desk, and shook Antoine. That coaxed the marshal out of his chair. Nadia slapped his burly arms away, not before Antoine mumbled, "King . . . and that party."

Angela shouted, "Let him speak! Antoine, go on. Nadia, *sit!*"

It was as if he hadn't missed a sentence in his narrative. "Senior year, I say, okay, so you're crowned Miss Howard, Homecoming Queen, and they invited you to DaFellaz thing? So what! So's every niggah in town who'll pay forty dollars at the door."

Tapping her pen against the peeling, rusty table, Angela pressed, "Listen carefully. Carl Davidson was in the DaFellaz? Dr. Les Collins? Oldheads from the seventies?"

He shook his head, eyes barely open. "All's I know is, these Omega Kap *muvfuckahs* couldn't seduce *me* the way they seduced my Jewel."

Now Angela couldn't discern whether the seduction was literal or figurative.

"Those niggahs and the white assholes on the Board of Trustees paid me to play ball at HU, Miz FBI-AKA. Not in the Ivies, or Stanford . . . or for Coach K at Duke. But King stopped my checks when I told him I was an academic all-American, too. Wanted to use my brain. Plus, I was scared of NCAA violations. Hell, like I really needed the money? I *came* from white money. But they also wanted me to be their pussy bird-dog. Fetch my own girl for those pieces of shit? Hell, no. So when I heard . . . they invited her, the other girls in the Homecoming Court, to the private *after party* they'd always have . . . maybe two hundred old-ass frat boys in the suite. I just snapped. But not like you say, or that transcript reads! That bullshit about me fraternizing with drug dealers . . . fuck that! I was getting righteous brothers and the community some knowledge. Stop the killing. Jewel gave me ideas about the Zulu young men, how they'd organize in Shaka's time. My girl was down with it . . . but then, with all her internships and the glitz these old Negroes promised . . . nah, she wanted to go pinstripe. I was the one gonna be an NBA millionaire and use my money do some good . . . but she was looking down on *me*. We fight. Break up. Get back. Fight. So I stray. What's a brother to do? She iggs me on campus, won't take my calls. Says I'm a stalker.

"The phone woke me up in my dorm. She was hysterical. Told me to come to the Omni Shoreham . . . I motor over there and push through all these drunk people, with King nowhere in sight, and bust into the suite's master bedroom. Just her in there . . . wearing her fucking Miss Howard tiara . . . *and a damn hotel bathrobe.* She's says she's *pregnant.* She doesn't know *who* the father is. And she's been having nightmares—says someone's *after* her in the nightmares *and* in real life. Figured she'd been doin' blow, maybe even basing. Those frat assholes loved to base back then. She's crying on me, saying how much she misses me. Kisses me, half-naked. I'm doped up from the trainers. We . . . we had sex. Party started moving to other suites on the floor . . . I told her I was going to her apartment on Fourth and W Streets, get her a change of clothes."

"When you left, someone *else* killed her? Scores of people in the hotel ID'd you. Panicked. Blood on your shoes."

"I was in that place a total of three fuckin' times, okay? When I came back the second time, with her change of clothes, we made love again, but she was different. Felt different, too. The sex. We fought . . . after we made love . . . fucked. I told her I wanted to marry her. She said she was in love with someone else. Got all hysterical again. Says I was just good dick! Screams that I'm like the African boys . . . and her daddy. Hate women to be independent. African men, they want the pussy *dry*. Dry as the African sky and wind, she says. 'Cause she's just property. And wet means power."

Nadia spoke up, "Her father abused her?"

"Everybody abused her."

And now, Angela was thinking: *No DNA profile on that fetus. And I'll be damned if it was Antoine's.*

Out of one trough of dry torpor, Antoine reached another peak of sobbing anguish. "She goes to the suite's minibar, takes out this open box of Arm and Hammer, scoops a handful *into* herself, screaming, 'Dry for you!' Then some shit in Zulu . . ."

Angela leaned back in the chair, stunned into silence.

Antoine whimpered how he ran away, betrayed, but still in love. He called some of his "friends" in the neighborhood, through a dormmate he kept calling String. These people were Dorry Davis's old Sherman Avenue Crew: Angela's suspects in the Venus Stalkers murders, before she discovered the truth about Trey. Antoine wanted the gangstas to help him put the beat-down on Bryce King and his cronies. Even the nihilistic drug dealers told him that was crazy. He returned to the suite, where he heard the shower running. He followed the noise to the bathroom of one of the suite's smaller bedrooms. Jewel was nude, head bloodied. Eyes rolled up in her head. No mutilations. Just a fractured skull. He said he wrapped her in towels and moved her to the bed, spattering her still warm, viscous blood all over his shoes, his clothes, and the clothing he'd brought for her previously. He said when he tried to wiped up the blood, a blind panic seized him. He escaped from the hotel, through the lingering crowds, driving wildly back to his dorm room. He said he blacked out and woke to find MPD offices aiming their Glocks in his face.

"Look at me, Antoine," Angela said. "Your appellate lawyer kidnapped and tortured a man. And he knew something terrible about the Zulu, didn't he? From you? Something Jewel may have told you? Answer me."

Antoine laughed. It quickened into hysterics. "The truth . . . drove me crazy. Drove Maynard . . . to *worse.* . . ."

"Maynard said something about someone murdering lies."

"The trial," Antoine panted, "that *devil,* he knew the evidence was planted."

"Planted by who?" Angela shouted, shaking him. "The police? The killer?"

"He knew they did *A Clockwork Orange* on my ass . . . made me crazy enough to cop on myself. Tainted everything, wrecking in my dorm room without a warrant, just like Maynard says. But that white-haired devil just grinned when the judge fucked me."

White hair? Angela thought. *Who had white hair?*

Nadia, fingers fumbling with the voluminous transcript, said, "It says here the Assistant U.S. Attorney trying the case was a woman, like his trial lawyer."

"*Wait.* Use the laptop, here . . . go in the Federal Rules Decisions and Federal Supplement–District of Columbia databases, punch in *U.S. v. Jones,* 'Jewel Ngozi,' 'exclusionary rule,' and 'fruit of the poisonous tree' as search terms."

Nadia got a cite. "Um . . . an evidentiary ruling . . . can't get the full text."

Angela shouted to a CO standing outside the door, "Officer, quickly—get volume nine ninety-two of the *Federal Supplement* from the prison law library!"

He rushed out as the marshal exclaimed, "This animal's going back in his cage, Inspector Bivens!" Indeed, Antoine's body literally spasmed with laughter.

"No!" Angela moved to Antoine's wheelchair; the marshal seized Antoine's shoulder. "Tell me if you've ever heard this word . . . from Jewel, when she spoke of her home, her nightmares, or even of this father you mentioned. Or from Maynard." He stopped laughing, swallowed hard, yet didn't respond. Then she whispered, "*Umthakathi.*"

Antoine screamed, as if his rib cage had cracked open just the way Jewel's had when the police found her. The force of his convulsion drove him forward, out of the chair; Angela threw herself back across the floor. Nadia fell to her side. The marshal maced Antoine and called for backup.

Three COs arrived through the metal door, followed by the one Angela had dispatched to the law library. He just dropped the book on the floor at Angela's feet. It was an olive-colored West Publication law book with a cracked spine and frayed cover. The *Federal Supplement,* volume 992. Nadia scooped it up and opened it to page 143—the case she'd found. Angela yanked it from her grasp; the trainee cupped both ears as Antoine's howls and shrieks made even the hardened marshal grimace. Not so with Angela. She read the case headnotes aloud, through the din.

"'Arguing against the United States' Motion to Suppress, Lorraine Stegmeyer, Assistant Federal Public Defender for the Defendant.' Okay. 'Arguing for the United States' Motion to Suppress . . .' *Oh, Jesus,* Styles was right—the devil, right in my face."

Angela pointed to the name. His final case before Clinton took office, but they *never* argue a small suppression hearing themselves. For some reason, this U.S. Attorney did. Alfred B. Whiting.

Antoine suddenly cried out for help—not from Angela. To Nadia.

"Yo, Porcupine! *Porcupine . . .* you can't let me die!"

Nadia cowered, perhaps for the same reason a chill ran up Angela's back. *How did he know what her name meant?*

"Porcupine, tell her—it wasn't just King who turned my Jewel against me!"

A CO jammed his nightstick under Antoine's jaw.

"Officer, no!" Angela yelled as she pulled away a CO who outweighed her by maybe a hundred pounds. She grabbed Antoine's shoulders. "Who? Tell me!"

"Thought he was righteous. Not like the rest of those 'Fellaz.' But he poisoned my Jewel's heart, too. King hooked her up . . . an internship, with the dude in California. In the House, but he was running for Senate in '92. Jewel'd never shut up about him. Like he was Jesus Christ Almighty!"

"Brian Buford," Angela whispered.

The marshal growled, "All right, take this asshole outta here!"

As Antoine was wheeled away, trainee and mentor could hear his shouts: *"Murder the lies! Murder the lies! The Lion comes to murder the lies! The Lion calls 'em up from the fire . . . to blind my enemies . . . to kill. You hear that Porcupine? Miss Porcupine?"*

A metal door down the corridor slammed shut, and there were no more cries.

Angela plunged her face into a cold stream from a rust-stained porcelain water fountain in a corner of the room. She lifted her head when she smelled cigarette smoke. By the cracked pane of the wire-latticed window, Nadia, hands trembling, was blazing up a Newport.

"Hey, no smoking in here, Miss Riccio," the marshal ordered.

"Then put me in prison."

Angela limped to her protégé's side. "Let's go. I want to talk to him. *Now.*"

A frazzled Nadia replied, "We don't . . . don't see King until Wednesday."

"I don't mean King."

32

THE SLIM, YOUNG WHITE MAN SITTING at the receptionist counter inside Brian Buford's third-floor office huffed, "Inspector Bivens, if you'd called first, I'd have told you that the Senator's on the Floor now—amendments to the Campaign Finance Reform Bill. See?"

The wall above the counter was thick with San Francisco 49ers, Oakland Raiders, Oakland A's, and San Francisco Giants paraphernalia, as well as Stanford, Berkeley, and San Jose State pennants. Stuck amid the kitsch were two monitors carrying C-SPAN's live Senate coverage, and there was Butch Buford, orating at an oak podium on the Democratic side of the aisle.

"And unless it's an emergency, we can't page him on the floor before a vote."

"Can't or *won't?*"

"Um . . . yah. *Li-sten* . . . maybe you can have a seat and wait for Mr. Andre Barnes, the Chief of Staff, to come back from lunch."

Nadia handled this one. "Look, it's not like we're the KGB or anything, but when we show our IDs and say we have to speak to the Senator *now*, it *is* an emergency." She leaned in his narrow face. "Got it?"

"Um . . . I can call the sergeant at arms. He can take you into the Democratic Cloakroom, maybe."

"We'll take the underground tram over," Angela said crisply. "Too hot to walk."

As the two women turned for the door, the aide called out, "Where were you guys when the Senator's son's school was vandalized? Yeah, Sidwell Friends School. Someone broke in, almost killed the poor janitor, and tore up ten gym lockers, including Kwame Buford's. Anyone even file a report? *Nooooo.*"

"Dude—we're the FBI," Nadia answered. "Not the cops."

Fluorescent tubes above the narrow tracks melded into a solid line as the subway tram rushed through the square tunnel toward the Capitol.

Angela spoke loudly over the noise in the open car. "What about Jones freaked you out so much? Be honest."

"He killed that girl . . . I think he's going to use what he said to convince us that he's crazy, or at least get us to convince a judge to stay his execution, pending our—"

"Try again, rookie."

"Ar-right . . . ya busted me. . . . Listen, only Ari, my pop, and my cousin Sophia call me Miss Porcupine, and that asshole Jones, when he looked at me, it's like he was looking through me. Maybe . . . maybe we should go back and find out why."

"Agreed. First we get some questions answered by the Senator. He opens up, then I can use his words on King. The key's been Jewel, all along. All along."

"What makes you think he'll 'open up' to you? Just 'cause he sent you flowers?"

"He will." *Kindred,* she told herself.

Nadia stewed in thoughts she now wouldn't share. The tram driver called, "Y'all ladies stoppin' at the canteen and post office?"

Angela replied, "No, the private elevators to the Senate Chamber."

"G'won wid yo' bad self!" the driver joked.

The tram slowed as it passed the Capitol's underground post office, coffee shops, and office supply depots. "Main elevators to Senate Cloakrooms and Chamber," the driver announced.

Angela and Nadia hopped out and presented their badges and IDs to a Capitol police officer, or CPO, guarding the bank of elevators reserved for Senators. As Angela stepped in to the next open lift, her cell phone sounded.

"Hello? I'm underground—you're breaking up," she said.

"Inspector Bivens, this is Andre Barnes, Senator Buford's Chief of

Staff . . . I was just informed that you were in the office bullying my people. I'm trying to get a handle on what you want regarding the deaths of Dr. Collins and Bishop Davidson. We cannot simply pull the Senator off the Floor."

"One way or another, we're not going to leave the Cloakroom, sir, until he speaks to us. Off the record. Perhaps it'll help if you give him the name Jewel Ngozi."

"Uh, wait. Access to Democratic and Republican Cloakrooms is restricted, even to you feds. Just . . . *damn* . . . just give us fifteen minutes. The President pro tem is calling a completion of debate on the amendments by two-fifteen, and the vote's likely going to be at two-thirty; we might be able to have a Senate page or one of our LAs get him out to you. After that, *no doubt,* I'm phoning your superiors." Click.

The elevator opened on second floor of the Senate Wing, Chamber level. Two CPOs and one of the Sergeant-at-Arms's doorkeepers met the two women. They seemed unimpressed by the FBI credentials. A doorkeeper pursed his lips and said, "You have to wait in the Gallery. Then one of us will come get you once the Senator responds."

"No way," Nadia quipped. "What a pampered millionaire boys-and-girls club!"

"And you have to give up your weapons. New rules."

Angela nodded and handed over her SIG-Sauer. What choice did she have?

A CPO ushered the women through a metal detector and down a polished marble corridor between the Democratic and Republican Cloakrooms: lavish lounges in which to relax, politick, or plot. Angela and Nadia joined on the tail end of a line of visitors waiting to head up the steps to the Gallery. Tourists: Asians and Europeans snapping photos, silver-haired pensioners in rainbow-colored culottes towing old husbands wearing sandals over black socks, a troop of Boy Scouts who smelled like wet hay, sweaty mothers with thighs puckered by cellulite and dads hiding beer bellies—tugging on kids sticky with spilled ice cream or soda. All happy to be indoors, surrounded by cool, ornate floor tiles and massive, sun-blocking velour drapes.

Nadia smirked. "Vapid losers. I think I'm gonna hurl."

"Nah, that's America right there, coming to see its government in action."

Nadia turned when she heard a baby wailing. "One in every crowd."

Angela turned, too, just as the line started moving up the stairs. A woman with long, flaxen hair, wearing a yellow tank top and red cotton shorts, passed a squealing, bald little child over the velvet ropes to an older woman whose hair rose in a blond-gray beehive. An empty stroller sat back beyond the metal detectors. The mother, with her gaunt, wiry frame, looked like a marathon runner. But the father really piqued Angela's interest. He was stocky, with a hint of sunburn on his forehead and cheeks. He smiled when their eyes met. Strange; with his wife right there? He wore a pale green Polo knit shirt. The jeans—creased, above cowboy boots. Pressed with an iron? And boots, in this heat? Most of the male tourists wore sandals or athletic shoes.

The couple turned and waved, and this putative grandma took the baby's hand to wave it back. The man held on to his video camera, though a tour guide admonished him about shooting, and the woman still had the baby's empty Snugli-harness slung close to her chest. The visitors filed into the Gallery; Angela used her ID to capture seats in the front row, though she offered the couple the two next to her and Nadia. The couple accepted. Angela smiled politely and leaned over the balcony's lip to view the activity below.

The Senate Floor resembled a shopping-mall concourse more than an august assembly of seated statesmen. People walked the aisles or congregated in the well before the huge burnished oak rostrum where the Enrollment and Chief Clerks sat. Buford had finished his speech and headed down into the well to admonish, backslap, cajole, and commiserate with colleagues. Leaning a little further, Angela spotted the long benches upholstered in red velvet where staffers sat. The doorkeeper who'd spoken to Buford's Chief of Staff appeared and looked as if he was handing a note to a stocky young black woman with long braids and Coke-bottle glasses who'd been tapping away at a laptop. The woman wrote something on a legal pad, got up, and sashayed down the aisle to the well, handing the pad to Buford.

Even at that distance, Angela discerned Buford's brow fold, his eyes narrow. He then looked up to scan the gallery. Angela sat, stone-faced, until his eyes found her. He lowered the pad and nodded to Angela. He whispered to the young woman, who promptly trundled back up the aisle. And between every subsequent exhortation or laugh or veiled threat in the well, Buford would look up.

"We have our answer," she said to her bored trainee. In a few minutes, the chunky young woman appeared in the Gallery, moving down to Angela's row.

"Inspector Bivens," the staffer said slowly and enunciating as if to compensate for an Oakland Ebonics cadence, "my name is Ayesha Coleman, one of the Senator's legislative assistants. He'll meet you in twenty minutes at Bullfeathers restaurant."

"I know the place. Thank you."

"You're welcome, Inspector Bivens. And if there's anything else you need, the Senator's placed me at your disposal. Here's my business card. My direct dial is—"

The tourist with the video camera elbowed Ms. Coleman's ample hip; he looked to be fumbling in the babyless Snugli harness still strapped to his wife. And now she was fiddling with *his* video camera; he rubbed up against Coleman again, with no apology. This time, Coleman's Oak-town showed.

"Um—excuse *you?*"

Angela squinted. In the dim Gallery light, the man's formerly prosaic expression had turned feral, bizarre. He rose from his seat.

Everything after that oozed into slow motion.

A BACKHANDED BLOW SMASHED INTO Coleman's face with such force that bloody teeth pelted stunned tourists in the Gallery's front row like hail. The poor girl's compact but rotund body crashed into Angela and Nadia like a bowling ball on two duckpins. Recoiling, Angela watched the female tourist rise to give an earsplitting war whoop. In her hand was what resembled a small piece of the video camera. Amid the silence of terror and frozen confusion, Angela heard one sole voice cry, *"Gun!"* And Angela's own weapon was locked up downstairs.

"Sic semper tyrannis!" was what Angela heard next, not from the man, but in a woman's shrill yet bloodthirsty pitch. This was John Wilkes Booth's rant at Ford's Theatre the night he murdered Abraham Lincoln. Shots rained down on the Senate floor. Rapidly. This woman had a 9mm automatic. Angela didn't contemplate how, because the man was now aiming his own weapon at her, and her mind muttered a negotiation almost inane in its simplicity: *But you can't kill me. I'm not done yet.*

Pop! Pop! Rounds drilled Coleman's body. Her thickness acted to shield Angela's own body, but the third shot—that bullet was meant for Angela's face. No escape this time, no improvisation or adaptation, and Angela saw her parents, her grammie, her nephews, all at once. All smiling. Yet Angela heard Nadia's voice next, screaming, cursing. Contemptuous of her own safety, Nadia swung her purse at the man's jaw like a medieval spiked ball and chain.

From above and behind Angela's head: *Pa-pop. Pa-pop.* Again. *Pop-pop-boom! He's killed Nadia.* But these didn't sound like 9mm rounds. Angela was buffeted and suffocated by Coleman's weight on her torso. Helpless. Bled upon. And Coleman's bowels were draining, adding to the misery and horror. Finally, screams from the crowd in the Gallery began. Another few shots, and the female shooter was toppling over the balcony rail . . . red globules trailing behind in a slow, thick leak, as if both she and her blood were weightless in a spacecraft. The man was gone, too.

With a grunt Angela pushed Ayesha Coleman's bulk off her. The young woman was groaning, gasping, spitting blood. Alive. *Thank God,* Angela rejoiced inwardly. She saw Nadia's flushed and panic-stricken face over the row, and she repeated aloud, teary-eyed, "Thank God."

"*Oh . . . oh, shit-Holy-Mary,*" Nadia panted, red hair a wild shag, eyes glazed and wide as saucers. "What the fuck . . . the woman shooter . . . she's dead . . . Capitol Police Tactical must've taken her out . . . b-but the guy . . . crazy asshole, h-he . . ." Angela shook her. "He went over the side, too. *Jumped.*"

All around was a cacophony of police-radio feedback, moans, shrieks, cries for help. She rushed to the balcony rail. On the Chamber Floor, people still cowered under chairs and desks. Bodies were slumped at the great rostrum and clerk counters. Some lay writhing in the well, the carpet soaked purple with blood. But Buford wasn't there. She remembered what he'd said at Collins's funeral: eye to eye, breath to breath, with the enemy on Koh Tang. *Shit, if he's not dead, then the asshole's got him.* "Nadia, stay here; keep this girl's head elevated."

When the trainee could hardly jerk a nod, Angela embraced her quivering body. "You did good, fledgling," Angela whispered in her ear. "Now take care of Buford's aide and be strong for the rest of these people, okay?" Angela pushed up the aisle to the flashing red exit sign.

Two Capitol Police Tactical Response officers wearing blue BDUs and helmets met her at the exit. She raised her ID when they raised their MP5K 10mm submachine guns. "Get some paramedics up there damn fast!"

They looked her up and down. Ayesha Coleman's blood washed her taupe suit skirt ruby, and they could smell her emptied bowels.

The officers told Angela that this was the temporary command post—the curtained vestibule between the Cloakrooms and the Chamber entrance. CPOs, MPD officers, and frightened tourists and staffers scrambled or huddled in every direction. No clear evac plan, but she did find what looked like a ranking Tac officer barking into a radio handset. Angela on his sleeve.

He clicked off the headset. "You're the FBI agent up in the Gallery? Okay, the sit-rep is that we got here within the last five minutes. Thank God a CPO nailed the female suspect . . . the male jumped. Some drapes and some bodies broke his fall, but we think his ankle or leg's busted up. He's armed. With what, we don't know. Something got past the detectors and—"

"He's got a hostage."

"Huh?"

"Senator Brian Buford . . . I'm . . . I'm positive." She swallowed hard. "And another thing, they came in with an older white female subject. Maybe five-five, one hundred sixty pounds, fifty-five to sixty-five, pink glasses, blond . . . with a baby and a blue Graco stroller."

"Jesus . . . all right, stay here. A Critical Incident Response Team from your Washington Field Office should be on the grounds just now and—"

"My weapon is in the sergeant at arms' cabinet, sir." She pointed. "And I can ID this woman and the man." Sudden anger welled up from her gut. "The *right-wingers* in Congress voted to keep the surveillance cameras in this building to a minimum, *sir,* as a fucking . . . fucking *rebuke* to the President when he closed off Pennsylvania Avenue to car traffic after someone shot at the White House." Her face was almost beefy red, her eyes wet again. "What goes around . . . comes around. Homegrown terrorists! Seal the exits, and *give me my weapon and a radio!*"

Nothing in Angela's psyche rang the bell of irony in the statement. Suddenly, *again*, there was no such thing as warlocks or magick.

"Okay, okay." He turned. "Bust open the cabinet . . . get the lady her piece!"

No more than two minutes passed, but it groaned on like two hours. Suddenly: "Shots fired!" a Tac officer shouted, holding his handset, which he passed to his commander. "Got a twenty on the male suspect!"

"Okay, moving to the North Wing," the commander relayed, "toward the West Front Terrazzo. He's down in the Brumidi Corridors . . . West Front!"

"Male hostage?" Angela asked.

The Tac commander answered with a grim nod.

Now it was blood decorating the walls, vaulted arches, and floors of the Brumidi Corridors, not pastoral frescoes, inlaid tile, and geometric lunettes. On another day, Angela could have walked the halls alone, imagining she was in the Vatican's Loggia. Today, she labored to keep up with the squad of Capitol Police Tactical Response officers as they attempted to flush this lone assassin into the trap doubtless being set on the outside by the CIRT and MPD SWAT. She stripped off her suit jacket and pondered the location of the older woman and that baby. Checkpoints choked off any egress by terrified tourists; every screaming child in every stroller was searched.

"Okay, we got him fixed at the West Front exit," reported an officer. The pops of gunfire ahead, in the glaring sunlight and dark shadows of the outer glass doors, confirmed it. "West Front Terrazzo . . . with a hostage. ID'd as Senator Brian R. Buford."

Angela moved to the Tac commander's side. "He's trying to get out? He must know by now it's impossible. He'll be out on a broad graveled walk with no cover!"

"Affirmative. No way off the Terrazzo."

"Unless that's what he wants. We gotta move."

By the time Angela made it to the exit, two Tac officers, crouched at the door, held up their fists. The signal to halt. Two more had already crept outside and were lying on their bellies, leveling their MP5K submachine guns, yet shaking their heads.

"What's going on?" Angela demanded. She pressed her face to the glass.

With his back to the sheer Capitol West Front wall, beyond frightened tourists and staff also hugging the ground, the man stood, displaying his pistol. His arm was locked around Brian Buford's head. And an old woman and a baby in a stroller stood next to him.

"Jesus . . . *no!*" Angela pushed through the door; the Tac commander, cursing, chased after her, his men flanking him. Angela halted, two-handing her SIG. She looked up; Tac officers and MPD SWAT personnel were in the windows about thirty feet above the man's head. Yes, no way out. This long, broad terrace ending in a wall was a stage.

Blood and sweat doused the man's face, trickling onto Buford's cheek as he mashed the pistol's muzzle into the Senator's temple. The older woman was clinging close beside the two men, lifting the baby out of the stroller and holding it up in front of her. Sacrifice or human shield? So they stood, rigid and clustered like a family posing for a macabre portrait. The baby wasn't even fussing; indeed, it cooed and gurgled, disturbed more by the heat and harsh sun than by what was unfolding all around it.

Angela called out, "Ma'am . . . please just come forward with the baby and—"

"*Shut up, you black bitch!*" She gestured to the man with her head. "My son's father, my husband, fought for this country in Korea and Vietnam. Twenty-five years he'd been disabled. Damn union bosses, niggers and

Jews, liberal baby-killers . . . took everything from him. And when his pride died, he died. We are taking *back* this country from the thieves. We won't wait until they're driven out . . . elections are bogus, and the thieves will multiply like roaches in the dark."

The man bellowed, "My wife . . . gave up her life today . . . I don't want my child living in the world like this!"

The Tac lieutenant whispered, "We'll get a shot before any of this goes down, trust me."

Angela didn't. And she could feel her pulse throbbing in her neck, her temples, as the man shouted, in Buford's ear, "Open your mouth . . . open it *now*, motherfucker! Carefully." He gestured with his head as Buford obliged him. "Mom . . . do it."

The older woman switched the baby to her left arm and reached into her camp-shirt pocket to produce something that glinted in the sun. A gold coin. Angela dipped her head, so slightly. *Oh, no.*

The women reached across her son and placed the coin in Buford's mouth. Angela heard the Tac commander say, in a lower tone, probably into his mike, "Does anyone have a shot?"

A blue MPD helicopter traversed the Mall, keeping the local news choppers, buzzing like flies to carrion, at bay. Another chopper hovered close, its shadow approaching. Sharpshooters, Angela figured. *I can't hear a damn thing from the rotor noise!*

The man hissed to Buford, "If you spit that gold out, nigger, you die."

With the coin clench in his molars, Buford growled back, "I'll die anyway."

The man laughed. "Not necessarily, asshole." He turned his head. "Mom . . . we prepared for this, right? It's time."

Angela moved forward; she couldn't hear from the chopper noise. The old woman didn't seem so brave now; she was crouching—still clutching the infant—and reaching into a yellow vinyl bag that looked as if it held spare diapers, bottles. Angela froze. *Sweet Jesus, here it comes.* Scopes were being aimed. Yet, slowly, the woman pulled out one of those small, canted plastic baby bottles. The sighs of relief from the corps of cops were audible. But then the women shook the bottle. Milky, frothy, and dripping with condensation like cold formula . . . *what the fuck?* She flicked off the plastic cap. Angela gasped. Replacing the nipple was a conical foil plug that looked as if it had a bent paper clip inserted through it.

"God, what is *that*," Angela whispered, aloud. Her only chance was a desperate bluff. She raised her SIG and slowly aimed—at the now squirming baby.

Both father and grandmother looked at her, mouths agape. Angela knew the Tac officers in the windows above would be dropping smoke and firing their rappelling lines.

"This child will die by my 'nigger bitch' hands, not by yours. Now put the baby aside." She glanced at Buford. Serenely, he closed his eyes slowly and opened them.

"You kill my daughter . . . this nation will rise up and tear your kind to pieces!"

"Yeah, but you'll die knowing it was me who murdered your baby."

The older woman had broken into tears and was now shaking so violently that it looked as if she'd drop the child. Angela's strategy was working on her.

"Ma'am, please . . . I don't want to kill her, but I will, to stop this!"

And suddenly . . . a scream. A man's scream. Echoing off the limestone and marble, until consumed by the humid air and boundless, hot blue sky.

"I am the Archangel Abdiel, and here I make my mark!"

The man shoved Buford forward. The glass in the windows above exploded. Smoke canisters and stun grenades and rappelling ropes showered down with the glass, but before it hit the ground, Angela watched the man reach across to his mother's outstretched hand, grip that baby bottle, yank out that metal pin . . .

A bright flash. A fireball. A delayed *foom*. A tenth of a second later, the concussion wave hurled Buford, Angela, and the other Tac officers back, hard, on the ground. When Angela looked up at the spot where a family had been standing, she saw only scorched stone. Three charred corpses—one very, very small. She sank her head to the gravel and wept.

Security guards and CPOs herded frantic staffers out of the Dirksen Building's East First Street, N.E., lobby as alarm buzzers screeched overhead. Struggling against the human tide was Samuel Ibhebesi, wearing a sweat-stained checkered shirt, battered straw fedora, and sandals that were ready to lose their soles and straps if not repaired. He removed his hat once inside and waddled up to a beleaguered security guard.

"Excuse me, sah? I am here to see Senator Brian Buford of California."

"Huh? What . . . listen, turn right around okay? This building's being evacuated!"

"B-but I have an appointment . . . the INS in California threatens my family and—"

"Did you hear me? There's been a shooting and explosion at the Capitol just now—didn't you see the helicopters, the police cars?"

The old man almost dropped his hat, stunned.

"Dead people, wounded . . . all on the Senate Floor," the guard revealed, against regulations. "We hear one might be Senator Buford . . . we don't know."

Samuel ground his molars. "Then . . . I will *mourn* him." He turned and stormed out, as if with the legs of a thirty-year-old.

34

"IF YOU LOOK AT THE NEXT slide on the wall screen, you see the blowup view of the weapon taken off the female subject from the Senate Gallery shooting. A complete semiautomatic nine-millimeter pistol: ninety-nine point two percent of the components are ceramics and composites."

Bureau of Alcohol, Tobacco & Firearms Special Agent Matt LaHaye's statement spawned murmurs around the ten-foot oval table, in a darkened room. Only Angela was silent, as was Victor Styles, who paced in the shadows, hands shoved deep in the pockets of his razor-creased suit trousers.

"The male subject was destroyed in the explosion." LaHaye gestured to the components with his laser pointer. "The material's an amalgam of General Electric's Lexan and Du Pont Arylon, with the barrel and chamber action reinforced with a derivative of the composite material used in the skin of the new F-22 fighter. The only metal on this weapon is the tip of the firing pin and the main action spring, both of which were concealed in the fake video camera, along with the two simple ammo feed clips, also made from this Lexan-Arylon mix."

Claude Baker of the Washington Field Office questioned, "You mean to tell me that the slugs and cartridge casings were composites, too?"

LaHaye nodded. *"That's* the real scary part. The rounds were hidden in the frame of that Snugli baby-carrier thing. Undetectable. With practice, it probably only took them sixty seconds to assemble the pistols, an additional sixty to load the rounds into the clips and then pop the clips in. Inspector Bivens's and Agent-Trainee Riccio's firsthand accounts confirm this. These people were soldiers . . . well-equipped, professionally trained. No matching prints, DNA, anything. Like ghosts."

"Hit the lights," Remo Donatello growled in the dark. The voice was tinged with the exasperated tone of a leader who knew damn well his Eastern European sabbatical was ill-timed, ill-advised. And who was ready to displace his guilt on the woman who'd put his child in harm's way. Yet again. Angela was the only person in the room perspiring, despite the frosty flurries from the air-conditioning vents overhead.

The overhead tracking snapped on; the blinds opened automatically to the sun-baked panorama of limestone and granite monuments. Angela was seated next to Lupo; ten other people were at the table, and aides ringed the room. Victor Styles still walked the cobalt-colored rug, and his distance distracted Donatello's eyes as the Director barked out command directives.

"I hope your families all have pictures of you on the mantel, because you aren't going home for a long time. In addition, all transfers, details, out-of-division assignments, are suspended unless I approve." He paused. "Anything to add, Vick?"

Styles bit his lip as he nodded, but he didn't speak for a few seconds. To Angela, he looked as if he were brooding, resigned. Wasn't this carnage his wet dream come true? A nation outraged at the right wing? One liberal Senator in intensive care, another dead, along with innocent tourists and staffers. The usually strident Fox News Channel, cowed. Talk radio brigands like Rush Limbaugh and Sean Hannity, now silent.

Woodruff Sessions, rocking in his chair, drawled, "We're waiting, Mr. Deputy Director."

"Yes . . . yes," Styles muttered. "Indeed, I would ask that your division, Woody, be put at the disposal of Scofield's CID, Lupo's ISD, and the joint Critical Incident Response Team, BAFT, and Secret Service commands. We are in need of your counterespionage and counterterrorism expertise."

Frank Lupo lightly tapped Angela's arm, which was still sore from her fall to gravel when the firebomb detonated. "I guess we're still in charge of the investigation, Tigress."

"Don't speak too soon," Angela whispered back to him.

Sessions protested Styles's directive. "Victor, under different circumstances I'd agree, but I believe the bulk of my people should be guarding the back door to the barn, from the terrorists on the *outside*—and those who've already infiltrated—while Frank, Bob, the AFT et al. hunt down our home-grown scum on the *inside.*"

"Terrorists are terrorists," Lupo suddenly broke in. "Whether named Abdullah or McVeigh."

Sessions retorted, "Frank, I pray that punting *that* distinction won't have dire consequences for us in the future."

Director Donatello waved his hands, expounding, "Before anybody gets more agitated over turf, you ought to know I was at Camp David with the President and the Attorney General until four A.M. The Speaker and Majority Leader Lott were there, and VP Gore invited someone from Governor Bush's campaign. Meaning, we all know it's white-knuckle time and we are *all* on the same page. Extremists turning the symbol of our democracy into a shooting gallery months before Americans go to polls? Nah, this isn't some third-world shit-hole subject to rebels or juntas every time somebody's pissed off. I personally assured the President and Ms. Reno that each and every Amesha Spentas cell will be exposed and smashed"—he glared at Angela—"and that the investigation does not again stray from agreed-on paths."

Angela glared back, but only for an instant. She was a good soldier. She looked down at her hands, humbly clasped on her briefing binder. Lupo nudged her reassuringly. It didn't help.

Styles now hovered over Angela's shoulder. "Think of this as mental sorbet," he said to Angela in a lifeless, tired monotone. "Clearing your brain's palate. Dump your South African–related leads, these peculiar interrelationships among victims Collins, Davidson, and Senator Buford . . . trips to holistic medicine shops." His voice trailed off.

AD Sessions spoke up, with AD Scofield nodding along. "Victor, may we get a clarification on—"

Styles cut him off with a look of blank ferocity. "The Inspector will be working with BAFT Agent LaHaye once more, along with Dick Wasserman in CID's Civil Rights Section. In other words, the task force goes back to what it was already tasked to do." Styles looked to Lupo this time, not Sessions or Scofield. "Acceptable to you, Frank?"

"Message received, Vick."

Angela protested, "Mr. Styles, sir, I still think we must study the victimology—the connections and commonalities among Collins, even Mr. Whiting, Maynard Mullinix, and the fact that these gold coins are ancient symbols, not U.S.-minted gold dollars as at the Capitol, other Amesha Spentas scenes."

Eleven perplexed frowns pointed in Angela's direction. Styles moved off and finally took his chair. Lupo whispered through gritted teeth, "Jesus, just let it go."

As Styles oddly looked away, nibbling at a thumbnail, Remo Donatello rose up. "We're finished with the briefing portion. Now, we're going into executive session with the assistant directors and our interagency liaisons. Francis, please dismiss your Inspector. Have her prepped for the operational meeting this afternoon."

"G'head," Lupo said. "I'll be out in an hour."

Angela stood, swallowed hard, and moved to the conference room door. But then she turned and looked to the Director. "Your daughter, sir . . . she reacted with a cool head, bravely, professionally."

"Duly noted," Donatello grumbled. He never even acknowledged that, regardless of what had led Angela and Nadia to the Senate Gallery, their presence there had saved lives. But he knew it. They all did.

35

SAMUEL IBHEBESI MOPPED HIS WRINKLED black brow with a crisp white handkerchief as he watched a stray dog greedily lap fetid rainwater from a discarded tire. Samuel was standing behind a huge, dented green Dumpster filled with putrefying garbage; against it lay an old Philco refrigerator. Samuel replaced his straw fedora on his head and cursed, "Fuck Simple City, *akotha*. American niggers. No respect for demselves."

"Simple City" was the neighborhood tag for this white-brick labyrinth of low-rise apartments. A familiar voice ended his thoughts.

"You look different, man . . . s'up? More healthy and shit."

Samuel squinted through the midday sun's glare at the outline of a tall, lean body, head sprouting a medusan tangle of braids, the end of each clacking with a small seashell or tiny steel beads. Samuel pointed to a crinkled Hecht's shopping bag at his feet. *"Ishungu* in there. Pain gone. I am strong. I feel young."

Stringbean Coy moved into the shade, shoving aside a rusted barbecue grill. *"Then why the fuck you need me?"* he exclaimed. But his anger evaporated when Samuel held up an index finger. A promise of pain. "Yo, man . . . I decided to hide it here."

Stringbean opened the door to the junked fridge. Samuel looked inside and nodded. Leering at him from the top rusted shelf were the bronze-tack eyes of a mahogany statuette. Bronze also sheathed the grain of its carved

205

mouth and teeth, making a smile like a jack-o'-lantern. Its hewn arms rested on its hips, a boastful presentation of the thick, erect phallus protruding from between its fat legs.

Samuel touched the fetish's smile. Gooey, coagulated blood oozed from the tiny bronze teeth onto his bony, callused fingertips. So he sneered at the grinning wooden imp, calling with his mind, in Zulu: *I sought refuge, not a vessel. I seek justice, not your feast. You serve me. The darkness.* "Dis place," Samuel said as he slammed the door, "is where fetish will digest its feast." He then aimed his filmy eyes at Stringbean. "Food. You bring food for my apartment, in Tupperware, like a woman? It smell like a white woman's. Where you get? You steal?"

"Got my mother, my bitches, cookin' for me, man. Washing clothes, too. Why?"

"You n'wash in days. You bring *other* thing I ask you to get for me? *Insila?*"

Stringbean hung his head to search his Nike sport sandals, as worn and torn as the dusty leather sandals on his master's clawed feet. Stringbean mumbled, "I don't . . . don't got it." As the old man's lip curled, Stringbean pleaded, "I'm sorry, shit . . . the witch, man . . . the muvfuckin' witch. 'Bout to cap me wid that Smitty .38. I musta dropped it in her shop. Or . . . or when I came back, to do her, maybe it fell out. Ya said y'only need a *little*. Even one damn piece of hair!"

Samuel grabbed Stringbean's grimy T-shirt, driving a man fully a foot and a half taller and almost sixty pounds heavier to his knees. "Den police find?"

Shaking with terror, Stringbean mumbled back, "Nah . . . nah, man. Five-O be all up in there, but ain't done shit but dust for prints."

Samuel hissed, "I send Lion's Regiment for it . . . and correct you mistake."

Samuel heard footsteps on the other side of the Dumpster; two teenage boys soon rounded the corner. Both wore uniforms: white spandex wave caps over their sweaty heads, drooping white nylon tanks, T-shirts draped around their necks like capes, baggy denim carpenter shorts sagging at their hips. One boy, sucking on the dripping remnants of a cherry Popsicle, lifted his tank top to expose a 9mm peeking up from his waistband. The stray dog, having drunk its fill from the tire, had the good sense to scamper away.

"What th'fuck, Bean?" one boy yelled. "Niggah you know you ain't s'pose t'come at us less you pay the toll, dumb-ass muvfuckah."

The "toll." Tribute, or a passport, for doing personal business in the territory of the Simple City Crew. These boys were merely the pages, look-outs. The Crew—Stringbean's buddies—were out selling their products. The word obviously hadn't trickled down to the youngsters that Stringbean was to get a pass, and when they fully comprehended that Stringbean was prone before an even older, feeble, crook-backed man, they burst out in laughter. One boy drew his weapon, a Browning, as he guffawed.

"You be suckin' *this* piece of shit's shriveled dick? Makes me sick, Gee!" He yanked the pistol's slide; his cohort mirthfully exhorted him to fire.

He did. At his own temple. Blood, brains, and bone sprayed the other boy's face. The other screamed. Then ran. Samuel had been shaking his dry *ishungu*, plucked from the Hecht's bag. He didn't laugh. He didn't sneer. He just sighed and said, "He tell others to leave us alone. No to come here anymore."

As Stringbean cowered against the Dumpster, Samuel dipped his fingers into the boy's head wound, collected the hot blood, and dripped it inside the gourd.

"Now, *thikoloshe,* my Ama Simba go to bring back *insila,* for justice."

Samuel stepped lightly over the boy's twitching body and moved up non-chalantly to the Metrobus shelter. Just another old black man, waiting for the Number 45 for Naylor Road, S.E., with an empty shopping bag.

Stringbean quickly sprinted away from the Dumpster. Not in terror, but disgust. *Old fool,* he thought. *Your time's already up.*

36

ON SULTRY SUMMER NIGHTS, GETTING AN outdoor table was impossible unless you rolled in very late, as Angela and her friends often did, after a house party or movie or date. Not tonight, with a nation stunned by the events at the Capitol. Half the tables were empty; the bookstore was quiet. Strollers in the Circle, amongst the other cafés, shops, bars, were few. There should have been hundreds.

Angela picked through the last of her mango chicken salad and said, "Daddy, Mommy, thanks for coming down. I don't know when I'll get a chance to see you."

Barbara Bivens shrugged. "Well, Pam asked for you. Byron junior wanted to know if you'll get another medal. How about that!" The laugh was tinged with a mother's fear. "Kobi loved the Buzz Lightyear doll you sent. You remembered his birthday, through all this horror."

"I'm a Rolodex, Mommy," Angela joked. "Aren't I, George?"

She nudged Vallas, who was seated next to her, nursing a Corona, lime wedge and all. Vallas laughed.

Dr. Bivens fussed, "I don't get it, baby—you show them there's something else out there beside these neo-Nazi scum, yet they shut you down, order you to ignore the obvious? So who killed Les, Angel? Do they even care?" He swilled the last of his wine.

"They care, Daddy," Angela answered softly, pensively. "But the Capitol attack trumps everything, consumes everything. I have my orders." She then drained her own chardonnay, smiled, and said, "So . . . dessert? Coffee?"

"Get a cup of decaf for your mom, and some key lime pie for me. We're going to check out this weird bookstore back in here."

"Two forks for the pie," Barbara added with a giggle.

"Then two damn pieces," Dr. Bivens batted back with mock outrage as he stood to help his wife out of her chair. The couple moved into the restaurant's eclectic bookstore, leaving Vallas and Angela alone.

A warm breeze tussled both the green elm leaves and Vallas's straight black hair. He pushed it out of his eyes, huffing, "You just lay down and take it, huh? Punt all your theories—not that you've shared everything with me—and march off like a good soldier."

"Shut up, George. That's what we do. And I am going to be a part of this war. I will not sideline myself in Dr. Sylvia Myers's office, babbling about living Zulu shadows, and eating mandrake root and nightshade." Angela ran her fingers down across a weary face. Makeup caked from the heat and the day that had started at 6 A.M. Layered, bobbed hair fallen and frizzed. Contacts blurred, dry and stuck to her eyeballs.

"Aw-ight . . . I feel you. But somethin' s'up whitchew . . . I feel that, too. You can't be movin' on two divergent investigations: your own personal one, and bustin' up these fools who shot up the Capitol. I know you, gurl, don't forget that."

Everybody thinks they "know" me, she mulled inwardly. "Thought I did, too."

"Angie, you say something?"

"No . . . just thinking." She was about to confess that she would indeed pursue this man who thinks he's a warlock, a necromancer, on her own terms, apart from Amesha Spentas, when her sore eyes caught Alvin and Sharon, strolling along the parallel-parked cars on Eighteenth Street. This time, they were looking right at Angela. By then Vallas had put his arm up on Angela's chair.

"Yo, the Mad Moon Man hisself!" Vallas called to Alvin. "The FBI's first and only forensic astronomer! S'up?" He extended his hand over the rail to the sidewalk; Alvin took it and shook.

Sharon fumbled, "We, uh, heard from Carmen you'd be here. Know you're busy . . . know what you went through in the Senate Gallery."

"It's okay," Angela said with a hopeful sigh. Somehow, pettiness was a waste. "Want to sit? My parents're here. I can go get them."

"Nah," Alvin said, fighting a lump in his throat as he looked at Angela. "We got reservations at Raku . . . lots of tables, too, alfresco. Folks afraid to come outdoors. But we wanted to stop by."

"You ain't afraid," Vallas remarked.

Sharon smiled. "Because we know we got an angel on our shoulders." When Angela mouthed a "Thank you," Sharon continued, "The partners sent everyone home today, like yesterday, out of shock."

"It's a full-time job worrying about m'gurl, here!" Vallas exclaimed.

"Uh-huh." Alvin nodded. "So—you reassuring her parents?"

Vallas pulled his arm off Angela's chair; Alvin's tone had gone cold quickly. Vallas said, "I gotta run to the boy's room. See y'all." He got up and edged past the waitress.

Angela sighed, shaking her head. "What's wrong, Alvin? You want to hash this out now, here? Well, I'm sorry I used you. Used you, too, Shar. As crutches, as foils."

"Angel," Sharon said, "you don't need to—"

"Let her be," Alvin cut in. "Gw'on."

"Alvin, you should have *known*. In six months—no real passion? I couldn't handle that. Warmth, yes, but not intimacy. And that night after Chi Cha, was that intimacy? No, not for me. I was wrong again."

Sharon's eyes narrowed at Alvin, but Angela wasn't going to sting her friend with the truth. And Alvin wouldn't have told Sharon; sweet men aren't always naive.

"Sharon, yeah . . . we stayed up all night, holding each other, fully clothed, dodging the truth. Listen, I want you both to know, I'm over Trey, and what he did to me. Whether I find a man to love me isn't important. What should be important for me, for you, as my *friends*, is how many people I can help, lives I can save."

Alvin's eyes got a little wetter. "Please give your parents my love . . . and you take care. *Please* take care."

Sharon leaned over the rail and kissed Angela's cheek. Angela replied, "Never stopped needing you, never stopped wanting to laugh at your dry little voice, your freckles."

Sharon nodded, then said, "Carm said she'd call. She's busy over at the Moultrie Courthouse . . . says some brother who killed her witness might have killed again, over at Potomac Gardens. Not even Brett can help her— everyone's on this Capitol shooting, the firebomb."

"So we survive, move on, huh? Not me. I'll see what I can do to help her."

The couple moved down the street to Raku's Asian bistro as Vallas returned from his putative men's room visit.

"Angie," Vallas said, squinting, "so you and him ain't—"

Angela held a palm in the air, fighting back her tears. "Not now, George. Please, not now."

Angela's parents stepped back outside, too, just as the hot breeze kicked up. "Couldn't tell, but wasn't that Professor Markham, and Sharon?" Barbara asked.

"No, Mom," Angela answered. "Looked like them." When Vallas grimaced, Angela patted his hand. "George, after we finish coffee, can you run me back to HQ? I need some stuff from my office to take home. Get prepped." She faced her parents. "Y'all have keys to my place. Don't want you to have to brave the Baltimore-Washington Parkway at night, after all this wine we drank."

"We're fine," Dr. Bivens replied stoically. "I-95 to Caton Avenue, Caton to Hilton Parkway, and home. Been such a long time, you've forgotten the route?"

" 'Course not, Daddy. *Memory* is what I live on now." She clapped her hands. "Now," she gushed, killing off the gray mood, "we need s'more forks to damage this kickin' key lime pie!"

37

AROUND NINE O'CLOCK, VALLAS FLIPPED on the harsh fluorescent lighting in Angela's office. Angela moved to her desk and floor lamps,
switched them on, then turned off the overheads. "Hurts my eyes, my
head," she told Vallas. Indeed, the glow was easier, comfortable. Vallas shed
his suit jacket and tasseled Italian loafers and crumpled onto the small sofa
under the window; beyond twinkled the lights of Pennsylvania Avenue, all
the way to the Freedom Plaza on Fourteenth Street, and the White House.
America's Champs-Elysées. Angela locked the door, as was her custom
when working late.

She'd already slung her suit jacket over her office chair. Her white silk
surplice blouse, which resembled a wrapped camisole, felt glued to her skin.

After catching a stare at the blouse, Vallas fawned, "No matter how
funky everyone else looks an' smells at the end of a hot, frustrating-ass shift,
you *always* manage to look together."

"In the eye of the beholder, George. Want a water or a Coke? There's
some in the minifridge."

"Nah, I'm cool." He swung his legs off the sofa.

"Well, then be a gentleman and grab me a Perrier outta there, please."

He did. She'd already propped her stockinged feet on her credenza. She
held the cold green bottle to her forehead as Vallas sat on the edge of
the desk.

"You ever think about Kristi?" Angela began drowsily.

"Uh-huh. Always smile . . . really bright. No matter how jacked up the situation. She'd always go on about you, about how strong you were one minute, then the next, girl shit, like how she's gonna shop at Banana Republic or Bebe to look just like you! My gurl was *fun*-ny. . . ."

Angela closed her eyes. Her voice was faint, strained. "I miss her terribly. I have nightmares . . . Pluto, shooting her. I have nightmares about a lot of things, George."

"Well, I just wake up, roll over, and think about the good times we had. C-1—best damn crim squad in the Nest, baby. Rockin' the slugs who slung the rock and 'love boat' and smack. Slammin' thieves, stone-cold killers. Then along you came, and *bam* . . . you made us better, stronger."

Eyes open, she tilted her head to him. "That's actually the nicest thing anyone's said to me in two days." The disingenuous "Well dones" from on high didn't count.

Vallas grinned his sexy grin; Angela moved off her chair and then commanded, "Turn your head. Otherwise, an FBI beat-down will follow."

He shrugged, twisted away from her. Angela was sick of the heat, the gritty discomfort. She yearned for a respite from the doubt, from pending confrontations. And, she prayed, from pending horror. No witches or archangels or politics. Or friends or family. For just a little while. *Lord, just a little while.* She hiked up her suit skirt and peeled herself out of her hose, dumping them in the mesh wastebasket by the desk. "Okay, all done." She yawned. Angela plopped back in her chair, resting bare, sore feet and legs on the desk.

"What?" Angela teased. "You think I was getting *nekkid* for you or something?"

Vallas leaned over, still grinning, "No doubt," he teased. "I heard the sisters love us white dudes with so-called Latino or Mediterranean looks, right?"

"Hmm . . . and where'd you hear this?"

"*Essence* magazine." He laughed.

"Damn, then it *must* be true, huh? Don't think you're as sweet as your mama's baklava, all right? Just talk to me. Nothing heavy. Put on the stereo, chill . . ."

He slid off the desk and stepped to the boom box, musing, "Wish we had some of my granddad's ouzo now, actually. Lord, we need it."

"We're already too buzzed."

Vallas thumbed through the CD case. "You ain't got no Outkast up in here?"

He did find something she'd like, however: an old Sade CD. He slipped it into the boom box and returned to the desk. Vallas, hands warm, moved over to massage the bones of her right foot, then her toes. It was a professional touch, like the trainer's in the Hoover Building gym. The song and his fingers were draining the tension from her legs, her hips.

"I beg your pardon, Special Agent Vallas?" Angela mock-protested. "I am your superior . . . and my feet are nasty."

"Nah."

"Then . . . awwww, that's good right there . . . grab this Body Shop lotion bottle out of my left lower desk drawer so you can do it right." He was already doing it right.

Gliding on dollops of peppermint-scented lotion, Vallas's olive-tone hands moved to her left foot. Kneaded her left calf. Then her right. Then he stopped, as if he'd reached an imaginary boundary: physical, emotional. Angela smiled, closed her eyes. And that was when Angela wanted a respite from boundaries.

Vallas rolled behind her, molding the tired muscles and ligaments along the nape of her neck to her shoulders, bare now because he'd pushed aside the blouse's loops, and eased down her bra straps.

"Careful," Angela whispered. "That arm's still sore, from the . . ." She couldn't even say *explosion.*

He kissed the bruise, then moved his mouth to Angela's neck. She heard his sigh. Felt his breath, his wet lips, his beard stubble, on her throat, her earlobes. His fingers moved slowly under the blouse, to her pulsing heart, lingering there as she grasped his encircling arms. He lingered on the lacy fabric cups of her La Perla bra. Vallas's touch oozed through the silk to her nipples. Incongruous sensations rushed through her: electricity, deep melting warmth.

Angela turned, raised her mouth up to his mouth. Up on her toes now. She snapped the window-shade bar; the shades popped down as he unbuttoned his dress shirt. His chest muscles and delts bulged through a white, ribbed tank undershirt. He yanked the shirt off, showing the thick, soft hair Angela imagined all Greek men had.

The hard chest, the soft cushion of hair over it, felt so good when Angela nuzzled it. Smelled so good: cologne, sweat. His nipples, peeking through the hair, tasted good. And when she and Vallas moved to her sofa, he tasted her nipples, lifted her out of her panties. Massaged her nubby wetness. She stroked him, too; it was uncircumcised, and she'd never felt that before. Lips and tongues seared one another, yet Vallas was now trying to pull away to sear her, lower. But she urged his face up, shaking her head. She just wanted to grasp, hold, feel, forget. *Just for a little while, Lord.*

"Angie, um . . . let's get dressed. I got some condoms, some brandy, at my place."

Angela touched a finger to his lips, made him sit still, then straddled him. He smiled, head dipped. Brash Vallas was suddenly shy. He shuddered as she guided him inside her. She didn't move, didn't grind; he didn't know whether he should thrust. She gripped his shoulders, then buried her face in his sinewy neck. They undulated slowly, fluidly, then faster. Harder. Then Angela heard him gasp, moan. She cried out, too, tears moistening her eyes. A guttural cry from Vallas met hers. She lifted herself off him as he came— hot, copious spurts, landing on both their bellies, his thighs.

"Oh, shit . . . s-sorry, Angie," he gasped as his body tensed.

"S'okay." Angela reached down into the slick, viscous heat between her own legs to finish herself. Her other hand cradled Vallas's head. A long moan, staccato whimpers. Twitches. Then thrashes as she came, panting.

They wrapped their arms around each other, her still astride him, semen oozing onto the throw covering the sofa upholstery and her not giving a damn. And they didn't move until there was a knock on the locked door.

"Maintenance! Hullo?" The voice had a Hispanic cadence.

"Aw, shit," Vallas whispered, frozen in fear.

Angela covered his mouth and bit her lip.

"Work late again, Inspector?" the voice said. "We come tomorrow. G'night!"

Vallas and Angela separated. He rolled onto the floor to grab his ribbed boxer briefs. Angela drew her arms around herself.

"Um, Angie . . . you okay?"

This time she smiled gently. "We had our 'little while.' Nothing more. Cool?"

He nodded. He crawled to the sofa, gripped her right hand. He lay his head on the edge of the cushion. Angela combed his straight black hair with her short, honey-brown fingers. And while she soothed him, she sat erect, eyes unblinking. Pretty, damaged, and yet still strangely functional. Like a piece of china with a hairline crack.

*   *   *

The Wedgwood plate had shattered into shards on the ceramic-tile kitchen floor. One sliver poked into the meat of Nadia's hand. Red blood on white china.

Nadia paced, barefoot despite the peril and the pain, tears streaming, saliva dripping. "I almost died!" she screamed, fingering her little cylindrical talisman. "And now you leave, you fucking *bitch!* You swore . . . you swore you'd never leave me again!"

The refrigerator was empty and defrosted; in the casting pantry all wicca were sworn to maintain, mandrake root shriveled, and the goddess's patchouli and bergamot spoiled. Half-packed shipping boxes lay around Arianne's condo, including the one Nadia had torn into—filled with the china they'd bought together during Nadia's last leave from Quantico. A stack of mail teetered on the kitchen counter. All unopened, save for one large, square envelope. Embossed. Engraved. Charlottesville, Virginia, postmark. It caught Nadia's eye as she summoned the composure to dig out the shard and hold her hand under the kitchen faucet's hot stream.

With wet fingers, she grabbed the inner invitation. Shipley-Neal Family Reunion. July 4, 2000. Monticello. Two P.M. Summer semiformal. All of these people were descendants of Thomas Jefferson, both direct and by marriage. It was patrician inbreeding, brought to scrutiny by the Sally Hemings affair. Arianne was supposed to attend either Virginia or William & Mary, as had generations of her family—her father's Shipleys and her mother's Neals. And Arianne was supposed to marry a Hampton-Sydney or Washington & Lee frat boy and receive Wedgwood china for her wedding. Instead, she escaped to New York, Sarah Lawrence College, and Nadia's lips. From Daughters of the American Revolution and debutante balls, to the wicca. And Nadia never asked why. But stuck in the RSVP card was a small pink Post-it. Nadia recognized Arianne's mother's handwriting. Tiny enough to fit on a Post-it. Psychotically neat. *Pls. come; we need you as we weather this double Negro storm of the Hemings thing and your aunt's nightmare with this boy, mercifully ending in his execution. Mother.*

Nadia recalled Arianne's remote comment from college, about how her aunt Mary Washington Neal Jones was always the iconoclast in the clan, relating at family gatherings her disgust at how the Neals had made their money in Alexandria long ago, on the flesh of black slaves. Neal & Co. The Shipleys considered themselves *innocent* Virginia planters and thoroughbred breeders—of horses, not slaves. Mary convinced her husband, a trucking magnate from Roanoke named Hank Jones, to adopt a nonwhite baby, before Arianne was born, and no one really spoke of Mary and Hank too much after that.

When the dagger of dread, of realization, speared Nadia's spine, the invitation dropped in the sink to pucker in the steam and scalding water. Nadia slapped her still-bleeding palm over her lips. She saw Antoine Jones's face, and she croaked, *"Miss Porcupine . . ."*

Dazed, Nadia stumbled into the bedroom. Both the pillows and heaps of clothes still on hangers stifled her cries. Antoine—"Shaka Seven"—was her lover's cousin? She swallowed the sick, bitter blindness that Angela must have tasted when she'd begun to unravel the truth about Trey Williams and his brother. But why was Arianne gone? Three days with no word? Not even a frantic call after the Senate Gallery attack? And the fridge, cleaned out, yet nothing really packed?

Nadia raised her wet, swollen face to grope for a tissue on the night table. Instead, her hand dipped into a cardboard box perched atop the clock radio. She sat up on the bed and pulled the box onto her lap. She couldn't even feel the pain of her cut anymore; the blood had coagulated. So she plucked out the tissue paper covering three photographs. *Very* old ones, which looked as if they'd been cut from rusty frames. Sniffling, winking out tears, Nadia found that all three were of the same person, from teenage boy to grizzled old man. There were smudged, penciled descriptions on the back of each picture. Nadia remembered Arianne's condemnation of the Shipleys' British cousins in history classes at Sarah Lawrence: "racist imperialist lackeys" destroying indigenous peoples. They'd served Queen Victoria, and then her son Edward, wherever the Union Jack fluttered over black, brown, and yellow people: from the heat and dust of India, to the mountainous frontiers of Afghanistan, to battling the "Fuzzy Wuzzies" and Islamic cavalry of the Mahdi before Khartoum, to the siege of Beijing during the Boxer Rebellion. Arianne Shipley, a witch, was the descendant of Frank Shipley, DSO, Twenty-fourth Regiment, His Majesty's Welsh Guards.

The first picture, dated 1859, was a tiny daguerrotype of a teenaged Private Frank about to be shipped to India, muttonchop sideburns just sprouting. Next, a larger portrait: a 1903 Eastman photograph of sixty-two-year-old King's Regimental Sergeant Major Frank, muttonchops snow-white. And with the third, the images of Antoine Jones in Nadia's head roiled, melted. 1879. Thirty-eight-year-old Color Sergeant Frank, muttonchops just touched with gray, assigned to Lord Chelmsford's campaign against the Zulu king Cetshwayo. The text on the back described the scene. He was displaying his trophies: a wrinkled, withered stump of an old man with rotted, pointy teeth, and a little naked girl, after standing fast against the Zulu Impi, in a meadow called Ulundi.

Nadia dropped the picture back into the box, her eyes flooding once more. "Goddess, what has she done . . . *Goddess, what do I do?*"

Nadia slid off the bed and returned to the kitchen to smash every remaining piece of china in that box.

38

CARMEN WILCOX'S NEW HEAT PUMP had blown a fuse in her re-habbed wood-frame row house off Grant Circle. The choice was between AC or lights and television, and thus the place glowed with candles. Angela was sitting on the hardwood floor in the living room; Carmen rested above her in a plush chair, plaiting and braiding her friend's sorrel-colored hair. A turquoise peignoir draped Carmen's curvy brown form; Carmen was not one for the cotton tank top and boxers Angela wore.

"Angel, Vallas is a white boy who works for you. Not cool. Can you trust him?"

"I don't know."

Carmen tugged at a stubborn patch of hair. "Listen, you're welcome to stay as long as you want. Mallory called me. They think this Stringbean's killed again, over in Southeast. Found his prints and a dead boy at the Potomac Gardens projects."

Sighing, Angela said, "I was ready to help you with that, but now . . . *Lord.* It's like watching some cloying romantic comedy on cable, then hav-ing the plot suddenly turn into *The Matrix.* I'm on my own now with this. Just like with Trey."

"Finding refuge in Vallas was not the answer. Maybe you should talk to Dr. Myers?"

"When I find what I'm looking for, that will be my therapy."

"I'm not messing with you, sweetie."

Angela kissed Carmen's hand. "I know."

Angela's cell phone, recharging on the floor by the chair, tweeted. Angela crouched to view the caller-ID readout. Unknown number. She answered anyway.

"Nadia is this you? What's wrong?"

"Ari's gone. And . . . and you gotta come. *Come now.* Youssa's shop."

"We went there with Detective Mallory. And your reassignment's effective tomorrow."

"Fucking Ari's been lying to me! I know it starts here, with Youssa!"

Click.

Yellow police tape remained taut across a picket of parking meters in front of Youssa's shop. MPD warning notices plastered the one intact plate-glass window; the place was dark but for a strange, faint red-to-yellow glow.

The door was unlocked, the alarm appeared deactivated. Angela's angry calls for Nadia brought glances from pedestrians still roaming the Georgetown sidewalks despite that late hour.

Angela hit the lights and locked the door behind her. The shop was how she'd left it, days ago. Same black smudges from MPD CSU fingerprint-dusting powder on the walls, cash register, and glass counters. Now she was certain Nadia had jimmied the lock, for the glow was from Youssa's iMac monitor. Someone had booted it up; the giraffe screen saver was the source of the glow. If the door had been unlocked for too long, the computer would have been pilfered by now. She noted the door to the fetish room. Shut and spotted with D.C. Health Department and U.S. Customs Service decals. And the whole shop smelled like chemical disinfectant. Incense, cinnamon, jasmine, and gingerroot—even the stale musk of the day fetishes—had been overpowered.

Suddenly, a hollow thud sounded from behind the door to the fetish room. Then another, and what sounded like a faint whisper. Angela grabbed the door handle and shoved, cursing, "Nadia, damn it, what—"

The stench rocked her back on her heels. Layered, rarefied: sickly sweet, like decomposition, upon a layer of burnt flesh, upon a waft of smoldering charcoal, upon a hint of sulfur. Reeling, Angela reached for the door handle, but a pall of smoke seemed to suck her inside the room as surely as it sucked the air out of her lungs. The door slammed behind her, as if the smoke were alive. And it glowed. Not from the fluorescent tube sputtering above. Rather, from orange flashes tinging the edges of a room that seemed now to have no walls, floor, or ceiling. Bordered only by what looked like insects—moths, flies—fluttering? No, exploding into sparks, glowing like wood embers. Then she heard male whispers, as in the tunnel under Rittenhouse Square. Her dry, tickling mouth formed a scream.

Out of the smoke, in an instant, she saw heads, shoulders materialize. Black faces, caked with gray soot. Yellow eyes with no pupils. Skin mottled, peppercorn hair dusted with that yellowish ash, paint? Angela jammed her hand into her shoulder bag for her SIG-Sauer. She collapsed before she could feel the trigger. When she hit a now firm floor, the smoke vanished, though the burnt stench remained. And the concrete was as warm as skin, not cold. Angela moaned, fearing her heart would explode.

"*Oh my God,*" Angela heard. It was Nadia's voice. The trainee found her mentor doubled over, beneath the popping lights. Trembling.

"Help . . . help me up," Angela muttered. She clung to Nadia's meaty, freckled arm and rose to her feet. "M-my head . . . I . . . must have had . . ." Angela now shook off the numbness of the flashback—hallucination? "Where were you? What the hell is—"

"I was in the alley," Nadia panted, eyes wide. "Ari was *here*. I knew she'd try to come here." Nadia produced a leather toe-ring sandal. "I chased her. Jesus, Mary, and Joseph . . . I chased her."

Angela drew a deep breath to slow her pulse. "Let's get outta here. Was Youssa . . . on the computer? It was on . . ." Angela looked around. Not only were the fetishes gone—presumably taken by MPD, or even the Health Department or Customs—but Youssa's scrapbooks had disappeared, too.

"What . . . what's this?" Nadia said slowly. She pointed to the remnant of a small, gray baseball cap on the floor. It looked as if it had been burned in a furnace. Only the bill and part of the front remained. The monogrammed logo *SFS* was still apparent. "Why would this be in here? Youssa lived with a woman. No kids."

She handed it to Angela, who was fighting to pretend that ghouls and smoke and stench were all in her mind. The intact piece of the cap wasn't even singed. It was as if a fiery knife had sliced off the crown and rear portions. Angela shoved it into her shoulder bag; the two women quickly moved out of the fetish room, back to the counter and Youssa's iMac.

Before Nadia could sit at the keyboard, Angela pressed her, "You said Arianne lied to you. What's going on?"

Angela'd seen the look on Nadia's face before—almost a year ago, in a mirror. A face battling to reconcile love and duty. Enduring horror. "Antoine Jones . . . she knows him."

"How?"

"I don't know. I don't fucking know!"

"Don't bullshit me! Does she know Mullinix, too? Where is she?"

"Look, I was at her condo, up on Florida and P Streets. She's gone and I don't know where, 'kay? So just . . . just *fucking* don't jump on me, aw-right? Just . . ."

As Nadia valiantly dammed up her tears, Angela patted her trainee's shoulders and asked, "You're being reassigned tomorrow, right?"

"I've got the holiday and about two weeks to spend with my mom in Southampton. Then I report to the Charlotte, North fucking Carolina, Field Office on July thirteenth for four weeks—mobile-home loan fraud in exotic Mount Holly and Gastonia, North Carolina . . ."

"Jaggle the mouse," Angela said, hoarse.

The monitor opened Youssa's Excel spreadsheet journal entries for merchandise inspected and appraised. Nadia said, "You think it's something else Mullinix bought?"

"No." *21 Octobre 1998. Un sachet de duex sachets.* "One out of a pair? Right there—a Zulu *ibheqe*. Someone was trying to offer her one for sale. My French sucks . . . put that Chapin School and Sarah Lawrence education to work."

Nadia clicked over to the final column. "It looks like . . . shit . . . the thing looks handmade, authentic, from the Polaroid sent. She says she wants to see it, but will only pay thirty dollars for it. The offerer—whomever sent the picture—said fine, wants to unload it. Youssa says here it's worth one hundred dollars. Calls the sender an idiot but is pissed about the secrecy. See? *'Par le poste, pas de nom.'* No name, by U.S. mail."

But the sender's return address was recorded and it splayed Angela's eyes: 1305 F Street, N.W., Washington, D.C. 20005. The address of the King Communications Corporation Building.

Angela spun the heavier trainee around on the stool to face her. "You aren't going to tell me why your girlfriend is interested in a Zulu bag, owned by Bryce King, are you? Am I going to have to go back to Lorton Prison to find out why?"

Nadia shook her head. "I swear . . . I don't know why."

"Then I have to ask *Mr. King,* personally. But now . . . look at me . . . I want you to go home, clean up, sleep, and quietly call around for your friend. If you find her, tell me where, then leave. If you can't by the time you have to leave, go anyway. No questions, no foot dragging, no drama. Do exactly what your father wants."

"Ari's a sister . . . in our circle, our coven, our sabbat. She wouldn't—"

"Your circle's broken."

39

THURSDAY, JUNE 29, 2000

MUSTAPHA DUNAI TOOK A WOLFISH BITE of his McDonald's sausage-and-egg McMuffin. He and fellow lot attendant Samuel Ibhebesi were sitting on the bench opposite their lockers, taking a break. Mustapha's black, narrow face brimmed with relish over American fast food. Samuel's square, wrinkled black face was empty, yellow eyes bottomless. They just stared ahead at the locker while a Styrofoam container of perfectly round McDonald's hotcakes swimming in imitation maple syrup and margarine went cold.

"Hey, Sammie," Mustapha said with his mouth full. "Pancake your favorite! You want me heat it microwave in the booth, huh?"

Sam didn't answer.

"You say nothing about thing in the Capitol? I leave Mogadishu to get away bombs and death, Sammie. So why you leave South Africa for?"

This time, Samuel faced his colleague, and the eyes weren't bottomless. Mustapha thought he saw what looked like gray disks, filmy, like the dun of cataracts where pupils should have been. He giggled nervously. Too little sleep? Exhaust fumes addling his brain? Suddenly, a pain doubled him over on the bench. It felt like someone had sliced below his penis's root, and acidic urine dribbled through the fissure. He saw Samuel clutching at his own genitals. Identical pain? No. Transferred pain.

Mustapha wheezed and was about to drop when he heard Samuel whisper, *"Leave, umtombi."* The pain abated as quickly as it had seized him;

mind refocused, Mustapha knew *umtombi* meant "asshole" in Zulu. And Samuel's eyes returned to their usual look. Tired, filmy yellow. But not gray like a ghost's.

Mustapha got up, cursing, *"Fuck you, Sammie!"* as he scampered away.

Alone, Samuel pondered the pancakes on that bench. Sweet, warm, buttery. Like her body. Her soul. These flavors helped Samuel will away the inner pain of rogue cells eating his bladder.

A bloodred Lexus coupe gunned down the ramp and screeched to a burnt-rubber halt. The window lowered, and a haggard, unshaved Bryce King—face hollow, as if slowly sucked dry—called to him, *"Umodi . . .* the snuff. *I need more, goddamn it!"*

Angela walked into her office, glasses perched on the end of her small nose, hands balancing a pecan roll on a stack of files. She stopped dead when she saw Lupo sitting at her desk. Marcus Johnson and Micklin milled in a corner with bashful unease. Vallas was sitting on *that* sofa, minus the throw. He wouldn't look at her.

"Close the door, Tigress," Lupo said slowly.

Angela kicked the door shut. Jerry was nowhere to be found. She plopped down next to Vallas on the sofa. "George, what's this all about?"

He looked down at his feet.

"Talk to *me,"* Lupo intoned. "I'm the one in charge, remember?"

That's when Angela noticed a large, flat, white box—the size of one of those bridal-gown boxes she figured she'd never own—leaning on the edge of the desk. On it was taped a label: EMBASSY OF THE REPUBLIC OF SOUTH AFRICA. Lupo noted her glance. "You can open your present later. To add to the layers of crap, I got the new D.C. Chief of Police calling me. Seems you've been trying to spin an unrelated local homicide—an African immigrant—into this Amesha Spentas investigation? Angie, you and these three young men are supposed to be on a plane to Atlanta with AFT Special Agent LaHaye, tomorrow, per your task force assignment, or did you forget?" He addressed the room. "Fellas, go back to work. *Real work."*

Angela faced Vallas. *"Et tu, Brute?"*

"Angie," he whispered. "I didn't say a damn thing." He sighed and moved out, just as Sylvia Myers waddled in. Angela shot to her feet.

"Angela," Dr. Myers began, pulling up a chair, "we are very concerned. Remember what I said about decompensating at the precise moment when we need you one hundred percent?"

"Who sold me out?"

"That's not important, Tigress. I can't have my premier divisional liaison running around telling ghost stories. Oh, yeah, I did get around to reading your field notes and 302s, pre–Capitol attack. I had to, because Bud White complained yesterday that you'd put an ISD encryption pass code on them? They're supposed to be available to everyone."

"Angela, was that some cry for help?"

Angela laughed. "Yes, Sylvia." She faced Lupo. "Are you going to relieve me of duty?"

"You know damn well I can't. But I want to know why you are still getting information pertaining to these bizarre South African leads of yours when you were explicitly, *emphatically,* told not to? What game are you pulling?"

"You should sit down, dear," Dr. Myers whispered. Angela folded her arms and remained standing.

Lupo's face reddened. "You must have a guardian angel, or else there is magic floating around, 'cause not an hour ago, the Director and Ms. Reno got calls from the Vice President."

Now Angela sat back down.

"Senator Brian Buford, fresh from the hospital, had breakfast with the VP and Tipper this morning at Blair House. After that breakfast, and based on Buford's personal recommendation, the VP wanted to make sure that, and I'm quoting from memory, that you have 'complete autonomy to interface with the Secret Service and Capitol Police to protect our public servants, and to bring the perpetrators of crimes against the people of the United States to justice,' and . . . 'to avenge the heinous deaths of Dr. Leslie Collins, Elizabeth Hooperman, Bishop Carl Davidson, and the attempted murder of my *friend and colleague* Brian Ross Buford.' "

Fighting down the bubbling acid in her throat, Angela muttered, "Then why are you here, too, Sylvia?"

"Because, dear—with this renewed pressure, conflicting orders, I am worried about your mental state."

A bit calmer, Lupo added, "Look, I don't interpret this directive from the White House as trumping your stated assignment post–Capitol attack, you get me? Me, I still want you on that plane tomorrow, but Styles, he's . . . damn . . . he's inclined to hold off, get clarification . . . jeez, he's utterly lacking in frigging balls, and I swear, Tigress, a month ago, that would have given me a good laugh. Now, it *scares* me. You'll stand by and await further orders. You will not discuss what I said with anyone outside this division." He rose and loped out, leaving Angela with Dr. Myers.

"Dear," Myers said almost sheepishly, "why didn't you just confide in me, come to me with your background, your research, on your dreams?"

"Because you'd have certified me crazy."

"Give me more credit."

"Who called you?"

"I said, people, or a person, who care about you."

"Then you might as well stay, report back to them, at what you see here."

Angela crouched down to open the large white box. The label said it was compliments of Her Excellency Helen Tambo, but one of Jan Durnkloopf's business cards was taped to the layer of tissue paper and bubble wrap. On the back, he'd written:

An aid in understanding the Zulu religion. More to follow, JDD

Angela carefully unwrapped the contents. It was an *iklwa*, its broad blade covered with cardboard for safety. The handle was thick, though barely a foot and a half long. She reached deeper into the tissue and lifted out an oval cowhide shield: tan, painted with white lines and dots. Small by any standard but large enough to cover her petite body when she stood. Still, it was very light. Angela waved it around and called it by its proper name, *isihlangu.*

"So, Sylvia, how did I know what to call this thing, huh? Having never done any research on these people, their customs? Or this sound, a sound I hear in my dreams, and awake, at *crime scenes."*

Angela slapped the flat side of the *iklwa*'s blade against the front of the shield. The thwapping noise wasn't as frightening as the next one. She beat the end of the spear's handle against the inside of the shield. It was the *thoomp-thoomp* she'd heard in the tunnel. And in dreams.

Dr. Myers sighed heavily, shaking her head. No words.

"Don't blame yourself, Sylvia. I was only following your medical advice. To stop indulging demons. And *listen."*

After a knock on the door, Jerry peeked in. "Special Agent Vallas wants to see you, Inspector."

"Tell him I don't want to see him. At all. Anything else?"

"A Ms. Keiko Johnson at King Communications Corporation called. She said Mr. King will see you today, briefly, and without his lawyers present."

"Good. And Jerry, please get Dr. Myers some water. She's looking a bit peaked."

The sun was a hammer and the sidewalk in front of the Marriott Courtyard in Foggy Bottom the anvil as a bellhop loaded the last of Nadia's luggage and gear into the trunk of an idling blue Crown Victoria. Nadia's eyes were dotted spindly red behind her dark Pradas, yet she could see that the tall agents sent to fetch her were staring at her thick body, shoved into a black tube top and gauzy drawstring pants.

"Not *ever* in your wildest!" she snapped, pointing for one of the agents to open the car door for her.

She climbed in and checked her watch. Time to call Angela. But her tweeting cell muddied the clear water in her mind.

"Naddy," came Arianne's faint, pained voice. "I-I need you. . . ."

40

TRANSUBSTANTIATION, WITH SYRUP AND MARGARINE

FOUR O'CLOCK. RELIEF FROM THE SUN and humidity arrived. Violently. Rain fell in sheets out of a black, roiling sky; Angela ducked into the Ready Park garage. Running the extra twenty feet to the main King Communications Corporation lobby would have drenched her. She sloughed off her damp blazer and undid two buttons on her blouse as she strode by the cars and other refuge-takers toward the metal door that connected to the lobby. A voice with an accent called to her.

"You need card key to get in that way, miss." The man had the name MUSTAPHA embroidered on his shirt.

Angela was about to flash her badge and ID, but Mustapha saw the SIG, holstered on her skirt waistband.

"I go get Sammie. My key lost . . . or you wait here for umbrella?"

He took off. The rain and thunder intensified, as if downtown Washington was dancing with a hurricane. After a booming clap of thunder, Angela heard shuffling footsteps; an old black man limped up the ramp. He was dressed like Mustapha, only he was barely Angela's height. Waxy, wrinkled, purple-black skin. His hair—tight, white, sparse peppercorns. And his eyes were yellow.

"Why you stare at me, Miss?"

"I don't . . . I mean . . . I'm sorry. Inspector Angela Bivens, FBI." She showed her ID.

"I am Sam. You look like you see a ghost. We meet before?"

"Um, no." She laughed. He wasn't smiling. Angela noticed that he was holding a McDonald's Styrofoam tray of hotcakes. Steaming, like the pavement cooled by pounding raindrops. They'd already been sliced up, like a mother would do for a child. Drowning in syrup and melted margarine. The old man skewered a sopping chunk with a plastic fork and sucked it in, never breaking withered, jaundiced eye contact with Angela as he chewed with very white, straight teeth.

"Is better reheated," he said. "Breakfast . . . I eat late. *Very hungry.*"

This old guy works a minimum-wage job? "Uh, card key?"

"Oh, yes—sorry, miss." He set down his meal, wiped his hands on a greasy rag from his back pocket, then ran a white card over the sensor. The door popped open with a rush of air-conditioned lobby wind. Before Angela could thank him, Sam was retreating into the bowels of the garage, chewing loudly.

King's office was on the tenth floor. The hulking security guards wearing maroon blazers and carrying two-ways were the last males Angela saw. Everyone else on ten was a woman, whether lounging in a tiny cubicle or a capacious, windowed office. Some were white or Latina; most were African American. All were beautiful. Most were dressed in BCBG, Guess?, or Lacroix. More mature women wore labels only advertised in Barbara Bivens's spare copies of *Women's Wear Daily.*

King's executive assistant, Keiko Johnson—an aloof and exotic mix of Asian and black—escorted Angela down a corridor lined with posters of KCC TV shows, on-air personalities, KCC hip-hop and R&B superstars, and action shots of Wizards games at the MCI Center. Perched on $300 Jil Sander mules, Keiko was at least four inches taller than Angela as she intoned, "This meeting is a courtesy, as this is not the official interview outlined in the court order . . . the one rescinded after the attack in the Senate Gallery. You may not record anything, and Mr. King may terminate the meeting at any time or break to converse with his attorneys by phone." They reached the outer doors to King's suite. "Mr. King has been ill, by the way, so you only have fifteen minutes."

"Perhaps we can talk at his home, then?"

"*No.* This suite has a bedroom, kitchen, exercise room. He's been here . . . a lot."

"I see. Thank you."

Keiko opened the double doors with a card key, turned, and swished back down the corridor to her office. King's walls groaned with original oils, acrylics, and collages by Jacob Lawrence and Romare Bearden; the windows lent a dark, rain-pelted view of the Shops at National Place and the National Press Club.

Angela roamed the office. "Mr. King?" No reply. The huge kidney-shaped redwood desk was piled with papers. Most Fortune 500 CEOs had naked desks. She noted two framed photos: one, King; his wife, Ramona; grown daughter; and teenage son. The other, the pledge class of 1974, Omega Kappa Fraternity, Inc., Gamma Chapter, Howard University. Young men with Afros shoved under gold berets, carrying the gold canes. In the front row: an intense, sanguine Bryce, the "playah" Les, a muscular, menacing Carl Davidson, and a smiling, mercurial Butch. Buford's leg was still in a cast from wounds received on Koh Tang; the Navy Cross and Purple Heart hung around his neck. Angela moved closer to pick up the photo, and her knee touched the gold wire wastebasket beside King's empty chair. She looked down, and immediately the stink of infection, of decay, masked by antiseptic, assaulted her nostrils. Spent medical tape and gauze, still wet with brown blood and viscous pus, were piled in the basket.

"Boating injury," called a wheezy voice behind her. "Before this tragedy at the Capitol. One that you could have stopped had you been on your job."

Angela spun around. King stood in the doorway of his washroom. He was more than "ill." He looked twenty pounds thinner than she'd seen him at Collins's funeral. Lips cracked, raw. Puffy flesh ringed lifeless eyes, and he smelled like an amalgam of dried urine and . . . *licorice. None of the people in this building have seen him in this condition?*

"I almost lost another friend that day." He brushed past Angela and fell into his office chair. She sat in front of the huge desk. As she did, King tongued a lump of something moist from the inside of his cheek and spit it out. From the splatting sound, he had missed his wastebasket, and Angela saw a stream of bloody saliva trail from his mouth. He'd been clutching a cotton oxford shirt at the chest. It was buttoned up to the top, and Angela noticed he had a dark T-shirt underneath.

"Mr. King, we can reschedule—"

"Naw . . . naw. You got that look. A young lady who wants questions answered." He coughed up phlegm, then chuckled. "Does Victor know your little ass is here?"

"My *little ass* wants to know, sir, how you know Youssa Ogamdoudou. How you know Antoine Jones . . . Shaka Seven. And how you know Jewel Ngozi."

"You said we were going to talk about the Archangels. This meeting's over."

Angela pulled the *ibheqe* Youssa had given her from her shoulder bag and tossed it onto King's desk. "Have you ever seen something like this?"

King recoiled, chest bellowing. Angela leaned forward, her fists on the edge of the desk, waiting for him to calm. And break. And tell her. Tell her *what,* she had no clue. But tell her *something.* Instead, he twisted away from her and dropped out of the chair onto the carpet. Angela swung around the desk; he was hemorrhaging from his mouth, his nostrils.

Angela pulled the almost comatose, limp King against his credenza, then rose and flung open the office doors. *"Ms. Johnson?* Call 911 . . . DCFD Rescue! And get security in here!" As she yelled, she yanked out her cell and hit a preprogrammed button. She then called, "Thirteen oh five F Street Northwest, need escort for EMTs."

When no one appeared in the hallway, she ran out, screaming for help. Keiko appeared, looking more bothered than frantic. *"Bitch, did you hear me?"* Angela shouted while she inserted the hands-free earpiece for her phone. "Your boss is unconscious!"

Keiko nodded and ran for help, mules clacking away. Angela clipped the phone to her skirt waist and turned back into the office.

Bryce King's body wasn't there.

She bounded over to the desk. There were drag marks along the carpet, and a small trail of blood, vomit. Then she heard a man's scream, from the suite's bedroom.

"Shit . . . *shit!* Mr. King?"

Two flashes of lightning, a boom of thunder. The lights flickered, blinked out. Just like in Philadelphia, and dread exploded into Angela's throat. She tore into the room in time for a flash of lightning to illuminate King's body being dragged, arms first, toward another door. Angela drew and cocked her SIG. Ready to charge. But then, another flash of lightning. Her heart almost stopped.

A glint from the storm, of tiny metallic teeth, serrated, like a piranha's, set in a small wooden face. As Angela gaped, a seemingly invisible force yanked King through the other doorway.

A hand patted Angela's back; she spun, barely in control enough *not* to fire. It was one of the burly guards, wild-eyed, winded, and confused, brandishing his radio and a huge Maglite flashlight.

"Seal the building!" Angela yelled to him.

As he shouted into his two-way, Angela tore away his flashlight and charged into the shadowy bedroom, toward the rear door. Bracing the SIG on the light, Angela shot a beam through the door, into what was apparently King's workout room, weights and treadmills visible, but no King, except for his muffled cries.

Angela saw a gloved hand attached to a bare, sweaty arm grab the door from within the weight room. She jumped up to rush the door.

BOOM! The door slammed in front of her with such force that the molding cracked. Angela fell backward into the guard's body. They exchanged nods; he threw himself at the door like a wrecking ball. The portal flew off its hinges.

They were met with screams and darkness but for a lone Exit sign through a tangle of stainless-steel weight machines. Angela aimed the flashlight at a grating, knocked off a large vent opening in the wall. Bryce King's legs stuck out of its maw, kicking, as if the building had swallowed him alive, headfirst. His agonizing cries echoed in the walls, punctuated by crashes of thunder. The guard stood transfixed in terror and disbelief, but Angela's training took over. Dropping both her weapon and the light, she lunged at King's flailing feet.

But King's body was sucked through the vent like an insect in a giant vacuum hose, leaving only a shoe in Angela's hand. The guard slid down beside her, composed enough to hand her her SIG. Other guards now crowded into the room, crowding at the vent's opening as they heard King's voice, tumbling down, away from them. Horrified, one guard dropped his Maglite down the shaft; it only seemed to ignite a smell that volcanoed up the shaft back at them. The stink of blood and emptied bowels. And something that Angela had smelled before. Dry. Musky. *Lions.*

"Where the fuck does this shaft go?" Angela shouted, springing to her feet. The lights flicked back on.

"Ventilation," one guard explained as Angela pushed through them to the hallway. "Fans are on the roof, but it goes down to an electrical room. In the garage."

Angela tore past the terrified workers for the elevator. "Have any MPD officers or FBI backup seal off the garage!"

She hit the emergency express setting; on the way down, Angela prayed. What was Nadia's sabbat incantation? *Goddess, protect me in your bubble of light.* The Lord would need all the help he could get.

She burst into the lobby. Two cops, Glocks drawn, met her. One panted, "We got the call . . . the electrical room's off ramp one, level two!"

"Okay, you guys hit the lobby exit to the garage. I'll take the stairs."

"What about backup?"

"Move!"

Angela opened the metal door and flew down the stairs, unconcerned that her heels would catch an edge.

Level two. She halted by the door. Sweat drizzled off her nose, onto her quivering lips. She puffed it away, grasped the doorknob, closed her eyes, counted to three. She eased open the door, slipped through, then let it close behind her.

The level was deserted. Just parked cars. Well lit. Quiet, but for approaching sirens and the rumble of the storm above. Angela saw the door with the yellow electrical warning signs, about fifty feet away in a corner. It was next to the elevator-cable motors. Suddenly the turbine kicked in. The once dead-quiet level whined with machinery as Angela inched forward, SIG ahead, eyes sweeping.

The door to the electrical room flew open. A figure rushed out. Spidery and black. Wearing shorts, a T-shirt. He looked seven feet tall. Hair like tentacles in silhouette. Did she expect a ghost? A demon-possessed Zulu warrior?

"Freeze! FBI!"

The figure leapt behind a concrete piling and fired at her. Two pops, like .38 rounds. They shattered the windshield of a Honda Accord; Angela returned fire.

She heard a male voice yell, "Freeze!" One .38 shot. Three pops from a Glock 9mm. Then, in a radio: "Ten-sixty. Ten-sixty!" It meant the intruder had evaded the police officers. Another male voice, to her left, softly begged, *"Miss . . . help! Help here!"*

Angela crouched to see the attendant Mustapha cradling the head of that small old man. Beside him was the crushed, cracked Styrofoam container of hotcakes.

"It Sammie . . . Sammie hurt! Said somebody beat him down when storm make lights go . . . when he hear noises! I came . . . *now guns!"*

The old man's lips were bloodied; air strained through flared nostrils. As one hand clutched his chest, he pointed with the other, in the direction of the electrical room.

"Somebody dead . . . in dere," he whimpered. "Dey eat him. *Eat him whole."*

Angela stood. The radio feedback and sirens were getting louder; the elevator turbine shut off. Three cops, one waving a shotgun, rushed down the ramp.

"Hold it," she called to them. She touched her finger to her now dry lips, then pointed to the electrical room door. The cops nodded and fanned out on either side of the door as Angela left Sam and Mustapha to meet them. Angela signaled for one cop to pull the door open, one to provide cover, while the third with the shotgun would enter with her. "One . . . two . . . *three.*"

When the door swung open, the animal smell was dizzying, but there were no lions. Just Bryce King, limbs twisted like a fallen puppet. His nose, his lips, and a piece of his cheek were being nibbled . . . by rats. Angela shoved away a cop who was about to blast the rodents with the twelve-gauge; they scattered of their own accord. Holstering her weapon, Angela touched King's neck. Miraculously, he had a pulse.

"Need evac—paramedics or EMTs in here fast!" shouted a female cop into her radio.

The oxford King wore had been ripped open, along with the T-shirt under it, exposing his chest. Angela flinched when she saw that the tee wasn't dark-colored after all. It had been a white undershirt, stained brown by old, dried blood. The flinch flipped from disgust to utter horror, and all the cops backed off. Pieces of macerated, infected flesh were where his areolae should have been, as if some monster had suckled from him. But—a monster with a .38? How could he work alone—and pull a body through a ventilation shaft, survive this fall ten floors down?

"Holy shit!" an officer exclaimed. "What is *this* sumbitch?"

He steered Angela to a corner of the foul-smelling room. There stood a wooden statuette. Leering with a painted face. Erect penis taunting everyone. And tiny metal teeth dripping with coppery-scented *fresh* blood. A night fetish.

"Oh, Jesus, no . . ."

Something else drizzled from the imp's mouth. Amber, viscous. Though sickened, Angela leaned forward cautiously, as if the thing were alive and would nip at her. The cops, confused, hung back as she fingered the liquid. It was tacky. She smelled it. *"What?"* It was a familiar smell. A happy one, incongruous with death. She touched it to her tongue, making the cops gasp. Sweet.

It was maple syrup, tinged with butter.

From in the garage Angela could hear Sam screaming, *"It eat him . . . it eat him up like Communion, body of Christ!"*

Five o'clock. The sun scared the thunderheads away. Swords of light pieced the garage's innards. Angela sat cross-legged on the hood of a parked car, waiting for Claude Baker's agents. On her lap, wrapped in plastic, was the night fetish. They stared at each other like old enemies. But only the statue had the answers. Hers would live or die with King, being loaded in a Medstar chopper on the roof, ten floors above.

41

"PLEASE DON'T HATE ME, NADDY," Arianne Shipley sobbed. Her otherwise sassy blond pageboy was matted with sweat. "Don't go . . . I'm so scared. He got Youssa, he'll kill me, too." Arianne dipped her head to her knees beneath the creeping shadow of Thomas Jefferson's statue, under the dome copied from Jefferson's beloved Monticello and University of Virginia.

Nadia fell to one knee and shook her lover's shoulders. "Why should I trust you? You lied to me. You abandoned me. Two of the worst things . . . the worst you could do to me and you know that!" Nadia gulped down tears and muttered, "But this . . . Antoine Jones, then breaking into Youssa's shop. Why?"

Arianne's wet face hardened. *"Oh, you know why, Naddy.* We divined it in our sabbats whenever you rolled up from your stupid little drills in Quantico. Those other little whiny debutante bitches couldn't feel *him,* my love for him in our spells, but you could, uh-huh. Not the love we share. I mean loyalty, dedication, devotion. That love. Seven is going to die and I was going to do everything in my power to save him. And if that meant using you, even Youssa, to force your . . . your *fucking idol* to face our world, our magick, dig up anything on Mullinix that would lead her to the truth, then—"

Nadia sprung to her feet, waving her hands. *"Shuddup, shuddup . . .* Christ, you've lost it!"

Several tourists noted the outburst; annoyed murmurs and eyes followed the young women on the limestone steps of the monument, gleaming in the wash of a waning sun as orange as Nadia's locks. The thunderheads of the late afternoon were only a gray line on the darkening eastern horizon, toward the ocean.

"Ari, did you sleep with him?"

"He's my cousin, Naddy."

"So he . . . he knows the craft? Did he teach you, or you him?"

Arianne sighed up at the hot sky and laughed tearfully. "That isn't the question she'd ask. *Angela.* She'd want to know if I knew who really killed that girl, the Zulu girl, soooo looooong ago. Not Seven, or Antoine, as you call him." Arianne then stood up. Both of her bare feet were almost black from dirt because she was missing a sandal. "Come on, Naddy, I took the Metro over here. My car's parked in Rossyln, in a garage; we can go away together. Bivens will find the truth, free Seven. And you can quit the FBI." She kissed Nadia's full lips, wetly. But Nadia shoved her away before a second kiss, in full view of the tour-mobiles and some titillated Marines on leave.

Face twisted in anger, Nadia muttered, "You left . . . you were on the run, you say? But why pack? And there was no food in the refrigerator—where did it go? I mean . . . oh, Jesus, Ari . . . what's happening? Youssa was murdered by the warlock. Did you know it would happen? Did Jones . . . Seven? Why didn't you come to me? Why rob Youssa?"

"I needed to see for myself if the warlock did come, baby. If he used that magick, the Zulu magick. The ghosts, in the vessel. They were there, but what came for Youssa was the asshole who's after me. Flesh and blood. His familiar—"

Nadia spun away, back to the darkening steps. "Aw, Christ, stop!"

Arianne stood over her, breathing hard, lips curled down. "Seven told me the warlock had help. They always have help. They pick a person with a rotted soul. This man was Seven's friend in school . . . or acted like it. He was nothing more than a fucking disgusting gangster then. A drug dealer, a waste now. A walking human ghost no one wants to see." She crouched in front of Nadia, whispering, "Evil men killed that girl. Seven was only trying to protect her."

"You have to come with me, Ari. You have to come and talk to Inspector Bivens . . . please, Ari." Now Nadia spurted tears, moaning, "I won't turn you in. I'm not going to be alone again. I love you. If you love me, you'll come with me."

"If you love me, you'll come with *me*," Arianne threw back, voice raspy. "My family avoided talking about Seven until I was five years old. I met him finally when I was thirteen, when he was on a college recruiting trip in Charlottesville, and Mom made Dad invite him over. He taught about the goddess, the craft—and more. African magick. Showed me books on voodoo, Santeria, the *orisha* Shango, who he said was a warrior god that possessed him when he played basketball like some demon. He even tried to teach real thug-life assholes about Shango. To reject what people like my family and their goddamn black lackeys like the ones who ran that college have done in manipulating them. Nah, not devil worship like old black people in Baptist churches say. It was about African and Caribbean heritage, culture. Indivisible knowledge, like the number seven. Seven is the number of the water serpent, ya know? Worshiped by their *sangoma* and the warlocks." Arianne kissed Nadia's freckled forehead, then fingered the tiny cylinder hanging at Nadia's breast. "This charm means I love you as I love the goddess, the earth, the rain, the sky."

"I can't go with you. I can't. But . . . I can't stay, either. I don't know what to do."

Arianne sat beside a now weeping Nadia, wrapped an arm over her shoulder. "When you joined the circle, you drank a drop of my blood in wine and ate a tiny fleck of my skin, right? What do you Catholics call it again? Eating each other symbolically?"

"I was a little girl, getting ready for my first Holy Communion, when they taught us about 'transubstantiation.' Means that when you take Communion, you really *are* eating the body of Christ, drinking his blood. That's how the covenant forms."

"Right. A covenant. Cannibals say that's why they eat their enemies. You absorb their strengths, not their weaknesses." Arianne caressed Nadia's cheek. "You haven't done that with Bivens, the FBI. You did it with me. You belong with me, not them."

Nadia stood up and stormed over to the Tidal Basin shore. Startled, Arianne ran after her. An embrace offered, an embrace thrown aside. All of this viewed by Stringbean Coy, who sneered at the two witches. Dykes. He promised himself that one would be dead, very soon.

42

ICU

MEDSTAR WASHINGTON HOSPITAL CENTER

THROUGH OPEN BLINDS, ANGELA AND Victor Styles watched the EKG and respiration monitor above Bryce King's bed beep, faint and slow. King's battered face was visible amongst a tangle of hanging IV tubes and lead wires; a nurse in blue scrubs, a mask, and hair cover adjusted the ventilator tube in his mouth.

The trauma surgical resident entered the darkened hall beyond the glass. He spoke in a near whisper. "Dr. Coleman's with the family; he sent me to brief you." The resident flipped through a clipboard. "The only reason Mr. King is alive is that he didn't fracture his skull in that fall. He broke just about everything else. Cervical fracture means a severed spinal cord for sure."

Angela said, "But I saw the pulse-oxymeter on his fingertip move."

"Involuntary muscle contractions. Plus, we had to remove his spleen, tie up his liver. He punctured his left lung."

"And the chewing marks?" Angela said softly, her own thumbnail between her teeth. Styles rubbed at his temples when he heard the word *chewing*.

The resident shrugged. "We hope to arrest the infection, but he's damn lucky he didn't get blood poisoning. We found some very strange stuff in his tox screen, too."

"Mushroom-based hallucinogen?"

"No . . . but an organic narcotic for sure, plant-based. Seen it before. Like some of these Central American immigrants when they chew coca leaves."

"Has he been conscious at all?"

"In and out. Mumbling. But look, no intrusions."

"I have to talk to him if he's conscious, even semilucid."

"Inspector, if his blood pressure keeps dropping, no one's going to be—"

Styles cut him off. "Thank you, Doctor. No statements to anyone. We've sealed the entire Critical Care wing of this hospital. Remind Dr. Coleman. All rosters and shifts are to be cleared with Claude Baker, Assistant Director in Charge of the Washington Field Division."

"Yeah . . . sure." The resident hurried away.

Angela faced Styles. "You have got to cut me more leeway from the main Senate Gallery shooting task force than what the Vice President already mandated."

"The Vice President's been misinformed. Donatello and the Attorney General are meeting with him tonight. We are full bore on Amesha Spentas. And you're overdue in Atlanta."

"This is not the Archangels. This was an attempted ritual murder, and that totem, that ugly little thing, was the calling card. Some sort of instrument."

"*Shit* . . . come with me." He pulled her into the trauma-staff lounge. "Your witness—this Samuel Ibhebesi—is down the hall in this unit. I suggest you roust the truth out of him when he wakes up."

"He didn't see any white males. I didn't see anyone planting a gold dollar. There were no explosives, no forced entry. One black male, six-four to six-seven in height, maybe two hundred pounds. And *that* statue."

"Maybe it's time you shared what you *really* think is going on."

"That was my question to *you*, Victor. Otherwise, why are you here, instead of Claude, the Critical Incident Response Team leaders, even Frank?"

Brett Mallory limped in without knocking. He was carrying two manila folders.

"Detective," Styles acknowledged. "As Chief Ramsey's been briefed, this incident's no longer within MPD jurisdiction. Nor is it a homicide."

"With all due respect, Mr. Deputy Director, I didn't think you got so directly involved with front-line investigations? And I saw King. Gonna be a homicide soon."

"What do you have for me?" Angela asked, interceding.

He handed her the folders as Styles slumped into a chair. "Forensic and print lamp material. Maybe you should sit down, too, 'cause this shit's gonna trip you for damn sure. Standard protocol to run the .38 slugs in any shooting within seventy hours of another. The .38 that fired at you and our people in that garage yesterday afternoon belonged to Youssa Ogamdoudou."

"Jesus Christ . . . conclusive?"

"Uh-huh. Matched the pattern on the slug we dug outta her shop. Your shooter . . . would be killer-kidnapper . . . stole her gun. Probably was the one who killed her. And we think we know who."

Styles rose slowly. Angela eyed him nervously, then prompted Brett.

"My theory? The same mope we were trying to track down for your girl Carmen. Devon Coy. Interfaced with your Field Office Crim Squad this morning—Coy drives a green hoopdy—a 1976 Plymouth Valiant, souped-up. A car matching that description had been reported as cruising the block around King's home off Calvert Street, Northwest."

"Still, Brett . . . the nexus?"

Brett smiled. "You ready for this? Two latents, matching his prints. One, at the crime scene in Simple City, some kid dead, head wound. Another partial thumb, at a B-and-E scene. Sidwell Friends School."

Angela faced Styles. She knew from the victim dossier that King's youngest son had just graduated from Sidwell. "Victor . . . I mean, Mr. Deputy Director . . . he's attending Yale this fall?"

Styles cleared his throat. Suddenly he looked ashy, rattled. "Yes. I wrote him a recommendation."

"I'm a Morehouse man m'self," Brett said. He cut off the levity when he saw Angela's head cocked back, eyes closed. "You okay, Angie?"

She wasn't. The cap remnant she and Nadia had found at Youssa's: SFS monogram. Sidwell Friends School? She recalled King's face when he saw the *ibheqe*. Her heart raced; she could hardly breathe once she lowered her head. "There's a cap in our lab . . . if we raise a latent print, I'll do an IAFIS search. There'll be a match."

Brett nodded. "I know my stuff's far-fetched but, hey—"

"No," Angela said, struggling to smile. "You're almost a for-real detective."

Brett laughed as he lumbered for the door. "Learned it from you, the hard way."

But Styles stopped him, voice choppy and devoid of mellifluous tone. "Detective, if you see Claude Baker's Crim Squad assistant, Special Agent

Rice, out there, ask him to call me on my cell, direct line, in ten minutes. *Not to come in here.* Just call."

After Brett left, Styles eased back down into the chair. Angela hovered over him.

"Victor, what is it?"

He looked up at her. Nothing feline or predatory about him. "Kwame Buford is in the seventh grade at Sidwell Friends."

"Oh my God."

Styles swallowed hard. "I need to talk to the Secret Service, coordinate with the Capitol Police . . . it's clear Brian Buford's going to be Gore's vice-presidential nominee and I—"

Angela crouched in front him. "Look at me! No bullshit, like with Pluto, then Trey. No bullshit, Victor! You knew all along this wasn't the Archangels!"

He shook his head, again swallowing lumps of air. Angela summoned all her strength and tugged him to his feet. "Come on out here . . . look at this man!" She pushed him back out into the hall; he offered no resistance. She pointed toward King, on the other side of the glass. "I showed him a little Zulu bag . . . the kind Zulu girls weave. The kind a girl like Jewel Ngozi would weave. And he passed out. Now you talk to me!"

Styles snapped out of his fugue; now, snarling, he was the one grabbing. He shoved Angela into an alcove by the water fountain, hissing, "I suspected these fucking terrorists all along until . . . until Carl Davidson's death. And then you wanted to see Antoine Jones in prison."

Angela shook herself free. "He knew her, Victor." Her chest was now heaving, and she fought to keep her harsh whisper down lest any passerby hear. "Did he kill her? Did he kill her, and frame Jones, and his friends helped . . . and now they're paying with their lives . . . because someone brought something very old and terrible from her Motherland to—"

"Shut up!" Victor spun around, scanning for anyone who might have heard his panicked yell, then, softly, touched Angela's shoulder. "I don't know about anything 'old,' or 'terrible.' But as for the rest . . ." His face went dead cold.

The resident reappeared, winded. "Mr. Styles, Ms. Bivens! Tried to find you!"

Angela gasped, "Did King code? Is he dead?"

"No . . . um, he's conscious, barely. His wife gave permission for you to talk to him . . . Dr. Coleman protested, but this is very, very—"

"Why?"

"Because he asked for *you* by name, Ms. Bivens."

Through a surgical mask, Angela whispered into Bryce King's sole unbandaged ear, "I know you can hear me. I tried to save you, I swear. I am so sorry. But I'm here for you now." She was dressed in scrubs, her hair tucked into a paper cap.

King's eyelids fluttered; Angela watched hopefully, but then he dozed again. Styles watched through the curtain wall, flanked by two other agents and Claude Baker. So did Ramona King, hands clasped together as firmly as Angela clasped her husband's.

Dr. Coleman, the head trauma surgeon, warned, "You see the EKG, his respiration, BP? You have one minute, then you have to leave."

Angela stroked King's fingers. "Mr. King . . . tell me about Antoine Jones . . . Jewel Ngozi? You know what happened to Les, to Carl . . . what almost happened to you. You want that to happen to Butch? No, you don't. We can stop this and—"

He stirred. Crusted eyes opened.

"I'll protect you." The ICU nurse stood by as Angela said, "I'm going to show you something. Be calm; it's just a photo." She produced a Polaroid: the night fetish with the engorged penis and metal grin. King's eyes suddenly widened, as if something he saw only in misty nightmares and daytime lapses had come to life; frothy bubbles formed on what was left of his lower lip. The EKG flashed and beeped furiously.

Dr. Coleman snorted through his mask, "Ms. Bivens . . . careful."

She took away the photo. "Mr. King, it can't hurt you anymore. You chewed the snuff to make it go away, because you thought it was only a nightmare. But the snuff made you weaker. Yes, we analyzed what you'd been chewing, finally. You thought it would make the nightmares go away. Something haunting you, like Jewel, the truth."

"J-Jewel . . . W-White-tink . . ."

"Alfred Whiting? Mr. King, I'm here. What did Whiting have to do with Jewel? He came in to take over Jones's murder trial from the Assistant U.S. Attorney; why?"

King's head dipped to one side. Styles's voice came over the speaker. "You'd better leave him, let him rest."

That voice wedged open King's eyelids. Angela pressed, "Did you hurt her . . . did you hurt Jewel?"

The next voice was Ramona King's. "What . . . Lord, what's she saying?"

"This interview's over, Inspector," Styles boomed.

"Did you hurt Jewel?" Angela repeated as Dr. Coleman pulled Angela away from the bed. He released her when King moaned and muttered faintly, "Yesh." Then his eyes closed and didn't open again.

Dr. Coleman shouted, "Nurse—start the drip, get the respirator back on him . . . everybody out! Get a code team standing by, stat!"

Angela roamed out of the ICU, tearing off her mask, her paper head cover. She herded Styles away from the group and a now hysterical Ramona King, back into lounge. She locked the door behind her, with Baker and several agents pounding on it.

Styles dropped his head into his hands. It was the first time Angela had ever seen him do that. "I will . . . will make myself available for a Section 645 hearing. Turn myself over to the U.S. Attorney—*if you deem it necessary, Inspector*. If you feel I am guilty of conspiracy to extort a federal official. Of aiding and abetting obstruction of justice, of aiding and abetting a conspiracy to deprive Antoine Jones of his rights under the Fourth, Fifth, Sixth, and Fourteenth Amendments."

Angela fell onto a cold stool, numb.

"You are, by now, aware of my . . . appetites. How they shift, capriciously from women to men, eh? I came upon personal knowledge and information of Alfred Whiting's appetite. That part, you already had a piece of. Yes, the man was a sexual sadist. And gay. Those two are not mutually exclusive. Yes, one of his 'victims' was Maynard Mullinix. Yes, the GOP wanted to keep this under wraps at all costs. Now, connect the new dots, Angela. King needed dirt, because King was trying to cement the frame-up of one Shaka Seven. That part, I have only come to accept. I always suspected it, but never had any proof, any reason to pull the suspicion out of the lockbox in my brain. It was a *reasonable* theory that Whiting would be knocked off by his friends, once they found out certain ugly truths. More than a Judas. A faggot."

"He killed her," Angela muttered.

"Only he knows." He was motioning toward the door. "If he ever wakes up."

"There is one *other* person I could ask."

"Leave him out of this."

"You are in no position to threaten me. Or tease, toy, cajole, use. Not anymore."

"I'm not. I'm *begging*. Please . . . please leave him alone."

Pitiful. Pathetic. Words Angela never thought she could associate with Victor Styles. She hobbled up to her feet when acceptance hit her like a bucket of freezing water. "You know Trey and Pluto's favorite song by the Rolling Stones, 'Sympathy for the Devil'? 'Just as every cop is a criminal / And all the sinners, saints.' The man was sedated, nearly dead. I couldn't use much of what he said against you anyway, should he die."

"Oh, it might be enough to get Antoine Jones a new trial . . . with my help."

Angela blinked moisture over her dry contacts. "So here you are . . . repentant as Othello in the final act, huh? I'm game."

"No game," Styles whispered to her, close. Then he quoted, " 'I took by the throat the circumcised dog / And smote him thus.' " He made a hara-kiri motion, as if he held one of his *hanto* knives.

Angela's voice sharpened. "All right, but you wouldn't have exposed yourself to this eight years ago without something to implicate King, and clear you—just in case."

Styles sighed, as if caught. "Checkmate. Ben Franklin Station Post Office, Department of Commerce Building . . . there's a mail drop. Ironically, Sessions once used it in conjunction with the CIA. It was retired four years ago—I made sure of that. But it's perpetual, like a safe-deposit box for Uncle Sam. I have the only key. In the bottom is a portfolio containing handwritten documents . . . and a few audio microcassette tapes— uh-huh, your old little trick. These materials date from 1991 to now. They'd help Mr. Jones, they'd hurt Bryce—should he survive. But I beg you again, leave Butch be."

"He's the next victim. Or his family. Somebody was casing Sidwell Friends. For King's son, maybe Buford's. So, no, I can't leave this alone. And you're going to help."

43

ANGELA SAT ATOP AN OLD TOWEL, on the stoop of her brownstone. Chin perched on her knees, eyes languorous, forlorn. Ten P.M. and seventy-six degrees. Her flip-flops felt as if they were sticking to the baked stone. Worse, the air was heavy with spent gunpowder. No one had told the children that it was in poor taste to fire bottle rockets, set off cherry bombs and firecrackers, days after the Capitol shooting and bombing. This was their dry run for July Fourth, making use of the cut-rate pricing at the firework stands that had sprung up on street corners over the past two weeks.

Three calls to Nadia. Three messages on a Bureau voice-mail account that would be terminated upon reassignment. *I need you, fledgling. I trust you. Bring in your girlfriend and make* her *talk to me.* Three calls from Vallas. One, pertaining to business: they would have to fly to Atlanta after all to an Amesha Spentas cell. The second, clumsily professing what sounded like love. The third, clumsily backpedaling on what he'd said in the second. She tucked her cell phone into her sundress's front pocket, chugged down the Zima she'd been nursing, and stood to wander back inside.

A silver, boxy Volvo 740 rounded the corner and swooshed to a stop. Angela ducked into the inner door and watched as the Volvo dueled with the curb. "Yuppies in this neighborhood still can't parallel park for shit," Angela thought aloud.

But soon she realized the Volvo had a black driver, with a white man in the back. Diplomatic plates. The rear window lowered, and a voice with a Dutch-Afrikaaner accent called, "Inspector Bivens. Please . . . accept a ride from me."

Angela emerged from the doorway. "You spying on me, Dr. Durnkloopf ?"

"On the telly, I saw how you tried to rescue the black media president, Mr. King. Like you saved Senator Brian Buford."

Angela hated how white South Africans pronounced *black* as "bleck." "So you lied—you weren't a diplomat by training. And you know *much* anthropology, right?"

"Correct. I did my training with BOSS. And I know much about what you're dealing with. *And,* I have emigration and citizenship files for you." He smiled and swung open the door. "I saw the image of the night fetish found by your Metropolitan Police Department at the site where Mr. King was thrown down a shaft and mutilated." When Angela stepped down onto the sidewalk to the idling car, Durnkloopf added, "Of course, the image of the fetish's phallus was pixeled out on Channel Nine *Eyewitness News,* but quite evident on Fox. I'm sure the FBI was quite piqued that the local police leaked this aspect of the case. Done by a large fellow at Chief Ramsey's press conference—Mallory of yours, no?"

Angela got in, with her keys, her phone. The car was cool; Durnkloopf smelled of lager. But his blue eyes were sharp, roving over Angela's form in the billowy dress. The Volvo sped off toward East Capitol Street.

"Please pass my thanks on to Her Excellency Mrs. Tambo for the spear and shield."

The Volvo tracked around Lincoln Park's statue of Mary McLeod Bethune, toward RFK Stadium, lit for a 2000 Olympics soccer qualifying game between South Africa and the U.S. national team. Durnkloopf noted Angela's admiring glance toward the bronze figure.

"A hero of yours? Yes, I read it in the dossier. Oh, we have 'intell' on you, too."

"She was a hero of our struggle here. As your dead regime made a lot of heroes out of ordinary folks, even children, in South Africa . . . so *fuck you and the BOSS.*"

"Right. We'll spin around the stadium, and I will make this quick, as my driver Isaac is eager to see the match. The *iklwa* you have, as well as the shield design, are smaller replicas of the set belonging to General Mavumengwana, last commander in chief of the Zulu Impi under Cetshwayo. Moreover, the blade's steel is from melted scrap metal belonging to the settlers fighting the Zulu under *my* hero, Piet Retief. The original iron in it, well, it was mined from rocks in Howick Falls."

"Interesting. So why give it to me?"

"I'm sure you'll find a use, Inspector. Just as I'm sure you understood the fetish's significance. You are doubtless sickened at the FBI's robotic insistence that the attack on Mr. King, like that on the others, was by the right-wing *kommandos* who attacked the U.S. Senate?" Durnkloopf then passed her a folder of old black-and-white photos; the driver hit the map light. "These are of a riot in Ladysmith, three weeks after the 1982 Soweto bloodshed. The police closed down the last sorcery market in Natal. An excuse for Communist extremists to stir trouble, considering they believe in witchcraft about as much as I do." He grinned, showing tobacco-stained teeth. "See right here—what the *sangoma* call 'fetishes'? That one in particular?"

A white policeman was beating a frail older black man with a long baton. The victim's face was turned away from the camera, and it seemed he was more concerned with protecting a statuette on the ground—identical to the one in King's building.

"Oh, no . . ."

"Oh, yes. Hard to identify the man in the photo. A harmless *inyanga*, an herbalist? Or maybe, an *umthakathi*. The tear gas didn't discriminate, nor did the police. He might have also been a *thikoloshe*. A 'familiar.' More a lackey than a black cat in human form, eh?" He was laughing at the end of that thought. "My cultural attaché says we're lucky to get these photos at all. You see, the myth is that other little fellows like this fetish can bend light. Daft, but that's the lore. For instance, a photo of something in that particular fetish's presence might look blank or undeveloped to us. I culled the records for a Zulu male who forged his identity and racial papers to obtain work permits in Durban; this took place sometime in 1987–89. He was wanted for questioning in the aftermath of a . . . well . . . witchcraft-related burning of a young woman. The Natal Constabulary surmised that the burning wasn't political. It was a warning."

He was giving her the pieces of the puzzle she could not get from Youssa. "I have to go home. I have to pack, rest. My superiors are sending me to Atlanta despite the attack on King. Then again, you already know that from your own 'intell,' huh?"

The consul general knocked on the driver's seat. "Isaac, back to Miss Bivens's flat, then to the match. You have a score?"

"Two to nil, the Yanks, sah."

"*Damn!* Well, I will e-mail you any information that isn't already burned in the CD I'm giving you, thus." He plopped an unlabeled CD holder in Angela's hand.

"Including background on a Jewel Ngozi, born in 1972? Our INS is very bad with information collection."

Durnkloopf nodded. "Worse than your FBI?"

"No, sir—our problem's interpretation, not collection. Do we have a deal?"

"*Deal?* What are you planning to do for us?"

She drew in a heavy breath. "Clean up your mess, that migrated here, from your country. And that started long ago, and that you will deny ever existed. Good night, Mr. Consul General."

"Of course. By the by, my sources tell me the police found a substance ingested by Mr. King." He shrugged when Angela's mouth hung open. "I am on your side. Tell your forensic laboratory it's called *umodi*. It's a Zulu snuff used by both the *sangoma* and the covens of *umthakathi.*" He handed her a Ziploc bag with a few pinches of what looked like wet tobacco. It smelled like licorice. "More potent than cannabis. Energizes you. Protects you. It's from the bark of trees near Howick Falls, home of the Inkanyamba. Only someone imbued with magic of that water snake can use this substance without peril. Used in conjunction with the so-called red mushroom, it can even heal broken bones, slow aging, maybe cure cancer, eh?"

"Where did you get this?"

"There's the rub, as the Dane said. Unless you sneak it in, only one place in this city. And now the proprietress has been murdered."

A throbbing pain erupted at the base of Angela's skull and crawled to her forehead, her temples. "God . . . *Youssa.*"

"Young lady, this woman Youssa was known by the staffers at many of the African embassies as the source of folk charms, herbal medicine, philters, trinkets. *Fetishes.* Some of our staff swear by them. Seems we don't practice what we preach." He scowled and rapped on the seat again. "Do we, Isaac?"

The Volvo pulled in front of Angela's building. Isaac got out and opened the door. Durnkloopf noticed Angela wince, reach for her temples.

"*Umodi*'s good for migraines, too. But be careful."

"Advil will do just fine."

"Isaac, see the lady to her flat."

"I can manage." As the glint of map light hit Angela's face, Isaac drew back, whispering something. Durnkloopf barked at him in Zulu.

"What did he say?"

"So sorry, miss," Isaac answered, head bowed.

Sighing with annoyance, Durnkloopf said, "He said you have the light of the Archangel in your eyes. Have a restful night, Inspector."

The Volvo zoomed off, leaving Angela on the curb, with her *umodi*. She tasted it before crawling into bed, and it dulled her pain, her fear.

She was drifting toward a welcome sleep when Ted Koppel recapped the evening's breaking news on ABC's *Nightline*. Angela hunched up against a mountain of pillows to watch. No mention of Bryce King on any national newscast save for his own network's and on BET, but on *Nightline*, Koppel announced that, because of the tragedy at the Capitol, Vice President Gore and Governor George W. Bush had agreed to forgo political games, at least for now. They'd made their choices for running mates public in a joint statement, rather than build hype before their parties' conventions in Los Angeles and Philadelphia, respectively. Governor Bush had tapped his daddy's Gulf War architect and darling of the right-wing intelligentsia, Dick Cheney. Gore, eschewing grandstanding for somber reflection, introduced one of his old Senate colleagues. No need for hype, because historic electricity crackled through the name: Brian "Butch" Buford.

Angela watched intently as Jeff Greenfield professed to Koppel, "Ted, Buford is an endangered species. An American statesman, in the nineteenth- and early-twentieth-century paradigm."

Angela hit the remote, threw off her quilt, and swung her little feet to the hardwood floor. Full circle, she rethought the dizzying truths suffered on Collins's examining table six months ago. Yes, life's clichés no longer applied to her: the center didn't hold, it bowed. "Good" didn't triumph over "evil." Good cheated. The butler did it, but he was avenging past horrors. *Hear my prayer, Lord. Deliver me from whatever monster is worse: the one that walks out there, or the doubt inside me.*

"Shit." Moonlight was cutting through her blinds like the sun. Angela could hear pops outside, saw red and green flashes through the blinds. More rockets, now, perhaps by African Americans in celebration of Gore's announcement, rather than the Fourth of July. Angela shuffled to the window and closed the blinds. She'd been yawning, eyes shut, so she never saw the pair of eyes staring, pressed against the window. Two stories up, floating. And she never heard, under the pop of fireworks and noise of evening traffic, whispers.

Ukwenza . . . ama zi . . . umthakathi . . . Ama Simba.

44

ANGELA SAT IN ONE OF LUPO'S Bauhaus leather-and-chrome chairs, sipping from a mug of chai tea Jerry'd fetched from Teaism on Dupont Circle. Restive, eyes darting. The morning side effect of *umodi*.

"Agent in Charge Walker over at the Secret Service wants to meet with you before you leave for Atlanta—and I said you were going to be leaving, right?"

"You gloating?"

"The VP's still anxious to see you do your thing, Tigress, but he's also been convinced that we have a case plan, and we must follow it. We're cogs in the machine, babe. Nothing more. That's how I plan to run the Bureau."

"And what does 'doing my thing' entail?"

He sighed. "Any word on King?"

"Lapsed into a coma."

"And this old African fart, the witness?"

"He's in the same wing—Critical Care. He's seventy years old. Bad heart. According to INS, he's Zulu, Frank."

"Your leeway is predicated solely on protecting Senator Buford."

Angela swallowed some spicy tea. "Which is precisely why Styles cleared my interview with Buford and notified Agent in Charge Walker."

Lupo rocked back in his chair. "Then why are you taking Vallas, Micklin, and Johnson?"

Angela stood. "We'll make our plane to Atlanta. We just have work to do here, first." Angela moved to the door.

Lupo pursed his lips, then said sourly, "My Roman ancestors had a saying, Tigress: '*Fiat justitia, ruat caelum.*' "

"Yeah. 'Let justice be done though the heavens fall.' "

"Try real hard to stick to the script. And stay out of trouble."

"I spoke with Ramona King," Butch Buford said somberly as he embraced Angela. She nodded; he didn't let go. "The whole world's lost its soul."

The sorrow clashed with Buford's attire. He looked young and hip in a summery Tommy Bahama print shirt, pleated shorts, and huarache-style sandals. He was on his way to a barbecue fund-raiser for the Susan Komen Breast Cancer Foundation in the sculpture garden at the Hirshhorn Museum; many of the guests were in town for the Fourth of July fireworks around the Washington Monument. It was Buford who'd convinced Bill Clinton not to suspend the festivities, as a show of unity and to honor the victims of Amesha Spentas, including his own junior legislative aide Ayesha Coleman.

Buford released Angela when his wife said, "Now I see why you sent her roses, Butch."

Dr. Cheryl Patterson-Buford had been standing beside her husband. She, too, was summery, festive, in a floral sundress. She was peach-skinned, like Sharon Boissiere, with freckles. Her brown hair was absent any gray; it was coarse but tied back with a coral scarf in a woolly bun. Each of her pedicured toes had some sort of ring or jewelry, like a Hindu dancer's. Unlike a Hindu dancer, she wore little makeup. And no smile.

"Inspector," Buford said, "meet my better half, Dr. Cheryl Patterson-Buford. She and my children didn't attend Les's funeral, thank God. But . . . to change the subject, my beautiful wife is the *most* painless dentist in the Bay Area!"

"Whatever you say, Butch. Honored to meet you." Her handshake was firm, yet cold. She didn't even look at George Vallas, who was shifting uncomfortably in his chair in the office corner. Micklin and Johnson were in the outer offices, questioning Chief of Staff Andre Barnes and Senior Legislative Counsel Betty Robinson. Buford had yet to ask Angela what the two agents were doing out there. He was simply happy to see her, unlike Dr. Patterson-Buford.

"Inspector, if you could check your calendar for October 2000, I am the cochair for our Links Chapter's Gala in San Francisco. I hope you'll consider being a guest speaker. Barry Bonds of our beloved Giants is our MC. We provide scholarships for underprivileged girls in the Oakland and Berkeley areas. Younger, *empowered* sisters like yourself make great role models for our girls, as well as prove something to the Marin County and Silicon Valley crowd."

"I'd be delighted." This queen bee's rap sounded too much the noblesse oblige of Trey's crowd in D.C. "Um, Dr. Patterson-Buford, I wonder if you could—"

"I'm on the faculty at Stanford Dental School," the wife said, cutting Angela off. "I'd read somewhere—*Savoy, Emerge*—you're friends with one of our university folks, on loan to Howard—Alvin Markham? He helped you crack the Venus Stalkers case."

"Yes, Doctor, but I really think that discussion's better left for another day."

Buford took Angela's cue. *"Cher,* could you grab Kwame off the computer game and see if Nicole and her boyfriend have cleared security? The kids always make us late." He looked to Angela. "My daughter's a junior at Cornell. Kwame's at Sidwell."

"Your son—has the Secret Service increased its detail on him?"

Dr. Patterson-Buford broke in. "If my husband's work threatens my children in any way, then my husband would leave political life, right, Butch?"

"Cher . . . ten minutes, no more."

This woman sure doesn't like taking orders, but she took these like a true political spouse. Dr. Patterson-Buford departed. *She didn't even thank me for saving her husband's life!* Pensively, Angela took her seat and revealed, "Sir, Special Agent Johnson's interviewing Mr. Barnes. Special Agent Micklin is doing the same with Ms. Robinson and by now has made a request for general records." As Buford rocked backward, stunned and slow, in his calfskin high-back, Angela said, "Mr. Barnes and Ms. Robinson have been with you for what, ten years, now?"

Face granite, the Senator shot back, "My staff and I are still mourning Ayesha Coleman. Now, if you would be so kind as to explain why this is going to help you protect me, find Les and Carl's killers?"

"Bullfeathers, remember? Mr. Barnes—and you—were all ready to sit down with me at Bullfeathers and talk about Jewel Ngozi. Not about the flowers you sent me in U. Penn hospital. Not about how the Archangels got explosives and nine-millimeter pistols past security. No. Jewel Ngozi. And, sir, I did get something disturbing out of Mr. King in the hospital before he slipped away. Something, I suspect, you were going to tell me."

She heard Vallas clear his throat. Angela motioned him forward. Buford watched in silent amazement as Vallas took surgical gloves out of a little plastic box he carried, snapped them on, then removed two long cotton swabs out of cellophane wrapping.

"Special Agent Vallas is going to swab your mouth for cells for a DNA profile."

"I beg your pardon?"

"Standard procedure."

"In what situations?" Buford pushed away from his desk when Vallas meekly approached.

"Jewel Ngozi, sir. She carried a thirteen-week-old fetus when Antoine Jones killed her. That . . . tissue . . . is likely in a Metropolitan Police Department evidence control storeroom and I will—"

"You will what? Are you out of your mind?"

Angela remained calm, detached. "What are you afraid of . . . sir?"

The Senator exhaled loudly and replied, "Nothing. I know the law, and the law will protect the innocent." He opened his mouth wide. Vallas, amazed, hesitated, but did his duty and placed the swabs in plastic containers.

"I'm not like these other pompous fools, Angela. I'm not going to throw you out or go whining to Donatello, or the White House." Buford sat back down. "Al Gore and I are going to remake this nation. A new covenant with the decent, ordinary people out there. And we're gonna need tough, righteous young folk like you at the top."

"I'm sorry, Senator. You have no idea how much respect I have for you, given what I see around me all the time. But are you about to offer a promise of a benefit, in return for something involving this investigation—here, in front of Special Agent Vallas?" She took out her cassette recorder, switched it on, and recited the date and time.

Buford smiled. "No. I'm stating an observation. And please, tell me exactly what's being investigated. I'm a little confused."

Buford's intercom buzzed. It was Barnes, complaining. Buford replied, "Cooperate with the Inspector's men, Dre. No matter how ridiculous the request."

"But they want to upload appointment diaries . . . and employment records, intern awards from the House, itineraries from, damn, eight years ago? You know that stuff's archived over at the Rayburn Building, if it even still exists."

"Dre . . . I have you on speaker."

"Shit."

"The FBI is our *friend,* Dre. Tell Betty the same. After all, the days of Hoover and COINTELPRO are long gone, right?" Buford clicked off. "I didn't know Jewel personally."

"So what were you going to share with me at Bullfeathers? I want to know what happened the night of October seventh, 1992, at the Omni Shoreham, because that bears on why Les and Carl and now, possibly, Bryce, died."

"She was murdered by her estranged boyfriend . . . after one of our parties. Actually, an after party up in the suites we usually reserved. Strike that. That *Bryce* usually reserved. Does this have to be on the record?"

"I can turn the tape off at any time."

"Then turn the tape off . . . please."

Angela nodded and did so.

"Wait . . . turn it back on for this." When he saw her click the record button, he sighed and recited, "I gave up a DNA sample willingly. I am not in custody, you have not read me my rights; accordingly, I do not plan to invoke my Fifth Amendment right to silence. And, by asking you to turn off this tape, I hope you won't construe I have anything to hide."

"As an attorney, you know the law makes no such construction."

"No. I meant *you,* Angela. Not the law."

"I'm turning the tape off now."

"Okay. Bryce King introduced me to Jewel Ngozi in 1991. She was a junior at Howard, I believe. Bryce had these proclivities . . . for young women." Buford's face softened. "I recall her face when she met me—she'd just been awarded a stipend for the internship. I mean, she was a four-point-oh student, excellent writer, ordered mind, fluid speaker, devastating debater. And ravishing . . . flawless cocoa skin. Tall, huge eyes, beautiful smile . . . damn . . . even when she wore sweats into the office on weekends, men would stare." Buford paused, catching himself. "I say this because, despite the accolades on campus and attention both complimentary and ill, she was usually melancholy. She thought she was ugly, stupid, that people laughed at her accent, her clothes. She once told me that Jones, or Seven, whatever, often denigrated her success, ignored her, while using her as a trophy. A near schizophrenic affliction, huh? She'd cry sometimes at her desk, in the open . . . I didn't have a spacious office when I was over in the Cannon Building. I'd hear her because sometimes we'd be in for late votes, special order speeches, committee work. She'd be sobbing, in Zulu. Sobbing for her mother."

"And not her father?"

"Apparently she hated him. He was some sort of political pariah. One of many reasons she was able to get asylum, get her scholarship."

"Interesting, sir." Angela leaned forward. "You said you didn't know Jewel well."

"So I lied. I felt sorry for this girl, all right?"

"And when you saw that Antoine Jones's lawyer had kidnapped Alfred Whiting, those feelings resurfaced?"

Tongue probing his cheek, he nodded.

"You never met Jones . . . Shaka Seven?"

"Met him often. He was a superstar. A scholar-athlete, turned arrogant, insane gadfly—even when he led HU to the Sweet Sixteen in the NCAA tournament. But . . . when he came by the office for Jewel, he was the center of attention, given his height and local celebrity status. I found him cruel, misguided. The next couple of times, well documented, he'd gotten through building security to come up to argue with her, threaten her. He'd quit our frat, changed his name to Shaka Seven, at that point. The real Shaka was a murderous dictator. Our young people seem to pull concepts out of their asses because they lack moral context. Well . . . he accused her of sleeping with me, his teammates, professors, his frat brothers . . . whatever."

"Whatever—as in King, Dr. Collins, Bishop Davidson?"

"He shot his mouth off, to that effect. That was more due to Bryce's reputation than Jones's psychosis, and I told Bryce that."

"And despite these rumors—"

"No rumors. *Rants.* On campus, I'm sure no one but his moronic followers and a few thuggish teammates took him seriously."

"Despite the rants then, Jewel and Antoine reconciled?"

"Apparently so. I remember . . . damn, August 1992? I believe Andre Barnes invited her to do limited part-time work in my office, because many of my regular staff were now doing advance work for my Senate campaign. Myself, I saw her *once* that late August, I believe, and offered her a chance to take the semester to come to California and work on the campaign. She said no, because of schoolwork, and she'd mended with Jones. By

Homecoming, I guess they split again. I was in the middle of a hard Senate battle with a well-financed right-wing scumbag from Orange County. Saw her before Homecoming at the Congressional Black Caucus Awards Dinner in September . . . seated at Bryce's fifty-thousand-dollar-donor table. That was also the first time I met Victor LeRoi Styles, by the way. But Jewel . . . she looked beautiful. Confident. No sadness. Seven was outta her life. Heard she was elected Miss Howard. Bryce invited her to DaFellaz affair. Saw her fleetingly at the event and then later at the after party. I left early. Had to catch a flight to San Francisco. Got a call from Les that the police had been at the hotel. Blood everywhere . . . my God . . . they'd arrested Jones for Jewel's murder. And that's it."

"So you had very little contact with her during the fall of '92?"

Buford nodded.

"And you mourn her to this day?"

He nodded again.

Her eyes drilled him nonetheless. "So I now ask you—did Leslie Collins have sexual relations with Jewel Ngozi?"

Jesus. Les was very busy with his practice in Philadelphia and—"

"And had enough free time to have several affairs. The last with Elizabeth Hooperman."

Vallas leaned forward, whispering, "Angie, chrissakes, wrap this mess up."

She repeated her question. Buford glowered and replied, "His dalliances were with women like Hooperman, *not* children like Jewel. To wit: very powerful, very willing, very wild *white* women, Inspector. So my answer is no, to my knowledge, he did not have sexual relations with Ms. Ngozi. Nor did he cause her any harm."

"Did Bishop Davidson ever have sexual relations with Jewel Ngozi? Or, in your words, 'cause her any harm'?"

"Again, not to my knowledge."

"And Bryce King?"

"Why are you so cold?"

Angela sighed and shot back, "I have to be, or else what's stirring inside my head right now, what I've seen, what I've experienced, would burn me right out. You recall what you said to me on the steps of that church in Philly . . . about looking into someone's eyes as you killed them? Because you had to. Cold necessity. *Because others depended on you.* So you don't insult me, Senator."

Buford perched over the desk, glaring. "No, to my knowledge, Bryce did not have sexual relations with that woman! Nor did he harm her."

"You mean *child. Girl.* Hooperman was a woman. And a mother. Now she's *dead* because of something *you* allowed those assholes to do!"

Vallas groaned and gripped her arm.

"Let go!" She stood. "None of them deserved to die, but damn it, you are better than all of them and you don't need to protect anyone. If you really think we are alike, then you know what you have to do! *No, Jones didn't kill Jewel, did he, Senator?*"

Buford drew back from the desk, then turned to his window. "You didn't ask the final question," he mumbled to the glass. "Did I ever have sexual relations with Jewel Ngozi . . . or harm her?"

"Did you?"

Angela heard a deep, troubled sigh. *"I wish I had.* When she'd cry . . . over Jones . . . maybe this . . . this baby she carried, for him, she'd say something in Zulu over and over again. And once I heard her say what I think it meant, in English . . ."

Angela muttered, " 'I ache for you.' "

The words seemed to chill him to the bone. He whipped around and sank back to his desk. Vallas moved to Angela's side. "Let's terminate this."

"Sit down, Special Agent Vallas." She then faced Buford. "Senator, I saw a recording of you on *The Charlie Rose Show.* You said denial is the eighth deadly sin. I know firsthand what that means."

"I say, I write, many things. I'm a politician."

"Thought you were a statesman." Now, without pressing Buford further, she wanted to leave. Unsated, tired. Afraid of the answers, she motioned to a relieved Vallas.

But as Angela moved to the door, Buford called, "When . . . when is Antoine Jones scheduled for execution?"

Angela replied, "July 23rd. When you win in November, *when you make history,* remember that date."

Out the door, she and Vallas whisked past bewildered staffers to collect Micklin and Johnson. Bigger, taller agents hung paces behind the shorter Angela. Silent, nervously eyeing each other. Finally, Micklin dared to tap her on the shoulder when they hit the elevator.

"Got some weird travel records for 1992. Can't believe it wasn't purged, but I think it's because it was in an old Federal Election Commission compliance file. King Communications Corporation paid for six plane trips,

United Airlines, from June to September 1992 for Buford and an 'unnamed female campaign staff member.' Five between Dulles and San Francisco Airport, one from National to LAX."

"So?" Angela huffed, still wondering why she'd let Buford off the hook.

"They were one-way tickets."

45

A CRESCENDO OF POPS AND BOOMS shuddered the Hoover Building as fiery blossoms exploded above the pinnacle of the Washington Monument. Its tip was just visible from Angela's office window; Angela, forehead to glass, closed her eyes when the last shower of light fell to the Mall. Her mind's ear heard three hundred thousand collective oohs and aahs at the fireworks finale, accompanied by the National Symphony Orchestra. Her mind's eye saw the traffic, adults dragging sweaty, sleeping children and lawn chairs. All scrutinized by exhausted MPD officers, nervous undercover FBI agents, and, clandestinely, FBI-HRT and shadowy Delta Force commandos. And there, under a Capitol Terrazzo defiled by blood and blast scars just a week prior, sat Al and Tipper Gore, Butch and Cheryl Buford. Casual, approachable—even animated. Your upper-middle-class, young-middle-aged next-door neighbors, now poised to leapfrog over Dubya Bush and a stolid, scary Dick Cheney.

" 'I ache for you,' " Angela muttered to herself as she fell away from the normalcy, both real and manufactured, beyond the glass, to her desk chair. And, recalling Maynard Mullinix's final words, " 'He comes to murder the lies.' *Shit* . . . Grammie, help me. *Someone* help me." Her answer was yet another vision, more sounds. Wings and breasts and pink shrimp cracking over charcoal on Carmen's back deck. Potato salad. Greens dashed with Texas Pete. Bushels of crabs. Bodies swaying to the music in the narrow yard abutting the alley. Two bodies, pressed closer than the rest. Alvin, Sharon.

Sighing forlornly, Angela returned to her desktop computer. She'd been running two files on a split multimedia screen simultaneously—a feat for the FBI's overpriced yet antiquated system. One side showed INS data and photos, the other, info uploaded from Dr. Jan Durnkloopf's CD. On the credenza, Angela's laptop screen buzzed with field notes and digitized crime-scene photos: the Blue Heron Inn, Rittenhouse Square, the old Neal & Co. warehouses, the site where Youssa's body had been found, Bryce King's office and the F Street parking garage. In Angela's throbbing skull, all these images melted together.

An incoming e-mail tone from the desktop rousted Angela from her painful trance. Durnkloopf was consistent. He'd just sent a PDF file of an old South African Ministry of Justice dossier on Jewel Ngozi. Most of the text was in Afrikaans, but some of it was redlined in English. As she read, she licked a straw clean of the chocolate goop that, an hour ago, was an arctic Frosty from the Wendy's across the street. The Natal constabulary had arrested Jewel in 1985 for organizing her junior high school's march protesting the shooting of a classmate by police in her township. She'd just turned fourteen and, though Zulu, was a student member of Mandela's ANC. Jailed again three years later, this time by Security Police: "Material Witness Custody." Jewel was a witness against someone named Elise Isambalala, age sixty-eight, for conspiracy to murder Nandi Ziwedu, age thirty-one. Isambalala was a self-proclaimed *sangoma.*

"Oh, shit," Angela cursed, Wendy's straw dangling like a cigarette. " 'Victim Nandi Ziwedu . . . Concierge-clerk, Royal Durban Palms Hotel. No ANC or Communist affiliation. Perpetrator asserts no political motive for fatal assault. Says Ziwedu was consort . . . to male witch.' *Jesus Lord."* Angela bit down on the straw as the English redlining ended with *Victim died from third-degree burns from tyre set ablaze. Isambalala executed 7 April 1988, precipitating Second Ladysmith Riots. First riots, 1982, ignited by similar purge of witches in KwaZulu Homeland after death of Lutheran minister Michael Dginshwayezi.* Angela whispered to herself, "Michael . . . the Archangel."

Angela flipped to one of the black-and-white photos Durnkloopf had given her. An old Toyota pickup truck had smashed through a stone wall. Natal police had gathered around it. It was captioned, in English: *17 December 1982, vehicle carrying Michael Dginshwayezi to chapel, wrecked on*

Pietermaritzburg Road. She leaned closer to the screen. A weird blood smear stained the passenger door of the pickup.

She looked back to the desktop screen. The rest of the info was in Afrikaans. She tossed the macerated straw in the wastebasket and fixed on the context of the words. There, the word *moedder* between *Jewel Ngozi* and *Nandi Ziwedu.* So Buford remembered correctly. Sort of. Her mother was burned for copulating with a witch? The police—whom Jewel hated—were protecting her? And there, the word *vadder.* Moses Ngozi, 25 Oktoberen 1925. *Afwezig zijn doden.* She accessed a translation utility; it took a while for the window to open. "Missing, presumed dead," she said.

Her body tingled. "Him. Warlock. Her . . . *father.*" Revenge. Murdering the lies.

A rap on her office door nearly jumped her out of her chair. "Go away!" she yelled.

George Vallas came in anyway. He looked and smelled fresh in a blue FBI polo and khakis. "S'up? I'm on call. All leaves and holidays canceled, remember?" He frowned when he saw that Angela was sweating, her movements jerky. "Sorry."

"No . . . no, it's okay. What do you want?"

"Just to say, apparently Buford didn't get a big hair across his ass for what you pulled in his office; haven't heard a damn thing from the Skipper. And, well . . ." He sat on the sofa and Angela prayed he wasn't going to get personal. "Sorry for clownin' you in Buford's office. Just would have been nice to get briefed in advance on how far you were planning to take this shit."

"Micklin and Johnson make any headway on Buford's old records?"

"A little. We gotta get ready for Atlanta, right?" He grinned, then said, "But we did find that Buford's San Fran trips didn't correspond to home visits. Check this out. He was going to a rented houseboat, in Sausalito. Rented under the AmEx card of one Andre Barnes. Unless that was their floating Bay Area campaign HQ, homey was settin' up a coochie palace."

"*Yeah.* Get Marc on that, even if we have to keep in contact with the Frisco-Oakland Field Office from the Metro Atlanta Command Center."

Vallas was fiddling with Durnkloopf's photos. "Hey, what're these?"

"Pass 'em here, George, okay?"

"Well, this one . . . this bent-up truck, man, this looks like the crime-scene stuff from Philly. I mean the blood, on the door." He handed her the photo. "See?"

Photo in hand, Angela slid her chair to the laptop screen and brought up a photo of the supposed "Chamuel" blood signatory on the wrecked EMS unit that had carried Carl Davidson. Angela looked back at her desktop's monitor. The pickup in that old photo. Identical smears. Again, her limbs tingled. "George," she murmured, "grab an Elmo out of the conference room and set it up on the sofa."

"Angie . . . I also wanted to talk . . . about us, know whut I'm sayin'. I think—"

"Goddamn it, George, get it!"

He bowed and ran down the hall, returning with the machine. The Elmo took the place of those old, clunky opaque projectors Angela remembered from high school. Angela slid the South African photo on the plate, then traced the outline of the presumed Hebrew *cha* on the plaster, in pencil. She did the same with the Philly crime scene photo, as Vallas scratched his head. Angela tilted her head, squinted, and said, "It's something. Not a symbol . . . something else."

"A face . . . looks a little like a face. Animal."

Angela tore a sheet off her legal pad and had Vallas hold it to the wall, over the penciled shapes. Then she took her Sharpie marker, outlined the outline, shaded it where appropriate, stood back. Had Vallas rotate it, until, with a shudder, she whispered, "Stop." He didn't hear, and the next time she shouted it: "Shit . . . *stop!*"

It was a lion's visage. "Simba . . . like Ama Simba." Lion's Regiment. Twenty years ago, they killed Michael, the child in her dreams. Now she had hard proof they stalked again. Controlled, like the fetish, by Jewel's father. She slumped at her chair. "Where're Marc, Micklin?"

Vallas came up behind her. "Where do you think? This building's empty because everyone's out on the street, Angie." He spun her chair around.

"Have you lost your mind?" Angela snapped.

"Have you?"

With Nadia gone, it was time to verbalize what she'd been dancing under his nose for weeks. "This pattern killer is . . . thinks . . . he is . . . a shaman of some kind. Zulu."

"As in witch doctor? This for real?"

"As in warlock."

"As in warlock like Maurice in *Bewitched*? Aw, no . . . this is going way, way—"

"Listen to me! I don't know who to trust anymore. You might go running to Frank or Dr. Myers, whatever. But I know who killed Hooperman,

Collins, Davidson, possibly even orchestrated Whiting's kidnapping. And, yes, what happened in Buford's office relates. All the way. Now, are you on my side? I gotta know."

He drew back, tousled his hair. "Yeah. But . . . Zulu. The snake, the gold under the tongue, the spear. Angie . . ."

"It's crazy, I know."

"That's not what I was gonna say. You mumbled 'Simba,' as in that faggoty cartoon Disney lion? That's a Swahili word. Yeah, like, I know more about the Motherland than Marc. He don't know shit if it ain't in Brooks Brothers or on ESPN."

Vallas's remark jogged Angela's mind—back to Durnkloopf's lecture at the embassy. "You are back in my good graces, Special Agent Vallas."

She pulled up to her desktop, reopened the translation utility. She typed in *lion*, then clicked the isiZulu language database. They waited.

Simba was Swahili, yes, but the Zulu word for lion was *ibhebesi*.

Face grim, voice faint, Angela muttered. "Go down and get a Taurus. We're going to Washington Hospital Center."

The nurse in Medstar's Critical Care ward checked Samuel Ibhebesi's vitals. The old man, wrapped in a blue hospital gown, snoozed peacefully. Because he was set for MPD and FBI questioning, uninsured Sam got a semiprivate room. The chart noted that he refused to open his mouth. The nurse would use this opportunity to open the sleeping old elf's mouth and see what the ruckus was about. Indeed, one of the DCFD EMTs who'd brought him in had teasingly sketched the old man's face with teeth like a shark's; a nurse who'd intubated him had nicknamed him Mack the Knife.

With a tongue depressor, the nurse parted Samuel's lips, careful not to disturb the oxygen tubes feeding each nostril. His uppers were white and straight, but she could tell this was a bridge of some kind that the admission staff had neglected to remove. Lazy, lazy, lazy—the risk manager would hit the ceiling over this. His lowers, however, brought a gasp. Razor sharp and yellow, like crocodile teeth. Uneasily, with curiosity sliding over fear, the nurse tapped the uppers once again. She readied a plastic cup for the denture, then, gently, she unsnapped it from Samuel's palate.

Not so gently, Samuel's jaws snapped down on her fingers, severing two of them at the second joints. His hand covered her mouth, just as her shock-delayed brain caused a scream. Samuel gulped down the finger pieces, and leaped off the bed, lithe and strong as a younger man. Pointed teeth bared like a wolf's, he twisted the nurse's neck till it crunched. Once he'd disconnected his IV and oxygen, he dragged her to a small half-cabinet, removed the shelves, cracked the dead woman's joints, and stuffed her in as if she were a contortionist. She'd keep until he could dump her properly. He found his clothes and his small canvas bag, supposedly containing toiletries, all packed by helpful police at his apartment. But in a side pocket, ready-packed, was a small gourd, stitched in beads, plastered with dead flesh. He shook it. Whispered. From his trouser pocket he pulled out three tiny jute pouches, the size of Sweet'n Low packets. By an air vent, he lit one with matches from the other pocket. He crept to the doorway to the hall, waited for the foot traffic to die down, and lit the other. In a whiff of blue smoke, the sacks disappeared. The third, unlit, he tossed into the cabinet with the nurse's mangled body. It would mask the smell of blood, evacuated bladder and bowels, until he decided what to do with her. He didn't care if they found her later.

Samuel loped out into the hall, yellow toenails scratching the floor, half-naked in a gown. Yet no one saw him. Not a soul, despite the flood of wounded or drunk July Fourth revelers. He sang a canticle as he hugged the wall down to the ICU, where Bryce King lay comatose. Helpless.

46

HELPLESS

"UM . . . HE CODED SEVENTEEN MINUTES AGO," the on-duty resident called to Angela as he bounded down the hall after her, toward Samuel's room. She was flanked by two police officers and followed by Vallas and an agent from the Washington Field Office. "But, ma'am . . ." He caught up with her, panting. "Ma'am, I don't see what this old man has to do with it."

Angela faced him at the door. "Doctor, please . . . go back with Special Agent Riggs here, make sure Mrs. King and her family are taken care of."

The agent yanked the bewildered resident back down the hall; Angela, Vallas, and one cop entered Samuel's room. They found a male nurse and PA replacing a ventilator tube, taping it to Samuel's closed mouth. Samuel was comatose, his heart rate dangerously erratic.

"What's this?"

The nurse answered as he worked, "No one's talkin' to ol' Kunta Kinte tonight. Unstable angina. BP's falling, pupils dilated. Plus, they found proteins for bladder cancer in his bloodwork. Confirmed a tumor when we catheterized him. He's a mess."

Angela sighed. "How long's he been out? May I see his chart?" The PA handed Angela the chart. Samuel had been mildly sedated for two days for a broken rib and internal bleeding. "Where is this Anne-Marie Sullivan, RN? The last to do rounds?"

The PA answered after checking her watch. "Off duty, right, Eddie?

Didn't see her when I started my shift, though. She's usually finishing up her paperwork then."

"Has he had any visitors today or tonight?" Angela asked.

Both staff shook their heads. "We're seven-to-seven graveyard on the holidays, sistah," said the nurse. "But, hey, we can check from the station terminal. Follow me." When the monitor at the nursing station kicked up one name, John Smith, nephew, the nurse mentioned, "Uh-huh, yesterday, four-twenty P.M. Musta been the real tall dude they say got jumpy when he saw the cops down the hall, guarding Mr. King. Said he looked like a cross between Coolio and Shaq!"

Vallas leaned over and whispered, "Uh, the INS printout we got coming up here says the man's a widower, child deceased—all other relatives still in South Africa. But he *is* from KwaZulu-Natal, Howick-Ladysmith Borough, green card issued seven, twenty-seven, '91."

"The address he gave," Angela noted, tapping the screen, "Eight oh nine Q Street, N.W. Apartment three. Shit, that's *Samuel's*, right?" Shaw-Trinidad. The "Jungle." The place where Youssa died.

"George . . . call for backup. ISD Code 371. *Now!*"

Most of the two-story row houses were boarded-up, with iron stoops rusted and mangled, bricks cracked, weeds and ferns choking the five-square-foot patches of supposed front yard. Just three blocks up Q Street sat new low-income garden apartments; three blocks up 8th, the row houses stood re-newed, proud, pristine, and festooned with yuppie Realtor signs that mostly read "sold" or "under contract."

Vallas pulled the Taurus up slowly—headlights off—as Angela checked the house numbers, skipping those where there was only a bare lot. Vallas punched the brakes and Angela would have jerked into the dash were it not for her shoulder harness.

"See that shit? Rats the size of damn cocker spaniels just ran across the street!"

"Park it here." Angela called into her throat mike, "Radio check, our ten-twenty is the eight hundred block of Q Street, Northwest . . . gimme a ten-ten in two minutes. Have MPD SWAT move up through the alley. Did you clear civilians from the block?"

Micklin answered, "Not too many of them. Some got scared when they saw us, and as for the ladies, I guess the fireworks put a damper on the ol' 'ho stroll.' "

"Nah, it was the rats," Vallas groaned. He saw rustling in the garbage-strewn gutter. "Or—you think we finally found the home of that big green mamba snake?"

Angela, Kevlar fastened, stepped out of the Taurus. "I'd rather face those rats than the snake."

Angela pulled her SIG; Vallas loaded twelve-gauge shells into a Remington assault shotgun, racked it, and followed her to a front double door. The glass panels had long been replaced with taped cardboard. A call came in on Angela's earpiece. Brett Mallory. "You coulda invited me to this party sooner, Angie. Guess what? Special Agent Johnson called me—the latents on that piece of baseball cap you had. They match my set for Stringbean Coy. We just got finished showing his mug to the day staff up at Washington Hospital Center. Four out of six people made him. Said he didn't even hang in the ol' man's room but for a minute . . . was asking questions about who was in the ICU."

Devon Coy. Antoine's teammate, friend—now thug. But a warlock? He wasn't African; even thinking it sounded insane. But she'd already thought and seen and digested so much insanity.

Mallory continued, "You're gonna need more backup, copy, Angie?"

"Negative. I'm already gonna have to explain why I pulled my team out here, plus one Crim Squad from the Nest, not to mention your people."

"Sucks ta be you, Angie. I'll be there in ten minutes, copy? Mallory out."

With a light affixed to the shotgun barrel, Vallas flashed a beam in the row-house foyer, through the door's one remaining piece of glass. Angela reassured him, "I'll deal with Lupo, the others. Let your big sister take the heat."

Vallas popped his chewing gum and grinned. "So what we did was incest?"

"Don't go there."

"Hey—you're only two years older than me, and but three feet tall, so ya ain't nobody's real big sis." He paused. "Nothing in the stairwell. Ready?"

She picked up her feet quickly as he easily forced the doors open, aimed the shotgun, then slid to the side. The cramped, hot foyer reeked of urine, spilt malt liquor, and fortified wine. Angela aimed the SIG as she edged up creaky stairs lit by three hanging bulbs. The shadows looked brown, not black. No TVs blaring or shouts—the usual. Just dead quiet, but for the distant pops and shrieks of kids using up their last fireworks. She froze in front of Apartment 3 when she saw that the door was ajar. Creaking on the ceiling meant that her backup and MPD SWAT officers were up there—she hoped.

Vallas flanked the door; they counted to three silently. Vallas kicked it wide and aimed the shotgun as Angela swept inside.

Nothing. Just furnacelike heat, the smell of fried grease, body odor. The glow from the streetlamp seeped in through smudged windows and torn shades; her eyes now accustomed to the brown murk, Angela eased down the hall.

"Check the kitchen," she whispered into her mike. Vallas didn't copy. She turned and in the meager ambient light saw Vallas tap his earpiece. Communications were down. How? She could hear him whisper harshly, "Micklin, you copy? Get your big ass up here. Micklin?"

"Quiet," she called, voice low, palm extended.

Vallas crept up to her. "Lost five-by-five on the channel."

She pointed to the outline of a door at the end of the shadowy, stinking hall. They moved toward it slowly, and as they did, the night swallowed them. Silence behind them, but in front, as they groped, they could hear noises beyond that door.

A cheap fan sputtering and humming. And then, faintly, a female's cry. Not of pain. "Uh-huh . . . uh-huh . . . uh-huh . . . fuck me . . ." A male groan. Mattress, squeaking.

"You gotta be kidding," Vallas said.

"Shush." Angela tapped her earpiece. Nothing. She cut a glance over her shoulder. No flashlights coming up behind them. They'd be hitting blind, without a coordinated attack. But she had no choice. This time she'd kick; Vallas would be ready to pump the room with twelve-gauge pellets. The blissful whimpers reached a climax, then broke to a shriek, *"Uuuummmnyama."* And the male voice screamed in horror.

Panicked, Vallas drew back, but Angela beat the door with her fist, shouting, shrilly, "Federal Agents!" Then: "Now, George!"

Vallas regained his wits and aimed his SIG as Angela smashed the door open with one kick.

A mist, a pall of lighted smoke, same as what had sucked in Angela in the fetish room, met the two agents. The nanoseconds passed like slow, dropsy minutes.

A black man, nude, writhed, screaming on the bed.

His hands flailing from his neck to his groin. Huge rats at his throat—gobs of thyroid, of bloody flesh, on their whiskers. His penis and scrotum torn off, blood gushing from his inner thighs.

At the open window, a small figure wrapped in a flapping open shirt, breasts lit only for a second, toes painted. Hand carrying dripping flesh. Flesh from the man. Then, suddenly, Angela saw only a silhouette, as darkness flooded back into the room. Before her brain could cause her to cry "Freeze," or even form any rational thought, the female leaped from the windowsill onto the roof of the next wrecked house, a mane of long black hair spreading on the wind, as Angela rushed to the sill to fire.

The only thing that fell after four 9mm rounds was the shimmery black hair: a wig, tumbling into the alley. And the mist sucked itself out as if the rusted fan on the floor had grown to wind-tunnel strength. Angela turned to see Vallas pump three shots into the rats. Three rodents were blown apart. A fourth and fifth burrowed to safety into the rotted plaster behind the bedstead.

Chest heaving, Angela rushed to the naked man, whose thrashing slowed, limbs dropping, still. That's when the static, then voices, returned to her earpiece.

"*F-fuck!*" Vallas stammered, breathless, spittle flying. "You *s-see* that? You *see?*"

Angela nodded, then, panting, called, "EMS . . . EMS emergency! Ten-seventy-five, ten . . . ten-seventy-five. Get up here now!" She shoved a wad of bedsheet into the gaping mess between the man's legs. "George! Help me elevate his legs, keep the blood in his chest, head! Compress the neck wound."

But Vallas, wielding the shotgun, was wandering, mumbling.

Angela sputtered in her mike, "Female suspect . . . on eight eleven roof! Do you have a ten-twenty? Repeat? Shit, answer me. Check the east alley. A black wig! Blood trails!"

Then, she heard, "Affirmative, this is Special Agent Goldman, C-3, MPD officers secured the wig. Negative on female subject. But . . ."

"But what?" She looked to Vallas, crying out, "George . . . *Special Agent Vallas!* Pull your goddamn self together! Shit, I need you!"

The lights flickered on; Micklin and Johnson stormed into the apartment with two SWAT officers.

"Get Vallas outta here!" Angela commanded. "Then help me with this man!"

Agent Goldman radioed, "We found . . . found male genitalia . . . *I think.*"

When Brett Mallory arrived, he had to navigate his MPD Chevy Malibu through four TV news trucks, microwave feeds high in the humid sky.

Reporters practiced and flubbed their phony camera "cutaways" as Brett saw that the object of their interviews was huddled in the back of an MPD unit, wrapped in a wool blanket despite the heat.

"Angie?" he asked through the unit's open rear window. When she didn't answer, he rose to see Marc Johnson sitting on the curb beside the police car, consoling Vallas, who was heaving some last few drops of vomit into the gutter. Even a hardened cop like Mallory, who'd himself been a victim of Trey and Pluto Williams's atrocities, could only shake his head, mute, at the sight of the stunned FBI agents, and the nude, mutilated man being zippered into a body bag too short for his tar-black legs and ashy gray feet.

Finally, Brett heard a faint voice from the unit: "It was Devon Coy, right? I'm sorry, Brett. We were so close."

"Uh, I think you should know—Chief Ramsey called me. He'd finished a conference call with Deputy Director Styles and Frankie Lupo . . . he said someone from FBIHQ was coming over to bring you in and—"

"That'd be all, Detective" came the stingingly familiar voice.

Expressionless, numb, Angela looked up to see Bud White standing on the sidewalk.

47

"SIT DOWN, ANGELA," VICTOR STYLES SAID somberly. Almost arthritically, he motioned to the chair in front of his desk.

"Victor," Angela began as she sat, "please let me explain why we went to that apartment."

Styles held up his hand. "It was a grand mess, and now the press is ahold of it. So Supervisory Special Agent White's going to clean up this matter with Devon 'Stringbean' Coy and that old man at Medstar while you're in Atlanta. Bob Scofield insisted on White's involvement, and the Director says that's the way it will be."

"I was supposed to be in Atlanta on Tuesday. They won't miss me."

"Two of our Learjets at National leave for Hartsfield Airport in an hour. This time, you will be on one of them. This time, no reprieve from the Vice President for you. No reprieve . . . for any of us." He paused and smiled. It wasn't his smirk; it was a weary, fatalistic smile. "I will watch your back here."

"You're going to a funeral: King's. You know damn well there will be one more. And it might not be Buford's. It could be his wife's. His daughter's. Even his son's."

"Woody Sessions's counterterrorism agents, in conjunction with ATF and the Georgia Bureau of Investigation, have credible intell leading us to believe that Amesha Spentas will strike in Metro Atlanta, full circle with the Olympic bombing in '96. Thus your presence there is now unquestionably urgent." He leaned forward. "The sooner you bust these pieces of shit, the sooner you get back here and finish whatever you started when you conceived an unauthorized strike team and hit that old man's apartment."

"Understood . . . sir."

"Be assured, Buford's Secret Service detail's been trebled; King's funeral's a private event at a crematorium in Annapolis. Even Buford's daughter's boyfriend has a shadow, and the son's going to a Boy Scout summer camp on the Susquehanna River for a whole month—with four agents, and our HRT as floating backup."

"In your wildest dreams, Victor, you have no idea what we're up against."

"That's why we have you. Now get out of here." Yet before Angela could rise, Styles added, "I will go to Buford's house next week. I promise. Talk to him about Bryce, about Jewel Ngozi. One-on-one." Styles sighed wistfully. "He and Cheryl rent the four-bedroom coach house on the Kennedy estate in McLean, Virginia, off Chain Bridge Road and Dolly Madison. Kennedy, as in Mrs. Robert Francis. Ethel. Butch apparently has a sense of destiny as well as duty."

"Good-bye, Victor. Please tell the Senator I *will* be back."

"How could he just fucking disappear?" Angela shouted through the windwash. She was on her cell's hands-free; Sweet Pea's top was down. The sun was blistering the upholstery as she snaked through on the Memorial Bridge into Arlington Cemetery. "Broad daylight? He couldn't walk; he's seventy years old. Eyes like yellow cataracts!"

Brett Mallory answered, "Homicide Commander Boone and the chief told me that we were no longer responsible for keeping an officer on the Critical Care ward, Angie. Someone from your HQ and the Nest was supposed to take over. So I'd pulled our uniforms outta there. I called that Russell-Crowe-wannabe-lookin' fool William White. By the time he called me back, the African'd been taken. Most of his clothes were still there. Someone'd disconnected the IV tubes, everything. Plus, his nurse on duty a few days ago—her husband reported her missing."

"Please find this guy, off-the-clock if you have to. I do not fucking trust that Bud White to do squat."

"I'll do what I can, baby gurl. Which means very little right now. Sorry."

She clicked off just as another call came through. Marc Johnson said, "Inspector, Vallas and Drew are already at the terminal getting stuff on board our flight. Your flight leaves ten minutes after ours, with the BATF and CIRT folks."

Nerves already plucked, Angela snapped, "I don't want to even talk to George, you understand? He froze in that apartment. He dropped the ball."

The young agent's tone sharpened. "We all aren't like you, all right? That was some mad, ghosty shit in that crime scene."

Angela sucked in a breath. "I'll see you in Atlanta, Marc."

Angela heard a sigh. "I was calling for another reason. More info coming in, from our check on Buford: the houseboat Buford's chief of staff was renting back in '92, in Sausalito."

"Go on."

"Houseboat's owner referred me to this fudge-packer named Sylvester St. Jermaine, who did the personal shopping, housekeeping, et cetera, on the boat, years ago. Said he remembers a lot of young girls coming aboard, cleaning up after them. *Very young,* from their appearance, the candy and soda consumed, MTV or *Video Soul* always on the tube. Said only one stuck out in his memory—a 'Fiona Apple–looking snow princess,' in his words."

"Totally unhelpful."

"Okay, white female, anywhere from underage to eighteen years old. Shoulder-length, straight, light brown hair, thin, long legs. Despite that Calvin Klein heroin-emaciated look, she was always ordering out; he'd see delivery receipts and containers from expensive Italian and seafood places. He's never seen Buford there, of course."

"Of course. Did you send him a photo of Jewel Ngozi?"

"Yes, through the Frisco Field Office. Negative on the ID."

As Sweet Pea pulled onto the George Washington Parkway, past the Pentagon, Angela's stomach sank. Maybe she should have been relieved? Maybe this "secret" died with King. But then Johnson said, "That white girl—he's pretty sure she was the last teenager there before Barnes terminated the lease. Says one thing really stuck out. Her eyes. 'Milky green,' he said, like the jade Buddhas he buys in Chinatown."

Angela felt a slight twinge in her spine. Something prurient, familiar. "Marc, thanks. You won't regret this."

"Nah, I'm sure I will at some point. See you at Hartsfield."

Seven minutes after Angela's Learjet lifted off from Reagan National, two pounds of C-4 destroyed a Planned Parenthood center in Augusta, Georgia. Five people, including two patients, died. At that moment, a hundred miles away, a more primitive pipe bomb full of masonry screws blew out the windows of the shared ACLU and People for the American Way offices on the ground floor of Five Dunwoody Plaza in Buckhead, less than three miles from downtown Atlanta. No fatalities, but the hot shrapnel inflicted hideous wounds on ten people. The previous day, those organizations had garnered harsh words from conservative native son Representative Bob Barr, along with Jerry Falwell. But now, even the most vitriolic right-wingers wanted the extremists rubbed out. They were a liability. Just as everyone wanted Antoine Jones gone. Another liability. On the Learjet, streaking toward Hartsfield International Airport, Angela listened to the reports of the carnage. Silent, eyes kept to herself.

48

MISSING YOU

NADIA RESTED HER BIKE AGAINST a shingled wall and entered the cottage through the screened-in sunporch. Her bikini was still damp and the bottoms sagged from the weight of her MP3 player. Her mother's attention was focused on the thirteen-inch TV, resting atop a plastic table. Nadia had been listening to Incubus's "I'm Missing You." She cut the volume and pulled out the phones when she saw what her mother was watching.

"Suspects have been identified as Scott David Wilmer, twenty-six, of Rochester, New York, Richard Carl Schroeder, twenty-seven, of Lavonia, Georgia, and Tyler Mitchell Boddie, thirty-five, of Alpharetta, Georgia." On a parking ramp under the Fulton County Courthouse, FBI agents stuffed three white males, cuffed, into a white van as Atlanta Metro Emergency Response Team officers brandishing Ruger mini-14 assault rifles stood, vigilant. *"FBI spokesperson Angela R. Bivens, who was witness to the Capitol Senate Gallery attack, confirms that Tyler Boddie is indeed a senior official in the Cobb County Sheriff's Department."*

"She did it. She . . . she cracked them," Nadia whispered as she eased onto the wicker love seat next to her mother. Angela, haggard, with sorrel hair yanked back in a bun fuzzed with flyaways, appeared on-screen, wrapped in an FBI field windbreaker that looked two sizes too large.

Angela recounted on-screen: *"Acting on tips and physical evidence in the*

277

Atlanta Metro area, we've broken the back of this Georgia cell, in connection with the Augusta and Dunwoody bombings, conspiracy to blow up the Martin Luther King Jr. gravesite, illegal weapons violations, as well as violations of the Free Access to Clinics Act, Domestic Terrorism and Hate Crimes Response Act, dating back to the Centennial Park bombing during the 1996 Olympics." Nadia grimaced as Angela spoke, as if she were an empath, feeling Angela's strain and bone-weariness. But she couldn't feel what was happening in Washington. An old African man, missing now for a week. A nurse, found in the back of an abandoned Buick off North Capitol Street, her limbs and ribs snapped like dry twigs.

Nadia reached for the cordless and began punching numbers. Marie Riccio yelped that she shouldn't tie up the line; they were expecting invitations to a lawn luncheon that designer Michael Kors was throwing in Sag Harbor. "You been brainwashed at Quantico, hon," she threw in. "Your father's dumped you here with me after exposing you to . . . to *that*. I want you to relax and enjoy some normalcy before he changes his mind and throws you back."

"Christ, Ma—you see this on TV? More important than your goddamn Upper East Side friends and goddamn Michael Kors."

"People have short attention spans, and are truth-averse. Things your father's finally begun to grasp, so lighten up. Now, for the party, be sure to wear the Kors sundress and those Jimmy Choo sandals I got on loan from my friend at *Vogue*, 'kay?"

Ignoring her mother, Nadia stayed on the line, finally reaching Angela's personal digital home answering machine, rather than her FBI-dedicated home voice mail. Before she could leave a message, a call-waiting tone beeped. She checked the caller ID: Arianne's cell number. She clicked over just as Angela's record tone sounded.

"Naddy . . . it's Ari. Please come back, baby. It's safer for us now. *I miss you.*"

Eyeing her mother, Nadia whispered, "Oh my God . . . where are you? What the hell is going *on*? First you act like some crazy woman, then you don't call?"

Marie Riccio lowered her sunglasses. "Is that *that* girl again? Jesus, Nadia—"

Apparently Arianne heard the mother's piquant comment. Nadia's jaw went slack as her lover screamed, "Fuck your mother, your father, the FBI . . . if you love me, you'll come back *now!*"

Then she hung up.

Nadia let the phone slip to her mother's hands. Nadia's brown eyes were blank, all the yearning or fretfulness sucked out of them. In a voice more rocky than ever, she said, "Ma . . . what time do you want to leave for this party?"

Marie kissed her daughter's forehead. "Eight, hon. And, please, I don't just want you to forget about this 'friend' of yours. She needs professional help. I *also* want you to forget Angela Bivens, too. Yes, her. Does your father know you have this . . . this *stuff* here? How'd you even get it onto the train, for God sakes?"

This "stuff" was a Kevlar vest, field windbreaker, and a SIG-Sauer 229 with one clip of live 9mm rounds. The fledgling had learned something from another mother.

"It's my gear, Ma," she muttered as she replugged her earpieces. "I'll put it away." She then set the MP3 on another file. Something familiar. "Freak on a Leash."

49

JEREMIAH WAS A BULLFROG . . .

ANGELA ROAMED, ALONE, UP A CROWDED concourse past the Delta Airlines gates. She swung her blue FBI duffel like a bored schoolgirl; a few passersby stopped, pointed, smiled. Why smile? Discomfited, by meeting an avenging angel? Flushed, by meeting a hero? The *Washington Post* and the *Atlanta Journal-Constitution* had used both monikers. *A hero is the wrong person in the wrong place at the right time,* she mused. *Nothing more.*

Two men in gray suits bounded down the concourse toward her. One had the telltale earpiece of a Secret Service agent. The other was a little doughy, maybe Latino or light-skinned African American, and wearing glasses.

The doughy man puffed, "My name's Anselmo Simms, Assistant Advance Team Manager to Senator Buford. This is Special Agent Tim Cooper."

"I'm very, very tired, gentlemen."

Cooper intoned, "Inspector, we're retrieving your personal luggage directly from the tarmac, as a courtesy. We've already cleared this with Assistant Director Lupo."

"Cleared what? I haven't even been debriefed and I need to speak to—"

Simms chimed in, "You've been invited to cocktails and Tennessee barbecue at Blair House, tonight at eight o'clock. Semiformal, summer-lawn attire; we'll get you home so you can freshen up and change. We have about three hours, but we want to get the press up there and briefed. Vice

President Gore and Senator Buford want to personally thank you for your heroism in Georgia this past week." Now Simms and Cooper flanked her and they walked three abreast up the concourse. "There's talk Governor Bush wants to fly you down to Crawford, Texas . . . but we claimed you first, eh?" Simms's laugh sounded more like a goose's honk.

"I have work to do."

Cooper said, "The invitation's through Deputy Director Styles. He said you'd understand."

Angela felt contempt trickle out of her smile. "Please tell the Senator we're still waiting, per his request," she said to the female Navy Petty Officer in dress whites. Dinner was starting in less than twenty minutes; the staff had cloistered Angela and Victor Styles away from the other 198 dignitaries inside the Commodore Matthew Perry Study in Blair House. This manse was the official residence of the Vice President, sitting on the grounds of the Dumbarton Naval Observatory off Massachusetts Avenue.

"In the meantime, I'd like another Perrier, no ice," Angela said. The petty officer looked over to Styles, who was dressed in a khaki linen suit and brown spectator shoes, as if out of a Ralph Lauren ad in *Vanity Fair*.

"Sweet iced tea this time," Styles said, "tickled with a dash of George Dickel. I foresee an interesting evening, don't you, Inspector?"

"Um . . . on second thought, I'll have what Mr. Styles is having. Please tickle mine a little longer." Angela then peered through the damask drapes at the tented veranda. The Vice President and Mrs. Gore were entertaining down there. When Angela had met the Second Couple in the garden, she found Tipper as funny and unpretentious as Dr. Cheryl Patterson-Buford was stolid and patronizing. Likewise, the VP wasn't the wooden martinet the press or the Republicans or comedian Daryl Hammond portrayed. He was as erudite and pleasant as his new number two.

Indeed, they hinted that "Joy to the World"—the "Jeremiah was a bullfrog" song, not the Christmas carol—would be the campaign jingle they'd unleash on woeful Dubya and scary Dick Cheney at the convention. Hope, energy, practical liberalism, *fun*. A CNN–*USA Today* poll had jumped them seven points ahead of Bush-Cheney—the biggest surge, in the shortest period, in any preconvention poll since 1972. Jeremiah was a leapfrog. Styles would have been bubbly under different circumstances.

Rather, his persistent, anemic monotone shocked Angela. "Bold work in Georgia. Heard you got your linchpin lead from old-fashioned, low-tech mail-cover surveillance." Mail cover was a little-used tool whereby the FBI simply walks into a local post office, demands to see all of a target's mail, including bills, and records the return addresses and postmarks. As long as the mail isn't opened, the practice is legal without a warrant. "But now—we have unfinished business, I suppose."

Angela was looking and feeling too much anger and frustration to speak it. "You told Buford we needed to speak frankly about Jewel, Bryce King? About a man on death row who has less than two weeks to live?"

Styles nodded meekly. "I had no idea it would come to this when I had them hunt you down on that beach at Assateague Island."

Angela lacerated him with her glare. "The truth's cruel, Victor."

The Petty Officer returned with their cocktails. Following her in was Brian Buford, looking like the happy warrior everyone thought him to be. No suit. A simple blue blazer, white flannels, sockless, in Italian loafers. He wore a maroon Bandit ascot tucked into his white linen shirt. He closed the library door when the server hurried out, then sucked down his own drink. Now the room smelled of single-malt Scotch.

Styles said, "Senator, per my phone call yesterday, when you congratulated us for the Atlanta success, we're long beyond posturing. There's a young man on death row who should not be there, and Bryce had something to do with it. If you were in complicity with this, we need to know now. That's all I'm going to say." He gulped down some tea laced with sour mash and left the room.

Everything cold, coarse, base, that Angela felt for Styles drained away, if only for an instant. "Did Mr. King kill Jewel Ngozi . . . and cover it up? Use you, Les, Carl, as alibis, and Antoine, alias Shaka Seven, as the patsy? This isn't on the record. This is between us. Kindreds, Senator. *Supposedly*."

"In one of your interviews, you praised Mr. Garvey as a hero and counted Mr. Brown as one of your friends, despite their flaws."

Buford's nervous chuckle seemed laced with as much self-approbation as Glenfiddich. "I have no real heroes, Ms. Bivens. Nor true friends." His smile sank. "But regardless . . . of what Bryce may have done, Antoine deserves to die. And I'll not come forward and gouge a scab off the past for that scum."

"You never slept with Jewel?"

"No. I told you that. *On the record.*"

"Yet, you loved her, didn't you?"

"Like a father would love a daughter . . . or, maybe back then, like an elder would cherish a protégé."

"I don't believe you. I still believe in real heroes. I'm not one, but you can remain one of mine if you do what's right. That will stop the killing. What happened in Georgia, or at the Capitol, isn't the issue, and I know you know that. Amesha Spentas didn't kill your friends. Someone's avenging Jewel. What you tell me tonight will help me find that someone."

Buford slumped into a walnut Queen Anne chair. "Being . . . unfaithful, to Cheryl . . . it *hasn't* been a conceit thing, or a power thing or some damned trite 'black man's weakness' thing. My wife no longer bewitched me. My family no longer held the magic it had. Not even my son, my daughter."

A chill danced up Angela's bare back. "Interesting you'd use those words, sir. Magic, bewitched. Jewel put a spell on you, eh?"

"Yes . . . but not what you think. She touched everyone, like some angel, all right? Maybe she had some feelings for me, but . . . but I had my own . . . entanglements. Someone else put *her* own spell on me."

Angela kept the houseboat card close. Better to let him spill his guts without playing it. But it rattled her that he'd use that word: *spell.*

"To Bryce, Jewel was another exotic piece of ass . . . nothing more. That's what she was to Antoine. They were simply bookends. Opposites on the same rotten spectrum. Using her." His eyes suddenly watered. "About a week before the Friends of DaFellaz event, Jewel said she wanted to indeed come back to work for me. She was in my office. Suddenly she got sick. Vomited. It was terror, despair, and, well . . . morning sickness."

Angela remembered the sour spittle, triggered by the gush of hormones, ordered by a tiny new piece of herself. And the despair. "There was never a DNA test done on the fetus," she said. "Bryce saw to that—part of his connivance with Alfred Whiting?"

The potential first African American vice president jerked a wounded nod. "Carl, man of God, bully, said that these little college-girl, gold-digging hussies have to be schooled, right? Just like when we were the BMOCs. Had to learn who was in control. Had to accept what happens when you give up pussy for access to 'great, powerful' men. Ha!" Buford paused, his voice fading. "Things got ugly. Someone got hurt. So someone . . . had to take the fall. Things were done, to make that fall complete."

Angela was now standing over him, shivering with anticipation. "Senator, are you confessing a conspiracy to obstruct justice? To cover up . . . a gang rape? Manslaughter? Maybe even murder? Look at me, damn it."

"This is all you get. Do with it what you will." Hopeless eyes corralled Angela's gaze. "Nothing will bring that poor girl back. And if you implicate me, all you will do is destroy the single chance for redemption that's taken four hundred years and oceans of blood . . . so much blood . . . to build. That's embodied in me, Angela. Only me, now."

"You sound like all of the rest of them." Angela scowled back. "Worse than Styles." Angela turned away, closing her eyes to drive back tears for a girl she had never known. A girl abused and exploited and terrorized such that she had to run from her homeland. Only to be used, battled over, abused once more and have her heart torn to shreds. First figuratively. Then literally.

She heard a low, long moan from Buford. Then the Senator suddenly hopped to his feet. "I'm the only one who's left to mourn her."

"Who'll mourn Antoine?" She moved toward him slowly as she spoke. Her big almond eyes covered by slit lids, once again, to dam any tears belying the sting of the coldness, emptiness, inside her. And the fear. Fear just like what she felt that hot night on the lawn at the Blue Heron Inn. Seeping into those empty spaces. "And someone else mourns her. Someone she was terrified of, yet who loved her more than any of you who either killed her or sullied her memory by what you did after she was killed. And he . . . *it* . . . isn't going to stop, until you have paid."

"One way or another, I'll do penance, contrition for my sins. But I will serve my country, my people, first. Let this end with Antoine . . . I'm begging you."

"My grandmother once told me that conceit is the worst sin of all. The 'well' of all sins: from little ones, like coveting, to big ones, like murder." As Angela searched Buford's face, someone knocked on the door. Memphis-style ribs and chops, the Gores, destiny, history. All calling. "And conceit even births bigger ones than murder," Angela mumbled as if to herself, "like surrendering to your worst self." She sucked in a breath when Buford approached, took her hand, kissed it lightly. Then he walked out.

Michael . . . as a child, or an old man, murdered by the creatures who killed your mother, would you embrace me now, conceit and all? Inkanyezi—*were you flawed, too, when they gave you that name? Crippled by doubts? God, truly let this be over.* At dinner, she flashed her brightest smile while her heart repeated that plea.

The only amenity afforded Lorton's sole remaining death-row prisoner was a radio, behind Plexiglas. Antoine Jones had a new cell: a pre-execution capsule with no sink or toilet. He had to ring a buzzer to wash his face. He seldom needed a toilet, because he refused to eat and took only three sips of water a day. He lay in the dark on a rubber-mattressed bunk, chanting over the "smooth jazz" elevator music meant to pacify him.

"*Uku-zi umthakathi. Ama Simba. Ama Simba.* One more. And her. One more. And her. The Lion . . . he comes . . ."

He finished with a shudder. Then he wept. To soothe himself, he mumbled a song his ostensible white mother used to sing to him when he was a lonely little boy, skin black as pitch, clothes green or pink or khaki or white. She sang it quite well, as all old Charlottesville debs could carry a pop tune from their "shag"-dancing and "beach music" days.

"Jeremiah was a bullfrog . . ."

50

ANGELA SAT ON HER FUTON, cradling her phone on her shoulder to squeeze a Nivea lotion bottle and slick lotion over her feet, her knees. Any unguent, any soothing escape. She'd already checked her digital answering machine. Eleven incoming messages, ten from Carmen, her parents, her sister. Number eleven would haunt her sleep. Not that she could sleep, after what Buford had said. After the Atlas-like weight he'd heaved onto her shoulders. Expose what happened, or vault it, like Bryce King's ashes in a mausoleum urn?

The sham on the larger pillow cushioning her head hadn't been changed in weeks. A faint touch of Alvin Markham's Bay Rhum aftershave remained, punctuating her solitude as she whispered another name, other than Buford's or King's. *"Arianne."*

Of course, there'd been no listing in the Hamptons for a Donatello or Riccio; the house was likely rented. There were hundreds of both names in the Manhattan directory; Angela got Nadia's mother's home number from the on-call staff at the FBI Academy. But would the trainee get the message? At the prompt of the voice-mail greeting on the other end of the line, Angela spoke.

"This message is for Nadia Riccio. It's Inspector Angela Bivens. Please ask her to call me, at home, again, private line. Nadia . . . no one's going to be safe, until we talk. Mrs. Riccio, *please* forward this message."

Angela closed her eyes, praying for sleep. One press of the stereo remote: an old Hiroshima CD and a smoldering stick of jasmine incense made up her Eucharist. But the prayers didn't catch the ear of the Almighty. *Arianne Shipley. Little fucking witch. Green eyes. Creamy jade. Milky jade . . .*

The ring tone for her other home line sounded. Angela clicked line two. It was Brett. "Angie . . . FYI . . . two updates. One, the old man, Ibhebesi. Found his hospital gown and ID bracelet not too far from where we discovered the nurse's body. The gown was covered in blood."

Angela shuddered. "Hers?"

"Unh-unh. His blood type. And get this . . . reptilian blood as well. Snake. We passed that info on to Bud White. He swears he cataloged it and shared it with Claude Baker's Crim Squad folks at the Field Office. He never called you, did he?"

"No."

"The old bastard's been eighty-sixed. No damn doubt. That much blood, in his condition? I say Stringbean took him out before Stringbean got himself nutted by that woman, or whoever. I say Stringbean was your voodoo boy, and whoever was helping him, maybe even this chick, did him in. Got ol' witnesses he was way into that black magic African shit at your alma mater. He and his boy, Antoine Jones."

She switched on the lamp on the night table. *"What?"* She could have kicked herself. Carmen had alluded to this, so had Antoine himself.

"Yeah . . . we shared that info with White, too. They was boys. Hooped together, according to family members." When all he could hear was Angela's strained breaths on the line, he said, "You want my second update? Got a single hair from that wig, the one at Q Street. Blond. Dye job, but definitely a Caucasian. Food in the fridge in Tupperware-like containers. But it ain't Tupperware. It's expensive microwavable shit from Williams-Sonoma. Ain't nothin' from no Williams-Sonoma in any house in that part of the Jungle, baby. This bitch may have had money as well as being a bloodthirsty sociopath."

Angela's eyes closed. *White girl in the window. Hissing like a cat as Stringbean lay convulsing.*

"Angie, you there?"

White girl, San Fran. Long legs. Creamy jade. Long legs.

Eyes opened. Very wide.

"Once in a bluest moon," huffed Angela's assistant, Jerry Lopes, as he clicked a computer mouse through a multimedia database, "I'm hoping we can work regular hours. Either that, or you are definitely going to have to resolve your trust issues."

Jerry was wearing a black silk shirt opened almost to the navel, pleated khaki shorts, and black leather slides. He stank with Gaultier for Men. He had been tending to his life outside the office, but he was devoted to his boss. She and Jerry were sitting at the flat-screened terminal in an ITC techie's empty cubicle on Sub-Four of the Hoover Building. The whole vast wing was dark and freezing. No sound but for a few on-call techies on break, or uniformed security walking the halls.

"We'll have to pull the records from the Washington Field Office's local background-check file. This isn't national stuff, especially if you want a photo." Jerry started typing. "Yeah, luckily, the Lowell School's one of those hinkty D.C. private schools that does these checks, then secretly feeds us the data. Private-school teachers aren't unionized and probably don't know what we're doing's a no-no under the Protection of Children Against Sexual Predators Act."

Angela sipped from her caramel iced coffee, then asked, "What's this notation here?"

"Chickie-gurl's pedigree. Went to that e-lite girl's academy, the Madeira School, in Fairfax County, before Sarah Lawrence, see? Wasn't that where Jean Harris was headmistress, before she shot that 'Scarsdale Diet' doctor?"

"Hold up now," Angela thought aloud. "Senator Buford's daughter attended Madeira. Hurry up with the photo . . . then merge it, compress it, fax and e-mail to the San Francisco Field Office under my ISD code."

"No cc to Supervisory Special Agent White?" When Angela jumped an eyebrow, Jerry chuckled, "Never mind. Hey, where did Buford get the ducats to send a son and a daughter to these schools?"

Angela smacked her lips after finishing her frosty, sweet coffee. "Silicon Valley law practice, plus his wife's a dentist and oral surgeon. Perfect couple. A real-life Cliff and Clair Huxtable. Too good to be true, maybe?"

"No, ma'am. He's for real. He's got our vote and he doesn't have to pander or fawn like Clinton. Treats us with basic human respect, which is all we want."

Jerry sent the data and the image, then phoned the San Francisco–Oakland Field Office's on-call supervisory Crim Division agent. It was only 9 P.M. out there. Angela got on the line and asked her to send someone ASAP to the last known address of Marc Johnson's gay admirer—the Sausalito caretaker—with Arianne's photo. Angela didn't care about security, or Buford's anonymity, or the late hour. She just wanted to sleep, in peace, without that feeling in her viscera, gnawing at her.

Angela slipped her bare feet back into a pair of sneaker mules. "Stay on this, Jerry. And Jerry, in my office I have some field notes on the C drive of my desktop. I want you to piece them into a coherent action memo. There are some attached files, some are INS, some are reformatted to our system, too. That source was the South African Consul General. Encrypt it. And then wipe what you've read from your mind."

"Wipe? Um, Inspector . . . this could take all night. You paged me at a friend's concert . . ."

"Jerry, *please*—help out the sister who's always had faith in you. Without Agent-Trainee Riccio, I have only you to turn to."

He nodded. "What do you want me to title the memo for retrieval?"

"Ama Simba."

"Okay . . . and that's spelled how? Forget I said that. Where're you going now?"

"To get some real food. Not this vending-machine stuff. Haven't really eaten much in two days." She reached into her small purse. "Here're my car keys; take Sweet Pea out if you need anything. I'll be okay. Page me."

Lacking the patience for the late-night paperwork involved in signing out a Taurus, and having no stomach for a D.C. cab, Angela headed for the Metro. Alone with the jolts, movement, flashing lights alternating with darkness—for her, hypnotic, conducive to reflection. And for a single woman carrying a 9mm, quite safe. Angela bounded onto the sidewalk along sweltering Pennsylvania Avenue toward the Archives–Navy Memorial station. She wasn't unmindful that she'd pass Styles's million-dollar condo or that Janet Reno's apartment was a mere two blocks away. Waking both with tales of her dreams, *amaphupho,* would get her committed to Bethesda Naval Hospital. So she opted for sweet relief, respite again: her taste for a train ride matched her taste for a midnight meat-loaf sandwich at Lim's Carry-out at 2nd and Elm Streets, catty-corner to her old dorm, Slowe Hall. Just like freshman year, 1985, with her roommate. Afterward, maybe decompress with some jazz at the rebuilt Bohemian Caverns on U and 11th, till morning. Or till Samuel's body was found. Or till someone from the San Francisco–Oakland Field Office confirmed or debunked what she dreaded might be true about Arianne. Or till Butch Buford pledged to reveal what his friends had done to a defenseless girl, eight years ago in a hotel room, and save Antoine.

The rush of air-conditioned blasts through the station's mouth felt good; she fed an old fare card through the turnstile. The motorman of the idling train looked asleep. He stirred and waved when he heard footsteps on the platform. Angela slid into one of four empty carriages and grabbed a seat as the recorded female voice warned to stand clear of the doors. Maybe not empty. When she looked up from snapping her purse shut, down at the other end of the orange-hued car she spied a slumped figure, white shirt stained and dusty. She heard what sounded like a paper bag crumpling, and the noise of clinking glass. The train swished off into the tunnel.

"Next stop Gallery Place–Chinatown–MCI Center." Not a soul embarked there.

But this time, the train restarted with a groan and a wheeled stutter. The lights flickered. Blinked out, as if out of service. Angela kept her curses to herself. A second later, bright lights and a smooth ride. And then—acceleration. Faster, tunnel lights swooshing by. She wondered if the other stations were closed. Was this damn train going all the way to Greenbelt or Hyattsville, nonstop? No, because there weren't any express trains on this line. Angela felt a rapid shudder as the train hurtled through the tunnel, slicing past the Mt. Vernon–UDC Station. Faster. The train took a curve; the whole left side of the car lurched up into the air. Screeching, scraping. Angela lunged for the train's emergency intercom. No answer from the motorman. And now the train roared through her stop, the Howard University station, shaking violently. Car lights surged bright, then shorted, exploded. Angela cried out as she tumbled to the floor.

Just under the rumbling, screeching, grinding, Angela heard *voices*. And she smelled a sickening musk overpower the odor of burnt air brakes and crackling ozone. Hot, dry. *Lions.*

Angela's throat locked in a silent scream as she watched the figure who'd been slumped over, whom she'd forgotten about in those first harrowing seconds of acceleration. It was standing. Arms outstretched. Face obscured by the nightmarish flicker and her own terror. The car surged as if revved by a giant hand. Safety glass cracked, brakes crackled, couplings smacked together and then twisted away. Seconds from derailment. But it wasn't until Angela saw *other figures* that she screamed.

Matted yellow paint covered a naked male body that advanced, gliding like a ghost. More figures appeared, painted in matted blue, orange, ocher. No ashy, singed look to these living corpses. They were refreshed, renewed. Hair caked with pigment, twisted into braids that looked like devil horns. Smiles bright with evil mirth. They stepped now, no longer floating. Stepping closer, in rhythm, unassailable, though the subway car was tearing itself apart.

Another curve. The car crashed into the tunnel wall, smashed onto the opposite side. Miraculously, bouncing back on the tracks. Angela saw raised spear points. From the floor, Angela pulled her weapon and fired wildly.

Something seized the train, like a giant hand yanking it back. The colorful ghosts evaporated; the force flung Angela into a seat support, head-first. All motion ceased.

The subway car was gone. Angela's feet were touching muddy earth. She saw fire glowing against a moonless night sky. Her jersey and drawstring capris were gone. Instead, she was bare-breasted, wrapped in a skirt of beaded leather and dyed homespun. Ears pierced with ceramic hoops heard the drums and the screams and doleful wails of men: condemned warriors, waiting to be impaled on posts and set ablaze. Stacks of their cursed iklwa—wooden shafts and smelted steel blades older than the oldest grandfather—were buried in the ground.

The mud hardened. It was day. Angela had become another woman, and the woman's son was crying. She kissed him, told him to remember, told him to call on her and she would always listen. She saw the regiments of the Zulu Impi moving in tight formation across a valley to face the white soldiers in red coats and knew they would be beaten if she did not prevail. She carried two gourds as she walked from her brave little son. In one, the water she'd drawn from the falls. The water of the Inkanyamba. In the other—her ishungu—are the small bones, feathers, herbs, roots, oils, that were her weapons. Then, on a *kopje,* or hilltop, she faced them. The last two warlocks. Crocodile teeth. Gnarled, bony arms and legs. They hurled invectives and spells at her. They wielded sticks wrapped in mandrake roots and dried brier vines. They, too, carried the water of the falls, but used it for fell purposes: animating the little fetishes at their withered feet. The statues came to life to claw and bite at the woman's legs. And the night sorcerers shook strange gourds and threw red dust that stung like wasps.

Bleeding from the bites, reeling from the spells and black charms, the woman still managed to close on one warlock and stabbed him through the heart with her own small iklwa. Then on to the survivor in a *pas de deux* of magick, set to imaginary music, ancient rhythms . . .

Angela woke up on a subway platform. The air was thick with ozone and leaking machine oil. She was aboveground; she made out a glowing sign: FORT TOTTEN STATION. Metro engineers in white hard hats, Transit police, and a few EMTs hovered over her. She jerked herself up, only to be leveled by shooting pains in her sides.

"Take it easy," an EMT said. His body was silhouetted against harsh spotlights.

"The motorman had a heart attack," a coverall-clad engineer added. "He's, well . . . dead. But we found your pocketbook, your ID. You're FBI."

"Yes. Am . . . am I alone?"

"No one else on Number 4034 but you, miss."

"What?" She tried to rise again. Only then did she realize she was on a gurney.

"The dead-man fail-safe locked up; our backup went off-line. Darndest thing I ever saw. Total system failure. Even more spooky because the automatic stops and emergency power cuts didn't take until you hit the Petworth station. You were maybe two seconds from a derailment or explosion. We had this train clocked at eighty-seven miles per hour at the U Street–Cardozo stop."

Angela heard a siren and then, strangely, a wry shout. "Take a look at this!"

Another voice: *"That* was in the motorman's cabin of Number 4034?"

"Looks like a tiki doll."

Angela watched a Transit cop walk by. It seemed like slow motion, and every step scraped Angela's eardrums. He was waving a small statue. A statue with a vicious smile. Crooked wooden teeth. A beaded neck. A night fetish. Youssa's words: they can control machines. Like ambulances. Now, trains. Angela's mouth formed words to speak. But her body felt as if it were sinking into the gurney. The floodlight faded to blackness.

This time, she saw another boy. Soft face, big-eyed. But not naked. Here, clothed like the other boys in the same khaki and red cap. A green shirt with embroidered badges. Baggy cargo shorts, neoprene sport sandals. A backpack. A Game Boy: Zelda enthralls him as the boys are herded toward a bus. Their sheepdog is a tall, young Asian man in a suit. An earpiece, Ray•Ban sunglasses. And he's watched by a tiny, old black man in grimy blue trousers. Sandals. Holding what looks like a gourd with one withered hand. Blowing a fine red dust into the humid air, off the waxy palm of his other hand. Angela sees a smile. Pointed teeth. Yellow. Dripping. Yellow eyes. *Those eyes.* The face. On the crest of that kopje? *No—at Thirtieth Street Station, Philadelphia. And in a garage. Him. All along. Samuel's alive!* The devil, right in front of your face, not in the details. And in her dream she heard Samuel mimic what the lawyer Mullinix had muttered weeks ago before he died: *"Child go, where children die."*

51

GEORGE WASHINGTON UNIVERSITY HOSPITAL

ANGELA'S BARE FEET DANGLED OFF the side of an ER examining table as a nurse in a floral scrub top took her blood pressure. That was on her good arm. Her other—still tender from the explosion on the Capitol Terrazzo—hung in a canvas sling. Her shoulder had been dislocated, and there is almost no pain worse than having two big interns popping a petite woman's joint back into its socket. Angela shifted painfully from sore ribs when Frank Lupo parted the privacy curtain and entered the glassed-in cubicle.

"Tigress, I spoke to the doctor. This is not going to be another Philadelphia escape, all right? I'm sending you home with your parents—they have been notified. Your sister, brother-in-law, and nephews are flying in tonight. Friendly faces while you mend up. And the quicker you mend, the quicker you get back into the field."

A familiar voice purred, "We know you're anxious to get back out, but—"

"Why are you here, Sylvia?" Angela snapped as the nurse hurried out.

Dr. Sylvia Myers had walked in behind Lupo. He nodded to her, so she replied, "The Assistant Director shared pieces of your . . . your case memo, titled 'Ama Simba.'"

"Like I said before, Tigress, we need you, one hundred percent, body *and* mind."

"Both of you get out," Angela muttered.

Rubbing his face, his chin, Lupo muttered, "Not that simple, Angie. And not what . . . *Jesus* . . . not what you think." He plopped into a chair next to Dr. Myers in the cramped, cold examining room. "It relates to Kwame Buford."

Angela's stomach sank. "It happened . . . it happened like in my dream. Oh, God."

Lupo recounted slowly, "Six fifty-five this morning, while you were sedated, the kid and his Boy Scout troop were headed to the Broad Creek–Susquehanna Camp in Cecil County, Maryland. Secret Service detail did a routine sweep when the yellow bus got to Baltimore for a potty and food stop at a Wendy's on Route 40. One of the agents, guy named Nuygen, got sick . . . convulsed, maybe hallucinated . . . then . . ."

"Oh, no, Frank, no!"

"He pulled his weapon, started shooting. His partners on the detail had to put him down . . . and when they did, somehow, Kwame was gone. Vanished."

"Like Alfred Whiting vanished in Bal Harbour."

Lupo nodded, then added, "A worker at the Wendy's claims she saw some old man hiding in the shrubs . . . decent description of the same black male who's still missing from Medstar, and if you recall, who matches the ID in that story you told our Philly agents a couple weeks ago, at U. Penn Hospital. The old man, in the tunnel."

"Samuel's alive. Samuel's *him* . . . not Stringbean Coy. *No.*"

"Yeah—whatever that means. So, how does a geriatric case with what—a bad ticker, cancer, arthritis, four fucking feet tall? How's someone like *that* doing *this?*" Lyso lowered his voice. "Your memo . . . after the subway accident, your assistant panicked—sent everything to me. Micklin took all your field notes off-line. Claude Baker went through the case file, too, before Bud White could get to it. We shared with MPD . . . MPD shared with us. I made Vallas, Johnson, Micklin, cough up anything they'd been doing for you. The memo is frightening, Tigress. As frightening as it is *incomplete*. Brian Buford . . . what is his involvement in this?"

"That's all you want to know? I'd have thought you'd have stopped reading when your eyes hit the word *witchcraft*."

"That's . . . that's why the doc's here. See, I don't think VICAP, another CIRT, the Child Abduction and Serial Killer Unit, will find this kid. We all now know damn well this wasn't the Archangels. Right, Angie?"

Dr. Myers spoke up. "I asked you not to assume or presume that I was your enemy, dear. Something was clearly invading your subconscious. We don't have all the answers, and very often we have to eliminate or exhaust all the clinically ordinary afflictions before we get to the extraordinary. If you want, the 'supernatural.' The brain can bridge gaps and act as a receptor to the most spectacular things. Especially a brain racked by emotional trauma."

"Maybe receiving, Sylvia. Maybe—remembering?" Angela eased down on the floor, slipped her feet into thin hospital slippers. "Frank, what else?"

"Info from your friend Mallory. Wood splinters in the tissue of a victim named Youssa Ogamdoudou's apparently matched tested fragments in Bryce King's wounds. The African figurine-thing in the subway car you were on had a . . . *shit* . . . a sales tag on it, from Ms. Ogamdoudou's shop. Plus an issue about fingerprints and a baseball cap . . . something at Sidwell Friends? You got a dead guy with his dick ripped off, who'd been stalking Kwame Buford, all this time. Now linked to a seventy-year-old serial killer you say is a witch doctor. *Santa Maria.*"

"Can I have my clothes?"

Lupo sighed heavily. "No. I said I want you rested, sharp. And I want a no-bullshit briefing. I don't care how *The Sixth Sense* or *Crossing Over with John Edward* it sounds. I just need something rational I can go to Donatello and the Attorney General with. We'll autopsy that Secret Service agent, and we'll find whatever wacky dust you claim was in these victims. Think Scofield and Sessions are surly now? Just wait. And the media's gone bananas. They caterwaul 'Amesha Spentas,' after we've declared we've broken its back in Atlanta. Imagine what happens when we come at the press with this: a voodoo 'Baron Samedi,' top hat and chickens and bones and all. African black magic! Nah, you're under wraps until we package this properly."

"It's *magick,* with a *k.* And Styles . . . he'll back you up. He'll 'package' it."

Lupo frowned. "I don't know what to believe right now." He looked to Dr. Myers. "Doc, a moment alone, please."

Dr. Myers got up, then called to Angela as she left the room, "I'm here if you need me."

Lupo's tone turned sharp. "What does a murder almost ten years old . . . a dead African girl . . . have to do with our kidnapped kid's father? Or a death row convict, Whiting, Mullinix? And of course all of Buford's friends. Knocked off, like Ten Little Indians. And there are tapes of interviews missing from the file—Jerry Lopes says you know where they are. Jerry also says some of the gaps in your memo—302s, field notes—you've encrypted them. Not to mention, Remo's pretty much walled off his daughter, so I can't interrogate her as to what the fuck is going on."

"Then get me a laptop with a modem. *And I'll find this boy.*"

"Done. But you are staying here for observation, up in a private room, under guard. I'll have a detail escort you to Baltimore for the rest of your convalescence with your parents. You stay in contact with me and me only. Fuck Vick Styles. He's glazed like some friggin' zombie now. It's you and me, Tigress, like Remo told us in the beginning of this crap."

Before he left—posting an agent to return Angela to her room—Lupo reached into his inside suit pocket. Two folded sheets of paper, stapled together. "On top, something from young Marcus Aurelius Johnson," he said, placing the sheets on the stainless steel sink. "The second page is from your *fanute* of an assistant. *Fiat justitia, ruat caelum,* Angela. I pray to God we find that boy, and get through this with our asses still hanging above our legs."

The first sheet was a one-page fax from the San Francisco–Oakland Field Office:

```
RE: witness saint-jermaine, ssn 064-111-0102. witness made
visual ID, related to unknown subject female age 16-18, tem-
porarily domiciled at sausalito marina boat-homes, july-
september, 1992. with facial age enhancement, match to known
female subject arianne v. shipley, age 24, ssn 234-43-9876.
```

Angela was afraid to breathe.

She fumbled for the second sheet. It was a hard copy of an e-mail from Jerry:

```
ITC helped me checked shipley lowell school reference. just
a hunch, like you get. she's from charlottesville, the daugh-
ter of a stella neal from charlottesville and a real estate
millionaire named baxter shipley, from culpeper. developer.
buys up old tobacco farms or sells own family's landholdings,
turns them into subdivisions with prefab, $750k "mcmansions."
brother-in-law to lucius neal, m.d., of charlottesville.
megawealthy orthopedic surgeon. both families related to
thomas jefferson, robert e. lee, the custises, the
washingtons. family tree like an octopus. here's where it
gets complicated. arianne's mother, stella, and her uncle,
lucius, are the siblings of mary washington neal jones, who,
with her husband, henry jones, became legal guardians in 1972
```

of black male toddler named Antoine, "adopted" from junkie
mother Alethia Carrier—Roanoke Women's Penitentiary. No
"Losing Isaiah" stuff here: birth mother got shanked in
prison. scandal in virginia country society. ironic b/c Neals
big in slaves. He was shaka seven! Those were the infamous
white parents who never came to his murder trial, cut off his
legal defense cash, thus he had to get a public defender! Did
I do good?

Again, the devil, in front of her face. The paper crumpled slightly in her
trembling little hand. *Yes, Jerry, you did good, and God save us all.* Pulse
doubled, adrenaline and dopamine flooding out pain, she grabbed the
agent Lupo had posted, Sheila Kelly, standing guard outside the examining
room door.

"Take me up to my room, now. And I want my cell phone and clothes."

"I was only authorized to get you a laptop with FBI remote access and
modem," Agent Kelly said, looking her up and down. But that look of dire
earnestness was mingled with a little fear. "All right. Clothes. Phone. But
you're getting in that wheelchair and coming up with me, Inspector."

"Nadia, I'm leaving you more messages on your private line at your mother's
apartment, and on your Sprint voice mail. Tell me where Arianne Shipley
can be found. Do not attempt to warn her, do not try to bring her in yourself. She is not the person you think she is. Kwame Buford, the Senator's
son? His life depends on your calling me. She knew his father, when she
was maybe fifteen or sixteen years old. And she's Antoine's cousin. That
part I should have damn known without even asking you. Use my cell."

Angela figured Nadia wouldn't buy the veneer of officiality; if Angela
was on active duty, it would have been "Daddy" on the line and Arianne
would already be *got*, as Brett Mallory said. Maybe instinct would call the
fledgling to the nest, to fight by its mother.

When Angela clicked off, she pecked, one-handed, on the laptop, navigating the FBI remote access log-on, working the touch pad to click on the
link to Nexis newspaper and magazine articles searches, cross-referenced to
FBI dossiers, IRS records, the National Crime Information Center. "Okay,
focus, Angie," she told herself. "Follow your gut. *Listen*. Neals, Shipleys.
Lord, this little heifer was fucking Buford when she was barely a teenager
at Madeira. Why, Butch, why?"

Her search turned up three articles on the Neal family. Two on the

Shipleys, and one FBI Economic Crimes/FHA investigation of Arianne's blue-blood father, Baxter Shipley of Charlottesville, for real estate fraud, mortgage-loan discrimination in central Virginia, regarding properties in Spotsylvania and Culpeper Counties and the Lake Anna area. Angela bookmarked that one. Another article from the "People" section of the *Richmond Post-Dispatch* outlined the Neals' and Shipleys' familial ties to the state's colonial and Civil War heroes, as well as a Shipley wing in Coventry, England, whose prime ancestor, a sergeant major in a Welsh regiment in the British army, wrote a best-selling memoir before his death in 1911.

"There are no such things as coincidences." There, one reference no one else would have tweezed out. A nexus. "He fought in India . . . China . . ." And was decorated—he received the Victoria Cross for service in the Zulu War, 1878–79.

Acid churning in her stomach, Angela clicked back to the information on the Neals. How they took in Antoine Jones to give him a better life. How they woke up one morning and did so, as if overcome by a spell to do right. To make amends.

Another nexus. And this one brought the acid up, spilling into the small green plastic wastebasket by the hospital bed. It brought her back to that clipping Youssa had shown her. Warehouses. A human corral. Slave pens. But this wasn't from the *Informer*. It was from the *Washington Business Journal*. Sanitized.

> Shipley Development, LLP to develop pre–Civil War warehouse properties owned by City of Alexandria into luxury condos. Property was condemned in quick-take, formerly owned by a real estate trust run by brother and sister Dr. Lucius Neal and Mary Washington Neal Jones. The sale was opposed by the NAACP and Virginia Historical Trust as property was former Neal & Co. slave pens.

Angela asked herself. "What did Mullinix rant? 'This was where children died . . . his children. Your children.' " And her dream. Samuel said it. Where children died. Illegally imported African slaves. Where Mullinix brought his gift. A gift to he who comes to murder the lies. But itself, was a lie? What was the lie? Jewel's murder, or this horrible thing unleashed in Samuel, to avenge that murder? She knew. "He's there . . . with Kwame."

She groped for her cell phone.

52

PRAYING THE WINGS UNFOLD . . .

ALVIN MARKHAM'S BLUE HONDA CIVIC pulled to the red light at 23rd and F Street, N.W.; Angela hunched in the passenger seat, looked to him, and smiled. "Thanks."

He was stone-faced. "Repeat what you told me. Just once. Not about a serial murderer or this ritualistic African animist stuff. Repeat what you said first."

Angela swallowed hard. "I was pregnant with Trey's baby. I found out when you and I were in Mexico, on our way to your asteroid crater, where the world ended for the dinosaurs. Three weeks after we got back, I went to Philly to get an abortion. I miscarried while on the table. My doctor was Leslie Collins. And I couldn't tell you."

The light turned green. Angela could see his face twitch slightly. "Right. And so here we are, full circle from Assateague, huh?" He gave her a glance. "You're something fucking else, Angel. And I am so thankful you are."

Her eyes moistened. Painfully, she leaned over to kiss his cheek.

Now smiling, Alvin explained, "Luckily, Special Agent Kelly remembered me from the Williams case. Plus she says I look like Lenny Kravitz, with glasses. Personally, I think I'm Eric Benet. Anyway, I lied and told her SAC Claude Baker was back in the lobby and it looked like some agents from the Nest were going to relieve her. Figured she'd get curious and take the bait. She hit the elevator; we hit the stairs, trailed out through the sublevels. Easy evasion, for an old Dungeons & Dragons master, like me. Still can't fathom how you move so fast with a dislocated shoulder."

"Discipline. You did this for me without even knowing the background, Al."

"Don't say, 'You're a good man,' blah blah, or, 'I don't deserve you.' "

"No, I'll say I'm lucky to call you a *friend*. And Sharon's lucky to have you as her man." She paused to reflect on those words, then said, "I don't want to tie up my cell, so hand me yours. I figure the nurse's seen that a lump of pillows in my bed has no blood pressure and doesn't take medication, so Lupo'll be calling me, a tad piqued. So—the Secret Service'll have a checkpoint on the Chain Bridge, therefore we'll go the back way: E Street, to the Roosevelt Bridge, to I-66, to Glebe Road . . . all the way to Dolly Madison."

She punched in a number. One ring, an answer. "Hello yourself, Mr. Barnes, and no, it's not a wrong number because you gave me this a week ago. This is Inspector Bivens. Are you in a secure place . . . where you can speak freely?"

"Uh . . . I read in the *Post* this morning that you were in the hospital."

"Do not use my name aloud. *I know where Kwame Buford is.*"

Dead air.

"And I know about Arianne Shipley. An underage girl. Eight years ago the Senator was having an affair with her. It ended around the time Jewel was murdered. I believe she was a junior at the Madeira School at the time? Now, do you want to save Kwame?"

"I'm in one of the bedrooms . . . your Bureau people and the Secret Service have a command post set up there in the den. Um . . . I'll talk to Butch, get you access to the grounds and the house . . . clearance from him directly to the task force agents in charge."

"I want a private talk with Senator Buford, understood?"

"Now look, if you know where Kwame is, you best damn better—"

"Shut up and listen! We can't fight the kidnapper until Buford talks to me. Set this up, Mr. Barnes. Now."

When she clicked off, Alvin mused, "The great sci-fi writer Ray Bradbury once said, 'Living at risk is jumping off a cliff and building your wings on the way down.' "

"Then I have a head start on the wings, Alvin. I'm an *angel,* after all."

Nadia, her mother, aunt, and cousins returned to the cottage, kicking off their expensive sandals and dropping into plush chairs cooled by breezes washing over Long Island from the Atlantic to the Sound. They'd just brunched at Bistro-One, a swank little place in East Hampton opened by one of Asia de Cuba's former chefs. Nadia could have settled for waffles at IHOP, such was her languor.

"Ma, I don't feel like going to the beach after what's been happening in D.C."

"Your father has several thousand agents to find that boy. He doesn't need you."

Nadia moped into the kitchen and dialed a voice-mail number on the cordless. Home, on West 94th Street, Manhattan. She hungered for even a lie from Arianne. *I'm okay, Naddy. I'll reveal everything, Naddy.* Instead, she got Angela's message. And dropped the phone onto the ceramic tile floor.

53

SENATOR BRIAN "BUTCH" BUFORD—WAR HERO, scholar, attorney, first black man to ascend to the U.S. Senate from California, less than three weeks from being nominated as Vice President, and likely the proverbial heartbeat away from the Oval Office, wiping clean the opprobrium of four hundred years of slavery and vile abuse, neglect, fear—wept. He'd been standing at his study's window, searching, through his tears, across a grove of lavender-bloomed crape myrtles, toward the old home of his boyhood role model, Robert F. Kennedy.

As Angela closed the study door, she saw the maddened or perplexed faces of colleagues out in the hall. Imagine the sight of a tiny black woman with huge almond eyes, face bruised, left shoulder and arm trussed—holding the combined leadership of the FBI and Secret Service at bay. And not caring what the hell they thought.

Thumbing red, dry eyes, Buford mumbled with a sniffle, "Are you saying Arianne Shipley's involved in this kidnapping?" He finally turned to face Angela. "And Vick Styles—why won't he take my calls? They say he's ill with a 'debilitating summer flu.' Did you brief him . . . about Arianne? Anyone in the Bureau?"

"No to all three questions."

"Oh . . . good . . . look, I'm . . . I'm sorry the agents roughed up your friend Mr. Markham out there, when you pulled in, but he had no FBI ID."

"He's fine. See, when this began, I left him alone out on a beach, to serve assholes like those in your living room. He stays here. Besides, your wife knows him, from Stanford." When Buford's mouth formed to speak again, Angela cut him off and said harshly, "Now stop bullshitting me, sir. It's my profound belief that Arianne Shipley may have knowledge of the kidnapper's motives. Why? Because she is Antoine Jones's cousin. Because you fucked her and dropped her the way Jewel was abused. Because you were what, thirty-nine, forty? And she was barely sixteen, *you piece of shit.*"

He fell onto a lacquered window seat. "She didn't . . . didn't act sixteen. I met her, her parents, at a Madeira Christmas pageant . . . I'd utterly, utterly forgotten she was related to the Neals, the same people who had taken Jones as a baby. No idea. She enthralled me . . . you wouldn't understand. But I had to break it off. Not only because it was wrong, but . . ." he threw up his hands. *"Where's my son, damn you!"*

"Clock's ticking—the first twenty-four hours of a kidnapping are critical. We can save Kwame's life . . . and Jones's, with the truth."

"You'd blackmail me—with my son's life? You bitter . . . cruel little—"

"Don't fuck with me! I can't save him unless I know what really happened in that suite eight years ago!"

Quailing, Buford mumbled, "First Les had her, all right? Then that fat piece of shit Carl. Bryce had her last and goddamn him for that . . . and . . . we heard all kinds of noise, commotion, screaming . . . shit breaking in the bathroom . . . we ran in, she was . . . God . . . unconscious, blood everywhere, her head, must have hit something."

"Where? The bedroom, the bathroom? King was with her?"

"I don't remember! Both . . . Jesus . . . that's when, when Les went back, checked her out. Bryce was standing there. She was dead . . . at least she didn't have a pulse . . . he said she didn't, he's a fucking doctor, he should know! That's when Bryce . . . he called a friend of his on the police department . . . used to be on Marion Barry's security detail, an MPD detective— and don't prick up your ears 'cause this man's long retired, all right? Died of cancer last year. They spoke, discussed what to do next. I mentioned Antoine."

"Mentioned to them, while they conspired? It was your idea to frame him?"

"Yes . . . *no* . . . look—I mentioned the insane things Antoine'd said about us—me, Bryce—and the fights he'd had with Jewel. I knew about her being pregnant." Buford covered his eyes, breath short, face wet. "He was

'Shaka Seven' now. Only tight with his raggedy-ass followers and the drug dealers and other neighborhood scum. Jewel was afraid of him. He'd cut his ties with his family . . ."

Angela moved closer to the window seat, by Buford's mahogany desk. "No. You named Antoine as a patsy because he'd been there that night, in the suite, in full view of your after party guests, belligerent, caustic, fighting with her—after making love to her, which is why she didn't want your 'Fellaz' paws on her!"

Buford nodded slowly. "He . . . he made it too easy for Bryce. Plus, Bryce and I had our friends on the *Post,* CBS, NBC. How do your think we could sanitize this whole damn thing? It was our party, a girl dies, and yet the story withers on the vine with everyone but the right-wing rags like the *Washington Times*! This was old-school scandal control, like some shit outta Sinatra and the Rat Pack! Even when Gore's people were doing background checks on me as a possible nominee, no one cared about that party! Nothing. *Nothing!*" His breath eased. "That's how good Bryce was. That's how awful we were. Lord, I mourn her, yes. When . . . when Congress broke for elections . . . I knew it was time to end it with Arianne . . . Jewel made me see how this shit was wrong, I wanted to protect her." He was bawling again, "I failed . . ."

Buford was shaking his head as Angela hammered him with words.

"Who tore Jewel's body up? Bryce? Les, with anatomical knowledge?" She grabbed Buford's shoulder with her good arm. "The Lion, as he calls himself. He is Jewel's father. And he called in his *own* friends to help. *Ghosts. Demons.* Not from hell. No, someplace worse. *Our minds,* with the help of ancient drugs modern science can't accept. He's come to set things right. He has your son."

Suddenly, Angela drew back, struggling to fathom, in her own mind, whether Sam Ibhebesi's accomplices were indeed drug-induced phantoms and not corporeal monsters that left spear points embedded in bone. Or brought statuettes to life, conjuring vermin swarms. Or spun ambulances and subway cars out of control. Or feasted on human flesh.

The study door burst open. Crisis Management Unit Chief Ed Groome and HRT leader Paul Trask stormed in with at least a dozen FBI and Secret Service agents.

"Take her out of here!" Groome commanded.

Buford, Angela's fallen hero, lifted his head, stood, and turned on her. "She knows where my son is! Make her tell you!"

Angela thrashed away as Trask grabbed for her good arm. "Buford—you fucking . . . bastard!" *Now, do I tell them about Buford's friends and Jewel? Now would they believe me? Now would Styles emerge and help? Would Lupo? No.*

The startled agents heard another female's throaty cry. "Get out! All of you! Butch, damn your soul, you stay. You, too, Ms. Bivens. You, too."

Angela looked up to see the oaken study door slam shut, and Dr. Cheryl Patterson-Buford standing, alone, eyes wet but wide. "That man and I have been partners, lovers, mutual cheerleaders, since Berkeley. I was a dental student and he was a law student. And he has always risen to meet his destiny . . . and I've looked the other way when he's strayed . . . and even, *God,* at something so horrible that . . . oh, Butch, may Jesus take me now if I let any of that cost the life of my baby, *my son!*"

"Doctor . . . what . . . what are you saying?"

"Baby, no . . . baby . . . please no," Buford pleaded.

"Shut up, motherfucker!" Cheryl hissed. "For years I've been psychotically quiet, forgetful, all to protect you, Butch. Fuck Bryce, the rest of them! That poor girl died."

"Doctor, he didn't hurt her, but he covered it up and everyone is in danger for—"

Cheryl Patterson-Buford was now shaking her head, weeping, yet smiling bizarrely. "You don't get it, do you?"

It looked as if Buford was going to rush to her. For an embrace? To strike her? His wet grimace, his body's contour, his pose—indicated both. But then he froze. Cheryl pulled up the rolltop on the matching secretary adjacent to Buford's desk. It was a finely carved piece, too similar to what Angela had seen in Trey's study, what seemed a million years ago. Glazed ceramic animal figurines made up a miniature zoo. The bigger animals were autographed "Kwame," and a few sat on the lid of an embossed leather humidor. Buford shrank into the corner as his wife, cursing silently, moved the little animals and opened the lid. "It was here, Inspector," she whispered.

Angela's heart crashed against her sternum as Cheryl lifted a little beaded bag out of the humidor. An *ibheqe.* Patterned like the old sample Angela'd received from Youssa. *I ache for you.* And now Angela knew it wasn't simply the ache of love. It was the ache of a new life, growing inside a woman's body. She could feel it herself as Cheryl murmured, face blank, over Buford's pathetic moans.

"Do you have children?"

"Doctor . . . no, I . . . but, I once . . . I mean . . . listen, we have to—"

"But you're a *black* woman," Cheryl said with a twitching, pained smile. "They've traced a certain type of DNA . . . in all humans . . . back, thousands of generations, to one female. One woman—in *Africa. Everyone* is our children." Her tears began anew. "So you've felt it—the tug and rip right here"—she patted her abdomen—"when your child is in danger, no matter how old they are." She broke down. Angela could barely brace her with one good shoulder as the mother cried. *"You find my baby! And if none of those motherfuckers out here will help, then you strap me and we'll go get him together!"*

"I-I will. I swear."

Cheryl spit at her husband. "You better pray he doesn't die. You better pray!"

Angela's knees went rubbery as Senator Brian Buford muttered back, "I couldn't have this baby . . . she didn't understand . . . it was an accident. I didn't mean to hurt her. Didn't mean . . ."

His voice faded as he crumpled in a corner. And Angela screamed out into the hall, "Seventy-five Jefferson Davis Highway! The same place we found Alfred Whiting . . . Code Red, five-ninety, goddamn you! Let's save this child!" And she repeated words uttered on Les Collins's examining table on a biting winter night. "This child is innocent."

I hope my wings have grown were the words she left unsaid.

54

THE TACTICAL CP WAS A CLUSTER of vans and Chevy Suburbans across a dusty lot from the old Neal & Co. hell houses, hidden by a rise of rotted storage tanks and stands of ferns. From there, Angela heard Paul Trask's burr in her earpiece. It was reminiscent of his assault on Trey's beach house. Now his team ringed the same crumbling pair of warehouses they'd stormed with Alexandria SWAT almost a month prior, when they had killed Maynard Mullinix. The same sun was battling back the night, burning holes through the chunks of mortar, birthing voluptuous shadows.

"Mr. Trask," Angela said over her throat mike. "I suggest two penetration teams, three agents apiece. No Ruby Ridge repeat, no Rough Riders up San Juan Hill shit. Get me in when they have a ten-fifteen. I can talk this monster's talk."

This time, it was the voice of Remo Donatello himself, cutting into the channel from the strategic CP, about a thousand yards north of a blocked Jeff Davis Highway: *"You ten-four that, Paul, you understand? No mistakes."* Angela wondered how this man could be oblivious to how his own daughter had enmeshed herself in what was about to happen. Yet Angela's thoughts were not on Nadia's relationship with Arianne. Or even witchcraft. They were on a terrified little boy, and she felt a tug in her pelvis intensify.

"Clear," Angela heard. *"Simon Alpha, Simon Alpha, cover and sniper sitref go."*

"Check, Simon Alpha. Simon Beta is . . . clear" came the confirmation.

"Infrared's no good in all this heat, but got a lotta movement within structure two . . . beneath second interior wall and loading-dock space . . . taking positions now."

Angela whispered over to Lupo, who had crouched beside her. "Please tell them to keep the choppers away. We can rely on satellite imaging. And . . . are they wearing gas masks? Tell them to be careful of any smoke or dust, anything bizarre, illogical, disorienting—they must take cover, assess, then react. Don't shoot."

"Illogical like what?"

She swallowed hard. "They'll know it when they see it."

Micklin knelt beside Lupo. "HQ confirms it. Next satellite doesn't come into retask reach for another hour. We're out of luck if we need sky-eye live action."

"You hear that, Tigress? Pass it on to Trask. I'll tell the Director."

"He already knows," Micklin said. "They fed a direct patch to the White House, too. The VP, the Attorney General—they're all listening in. God help us."

Lupo exchanged an uneasy glance with Angela. "Important career tip."

One of the HRT agents inside had crawled through the broken bricks to a cracked doorway painted in foul graffiti. He could hear noises: rustling, scratching. Angela heard, or maybe wasn't supposed to hear, *"Send up pee-wee Bivens. Tell her to stick to marked ingress . . . heard she got a busted flipper—can't get Kevlar on."*

Angela frowned until she heard a female voice. *"This is Simon Alpha sniper, on scope. Don't worry, ma'am, I'm the angel on your shoulder . . . and I'm only five-three myself."*

Angela moved across the lot, through the tangle of ferns and stacks of refuse. Closer now—just on the other side of where an army of river rats had surged a month ago, driving Angela and Nadia before them. One of Ed Groom's men, clad in a black HRT helmet and a blue Tac windbreaker, ushered Angela to a hole in the warehouse wall, marked by fluorescent tape. He took her earpiece, handed her a helmet, and helped her secure the attached gas mask and goggles.

POP-POP-POP! Then shouting. *POP-POP-POP!*

Angela fell beneath a column; three HRT agents rushed ahead of her. She heard Trask yelling, other voices barking orders, frantic. Scared. That's when she saw the mass rolling past her, back to the river. Rats. Thousands.

Beneath the shouts of utter confusion, she could hear dying, vicious squeals. She watched brown, matted fur bristling with teeth and wormlike tails leaping, writhing, blood flying as the rounds hit. Yet soon she also heard splashing on the shore. The survivors were drowning themselves in the tidal shallows.

She heard in the helmet receiver, *"Egress! Egress, Simon Beta, before you shoot each other!"* Something dry, living, hit her cheek. Then another and another, pelting her from out of the shadows, avoiding the killing beams of fiery sunlight. Instinctively, she reached up to swat the pests away. Wrong shoulder, wrong arm. She cried out in pain, and that cry morphed to terror, as clouds of silver-brown moths flew out of the cavernous warehouse, into the hot sun. Over the Potomac, gangs of brutish seagulls intercepted what the heat didn't kill.

As quickly as it began, the storm of vermin and insects ended. Dead quiet. Then . . .

"Simon Alpha four, clear . . . we got something!"

Angela stumbled forward, braving a possible friendly bullet from lingering confusion. She found the HRT agents circled around a dirty khaki and red cap, with a Boy Scout insignia. A Game Boy. No blood. Nothing else.

Trask entered with underlings. "This was planted here," he said. "We've been had. Christ, Bivens!"

No, no, no, Angela raved inwardly. *This was the place children died! Bought and sold! Even Mullinix said it!* But, another thought. Mullinix also said everything was a lie. Why did these creatures swarm and kill themselves? Where else would a child die? Hospital? Angela paced the wreckage as she heard the murmurs of frustration, aimed at her, and those murmurs were being tracked all the way to the West Wing of the White House.

"Wait," she whispered to herself. *His* child. "Sweet Jesus!" Angela shouted.

She rushed up to Trask, breath driven from her small body. "Code Red-Delta-Five . . . HRT . . . MPD Tactical Response . . . get them . . . all up there! Omni Shoreham Hotel . . . off Rock Creek Park. Stephen Decatur Suite . . . *Now!"*

"Hold that Code RD5," she heard, in Donatello's voice. Three agonizing seconds later, in an inexplicably small voice, the Director said, *"Lancelot and Guinevere say go on Code."* Lancelot and Guinevere were the Secret Service code names for Buford and his wife.

*   *   *

Rosario Camacho had joined the housekeeping staff at the Omni Shoreham just three months ago. But she was pixieish, energetic, and spoke decent English and thus got a plum assignment to the big suites on the eleventh floor. The last thing little Rosarita saw before she died was an old black man, bounding down the tapestry-hung corridor toward her cart. Striding, even, as if with a young man's legs. With one frail hand, he dragged, effortlessly, a squirming, sizable black boy. In the other, he carried something that looked like a paddle. It wasn't, and the *iklwa* ended Rosarita's life from a single thrust to the throat.

The old man kicked in the door to the Stephen Decatur Suite, flung the boy onto a king-size, canopy bed. When Kwame jumped up to escape, Samuel smacked him unconscious. He then dropped to the floor, emptying out a small jute sack he'd tied to his waist: an *ishungu*, full of dry bones. The one full of wet matter was gone, and Samuel cursed his missing *thikoloshe*, his familiar, Stringbean, for its likely theft. It had been his only effective weapon against *her*. But he had others. More than the black and red dust. Spells, charms. And, in the *ishungu*, he had the bones. His army. Ghost warriors. Ama Simba. He poured blue ash from a tiny cloth pouch and drew his charms on the carpet. He sang. He sang for the *amafufuyama* to come, gird him. Complete his revenge. He really did love the only daughter he had ever known. Even if she'd run away from him. She was all he had left of his tortured wife; Jewel was his seed, and seed-bearer. His kind's hope for renewal. To live forever. The fortified *umodi* he took would afford him enough strength to face the white men's guns. His bladder was eating itself anyway. They would get no satisfaction from imprisoning him, along with the young fool now awaiting a lethal needle. Divining and canticles complete, Samuel waited for his enemy. He didn't have to wait long, for the sirens and beat of helicopter rotors soon rattled the suite's picture windows.

On a landing in the emergency stairs between the tenth and the eleventh floors, one of Paul Trask's HRT reported that the dusk's cooler temperatures allowed a decent thermoscan on the eleventh floor. Two bodies, in the Decatur Suite.

"You all go first," Angela said. "But if there's a negotiation sit-ref, let me in."

Trask's original orders had never been adjusted. He grunted, "Yes."

With HRT agents moving up the stairs and the elevators, and MPD Tactical Response–SWAT personnel now on the roof, Samuel was trapped.

He had to know he would be. Angela figured it would end in ritual murder and suicide, so she was Kwame's only hope. After an hour of positioning, she was called up to the eleventh floor. She'd been up there once before, she mused. A prized invitation to the infamous after party, 1994. Yes, someone could be raped, mutilated, in that indoor Mardi Gras and no one would know. But would three prominent black men really stage a gruesome homicide, rip up a girl's body, just to protect their great black hope, Butch Buford? That wasn't important anymore as Angela inched down the hallway behind two HRT agents. One pushed a bulletproof shield ahead; the other flanked him with a curious tube weapon that shot nonlethal beanbags laced with a morphine-base powder. At least Trask was using his head. Other teams were breaching the doors to connecting suites; one way or another, it would be over in minutes.

They reached the door to the main suite. Even above the patrolling choppers, they could hear Samuel singing, *"Uku-zi umthakathi." Take him alive. Make him tell me what I dream, what I feel.* The HRT agent with the beanbag gun counseled, "Aw, man—put your helmet and mask back on, Inspector!"

A new sound hit Angela's ears. Hard things, like giant dice, rolling and thumping onto the rug. Then, abruptly, she heard a sharp crash inside the room, then shouts and barked orders: *"Freeze! FBI!"* She dropped the helmet and mask.

"Shit, we're a go!" hollered the agent, who kicked open the door, shoved Angela aside, and charged in. The shield bearer leaped in to provide cover; Angela was limp against the corridor wall, shoulder throbbing.

There was no noise from the suite.

She entered. A cobalt-blue, breath-sapping smoke rose from the floor. She had nothing to cover her mouth; five more agents stormed in and shoved her away, once again, but she kept walking, to the bedroom, and the place where Jewel had died.

There was Samuel—chest heaving from his *umodi* high, touching the point of an *iklwa* to Kwame Buford's tender neck. The beanbags had been spent. They had missed. And now a dozen MP5Ks were aimed at old Samuel Ibhebesi. He hadn't counted on the gas masks; Angela had neglected hers. Yet he smiled as she swayed, eyes clouding. Why? Wasn't he trapped?

"Bones on de floor," he snarled, pointed teeth bared, " 'ave power of fetish."

Indeed, the HRT agents didn't fire. They didn't move at all: fingers on trigger guards, breathing, blinking under their mask goggles. Yet frozen.

"Now," Samuel said, "ghost warriors. Ama Simba. Shaka's fruit. Fist of *mfecane.*"

Angela saw them rise from the smoke. No bright pigment slathered on them, as on the subway. No, gray soot covering dead flesh. Blank, dead eyes. Rawhide shields, menacing *iklwa.* But as motionless as their modern counterparts brandishing machine guns and strapped in Kevlar. Perhaps awaiting Samuel's order to kill?

"You followed me . . . to Philadelphia . . . on the train."

"To find Collins. And maybe, I kill you, too."

"Why?"

"Why? *Izi mphabany uku i myaze! Myaze, inkaneyzi!* Archangel. *Sangoma* whore!"

"No." She was reaching into her sling. "Stop . . . calling me that . . . I am Angela Renee Bivens."

"Voice, voice of Umnyama, evil one, spell of Inkanyamba, the spirit of de river falls, both bring me here, to America, to dis room, I hear t'rough *amathambo* . . . bones of Ama Simba . . . it say, you *inkanyezi.* You die, too." His feral look suddenly melted with sadness. "My child dead. My seed, it end. So Buford's seed end. Last lie. Murdered."

Dizzied but undaunted, Angela stumbled toward the old man, through the demonic soldiers and the HRT agents as if she were negotiating a giant chessboard and they were the pieces. "No . . . you . . . are . . . just . . . a man."

With one hand on the spear handle, Samuel opened his other hand to reveal a flat gold slug, ready for a dead child's mouth. "Den we die . . . like *you seed die at Collins's hands!*"

His craggly knuckles were tense on the spear's short handle. Angela had only a second to pull her 9mm—with her left hand—and fire. Angela was right-handed. Yet in that instant, Samuel winced; his shoulders sank. He became enfeebled, old, diseased once more. His power, his resolve, were sucked away. Or stolen.

Even shooting left-handed, Angela tagged him cleanly with a wounding shot to the shoulder, spinning him into a floor lamp. As the lamp and the old man crashed to the floor, the weird smoke dissipated, and with it went the Ama Simba, with a whisper. Angela dropped to one knee, sapped by Samuel's conjured smoke. She was too weak to press forward, to cry out, when Samuel, moaning, tried to hobble to his feet, grope for help.

The HRT agents snapped out of their daze. They only saw Samuel, using the *iklwa* handle to prop himself up. And they opened up on him. The Lion, the warlock, was dead.

55

ANGELA EASED ONTO THE SOFA IN her office; Jerry handed her a plastic cup of water and departed. She downed two Advils and looked over at Carmen Wilcox. "Glad you came by. Sorry I had to work on a Saturday; we could've gotten our toes done together down at that new Vietnamese place on E Street."

Carmen smiled. "Next weekend, then. And, Angel, I'm *ashamed* I wasn't there for you. Ashamed I fronted about my doubts."

"It's in the past."

"So much hurt packed into the past already. Listen—how's the shoulder?"

"Stiff." She tried to rotate her arm. "I popped it back in myself, ya know, like Mel Gibson in *Lethal Weapon 2*!"

"Oh, chile, stop!"

They shared a quick laugh, then a second of stern silence. Carmen spoke first. "So . . . you were in Styles's office for a couple of hours yesterday, huh? Mallory told me."

Angela swung her legs onto the sofa, grunting with residual pain. "Classified, Carm. Brett shoulda known better. Be glad Stringbean Coy's off the street."

"Uh-huh, but . . . all of sudden, Antoine Jones gets a stay from the D.C. Circuit, U.S. Court of Appeals, then a new trial based on 'new' evidence that can only be viewed in camera with a federal judge, under Justice

Department supervision . . . ACLU and Southern Poverty Law Center posts a bond pending the new trial this afternoon. Very fast. And he's free. What's really going on, Angie-boo?"

"I saved a man from lethal injection. Now his white family's disowned him. They, in turn, are still missing Arianne Shipley. Maybe she's dead, I dunno." Angela sighed behind the mask she'd plastered over her soul. "It's done."

Carmen shook her head. "No, baby—it's connected. Rumor is, something was sent out of Janet Reno's office on Friday, to a grand jury over at our favorite courthouse on Third and Constitution, under seal."

Angela slid to her desk to boot up her desktop computer. "You said it—rumor."

"No. Very well-placed sources, according to folk I know in DOJ. Bryce W. King, Leslie Collins, Bishop Davidson, all implicated in murder, conspiracy. Lots of hush-hush stuff on the GOP side regarding Alfred Whiting's role in this supposed conspiracy. All related to that dead African girl. Did he do it, Angie-boo? Did Brian Buford finger his own dead friends? Is that why Jones is out?"

"Carmen, Buford has no friends. His wife is leaving him; he might not see his son and daughter again. What he did, whom he fingered—does it really matter now? Lord, I don't even know what matters now . . . except we saved lives."

"At what cost—scattered street riots, all hell bustin' loose on TV talk shows? Buford's even saying he's going to resign from the Senate. Another one of our heroes, just shot down. This time, it's figurative. And, Angel, I pray you didn't help pull the trigger."

"You don't know *everything*. I can't tell you *anything*. *Please* stay my friend."

"Honey . . . I know it sounds like I'm flippin' back on you, but Al Gore's having a press conference tonight. He's lost his *flavah* again, and the *Post* already leaked that he's gonna replace Buford with Senator Joseph Lieberman, from Connecticut. The convention starts at the end of next week, and a poll today's got him five points down—a net loss of twelve. Lord have mercy—George W. Bush in the White House?"

Jerry buzzed Angela's desk. "Inspector, it's Assistant Director Woodruff Sessions, secure line three."

"Carm . . . I'm sorry . . . I gotta take this in private. Felix at eight, right?"

"We can try another spot. I know you and Trey used to hang there, so—"

"We have to overcome the shadow of the past, sweetie. See ya tonight."

Carmen kissed Angela on the cheek and left. It was a quick peck; Angela prayed the distance would close. She picked up the handset. "Mr. Sessions, you on duty this weekend as well?"

"Just taking the time, Ms. Bivens, to cogitate over this matter with Brian Buford: how it pertains to this Jewel Ngozi's murder, of which Antoine Jones was pretty much cleared, pending his new trial, of course. And how it relates to her father, this Zulu man. The paperwork he presented to INS was forged, fake, y'know. Can't seem to get any answers from the South African Consul General, Mr. Durnkloopf. Love ta clean this from the heels of 'er boots before the election catches up with us."

"What is it you really want?"

"Just continuing a past thought—e.g., your ties to Victor Styles and *his* role in this awful sequence of events. And your future role—in case there is a change in administrations, a new Attorney General. We will remember our friends, m'dear."

"Well, sir, you and AD Scofield will get copied on my final report on Kwame Buford's kidnapping. Nothing redacted or expurgated. Is there anything else?"

"No, ma'am, and you have a great and productive weekend. Oh, by the way—Bobby Scofield says he's keeping Bud White detailed to FBIHQ indefinitely. Bud says he's got some interesting background on this Antoine Jones's activities in college. You might want to stop by Bud's new office and give 'im a holler."

"I'm entering that on my calendar as we speak, sir." Angela hung up. What did Donatello say about candor not being a virtue, as the election approached? *I've accepted that. God forgive me.*

Felix's panel windows were flung open to admit the throngs on 18th Street, N.W. This night, it was a cool relief. Sixty-five degrees. Comfortable humidity. And at the bar, Angela drained her Cosmopolitan and ordered another while a slender black woman finished her rendition of Angie Stone's "No More Rain (in This Cloud)." The drowsy, neo-soul syncopation was just what Sylvia Myers might have ordered.

Second Cosmo finished off by 8:25 P.M. Still no Carmen or Sharon and Alvin—they were comfortable announcing themselves as a package. People who didn't have to work on Saturdays had no excuse to be late. As for her cohorts in the Bureau, Vallas said he couldn't make it and didn't say why.

Micklin didn't go to Adams-Morgan. He preferred hanging with his Mormon cohorts at any Applebee's or Golden Corral he could find in the strip-mall desert outside the Beltway. No, it was just Angela and cocky Marcus Johnson, and to pluck Angela's nerves even more, the singer had decided to switch from covering Angie Stone and Jill Scott to a retrospective of Shirley Bassey's James Bond tunes. The crowd was getting younger and whiter; after all, this was Felix, where *Thunderball* and *Dr. No* played perpetually on the club monitors, except Sundays. That was *Sex and the City* night.

"I brought your mail, by the way. Usual stuff, but you got a UPS package." Johnson took a sip of Heineken, then explained, "Don't worry—it's been fluoroscoped. Looks like photos, newspaper clippings, small books. Sender's Abamye Modu—Youssa Ogamdoudou's roommate, girlfriend, whatever. Note pasted to the box says, 'Youssa would want you to have it,' whatever that means. It's in the car. Want it?"

"Not yet. Just want to chill." Angela pulled out her compact and touched up her face, moistened her lips with a fresh stick of M•A•C's Pomegranate.

Johnson looked at her admiringly. "Hey, we had a hell of a month, huh? Always had lots a respect for you; sorry I haven't shown it. Even when I was Frank's monkey back when we were all at the Nest last year, you treated me well. Still do, even though you're all blown up on the news and get your drinks damn comped at places like this!"

"I haven't changed, Marc." *Hell, no,* she told herself. *Who am I, now?*

After parsing her smile, Johnson flirted. "How old are you again? Twenty-five?"

"Don't push it, Marcus." She laughed. "And don't even start pressing me about Vallas. I heard you and the others in the canteen, talking out your necks about things you have no clue—"

She cut the levity off when her glance shifted over Johnson's shoulder, out to the sidewalk. Across 18th Street. Nestled between the bar Columbia Station and a dance club called The Crush was a small lounge called Georgia O'Keeffe's. At the door, towering over two clinging white women, was Antoine Jones.

Angela squinted hard. A flash from headlights illuminated the face of one of the girls, who was turning toward Felix's bar. Her green-eyed stare seemed to peel through the crowd and the traffic, straight to Angela.

Arianne Shipley.

"Oh my God . . . Marc, wait here."

Angela jumped off the bar stool, pushed through the bodies, and ran across the gauntlet of glaring headlights and blaring car horns. A very tall woman, almost as tall as Antoine, blocked her path. Nothing "lipstick" about her; this was the bouncer-ette. O'Keeffe's was a "membership" bar, and most of the members were lesbians. The bouncer-ette didn't recognize Angela's face from the TV or newspapers. She must have been the only one in the city who didn't.

"Can you give Arianne Shipley the message that FBI Inspector Bivens will be waiting out here for her to come out. She's with Antoine Jones, whom I'm sure you've heard of from the news."

"Yes, I have, but I don't know any Arianne Shipley. May I see some ID?" Angela realized her badge was back in Felix.

"And the member who went inside with her guest isn't 'Arianne,' it's Alice."

"Do you know her girlfriend, Nadia Riccio?"

"Who? Okay, miss, Alice's girlfriend is with her tonight. And as far as I know, she met that guy Jones through a prison pen-pal thing. Now if you please . . . if you are in the FBI, then show ID, a warrant, or exigent cause, or you move on. I'm a second-year law student at American University, *little girl,* and I know my stuff."

Angela backed off, numb, as Johnson sprinted across with her bag.

"Problem?"

"Um . . . no, Marc . . . I got to get out of here. My laptop's in your car."

They moved quickly up to Columbia Road to the space Johnson bogarted with his FBI parking decal. Angela's mind spun like a propeller, churning wind but nothing else. *Alice? And Nadia's never been there?*

"Here's that UPS package, by the way. Small but heavy. You gonna be okay?"

"Look, thanks." For some reason—adrenaline, Advil mixed with Cosmopolitans, a brain distracted—she bussed him lightly on his surprised lips. He was still grinning as she hiked away, briefcase slung over her good shoulder, toting the small box. She slipped in the cybercafé on Columbia Road next door to Bedrock Billiards and found a quiet corner near the rest rooms: no espresso, no Natalie Imbruglia on the speakers, no interruptions. She unpacked her laptop and started to enter the FBI remote site.

Arianne Shipley had no aliases. No criminal record, not even moving violations or DUIs. Given her experience of the previous year, Angela checked birth records to see if she had a twin. She was an only child. Not until close to 10 P.M. did she call Nadia; Angela already had four messages from Carmen on her cell voice mail.

Finally, the familiar raspy voice answered. "I was going to call you, I swear to God. I'm in North Carolina . . . at a Fairfield Inn by Charlotte Airport, can you frickin' believe that? I'm so sorry that—"

"Nadia. Listen—first, it is so, so good to hear your voice again. Second . . . I saw Arianne Shipley. Her parents are still looking for her, right? So is MPD, and I'll bet you haven't spoken to her in a long, long time."

"Um . . . Angela, wait. I spoke to her. She called me, from a pay phone in Virginia. She was really excited about Antoine getting out. I got so scared."

"Nadia, honey, slow down—I saw Arianne walk into Georgia O'Keeffe's with Jones and another girl."

After a tense pause, Nadia sputtered, "Ari's never been to O'Keeffe's. Isn't her scene. Lipstick Eurotrash Embassy Row types and bored rich bitches who think they're dykes!"

"I saw her, and they said her name was Alice."

"Where are you right now? What the fuck're you saying to me?"

"Who is Alice? What games is she playing on you, Nadia?"

"Fuck you!" But Nadia didn't hang up. Angela heard labored breathing, then: "Alice. Did she say her name was Alice? What's this gotta do with Antoine? Did you sic the cops on her?"

"No . . . Nadia . . . think."

"Christ . . . *fuck* . . . she mentioned someone named Alice when we were in Sarah Lawrence, 'kay? The person was like an ancestor. And her grandmother's named Alice. She was saying everyone in the damned family was named Alice. She's related to all kinds of famous people. Look . . . I gotta go."

Click. Nadia was gone.

Cursing, Angela twisted away from her laptop screen. Her eyes caught the brown-wrapped package, set on the adjoining table. *Ancestor—Alice?* Angela grabbed the box and tore into it.

Youssa's life unfolded before her eyes. Snapshots of Burkina Faso: dusty, red clay streets, clapboard and tin houses, skinny cattle, skinny dogs, skinny people. Soldiers. But she, smiling. Her arrival at Dulles. Real estate closing on her shop. There must be more. Yes. Angela drew back. A group photo at the shop counter. Youssa, tall, black, clustered by shorter, smiling white girls. A wiccan field trip? There, third from the left. Arianne. Other little preppies from the circle at Chi Cha's. No Nadia. The date, 5/99: Nadia was at Quantico. But someone—Youssa?—had circled Arianne's face with a ballpoint. Angela rummaged further through a layer of newspaper clippings to the prize. The scrapbook.

There was the article in the *Informer* on the Neal & Co. slave pens. Two leafs over, an unseen story on Old Michael, the pastor. His death: a column and blurry photo from another South African daily. Luckily in English and not Afrikaans or Zulu: *Suspects detained in alleged malicious driving and motor car manslaughter charges. Released subsequent to inquest indicating mechanical failure.* Photo: two men. One older, face obscured by a wiry arm. Another, young. Angela leaned closer.

Antoine's face, on a shorter, stouter body.

Youssa, my God, you knew all along.

Hands trembling, heart pounding, Angela was terrified to turn the pages, yet could not put down the scrapbook. Two more leafs of innocuous clippings and banal vacation postcards later, Angela found a photocopy, likely from microfiche, of an old obituary. The photo had the banner: *London Times,* April 7, 1911. *Coventry: Funeral procession of Sgt.-Mjr Frank Shipley, DSO, Victoria Cross, Welsh Guards, 24th Regiment of the Foot and Coventry Yeomanry. Author of memoir* My Years in Service. *Attended by current & retired officers & H.R.H. George, Prince of Wales, & young wife, Alice Shipley.* The copy quality was poor; harder, still, to discern faces under veils, feathered regalia, and bearskin hats. The piece continued on the next leaf. Slowly Angela read aloud, " 'Sgt.-Mjr. Shipley & second wife, the former Alice Brunnell.' " She was much younger than he.

And had the face of Arianne Shipley.

The exact face, not a genetic resemblance. The sight drove Angela into the ladies' room, straight to a sink, where she vomited. *Michael . . . who are they? What are they?* Mullinix was right. He came to murder the lies. But that, too, was a lie. *Michael, what did he say, before he died? The lion, the crocodile.* A coven. *Jesus, there were two of them,* as on the kopje, fighting the *inkanyezi.* Two, and Arianne.

Angela splashed cold water from the adjacent sink onto her face and muttered to her reflection, "Did I fail . . . *twice?*"

56

THE HAMMER OF THE WITCHES. As a teenager at Chapin, Nadia had taught herself that this tome, written by misogynistic gay German monks in the fifteenth century, was a lie. Catholic propaganda, all aimed at control. The wicca had always been benign spiritualists, herbalists, healers—sisters conveying the goddess's sweetness in the trees, the earth, the sky. By no means un-Christian. But there were always a few, in each generation, who perverted the Rede to the black sabbat. That's why she'd accepted her little medallion when she'd learned the craft. That's why she now fingered it with one hand, while the other steered her rental car through late-night traffic as she rocketed past the glowing, fanciful, yet soulless skyline of Charlotte, North Carolina. The green sign ahead: I-85 NORTH—GREENSBORO. Fighting back tears, she figured it would take her five hours in the dark to reach her destination, and woe to any state trooper who tried to pull her over. At least, not before she drank the last of the tea she'd brewed and placed in a thermos on the passenger seat.

Angela cradled her phone between her head and good shoulder as she pulled on a pair of jeans. Her laptop still crackled with information; her heart cracked with fear. Brett was on the line, groggy and bellowing in disbelief.

"You want me to *what?* Put out a citywide on Shipley based on the

Ogamdoudou homicide . . . post that to the Maryland and Virginia State Police? Didn't your report state the old man snuffed her with Stringbean's help? Hell, now you sayin' she was the harpy who ripped Stringbean's balls off?"

"Copies of supporting materials're here in my apartment. In the meantime, I am going to rearrest Jones on federal charges, get the U.S. attorney to go to court to vacate the stay of execution and new trial for Jones. I faxed the female subject's photo, dossier number, et cetera, to your office. Relay them to a Detective Goins at Philly PD Homicide, and to the Talbot County PD. There might be witnesses, anything, to put the female at these crime scenes. Have them use the facial variation software, adjusting for hair length, hair color, but *not* eye color."

"Hold up. Do I need to wake up Lupo . . . or better still, your shrink?"

"Are you going to help me?"

"Why don't you let me get outta bed first. You sit tight."

"Can't. As I said, I'm visiting Antoine. Haven't seen him for a while." *One hundred twenty years, to be exact,* Angela thought as she clicked off.

She tossed the phone onto her futon and slipped a cotton tank top over her sore torso. Water, three more Advil, and then, one pinch of the *umodi* she hadn't flushed down the toilet. She checked her SIG, snapped it in the holster. Then she walked to her closet, closed her eyes, drew in a deep cleansing breath. Eyes still shut, she opened the sliding door and dropped to her knees. Eyes opened, she reached behind her multilevel shoe rack for a large, flat white box.

"Grammie, tell me this isn't happening." Angela smiled. *I'm here talking to a ghost,* she mused. *I shouldn't ask what's real.*

She pulled out the *iklwa* that Durnkloopf and Ambassador Tambo had sent. A gift. Now she realized it was a tool, as was *she*. She smiled again, mulling over the irony. South Africa was a troubled, flawed emerging nation, killing the old, the supernatural, for the vagaries of the modern, the technological. Angela was a child of the technology, and just as flawed, wrapping a symbol of the supernatural in a modern newspaper, placing it in an old tennis-racket shoulder bag, then bounding out of her apartment for Sweet Pea. Old and new meshing. Indeed, on her computer, under the *Boondocks* comic strip screen saver: SEC and Virginia corporate filings for Shipley Development, LLP. The family was selling off lots carved out of an old farmstead. Fields long fallow, manse long abandoned. Ten miles northwest of Thornburg, Virginia. Equidistant between the bloody

Fredericksburg and Chancellorsville Civil War battlefields. Perfect place to celebrate an ancient sabbat dedicated to the Umnyama. The Darkness. Attended by the *amafufuyama*. Ghost spirits living in the burned bodies and wet bones of the Ama Simba. The Lion's Regiment had deserted the Lion in that hotel suite, when he needed them the most, and Angela accepted the only possible explanation: they were never serving Samuel in the first place. He was a foolish patsy. The false patsy was the real evil.

Yet no prayer, no call to Michael, to her grandmother, could still Angela's shivering body as she steered her VW across the Potomac toward I-95, and a farm called Alice's Close.

57

FOREVER . . .

TWO A.M., AND A MILE FROM the Route 606 exit off I-95, clouds materialized from nothing to engulf the bright stars in the Milky Way like stygian amoebas. Quickly, the clouds opened up, sending down sheets of hot, stinging rain before Angela could pull over and raise Sweet Pea's ragtop. It took another forty minutes, headlights barely piercing drops that plummeted like buckshot, for Angela to find the junction of Routes 606 and 648. There, in a deluge falling through a curtain of palpable country pitch-darkness. Suddenly, a lit sign seemed to jump into the VW's enfeebled headlights like a deer: SHIPLEY DEVELOPMENT, 26.9 ACRES FOR SUBDIVISION, (804) 555-3400.

Angela killed the headlights and eased Sweet Pea off onto the shoulder. The racing water erased any telltale tire ruts at the entrance to what looked like a dirt feeder road to Alice's Close. With eyes now adjusted to the dark, Angela sucked in a moist breath and rolled down the window. She could see a faint orange glow dance on the rim of a ridge, maybe a quarter mile up that muddy road. She exhaled and checked her flashlight. The big Maglite would be her only other ambient guide, aimed down, for stealth. Angela slung the tennis bag over her shoulder and stepped out into the rain.

Angela slogged, soaked and chilled to the bone, in the murk. First parallel to the feeder road, then down into a hollow. A truncated flash of lightning on the horizon made the clouds glow red for an instant. Angela discerned the black outlines of two structures. Then darkness struck back, and all she could see was the muted flashlight beam before her, pointing out flooded gopher holes, or anything that might be lurking or slithering in the wet, ankle-high alfalfa and dandelion. Above the *boosh* and thump of her pulse in her throat and her heart in her chest was the deafening patter of rain on the dogwoods, drooping live oaks, and erect pines. The sting of wet wind, rumbling in the sky.

As Angela rose out of the black hollow, those sounds quieted. The storm was abating to a gentle rainfall. Soon, an intermittent drizzle. Angela switched off the Maglite and stood as still as she could, though she shivered maddeningly. Yes, she was cold, but terror had bitten right into her spine, for now she couldn't hear what she'd expected to hear, once the rain slackened. No symphony of crickets and frogs. No stray patters on leaves, even though the acidic rain still fell. The air was wet and dead.

That's when she saw the orange glow again. She was much closer now, maybe only forty yards away. The light came from *inside* a clapboard tobacco barn, and it oozed out onto the road. With those tiny dribbles of light, and with senses heightened, not dulled, by the *umodi*, Angela could just make out the ancient, faded painted ads on the barn wall: Gold Medal Flour, Winston Cigarettes. Beneath the wall was a wrecked tractor surrounded by a rusting, junked car chassis. As soon as she girded herself to clamber up the hill to the road, the moribund air stirred, from a flurry to a gust. Howling through rotted barn planks like a ghoul's shriek. And that wind grew hotter, drier. It stank, like lions.

Her quarry was in the barn. She could smell them in there, but she couldn't take them. Not yet. She had to find a place to plan. She turned and saw the shell of an old house only a dozen or so dark yards down the soupy road. With one stray lightning flash in the clouds, she could see that the brick chimney and brick facing was crumbling, the porch about to fall. Vintage Virginia, perhaps pre–Civil War. The past inhabitants must have been able to sit on that porch and watch the carnage of Chancellorsville or hear the distant rumble of the cannon at Fredericksburg. Angela humped over the wrecked wall. Rainwater dripped through a gaping crater in the roof. Angela let down her shoulder bag and removed the *iklwa*, then unholstered her SIG. She stood slowly and stepped forward, bracing the barrel of the 9mm on the spear handle. Practicing.

Then she smelled something other than the musty wind. The odor of candle wax, spent kerosene. She went into a deep tuck on the plank floor, groped for the Maglite. Could she risk a split-second beam? She decided yes, and in the light, in the corner under a wrecked staircase, she saw dozens of smoldering candlesticks and lanterns, all seemingly extinguished by the rain. All around a platform of quilts and bare mattresses. The malodorous wind stilled.

"*Shit,*" Angela mouthed, rolling to her belly, aiming the SIG-Sauer. But there was no one there. Until she heard a whisper.

It was in her ear, then on her neck, like a breath. She swung around, on the floor, in the dark. Nothing again. But the orange glow in the barn had melted into the dark.

Behind her, a muffled, dull sound, like voices through a wall. Slowly, she rose, looked back over her shoulder. Something alive was crawling along the old fireplace mantel. A raccoon? A muskrat? At least it wasn't whoever had lit those candles.

Relieved, she reholstered the SIG as she turned back around, only to see Arianne Shipley's face rushing out of the shadows toward her.

Angela reeled backward. She lost her footing and hit the floor. The rotting, termite-chewed planks cracked, collapsed. A black, wet maw of roots and mud walls swallowed Angela as she fell. She hit the soft ground with a thud. She heaved for a breath and groped in the slime for either pistol or spear. She had neither. But she did look up.

Two faces, now. One male, one female, peered down. A hand showed something that looked like a gourd. And when the hand shook it, the pain sawed through Angela's uterus, into her stomach, like a blowtorch-heated, serrated blade.

Micklin jimmied the lock to Angela's apartment door; two of Brett Mallory's men shoved it wide open. Instantly, Frank Lupo moved in with five agents. Bud White brought up the rear.

"Tear this place apart!" Lupo barked to FBI people and MPD cops alike.

Ten minutes later, Lupo was reading a hastily typed memo, gasping at each word. White demanded to see it just as Vallas shouted from the bedroom, "Skipper! Better peep to this!"

Lupo rushed in, with Brett elbowing White out of the way. Vallas had dissolved the screen saver on Angela's laptop, revealing the location of Alice's Close.

"Jesus," Lupo muttered. He yelled out to Marc Johnson, "Call the pad at Andrews and get me *anyone* at Fort A. P. Hill in Virginia. Tell 'em choppers're coming!"

Brett said, "You aren't gonna call the locals, Virginia State Police, your HRT?"

"Yes to the State Police. Otherwise . . . this stays in the family."

White seethed, "Frankie, what the hell is this? I gotta brief Scofield and Sessions!"

"You pull out that cell phone, I break your fingers!" Lupo looked to Vallas. "Gather up this shit and get to the car. I want an ISD weapons check in one hour."

"This means your ass, Lupo!" White hollered. "We need to run this through channels—you know that!"

The taller Lupo bent to look White in the eye. "What I know is," he said, almost whispering, unblinking, "I will end your bullshit career tonight, Buddy, if you fuck with me." Lupo looked to Brett. "Detective, c'mere. I'm thinking you could keep Agent White here company while we get our tac plans together. Maybe brief him on Metropolitan Police Department–FBI procedures—over breakfast."

Grinning, Brett pushed his massive chest up against White. "I think you'd best stick around and shut up."

58

NADIA PULLED THE RENTAL CAR onto the gravel shoulder, high beams searing flying insects and illuminating Angela's VW. Nadia tried Angela's cell one last time; she couldn't even get a signal, as if the clouds were deflecting the microwaves. Not even the FM stereo worked. Just static. With a final plea to both mothers, Mary and the wiccan goddess, the trainee removed a small flashlight and a SIG 229 from the glove box, then moved out of the car to the soupy feeder road.

She pushed up the muddy road, jerking the light from side to side, keeping the pistol down, praying her shoulders would stop trembling. The skinny elms lining the road rustled and swayed in waves, like cilia in some wormlike gut, fanning food forward. As she stepped faster, shaking off the chills and stray raindrops, two buildings slowly came into view. She hiked faster, blindly, until she came, panting, to what looked like a weed-choked ramshackle barn, and the house Arianne had once described as something out of an old Currier & Ives engraving that looked like a bomb had hit it long ago.

Yet, the trainee was too inexperienced, too *scared* to notice, as her mentor had, the lack of animal sounds on a midsummer country night. No owls, crickets, frogs. But on that silence floated a faint woman's guffaw. Nadia stopped and, just as faintly, answered, "Ari? Oh, Jesus . . ." Then, shooting the flashlight beam wildly, louder: *"Ari?"*

Another disembodied voice—a female moan. Nadia gasped, swung the light. Again, she was answered by silence and the molasses-like shadows. But now, tiny flickers of light sparked in the barn and grew to an orange glow. Nadia killed her flashlight. Too late. She felt dizzy, nauseated; the road seemed to liquefy underfoot, and she heard the laughter and whispers of men. Warriors . . .

Antoine Jones, Shaka Seven, stood naked and ankle-deep in rotted, wet hay. A circle of chipped clay smudge pots smoldering with incense surrounded him, and behind that, a semicircled audience of mahogany and teak night fetishes. Antoine's penis was engorged, like the wooden members on the gang of cruel-looking, inanimate little statues. Also nude, Arianne applied the last touches of oils, ocher and yellow pigment, to Antoine's body. Around her neck hung a garland of herbs, twisted roots; around Antoine's, a necklace of hyena teeth and buzzard's feathers, interlaced with quartzite, rubies—and gold slugs like the ones found under Les Collins's and Carl Davidson's tongues. Angela lay against a post supporting one of the barn's few remaining crossbeams, nose bloodied. Unable to move.

Both warlock and consort turned to face her after a kiss. Antoine smiled with straight white teeth and spoke to Angela. "My name was the name of the Zulu king we made. My coven. I'm the last one. My brothers began to die the day Shaka's brother, Dingane, betrayed the King, impaled and burned our protectors, the Lion's Regiment. We swore revenge on Dingane's seed: Mpande, and Mpande's fat son, so-called Great Fire, Cetshwayo." Angela grimaced when he gestured to a plank rail. The *iklwa* lay on top. Her only weapon. "Fuck if I know how you got that thing. The Boers stole the steel smelted from our clay kilns, iron ore from the hills around Howick Falls—to make motherfucking horseshoes, buckles! That's the shit you're defending?"

"Who . . . who are you?"

"Ngapathaki. The Crocodile. The Lion was a weak old fool. He thought he was the last. I'm forever. I spoke the *mfecane*. The Lion's a vomit stain. His *thikoloshe* was *mine.*"

"The familiar," Angela muttered. "Stringbean . . . he worked for you, not Samuel?"

As Arianne smirked, Antoine nodded and said, "From the beginning. From college. Devon was my boy; front court with me. He helped me start a student group to counter the frats. Oh, no 'Groove-Phi-Groove' shit for us. We were called the Ama Simba, like the warriors, whose bones the Lion held *all* this time, thinking that *he* controlled them. But ol' String was getting sloppy; even Samuel was getting jumpy with him. So, there is only one way to silence the familiar in this life and the next." He mugged at Arianne. "Take his manhood, right, baby?"

She didn't agree fast enough; annoyed, he smacked her down to the straw. As she cowered, he moved to Angela. His penis was inches from her face. She winced, tried to jerk away. *I will not die like this,* her mind resolved as it labored to retreat from her body, from the degradation and pain that was to follow. But Antoine didn't force himself on her paralyzed body. He crouched, hand on her shoulder, and whispered in her ear, "I couldn't die before my seed was planted. So for my plan to succeed, Samuel had to succeed. At least for a while. So the witch Youssa had to die; she's ol' Sam's enemy, too. Too bad you didn't fully accept her before then." Angela could not stop her tears as he murmured coarsely, "Wanna know real fun? Those motherfuckers Samuel killed—*they were framing me for a murder I was going to commit anyway.* Yeah, as of tonight, like the storm, my seed's flooded Arianne. She'll have a daughter, who'll bear a son, who will be *me*, again." He stood up. "A son, like the *inyanga* Michael? Unh-unh." Arianne handed him an *ishungu*. One Angela had seen in the tunnel under Rittenhouse Square, then wielded by Samuel.

As Antoine swished the wet contents around, Arianne hissed, "The ultimate *insila* . . . the Lion stole it from Collins's office on a snowy night, right? Stringbean stole it from the Lion. The offal that would have been *your* son, you pathetic, bitter little *bitch!*"

Angela screamed—hoarse, raw, anguished—when her mind fully comprehended what Arianne was saying. Antoine capered back inside the circle of candles, gleeful with her misery and mocking her cries, to Arianne's amusement, until his face curled in a sneer.

"You failed tonight. You failed a long, long goddamn time ago. Took my spirit a long time to wait, to search. The Lion thought he was so powerful when he killed the old *inyanga* . . . Michael, the 'archangel.' He did so with my help. Senile niggah couldn't even recognize me now. But he's an infant, compared to me. I faced the *inkanyezi*, on that hilltop with my brother witch, as the Impi and British clashed on Ulundi . . ."

"*Nooooo!*"

"You see it every night you close your eyes. The blood's in you. Diluted but there. My brother witch died after we spoke charms and spells ensuring victory for the British. Ensuring final revenge on Cetshwayo. You killed him. And you weakened me. I couldn't even savor the sight of the *amabutho* cut down by rifles, of your son watching you die. No, me and my daughter, seed bearer, were taken by Cetshwayo and would have died, but for a British soldier named Frank Shipley. There, my spirit saw an opportunity. Convergence. Her world"—he pointed at Arianne, who was now holding Angela's head by her hair—"and mine. And *yours*. I tracked Samuel's seed, and seed bearer, Jewel. Wooed her, fucked her. She was only trying to escape from Samuel. From superstition, fake magic mumbo-jumbo, right? But I didn't count on her falling for Buford, falling in with King, Collins . . . dog-shit fools drunk with power, lust, greed, ego. Yeah, nothing's changed since Shaka's time."

Antoine cocked his head to the hole in the barn roof, voice soft. "I wanted to tear Buford's baby out and replace it with mine, I was so angry. But my only real choice was tearing it out, period. See, when I left the first time, the sow got drunk, let them all pull a train. Buford stopped it, then they argued. He pushed her, too hard. Jewel busted her head open." Antoine's gaze lowered again, to meet Angela's tortured face. "They did things to her body, even planted a .22 String'd been holding for me, in my dorm, all to implicate me. Yes, I did come back to add *flourishes* to their work. Umnyama compelled me." He sighed. "But I ended up on death row. Mullinix failed me. So I'm full circle. I used the Lion's blind revenge, to punish the pieces of shit who deprived me of my prize. And I used their deaths to flush you out, to free me. Made easier because Arianne's lover was placed under your care. I knew everything you were doing."

Arianne grimaced at Nadia's mention, but quickly released Angela's scalp and crawled to Antoine's flexing thigh. "Do it," she said dryly. "Sun'll be coming up soon."

Antoine reached for the *ishungu,* uncorked it. Angela instantly suffered a bubbling nausea. Antoine raised the beaded gourd above his head. "It'll slide down my throat like a raw oyster in a bar, and you'll be gone. Thank me—you'll be free of the whore's spirit. But then, well, we'll kill your body. Maybe, your friends next? Family. *Finish what Trey Williams couldn't?*"

Angela heaved a bloody gob of spit at the couple and chanted with alien words that seemed to spring from her mouth, though she didn't understand them: *"Myaze Inkanyamba, Myaze Inkanyezi."* She repeated them, louder. And they made Antoine's ears trickle blood.

He dropped the gourd. *"I'll cut your goddamn intestines out and hang you with them from these rafters!*" He grabbed the *iklwa* and raised it to heave at Angela's chest.

A gunshot echoed in the barn, like the one that had saved the warlock in a *donga* long ago. Nadia, 9mm shaking in her hand, screeched down from the hayloft, "Don't move . . . drop that fucking spear . . . Ari, get up! Get the fuck up and stay in the light!"

"Baby, *no!*" Arianne shrieked back.

"Shut up, damn you. Do it!"

Antoine lowered the *iklwa,* but as he raised his hands again, he blew into the air with a great puff, and suddenly both Nadia and Angela smelled a rotten-egg stench, then something like burnt flesh and lions. Angela's eyes stung with the sight of dozens of dead faces. No pupils. Spear handles pummeled shields. Moving on her, as she lay helpless. *POOM!* Another step. *POOM!*

Nadia, high above, saw nothing, yet sensed what Angela sensed. She'd taken a tea of mandrake, nightshade—the protection Mullinix had sought—as she'd driven from North Carolina. She was immune to the spell; she'd recovered outside when she'd first inhaled the hallucinogenic extracts laid around the barn. And she'd learned well from her teacher. "I know you called them!" she shouted to Antoine. "Now call them off . . . or I'll kill her." She was aiming her SIG at her lover, and the seed she carried.

"Naddy?" Arianne whimpered. "Sweetie . . . I love you. There's room for both of us here, Naddy. He just wants a baby, not me. *I'm yours."*

Tears squirted from Nadia's eyes, her grip loosening on the wobbly pistol.

Angela's eyes closed—her strength, her spirit, sapped.

But Nadia called to her, "Remember what I asked you . . . what was it like . . ."

Angela, coughing out what seemed to be her last breath, answered, "To kill someone . . . you love?"

Nadia emptied her clip into Arianne. The shots echoed across the hills in the hollows, drowning out Antoine's howl. Nadia clenched her eyelids for the last five rounds. She didn't even see Arianne drop.

Now it was Shaka Seven who screamed in horror as the Ama Simba disappeared in the blink of a smoky eye. Nadia collapsed, but Angela wobbled to her feet.

"We are forever!" Antoine screamed defiantly, as if words could hold her at bay.

They didn't, and Angela whispered words spoken long ago, *"Forever . . . ends here."*

She lunged for the *iklwa*, pulling it away before Antoine could reach it. For an instant, they stood toe-to-toe. Angela, hesitant. Perhaps doubting this was "real." Antoine's eyes darted to Angela's 9mm, lying beside Arianne's lifeless body. No more spells. Angela saw the emptiness in his eyes. She'd seen it before. In Trey's eyes.

She plunged the blade—made from the old Voortrekkers' steel—into Antoine's chest. She didn't let go, making sure his last breath blew into her face. It took a revived Nadia to pull her off, and the two women embraced until a pinkish glow kissed the fields to the east, followed by the first mourning dove's coos. Angela and Nadia staggered to the house, returned with kerosene lamps. Nadia tossed her SIG into the drier straw. Nothing was to be recounted or remembered. At least, such was Angela's prayer.

An hour later, mentor and protégé limped down the feeder road, puddles drying with the heat of both a new day's sun and a raging blaze behind them. A caravan of sirens broke the morning calm. And nothing would be recounted. Witchcraft was the alchemy of self-interest. Of politics. Of quieting the voices of the past.

59

A PRAYER FOR DELIVERANCE

GARETH MONTGOMERY ROLLED OVER TO FIND his bedmate gone. "Angie?" he groaned. "Girl . . . come on back here and spoon me."

Angela roamed into the bedroom, buttoning her blouse. "Wake up, sleepyhead. It's seventy degrees and a pretty day."

He peeked at the clock. "*Shit!* Gonna be late picking up Dad at Dulles. Coming *bahk fe hoam.*" Gareth parodied an exaggerated Jamaican patois. One wing of his family was West Indian. For Angela, it explained his stubbornness. And the inability to buy anything other than a cheap alarm clock from Target. But the brother could burn in the kitchen: jerk chicken, oxtail stew, and *esceviced* snapper to die for!

Gareth limped into the bathroom to brush his teeth while Angela finished with her makeup. Through a mouth of minty Colgate foam he complained, "We wouldn't have to play musical beds if you'd just come off the cash for that house up on South Dakota Avenue with me." He spit and smiled.

"I don't buy real estate with someone I'm not legally bound to, cool?"

"That a hint for a diamond solitaire? Can't fence a brother in, now!"

She winked. "Well, we have nothing in common anyway. By the way, how's it working out—you and your harpy sister at *Time*'s D.C. bureau, together in the same newsroom? Y'all twisted siblings are the black 'Mel and Susan Profitt' of the press."

Gareth pursed his lips, then wriggled out of his boxers and yanked back the shower curtain. "Kevin Spacey, Joan Severance, played the freaky siblings on CBS's *Wiseguy,* second season, 1988. And you say we got *nothin'* in common! Hit me with a *hard* one next time!" He twisted the hot-water knob. "Now let me flip this on you—speaking of freaks, you seen Victor Styles lately?"

"Conversation's over. Got a briefing at the U.S. Marshals' HQ in Crystal City in half an hour, and you know the traffic."

"Styles has come out of retirement," Gareth said, stepping into the shower. The mist was rising. "Now he's CNN's go-to pundit on the Bureau and Justice Department under Ashcroft. Your Attorney General boss, who lost an election to a dead man, is a racist Holy Roller. Did he *really* have janitors cover the breasts of the statue of Justice in the Great Hall? Isn't that where you got your medal two years ago? Baby, you shoulda quit the FBI back when Lupo had you and Vallas guarding ballot boxes down in Palm Beach County, Florida, after the election."

"Mr. Ashcroft's not the ogre you think he is. You are supposed to be objective."

"Mister? Aw, *Lawd!* By the way, why you so frosty with Vallas?"

"You're steaming the mirror. I'll see you after your taping—my place?"

"My dream guest on the show: Butch Buford. Hear he's working as a teacher."

She ignored the name. "Have an eventful day, Mr. Montgomery."

"Have an *un*eventful day, Madame Special Assistant to the Director. Girl, you are only thirty-four, with that title? I'm forty, and still low on the journalistic totem pole." After a pause, Angela heard, under the spraying water, "And I love you."

"Love you, too, sweetie." Angela repeated it over and over even when she was merging Sweet Pea—ragtop down—out of Gareth's condo garage onto Wilson Boulevard in Arlington, then down to Route 110, the freeway that paralleled the George Washington Parkway as far as the Pentagon. Stopped in a traffic tangle, she checked her palmtop. At three she was meeting Carmen at Hecht's downtown to help Sharon register for her bridal shower. Her fiancé, Alvin Markham, was flying to L.A. that morning to do some Hubble telescope research at the JPL in Pasadena, before returning for a full-time post at Howard. Just what Angela needed, now that her schedule was burdened with administrative duties. *That* wedding, and the reemergence of Styles. Landing on his feet like a cat. No, she hadn't heard from him.

Not since Frank Lupo had stepped down as interim Director, returning to his previous post. Not since Woodruff Sessions had ascended to Deputy Director, under John Ashcroft's aegis. Not since the new president of the United States, George W. Bush, had named Houston native Junipero "Pete" Garza the new Director of the FBI. Garza was a DA for Harris County, Texas, and former Chief Counsel to the Texas Rangers: the law-men, not the baseball team Bush once owned. No, she hadn't heard from Styles since Garza'd promoted her, to everyone's shock, as his Special Projects Assistant. Garza was surprising a lot of the right-wingers who'd once cheered his appointment. But it didn't surprise Victor Styles. He'd sent an engraved congratulatory note on Crane vellum paper: *So you survive. And rise. Witchcraft . . . or merit? I say both. Best wishes.* His signature was in calligraphy.

Thirty-seven minutes of bumper-to-bumper snarl later, and jumping radio stations between Russ Parr and Olivia, and *The Tom Joyner Morning Show,* Angela neared Boundary Channel Drive and the Pentagon. Larry King's grating voice sounded on the stereo: *"Tonight on CNN, eight Eastern, join me and my guest,* Time *magazine reporter Gareth Montgomery, as we discuss shocking developments in the Chandra Levy story, then at nine Eastern, I urge you to stay with CNN as Mr. Montgomery joins Wolf Blitzer for an in-depth interview with former FBI Deputy Director Victor Styles, now Executive Director of the Center for Justice and Policy Studies. Ghosts of the FBI: an exposé, from Martin Luther King to the Robert Hanssen spy debacle. Tonight . . . September eleventh, 2001 . . . only on CNN!"*

Enough of that. Angela switched to the "Oldies 100," WBIG FM. Some chatter, mindless pop. Her cell phone beeped. On hands-free, she listened as her assistant, Special Agent Nadia Riccio, sputtered frantically, "Oh my God . . . Angela?" Nadia's voice competed with Sweet Pea's ancient speakers: Three Dog Night's snappy electric-piano intro to "Joy to the World." That was the abortive Gore-Buford campaign's song. Favorite of Antoine Jones's. Angela bopped her head and belted soulfully out to the bright blue sky, *"Jeremiah was a bullfrog / Was a good friend a mine."*

Microwave static dismembered Nadia's words: "Report HQ . . . ASAP . . . plane crash . . . *Oh my God* . . . aw, no, no, no . . ."

The traffic opened up a little—because commuters were pulling onto the shoulder of Boundary Channel, to a dead stop. All seemed to be on cell phones or riveted to car stereos.

Listening.

There was a low rumble in the sky.

Angela called out after humming with the song, "Nadia? I can't hear—"

The rumble became a shriek. The shriek became a roar. Overhead, a shadow appeared, like a giant circling condor. Darkening Angela's face.

That was the last thing she saw before the VW skidded across two lanes and smashed into the concrete divider. "Joy to the World" cut off.

The elder Zulu *sangoma* have a saying: *Inkanyezi d'basi u unkubutho siphulu, si ngom a ene.* "When men indulge their rage and cruelty, only the archangel can deliver us."

A B O U T   T H E   A U T H O R

CHRISTOPHER ALAN CHAMBERS, a Washington, D.C., native, is a former attorney with the U.S. Department of Justice. He's a pharmaceutical industry consultant and teaches communications at Central Piedmont Community College in Charlotte, North Carolina, where he's working on more Angela Bivens novels.